THE AFRIKAANS

THE AFRIKAANS

NICK PIROG

DECIQUIN

"Where there is a sea, there are pirates."
—Greek Proverb

"They should have picked a different ship."
—Thomas Prescott

DAY 1

DECK 6

5:58 A.M.

THERE WEREN'T many people about, but then again, it wasn't yet 6:00 in the morning. However, there was a couple just off to my right. The woman was resting her elbows on the ship's sleek oak railing, squinting at the brightening horizon. Her hair was braided with a bunch of multi-colored beads and she had donned an unflattering tie-dye dress, a purple sarong around her waist, and lime-green flip-flop sandals. It looked like a rainbow had thrown up on her. The man next to her, as if to compensate for his wife's loud outfit, was dressed in a whisper. White T-shirt feeding into XXL equally white Bermuda shorts. He appeared slightly less enthusiastic about being wrestled from a Mai-Tai-and-lobster-tail-induced coma to watch the sun rise above the glistening sea.

The Campers, like many of their brethren on the *Afrikaans*, reeked of overfed, overindulged Americans, and initially, I'd guessed they hailed from somewhere in the Midwest. Wisconsin or Iowa. Somewhere with a prevalence for quality cheddar. In fact, they were from New Mexico.

Susie Camper took a large bite of danish—something red in

the middle—wrestled it down, and asked, "Where's your better half?"

"I couldn't shake her out of bed."

Frank gave me a look I decoded as, "Exactly where I should be right now."

On the subject of my seafaring cohort, when I was initially given the eleven-day African cruise, my better half had been my then-girlfriend Erica Frost. But sadly, a month earlier the two of us had gotten into an argument over which Tom Hanks movie we liked best. She'd said hers was a toss-up between *Philadelphia* and *Forrest Gump*. I'd said *Joe Versus the Volcano*. A big fight ensued, and two days later relationship 7b was all but over.

There had been just enough advance notice to make the necessary changes, and I'd found a replacement at the eleventh hour. Her name was Lacy. Dirty blonde hair, ice-blue eyes. A body shaped by hours in the pool. By most people's standards a total babe. Who just happened to be my sister.

Anyhow, this was day six of the aforementioned eleven-day cruise aboard the *Afrikaans*. Our first port of call had been Mombasa, Kenya, where we spent two days exploring the local wildlife preserves. On day two, Lacy and I had been in the same safari jeep as Frank and Susie Camper. Frank and I drank beers and talked about guy stuff—you know, cars, guns, Carmen Electra —while Lacy and Susie gushed over the small critters and swapped medical histories: Susie battling type 2 diabetes, and my sister, multiple sclerosis.

The only downside to the experience was that we'd been stuck in the same Jeep with a couple from Georgia, Gilroy and Trinity. I think their names said it all.

If my memory serves me correctly, Trinity had said in her high-pitched southern drawl, "That little baby hyena is just precious."

To which Gilroy had responded, "Would you like me to buy you a baby hyena, *baby*?"

Barf-o-rama.

Day three brought us to Zanzibar, Tanzania, where the four of us rented a Jeep for the day and drove to a series of small huts along the coast drinking local beers, sampling the various local cuisines, and trying to avoid the local primates' feces grenades.

After a day at sea, then a quick stop in Mozambique, we spent yesterday at sea as the *Afrikaans* began its three-day voyage south to the first port of call in South Africa: Richard's Bay. We would then make stops at Durban and Port Elizabeth, and finally spend the last two days in Cape Town. Susie and Lacy had scoured several brochures from each of these stops, and I was certain Frank and I had our days booked solid.

But, back to the present.

As the horizon began to lighten further, I noticed a solitary man thirty yards to my left. In the soft glow resonating from the cabin lights, the man's skin shone a midnight black. That the man was alone was not an oddity. I mean, here I was by myself. I was within relative proximity to my fat friends, but I had come out here alone. But the fact that I hadn't seen the man before *was* odd.

I should mention that the *Oceanic Afrikaans* was a small luxury cruise liner which, according to Susie, was home to 208 guests, mostly American with the occasional European or Australian thrown in the mix.

The point I'm driving at here is that the *Afrikaans* was an intimate setting, and over the course of the past week I had had a conversation with, said hi to, or at the very least, taken notice of every guest on the ship.

That was until now.

There was a slim chance the man was part of the 164-person crew—which was multinational, and according to the county of origin listed underneath each crew member's badge, had more countries represented than the last Olympics—but I'd encountered most of those people as well, and I would have recognized this guy. For one, he wasn't South American black or Caribbean black, as were most of the black crew members. He was African black which was the single continent the HR department of the *Oceanic Afrikaans* had neglected when hiring for their "African" cruise. This *should not* have mattered. But again, it did. And second, the man's left ear appeared to have been badly burned, melted down to a small asymmetrical mass.

The man was dressed in khaki slacks with an accompanying white button-down. A bit overdressed seeing as how it was already a baking 78 degrees. But, then again, he could easily be used to 120-degree heat in the shade. Or wherever people go to hide from the lions. All sweeping generalizations aside, he had one of those cheap black watches on his wrist, a Casio or a Timex, and he'd checked it six times in the three minutes since he'd arrived.

Because I'm one of the friendliest people on the planet, I yelled at him, "Don't worry, it's coming!"

Actually, I'm not that friendly, but this lone man leaning against the railing looking repeatedly at his watch was making the hair on my arms stand on end, and I wanted to see how he would react. I was probably just being paranoid. Which, I should point out, I am *very* good at.

The African man glanced in my direction but said nothing.

I prodded, "The sun. Don't worry, it's coming. It's one of the few things that never disappoints."

He made no reaction, and I figured I might as well be speaking Latin. What matters is that I wasn't speaking Swahili, or Zulu, or one of those other African languages that sound like someone is trying to purge their Adam's apple.

I turned my gaze back to the horizon. A soft halo of red had begun to form over the silent water. It quickly turned into a ring of pink as if Saturn were rising from the ocean. In the soft light, I noticed three small boats. They were miles away, looking like three buoys drifting in tight formation. Fishing was a billion dollar industry in South Africa, but I couldn't help wondering why these tiny boats were so far out to sea.

Over the course of the next three minutes the sun rose to its full form, and the day officially began. More importantly, the lone black man stopped looking at his watch and appeared to relax. And most importantly, the fishing boats appeared even farther away than they had minutes earlier.

"Would you like to hit the buffet with us?" Susie Camper asked, turning in my direction.

"Now that's more like it," Frank Camper added, turning his frown upside down.

I laughed and told them it was a little too early for breakfast. What I didn't tell them was that it was a little too early for me to watch them gorge themselves on plates stacked high with eggs benedict, bacon, sausage, ham, and various other HDL-clogging delights. Then head back for seconds, thirds, and fourths. I mean Frank was a great guy, but his blood was probably doing the steeplechase in his veins as we speak.

I was more of a Honey Nut Cheerios, grapefruit half, apple juice guy myself. With the occasional Chocolate Chip Eggo thrown in the mix. At thirty-four, I was feeling the aches and pains most people feel in their fifties. But, then again, I'd been running six miles every day for the better part of my life, been shot twice, fallen off a cliff into the Atlantic ocean, collapsed a lung, and most recently been attacked by a pack of wolves. I didn't need to add bacon to that list.

As the Campers departed, I watched as Susie grabbed a big chunk of Frank's left buttock and he draped his large, rotund arm over her shoulder. That, my friends, was close to five hundred pounds of true love. This got me thinking about my love life. My last three relationships hadn't exactly ended in disaster. Okay, two of three had, but the last one was pretty good. And, had she not blamed me for getting waffle crumbs in the butter, or blamed me for repeatedly getting water on the bathroom floor, we still might be together. Of course, I was to blame for these things. But some things, for instance, the movie sucking, or not being able to call her when I didn't have cell service, or the plight of the polar bear, I was not to blame for.

A light beeping broke my reverie.

I glanced to my left. It had been the man's watch alarm, his small black Casio. It beeped once more. The man looked at his watch, then peered over the railing at the rippling water below. Almost as if he were expecting a package from a dolphin at this exact moment.

Without being too obvious, I leaned over the railing and looked down. No dolphins. Just a seventy-foot drop into a frothing blue chasm. When I looked up, the man was clambering up and over the railing. I opened my mouth to yell at him, but he'd already jumped.

UPPER CREW DECK

6:04 A.M.

WHEN THE BRITISH EAST INDIA COMPANY tried to expand their trade routes into Nepal and beyond, they encountered the Gurkhas. The British were so impressed by the Gurkhas' fighting skills, it was suggested these hill men should be recruited into the British Army. In 1816, the first battalion of Gurkhas took form. Today, these legendary, British Army-trained soldiers can be found using their skills in all manner of security detail on land and at sea.

Master-at-Arms Ganju Thapa pulled the sleek black radio from his hip and asked, "What deck?" He'd heard the three blasts from the ship's whistle. *Man overboard.*

"Deck Six," came the voice of Michael Stoves, Security and Safety Officer for the *Afrikaans.* Stoves was technically Thapa's superior—although you never would have guessed it—and he did a fine job with the day-to-day security and safety of the passengers.

"He didn't fall?"

"We have several witnesses that claim he jumped."

"So circle around and get him."

"It isn't that easy."

Of course it wasn't easy. It would take twenty-five minutes for the cruise ship to circle back to the man. But the water was warm, and if the sharks didn't get to him, then there was a good chance they could recover him. "I don't follow."

"Walk to the starboard side."

Thapa walked out of the bathroom and peered out the small window. Stoves said, "Do you see those small specks on the horizon?"

Thapa could indeed see three small specks bobbing on the horizon. "Affirmative."

"They are headed right at us."

Thapa was silent.

"Did you hear what I said?"

"Yes, yes. Give me a moment. I'm thinking."

Stoves did not give him a moment. "Should we mount the LRAD?"

The LRAD, short for Long Range Acoustic Device, was a sonic weapon that blasted high intensity sound waves at would-be attackers, scrambling their eardrums and driving them away. The device had been used successfully by many freighters and a couple of cruise ships to ward off pirate attacks.

"How far away are the ships?" asked Thapa.

"Four miles."

"They're probably just fishing boats that happen to be headed in our direction. I advise to circle back for the man."

There was a long pause. "You sure about that?"

"Absolutely."

"Should we radio it in?"

"Not yet. I'll be up to the bridge shortly. If the boats are still on their way, we will go to max speed, and I will man the LRAD myself."

"Roger that," Stoves replied, ending the transmission.

By law, guns were not allowed on the boat. But this was one of those few moments when Thapa was glad he had a small arsenal tucked away. He felt for the small key around his neck. In the three years he'd been master-at-arms for the *Afrikaans*, he'd never once had occasion to use the key. But today he knew he would not only have to use the key; his loyalty, his integrity, everything that had made him a part of the legendary Nepalese Gurkhas for nearly three decades, would be put to the test.

LOWER CREW DECK

6:05 A.M.

BEN—AT least that's what it said on his name tag—looked down at his beeping watch.

It was almost time.

He peered up from the swimming pool. He saw no one. He dropped the long silver pole with the debris catcher and watched as it sank swiftly to the bottom of the turquoise water, listing toward the edge closest to him. Ben walked past the hot tubs, past the gleaming bar and its twenty askew stools, and pulled open the door marked Deck 7. He stepped into the elevator and pushed the button for Deck 2. He exited and walked briskly to the crew corridor. He made his way to his room and silently opened the door. His roommate, a thirty-something guy named Joe, turned over and said, "What time is it?"

Joe was one of only a handful of white crew members. White, like *Ben's* father. According to his mother, his father had been a mercenary. A man who had taken his mother by force. Ben's skin was a soft nutmeg, seven shades lighter than every person in his village, and he easily passed for Indian, Mediterranean, or even American, which is why he suspected he was picked for this mission. Ben found it amusing that he'd ended up taking on the same occupation as the man he so much despised.

"A little after 6:00. Go back to sleep," Ben answered in near-perfect English.

Ben didn't mind Joe. All Joe cared about was getting drunk and getting laid. They worked like dogs of course, sometimes sixteen hours a day, but the little free time they did have was used very efficiently. Joe more efficiently than anyone. Joe had even gotten Ben laid once. He'd been sleeping when Joe had entered with two women. They were both in their mid-forties. Australian from what it sounded like. The lights had dimmed, and a moment later a woman sat on his bed, pulled off his underwear, then straddled him. Yeah, Joe wasn't all that bad. A shame he would have to die.

Joe pulled the covers up over his head and quickly fell back asleep.

Ben pulled out his luggage and pried off the plastic cover revealing a small compartment inside a false bottom. Seven days earlier, when he'd reported for work, he'd watched as head of security for the ship, a man everyone called Stoves, spent twenty minutes inspecting his luggage and room looking for any contraband. He, of course, found nothing.

Ben folded the heavy plastic lid down and retrieved the small pistol. Then he looked down at his watch and waited.

———

Thapa bypassed the group waiting to board the elevator and headed up the winding glass staircase. He exited the stairs on Deck 7 and made his way to the port railing. The sun was a couple of inches off the horizon, and he squinted into the reddening water. The ship had begun its large arc back to where the man had allegedly jumped ship, and the fishing boats were slightly off starboard. They were closer now, maybe three miles off.

Thapa ran to the radio room, walked past two staring officers, and stuck his key into a black door that hadn't been opened since their last inspection. He opened the door and entered the small chamber. His radio squawked and he hit the button to silence it. He needed to concentrate. There was a long safe at the back, and he entered the ten-digit code from memory. The safe whirred open, and Thapa appraised the various firearms. He opted for the Beretta 9mm pistol, slipping it into the small of his back.

He closed the door, feeling the stares of the two men. He exited the radio room, walked the thirty feet to the bridge, and pulled the door open. The bridge was mostly comprised of electronics: radar, weather, computers for anything and everything. Looking out on the water was a series of rectangular windows, each with their own set of industrial black window wipers. Seven white uniforms—the captain, the first officer, the second mate, three additional officers, and Stoves—were observing the approaching boats.

"Where have you been?" Stoves asked. "We need to abandon course. We need to mount the LRAD and send out a distress signal."

"I advise you do no such thing," replied Thapa.

Stoves looked puzzled. He looked even more puzzled when Thapa pulled the Beretta from the small of his back and shot him between the eyes.

SUITE 03
6:16 A.M.

I WOULDN'T SAY I knew something was wrong the moment I'd laid eyes on the African gentlemen, but really I had. Just one of those sixth sense, pit-of-your-stomach feelings you get from dealing with sick individuals for a third of your life.

Now would probably be a good time to mention that in another life I'd been a consultant to the FBI's Violent Crime Unit. Although, these days it felt as if it were two lifetimes ago. Almost as if I'd stumbled into one of those psychic huts, and the crazy woman told me in my previous lives I'd been an otter, a Russian immigrant, and something in the general proximity of a detective. But, as I said, that was in another life.

After the man had jumped, I'd watched as a group of three people ran to an officer walking along the track and animatedly recounted what they'd seen. He instantly pulled the radio from his hip and began speaking. A moment later there had been three loud blasts.

I wasn't overly concerned until the boat started into its wide arc. This slow turn to the left led me to believe some idiot had decided to circle back and pick up the jumper.

Here are a couple of simple rules I live by:

1. Waffles are delicious frozen, cooked, or burned
2. Never stretch before a run, you might pull something
3. Always add a smiley face to sad texts, e.g., *Dear Erica. This isn't working out. I'm taking my sister on the cruise instead :)*
4. Don't watch *The Walking Dead* while you're eating
5. If someone wants to jump to their ultimate death into the Indian Ocean, let them

What concerned me more than the captain's judgment were the three fishing boats, which I hardly believed carried so much as a single fishing lure. No, I suspected there were far more expensive toys on those little boats. The kind of toys that put holes in people. The toys that had put two holes in *moi*. Which might have been the reason I had sprinted down the stairs to the room I was sharing with Lacy.

I pulled my blue *Afrikaans* ID card from the side pocket of my red board shorts and slipped it in the reader. The photo they snapped of me on arrival took up the better half of the left side (I might have been picking my nose in the photo). The light turned from red to green, and I pushed through the door. The 477-square-foot suite was one of six presidential suites aboard the ship. It was carpeted in thick scarlet shag. The tables and cabinets were trimmed in a light oak. There was a walk-in closet and an impressive bathroom with a state-of-the-art Jacuzzi tub. Two leather couches and a set of ocean-blue designer chairs surrounded a fifty-two-inch flat screen. The TV was set on the default channel that displayed a continuous loop of how much fun you were supposed to be having on your cruise.

Since this was my first cruise, I didn't have much to compare it to. But Lacy—who had been on a number of different cruises and always joked about how tacky and over-the-top they were, almost like she was stuck in the middle of an off-off-Broadway production—had marveled at how "classy and tasteful" the *Afrikaans* was.

On our initial walk-through, Lacy had remarked, "And not one palm tree." Apparently, the other ships were chock-full of these.

The point I'm driving at is if your run-of-the-mill cruise ship was the Best Western, the *Afrikaans* was the Ritz Carlton. If your average cruise ship was a peanut, the *Afrikaans* was a macadamia nut. From the bellhop with white gloves who had greeted us on our arrival, to never-ending caviar, to heated toilet seats, to fresh flowers in your suite every afternoon, the *Afrikaans* was the epitome of luxury.

Damn shame I would be jumping off it any second.

I made my way to the large plate glass window that stretched the length of the room and pulled apart the thick ivory curtains. Bright light filled the suite, clawing its way to the king-size Tempur-Pedic and the lump in the top right corner. "What the hell are you doing?" the lump grumbled.

Lacy was not what you would call a morning person. For eight years, from seventh grade until her junior year at college, by 6:00 a.m. Lacy would have a mile in the pool under her belt, then crank out another two over the course of the next hour. She was diagnosed with MS her junior year at Temple University and they decided it would be in good taste to strip her swimming scholarship from her. I'm not sure she'd been out of bed before noon since.

I peered out over the water. Saw nothing. I walked over to the bed and said, "You need to get dressed."

She opened one eye. "What's going on?" It must have been something in the tone of my voice.

"I think, although I'm not positive, that some angry fishermen want to take over this boat."

She sat up. She was still wearing her lime green bikini. "What kind of fishermen?"

"The kind that don't fish."

She picked up some tattered jean shorts and began to shimmy into them. Her eyes opened wide. "Do you feel that?"

I'd felt the teeter-totter of the ship for the past five days and I could feel little else. I shook my head.

"We're slowing down."

She was right. The boat was slowing. I walked back to the window and peered down at the water. The usually large wakes that fell away from the hull were slight, barely making ripples of white water. I guessed the boat would be at a complete standstill within minutes. And I had a bad feeling about what would happen shortly after that.

I said, "Hurry up."

She nodded.

I grabbed the small backpack we'd taken on the safari—it still had a couple water bottles, a few energy bars, a deck of cards, and suntan lotion—and Lacy's zebra-striped fanny pack with her medicine and said, "Let's go."

We were walking out the door, when Lacy turned and said, "Wait! Where's Baxter?"

Baxter is my sister's dog, though "dog" is a bit of a stretch. Technically it *is* a pug, but it looks more like a wadded up newspaper. Lacy hadn't planned on bringing Baxter on the cruise seeing as it wasn't allowed, but when she'd gone to unpack her luggage, she'd discovered the little stowaway. Did I mention that Baxter was narcoleptic? Well, he is. He would fall asleep on a whim. During a walk, chasing after a rabbit, taking a dump. Didn't matter what he was doing, he would just turn to jelly and flop over on his side. It used to be for a couple minutes at a stretch, but as he'd aged, the *naps* had gotten longer and longer. His record was 51 hours. He was also a concerto of barks, snores, and farts. When he licked you, he left this residual slime that smelled like rotten tuna fish, and you'd have to wash your face with lye to get rid of it.

Anyhow, Lacy wasn't exactly sure how Baxter had gotten out of her fiancée's car at the airport in France and into her luggage, let alone passed through security, but she'd long ago stopped trying to figure out how he got into the places he did. He'd been in two Kibbles commercials without her even knowing. Checks came in his name each month.

"Shit," I muttered and started searching.

It didn't take long to find him. He was asleep in his water bowl, his face submerged. Lacy held him up to her ear, cocked her head to the side, then smiled. "Alive."

I gave her a very enthusiastic thumbs up.

We made our way into the hallway and up the stairs. We didn't pass anyone as we ran up the two flights to Deck 8. We pushed through the door leading outside and then navigated a small set of stairs that led to the sundeck at the far back of the ship. It was the highest point on the vessel, offering an unobstructed 360-degree view.

Lacy and I gazed out over the water.

If the *Afrikaans* was at the center of a clock face, numerals two, three, and four would be fishing boats. *Quickly* approaching fishing boats.

"How long do you think we have?" asked Lacy.

The cruise ship was now at a crawl, and I guessed we had two minutes before the boats reached the ship. We were what people refer to as a sitting duck. Which brought about a couple of questions: *why weren't we trying to outrun these pirates?* and *what evasive action was the cruise ship taking?* I would have felt a tad more at ease if there were a bunch of officers aiming RPGs at the incoming boats. There weren't.

"Five minutes tops," I answered.

Lacy said what we both were thinking. "Lifeboat."

I nodded.

"Think we can get one in the water in time?"

I gave one last glance at the fast approaching boats and said, "Let's hope so."

———

When you initially set foot on a cruise ship, one of the first things you do—are forced to do in fact—is a lifeboat, or muster, drill. Everyone puts on their life jackets, they blare this obnoxiously loud alarm, and everyone is mandated to reenact the *Titanic*. In hindsight, I probably shouldn't have played Angry Birds instead.

The lifeboats were situated at the back of the ship where Deck 6 and Deck 7 tapered inward. Each boat was roughly sixty feet long, white on the bottom, orange on top. They looked less like boats and more like the escape pods you might see on an interstellar spacecraft. There were eight in total, four on each side, and I deduced each boat was capable of holding more than fifty people. I figured we had three minutes to somehow get one of these things lowered into the water. And it would be favorable if we were in it when that occurred.

Lacy raised her eyebrows and said, "Uh, how, exactly, do we get that thing down?"

I was under the impression that while I'd been sleeping she'd been going over our cruise ship safety procedure. "Didn't you go to the safety drill?"

"I took a bath and finished up the *In Touch* I bought for the plane ride."

We Prescotts *really* had our priorities in order.

Each lifeboat was sandwiched between two hydraulic arms. There was a heavy chain attached to both the bow and stern of each boat. I searched high and low, but I couldn't find any buttons, levers, cranks, anything that would denote it controlled the lowering of the boat.

Stymied, I said to Lacy, "Stay here. I'm gonna go snag Frank and Susie."

Luckily, the Veranda Cafe was on Deck 7 and more importantly, the *Get the Worm* breakfast buffet. If there were any two people on the boat that knew how to get this thing down, it was the Campers.

Lacy nodded.

The Veranda Cafe was completely outdoors, covered by an enormous domed white tarp. Tall metal chairs surrounded tall glass tables. There was a large buffet set up, everything you could imagine: eggs every conceivable way, sausage every which way, bacon, French toast, pancakes, muffins, cereal, yogurt, and every fruit imaginable.

There were four people eating: an elderly couple and the Campers.

As I passed the buffet, I grabbed an apple and a piece of French toast.

I bypassed the old couple, wolfed down the French toast in two bites, and approached the Camper's table. Frank had three plates cast aside, each splattered with remnants of syrupy goodness, and Susie had the better part of a whole pig in the form of a heaping pile of bacon. She snapped off a piece in her mouth and said, "Got hungry, did you?"

I leaned forward and quietly explained the situation. Frank had only known me for five days, but he could tell I wasn't bluffing. They both jumped to their feet. What I didn't expect was for both to run to the buffet and begin filling tote bags with everything they could find.

I shook my head and told them to hurry. I turned and made my way to the old couple. They were both eating Cheerios and staring blankly at each other. I had seen them in and around the boat, mostly sitting in the shaded area around the pool playing cards. I said, "Not to interrupt your breakfast, but we are about to be boarded by a bunch of pirates."

The woman looked up at me and in a heavy Boston accent said, "First, this damn heat. Now, pirates." She shook her head, but didn't look overly concerned. She went back to her Cheerios.

The Campers—their tote bags slung over their shoulders, an entire pineapple poking from the top of Frank's—followed me from the cafe, down the stairs, and to the lifeboat.

I figured we had used up most of our allotted time and the

pirates would be reaching the ship any moment, if they hadn't already. Frank and Susie had both attended the safety drill and Frank knew exactly how to get the lifeboat down. "Follow me," he said.

We followed him to a small, glassed enclosure splitting the four lifeboats. It looked almost like a hockey penalty box. Frank tried the door. Locked. I pushed him aside and kicked the door until it opened. Frank fiddled with buttons for half a minute, then the lifeboat closest to us began to lower. The four of us shared a quick smile.

I told Frank the plan. The three of them would climb in. I would lower the boat the rest of the way, then slide down one of the cables. Frank would set course for land, we'd play cards, eat pineapple, and have a great story to tell in three days.

When the boat was level with us, I tossed in my backpack and the fanny pack. Susie did the same with their totes. Lacy gently set the now wide-awake Baxter in the boat and started in herself.

"Stap! Turn rand!"

The four of us turned and stared at the man pointing the machine gun at us.

So close.

THE BRIDGE

6:14 A.M.

THAPA STARED at the blood pooling around Stove's head. He had killed before. He had killed often. But never in this fashion. And never for money.

The six others in the room had yet to speak a single word or make a single movement. This may have been related to the gun Thapa swept continually at the group. Captain Holstrond, a tall Norwegian who had commanded the ship for fewer than six months, finally spoke, "What do you want?"

What did he want?

He wanted his son to have a long full life, one he couldn't possibly have without the operation. His fourteen-year-old son had been crippled in a trip up the treacherous Himalayas, carrying luggage for spoiled Americans who paid hundreds of thousands of dollars to climb his native mountains. He wanted nothing more than for his son to walk again. That is what he wanted.

"No talking," he said, waving his gun at Holstrond.

There was a clamoring of feet, and seconds later the door to the bridge was wrenched open. Four Africans entered. The lead pirate had a shaved head and a coarse black beard. He had twin scars running diagonally across his cheeks. His eyes were stained red and glowed against his shiny, black skin. He swept his machine gun over the six men, then made his way back to the door and waved. Two more pirates entered. The first man wore a military-style beret and mirrored aviator glasses. He had smooth, freshly shaved skin and a small puff of a goatee clinging to his chin. He was wearing military fatigues. He smiled, revealing white teeth with a small gap between the front two. He turned to his side, revealing a large pistol and a bowie knife on his hip. He had a machete hanging off his back, splitting his shoulder blades.

The second man was older. He had a heavily receding hairline; what remained was spongy, black, and dotted with white. He had a mangy beard of the same malleable curls of salt-and-pepper which, combined with his spectacles, gave him the look of a tenured college professor. He was dressed in a white gown, zippered high up his neck, its final resting place hidden within his spotty beard.

There were now fourteen men crammed into the bridge. Six pirates, six officers, and Thapa. Plus, of course, the dead Stoves.

The older man took a couple of steps forward. He glanced down at the fallen security officer. He leaned down on his haunches, said a couple words in his native tongue, and slid the man's eyelids shut with his thumb and index finger. He stood, appraised Thapa, and said, "Death is not the worst that can happen to men." The man's voice was deep, the words heavy, made of molasses.

Thapa had heard the adage before. Plato. It did not cleanse him of any of his guilt.

"I am Baruti."

Thapa took his hand.

Baruti cocked his head at the other man and said, "He is called The Mosquito."

Thapa had heard of this man. He was a horrible man. He had done horrible things. Thapa could feel The Mosquito's gaze behind his mirrored glasses devouring him.

"He is a man of few words, but trust me, you want him on your side," remarked Baruti.

Thapa wasn't sure about this.

"I trust you got the money."

Five hundred thousand dollars had been transferred into a bank account known only to him. He had checked the account this morning in the ship's computer center. The money had been there. Gaining interest at this very moment. The money, not Plato, made him feel better about the latest life he'd ended.

He would get another half million in three days' time. Enough to cover his son's surgeries, their move to England, and to live modestly for the rest of their lives. Stove's life would be the last life he took.

"Show me the deck plan."

Thapa nodded to Holstrond, nearly unable to meet the tall man's accusatory glare.

The captain retrieved a thick black binder from beneath the electronics and reluctantly handed it to Thapa, who in turn handed it to Baruti.

Flipping through the binder, Baruti pointed to one of the pirates and said, "Take any passengers on this level, here. Leave a man at the door. Then clear all suites on Deck 6 and lock the passengers in the four presidential suites, here. The same for Deck 5." He spent the next five minutes detailing where he wanted the passengers and crew taken.

Three of the pirates left, leaving Baruti, The Mosquito, and the pirate with red eyes behind. Baruti pulled the large metal briefcase up and laid it on the Captain's chair. He clicked it open. Inside were a laptop computer and a number of other electronics. He handed a small, sleek video camera to Red Eyes, then he nodded to The Mosquito.

The Mosquito smiled, pointed his gun at the six officers and said, "*Wak.*"

Thapa watched as Holstrond and the others exited the bridge, The Mosquito and Red Eyes nipping at their heels.

Baruti stared at Thapa, then pointed at Stoves and said, "Throw him overboard."

————

"Ben" made his way gingerly up the stairs. It still hurt to walk. But at least he no longer felt like there was a fireball in his stomach.

His watch had beeped a second time eight minutes earlier. That's when he'd slipped from his room and made his way up the elevator to Deck 5 and walked to Suite 218.

He knocked on the door. No one answered. He pulled the card he'd *borrowed* from one of the maids and slipped it into the reader. The light turned green and he eased the door open.

He slipped into the foyer of the balcony suite. He pulled the gun from his waistband and clicked off the safety. That's when the lamp hit him. He grunted and fell backwards into the wall. A blur rushed past him, and he reached out and clasped a handful of hair. The woman screamed. She thrashed her arms and legs, and lightning struck Ben's cheek. The bitch had scratched half his face off.

He pushed her off and stood. That's when she'd kicked him in the balls. He'd never felt such pain. He crumpled to the floor and watched through half-open eyes as the small feet scampered out the door.

When he was finally able to stand, Ben took a deep breath, cupped his tender balls in his hand, and walked the final steps to the bridge.

————

Thapa watched quietly as Baruti silently studied the deck plans, which he had been doing since Thapa had returned from tossing Stoves' body over the side of the ship. A couple minutes later, the door opened and The Mosquito returned. He was alone. The two pirates conversed in some African dialect for several minutes. Their conversation was interrupted by a thin rap on the window. All three turned. A member of the crew stood at the door. Thapa remembered him: Ben.

He had streaks of blood running down his cheek. How had he escaped the pirates? And why was he at the bridge? Thapa glanced at Baruti and The Mosquito. Neither looked alarmed.

Ben was one of them.

Baruti opened the door and Ben entered. "Kimal, it has been too long."

Kimal gave a slight bow and said, "Yes, it has."

A wave of disappointment swept over Baruti's face.

Kimal looked down at his feet.

The Mosquito pushed forward and said, *"Whey de gurl?"*

Thapa noticed Baruti shoot The Mosquito a look of disapproval, then utter something in African.

The Mosquito gave a sideways glance at Thapa, then turned to Kimal and began speaking in African. Kimal responded likewise, ending his statement with a shrug.

The Mosquito touched the blood on Kimal's cheek and stuck his fingers in his mouth. *"And dis?"*

Kimal spoke and Thapa could tell from his animations that he was saying that he fell. He took a step forward to mimic falling and grimaced.

The Mosquito stuck out his right hand and grabbed Kimal's groin. Kimal let out a wail. The Mosquito pushed Kimal to the center of the room and yelled, *"You liya!"*

The Mosquito removed the machete from his back. Thapa thought for certain he would slash it across the man's neck. But he didn't. He pressed the blade against his throat and screamed, *"Fine hur!"*

SALON MUSA

7:01 A.M.

SALON MUSA RESEMBLED, well, a salon. It was all mirrors and that foggy green glass that reminded me of green beer on Saint Patrick's Day. Everything was in threes. Three chairs in the small waiting room, three haircutting stations, three hair-washing stations, and three hair-drying stations. The only thing missing were three hairstylists, but as we'd been marched through the door I'd noticed the salon hours were 8:00 a.m. to 7:00 p.m.

Speaking of the door, you could see the outline of the pirate leaning against the door through the foggy green glass. At the lifeboat, after the four of us had turned around, the African had pointed his gun at us forbidding us to move. He was clad in cut-off military fatigues and a ratty muscle shirt. His hair was tied down in thick cornrows. His teeth were capped in gold. He could have been any rapper in America.

The radio on his hip chimed, and he held it to his ear, then spoke into it. In English, broken but still understandable, he said, "Four by de lifebats." Then he proceeded to speak in his native tongue, which was full of clicks and clacks. After his conversation, the African waved his gun at us and said, "Walk dat way. Don make mey shoot you."

Leading us around the outside of the ship to the front of Deck 7, he then ushered us into the salon.

And here we were.

There had been two women sitting in the waiting room when we'd arrived. To say they were startled when the four of us marched into the salon ushered by an African holding a machine gun would be an understatement.

Minutes later, the six of us had been joined by the old couple from the Veranda Cafe. The door opened and the woman stopped cold. "This is the worst salon," she said, shaking her head. "This is nothing like the salon I go to in New York. No, I don't like this salon at all."

The old man rolled his eyes.

A minute after that, we became ten.

The door opened, and a tall man with a curvy woman walked in. Both were dripping wet. The man was dense like a linebacker, his barrel chest covered in thick black hair, and he wore those tight swim trunks Europeans are known for. He also wore a defiant sneer, his enormous, retina-scorching white front teeth grinding together. The woman was a bottle blonde, almost a bottle white, and was clad in the skimpiest bikini ever made, the white fabric just partially covering the nipples of her three-sizes-too-big, surgically-enhanced breasts. Both held champagne flutes in their hands. Mimosas.

The tall man was barking, "Do you know who I am? Do you know who I am?"

I don't think Lil Wayne knew who he was or much less cared. I, unfortunately, knew who he was and I *did* care. Well, I cared that I was locked in a room with him. Yes, that's right. Gilroy and Trinity had joined the party. I looked around for some peroxide I could drink.

After the initial shock had worn off, compulsory introductions were made.

The two women, Berta and Reen, were from Oregon. I guessed

they were sisters. They had an appointment at 8:00 a.m. to get their hair done, but they'd been so excited they'd been in the waiting room since 6:00.

The old couple was Walter and Marge Kohn from Boston and New York. They had houses respectively in each. They, or at least *she*, hated everything that wasn't made, located, or associated in some way with either of the two cities.

And then you had Gilroy and Trinity. Douchebag and Bimbo.

"How did this happen?" asked Berta. Or Reen.

Gilroy shook his head in disgust. "I'll tell you how this happened: the people that run this ship don't know their ass from a hole in the ground. That's how. We're out here in the middle of fucking nowhere. A boat loaded with *multi-millionaires* such as myself. What do you think is going to happen? We should have had military chaperones at all times. That's the truth. This area is crawling with pirates. I knew this was going to happen. I knew it. I fucking knew it."

He was silent a moment, then added, "Shit, these guys are probably going through our rooms as we speak. I don't know about ya'll, but I got a twenty thousand dollar designer watch in there and a couple hundred thousand dollars cash. Ah, shit. If these guys get their hands on my Black card, there's no telling what they can buy. I mean there's no limit. They could buy anything."

I was tempted to tell this buffoon that if he knew this cruise was so dangerous, then why did he sign up for it, and that no one told him to pack his designer watch, and surely no one told him to bring a couple hundred thousand dollars cash, and if one of these pirates with eight names got hold of his Black card and tried to buy, oh say, a machine gun or a nuke, American Express might find the purchase suspicious.

"Actually, these waters are extremely safe," said Frank. "Off the coast of Somalia and up north you might have to worry about pirates. But not down here. This is freak."

Gilroy took a swig of his mimosa, but said nothing.

Reen—or Berta—said, "How do we know these guys aren't Somalians?"

"They're not," replied Frank. "And it's *Somali* not Somalians."

"Where are they from then?"

"I'd guess South Africa, Mozambique, or Zimbabwe."

"And how would you know that?" shot Gilroy.

"Easy. I overheard him speaking Zulu. Those are the countries that speak Zulu."

"And how exactly would you know what fucking Zulu sounds like?"

Frank blinked a couple times, then said, "There are three distinct clicking noises in the Zulu language: one that sounds like the sucking of teeth, one that sounds like the popping of a bottle, and one that sounds like the walking of a horse. And I know because I watched a show on it."

Gilroy sank into his chair.

I almost started clapping.

"Aren't Zulus cannibals or something?" asked Reenerta. "Are they going to eat us?"

"I don't think they'll eat us," Frank said with a shake of his head. "That they speak Zulu doesn't mean a lot. Most of the people in the eastern provinces speak Zulu, from the small villages to the big cities. And he had a passing understanding of English which means he's been around white people at least part of his life. Probably a hired gun, a mercenary."

Susie turned to him and asked, "Do you think they'll hurt us, baby?"

He shrugged.

Gilroy grunted and said, "They're not going to hurt anybody. They'll take everything they can find, ransack the rooms, then be done with it."

"You can't be sure of that," Susie rebuked.

"Sure I'm sure. They'll take everybody's money, take all the jewelry from the boutique, and then scram."

"Ransom."

The word chilled the air. Hearts paused. Buttholes clenched. Mouths went dry. I turned to Lacy. Her eyes were still red and puffy. She'd been crying since having to leave Baxter in the lifeboat. In fact, "ransom" had been the first word she'd spoken in over an hour.

"What? Somebody had to say it," she said, wiping snot from her nose.

I'd been thinking it since I'd seen the man jump overboard.

"Fine by me," Gilroy said with a flash of his prized Chiclets. "I've got ransom insurance. When you are in my financial position you have to, you know. Got to have ransom insurance." He looked around the group. "Don't tell me none of you guys have ransom insurance."

Trinity looked at him and smiled. "You have ransom insurance, baby. Oh, you think of everything." Her boobs jiggled as she hugged him tightly.

I didn't hate it.

The next ten minutes were spent listening to Gilroy recount how he'd gone about getting ransom insurance, which company insured him, and why all of us were idiots for not having it. By the end of his diatribe, I was ready to knock on the door and ask Lil Wayne if I could borrow his rifle for a second.

Lacy whispered, "I hate him."

After Gilroy wrapped up his presentation, there was a subdued quiet. Susie broke the silence with, "I hope the pirates get done before lunch. They were supposed to do cheese steaks."

Lacy and I looked at each other, both fighting down smiles. That was our Susie.

Marge Kohn had an opinion on this matter and said, "You want a good cheesesteak, you go down to Riverfront and 143rd in Queens."

"134th," corrected Walter.

This led Gilroy to tell a seven-minute anecdote about cheese steaks. I thought being in a Jeep with this guy for eight hours was bad enough. This was going to be torture.

I noticed Lacy staring directly across the room where Berta and Reen were sitting. I followed Lacy's gaze. Reen was holding Berta's hand. Stroking it.

I mentally drew a line through the word *sisters* in my head. And I once called myself a detective?

Lacy asked, "You were getting married later today, weren't you?"

At one point, on the first day, Lacy had stumbled across a group of fifteen lesbians. One of the couples was rumored to be having a civil union ceremony held sometime during the cruise.

I'll blame the pirates on my taking this long to piece this together. I mean, come on, the frumpiness alone should have been enough.

"Later tonight," Berta said with a smile. "In District 9."

District 9 was one of the clubs on the ship, which I could only assume was named after the Peter Jackson directed movie of the same name. The movie is an allegory of modern day apartheid in South Africa, of course, this time, with aliens. If you haven't seen it, it's pretty good. The movie, not the club.

Marge leaned toward them. "Which one of you is getting married?" she asked, revealing she was capable of smiling.

"We're getting married…to one another."

Marge looked confused. Walter sighed audibly and said, "They're lesbians."

"*Lessssssbbbbbbbbbbbbbiannnnnnnns?*"

Something tells me Marge didn't watch much *Ellen*.

Reen patted Berta's hand and said, "Oregon doesn't recognize same sex marriage, so we decided to have a civil union ceremony. This cruise was going to be our honeymoon, but then Berta had the idea to have the ceremony on the ship."

"I think anyone should be able to marry anyone," remarked Trinity.

"Now don't go saying that," Gilroy said, patting Trinity's leg. "Marriage is the union between one man and one woman. We can't have anyone just up and marrying. Soon you'll have men marrying goats and women getting married to trees."

Susie leaned forward and said, "And just out of curiosity, how many of these one-man-and-one-woman unions have you had?"

After being in the same Jeep as Gilroy for eight hours, Frank had decided to Google him when we returned to the ship and see just how full of shit the guy was. The verdict: half-full. Gilroy Andrews was an extremely successful oil driller in Georgia. Or had been. He'd once been worth around twenty million, but after four divorces and a half dozen ill-advised drillings, his net worth was down to around three million.

Gilroy shot Susie a look but said nothing. I doubted Trinity knew she was well on her way to being number five.

The subject changed when Susie slapped Frank's leg and said, "My insulin."

Frank puffed out his cheeks and said, "Shit."

Lacy cut her eyes at me and I knew she was thinking about her own meds, which were in her fanny pack, which was in the lifeboat. She'd been so preoccupied with leaving Baxter that she hadn't thought of her meds. Multiple sclerosis is an enigmatic disease. There is no known cure, and even the cause is something of a mystery. Over the course of a day, Lacy took ten different pills. On her current regimen she'd only had one flare-up—a three-week bout of severe dizziness—in the past year and a half. If she missed a couple doses, or even a couple days, nothing might happen. But then again, something might.

Susie, on the other hand, had diabetes. And Susie just so happened to be the worst diabetic *ever*. Most people with diabetes could control it by taking insulin once or twice a day. I had watched danish-and-Pepsi-loving Susie shoot up five times yesterday and six times the day before that.

Susie put her head in her hands and said, "Oh God."

We didn't have time to sympathize or strategize or even ponder the impasse. The door to the salon opened, and a man stepped in. He was slight with black hair and silky brown skin. I thought for a moment he was there to rescue us, but it only took an instant to realize he wasn't. He was one of them. He was their inside man. He was the reason we didn't try to outrun the pirates.

Ganju something-or-other was a security officer. I'd run into him late one night. He was having coffee at the twenty-four-hour cafe and watching a soccer match on television. He was intensely invested in the game, his entire body applauding and condemning each touch of the ball. I asked him who he was rooting for. Manchester United, he said proudly. I was curious how this tiny brown man, obviously not indigenous to the UK, had become so enchanted by this team, and inquired as much. And that is when I learned about the Gurkhas. I asked about Nepal and he answered in clipped sentences. I asked about Everest, which elicited not an angry response, but a heated one, and he explained that his son, a Sherpa for the rich climbers, had been crippled by the mountain. He asked me where I was from, and I told him, but I knew he was just being polite. I could tell from personal experience—say, when Erica wanted to talk and I wanted to watch the last ninety seconds of the Seahawks game in fucking peace—that all he wanted to do was watch the match. I told him his next twenty coffees were on me, slipped him a hundred dollar bill, and left him alone.

Now he stood in the entrance, Lil Wayne standing just behind him. He was holding a pistol in his right hand and a small metallic object in his left. The object made a soft clicking noise. It was one of those counters you sometimes see bouncers at clubs using. The sound of ten clicks filled the silent room.

Then as quickly as he came, he left.

DECK 6

DECKS 4, 5, and 6 were passenger decks, home to the hundred suites and six presidential suites that collectively housed the 208 guests of the *Afrikaans*.

Thapa approached the two presidential suites, 05 and 06, situated at the bow of Deck 6. He'd been inside each of the suites a handful of times and he was always amazed at how spacious they were. Although he didn't know the exact cost, Thapa had heard the rate to book one of the six suites for the eleven-day cruise was well over twenty thousand dollars. The last time Thapa had set foot in one of the large rooms was a year earlier when he'd been summoned by a maid who had overheard a woman screaming. Thapa had slid his master key into the door and barged in only to find a man and woman both clad in leather, the man holding a large whip in his hand. Yes, that had been quite an experience.

There were two pirates leaning up against the outside wall, and they were conversing in broken English.

One of the pirates was the darkest black man Thapa had ever seen. The other, possibly the lightest. They were obviously both from Africa, but different parts. That's why they were conversing in English. The universal language of money and, as such, mercenaries.

Thapa nodded and both jutted their chins upward in response. Friendly, these guys were not. Thapa slid his key into the door. Remembering the passengers were now *hostages* and might be even less friendly than the two African pirates, Thapa pulled the Beretta from his hip. He pushed the door in and took two tentative steps forward.

Hushed voices went silent and Thapa watched as countless heads whipped in his direction. He heard a "Thank God" and a "We're saved." Several women began weeping. Of course they would *think* he had come to save them. They would think the brown man they'd seen walking the ship for six days had somehow overcome the even darker men and was here to free them.

Two men stood directly in front of him. One of the men, a bookish-looking guy wearing a white tank top and briefs, threw his hands up and said, "What took you so long?"

The other man, clad only in boxer shorts, attempted to rush past him. Thapa stopped him with his arm, pushed him back, and then pointed the gun at his chest. "Step back," Thapa said calmly.

The man's eyes widened. He waddled backwards as if pulled by an unseen hand. "You bastard. You're one of them," he cried.

Yes, he *was* one of them.

God save him.

The hostages' eyes bore into him. He noticed a woman—a large woman who had been friendly to him on the elevator—wearing a T-shirt and big white panties. She was lying on the ground, pulling her shirt down over her privates, tears dripping down her cheeks.

Thapa took a deep breath and did what he'd come into the room to do. For each person he saw, he clicked down the small metallic tab. The two men in front of him, *click, click*. The large woman, *click*. Eight sitting on the bed where he'd found the man lashing away at the woman with the whip. Five sitting at the table. Ten on the couches and chairs. One in the bathroom. Twenty-seven clicks in all.

Thapa exited the room and walked directly across the hall. The people were different but the faces were the same. Twenty-five clicks.

Thapa made his way down to Deck 5 and repeated the procedure. Deck 4 was a passenger deck, but it was also home to half the crew accommodations. Since there were no Presidential suites on Deck 4, the passengers had been crammed into the four double suites. Thapa clicked these people off.

The opposite side of Deck 4 was the Upper Crew Deck, home to the forty cabins of the higher-ups: the captain and his team of officers, the guest relations and entertainment staffs, theater techs, photographers, and outside concessionaires that worked the gift shops and salon. These folks were a revolving door of faces, and many only worked a single cruise before moving onto greener pastures. Although Thapa was considered one of these bourgeoisie and his cabin was nestled between those of two officers, he couldn't have named half the faces he clicked off. And he knew none of the faces could have named his.

But the faces on the Lower Crew Deck were a different story. As Thapa took the elevator to Deck 2, he could feel his stomach tighten. He would soon be forced to confront his fellow crew members: the hardworking cooks, waiters, busboys, bartenders, maids, casino workers, and maintenance workers that truly made the ship run. Thapa had worked with many of these people for three years, and he would have to watch as they slowly comprehended what he'd done. What he'd *become*.

Thapa advanced to the crew break room. There were two pirates near the door leading to the room, which was filled with couches, flat screens, a stocked bar, foosball, pool, and ping-pong tables, and a small attached fitness center.

Thapa pushed into the room. The crew members who had

been working were dressed in their different uniforms: white coats for the kitchen staff, black for the dealers at the casino, red for the waiters and waitresses. The others were all dressed in their sleeping attire: boxers, T-shirts, panties, pajamas.

There was a moment of silence as everyone took in Thapa's presence; the silence broke when the ninety-plus individuals broke into wild applause. Thapa watched as they high-fived, many turned to one another and hugged. Some kissed. A guy sitting on the edge of the couch with a beer in his hand, set the beer down, and lunged toward him, his arms outstretched. A bartender named Joe. He was tall, built like a rock, charismatic, good looking, a free spirit. Everybody adored him. Thapa couldn't count how many of Joe's hugs he'd had to ward off. But every so often Joe would be successful, sneaking up from behind him, wrapping his large arms around Thapa's small body and lifting him off the ground in a tight squeeze. As humiliating as Joe's hugs were, Thapa always found himself feeling a bit spryer, a bit younger afterward, almost as if Joe had passed some of his zeal for life into him.

Thapa drew the gun from his side, but he was too late. Joe was already dipping to engulf Thapa in his muscled arms. Thapa brought his left hand up, the one holding the clicker, swept it across his body, and struck Joe in the throat. Joe's eyes bulged and his hands flew to his throat as he crumbled to the ground.

Thapa still remembered the day one of his instructors had taught him the blow. His instructor, a retired British Special Forces officer, had said of the strike to the Adam's apple, "He won't die from the blow, but for the next couple minutes, he'll wish he had."

The ashen faces of the crew traded glances between their writhing leader and the man who had betrayed them. Thapa quickly clicked off the men and women, then left.

Finally finished, Thapa walked outside and leaned against the railing. As of the last port there were 381 people aboard the *Afrikaans*.

He looked down at the clicker.

380.

Someone was missing.

———

Kimal averaged five minutes to a room. More than enough time to peer into every nook and cranny. He exited room 218 and walked directly into room 219. Kimal hoped he would have the restraint not to kill the girl if he found her. His testicles were still aching something horrible.

He completed his search and moved onto the next room, then the next. Between rooms 206 and 204 there was a door. Kimal pulled the door open. There were two maid carts and a cart full of towels. He looked around the small room for any place to hide, but unless the girl had turned herself into a mop, she wasn't there. He turned to leave, then decided better, plunging his hand down into the towels and fishing around.

Nothing.

He shook his head, closed the door, and walked to Suite 204.

Had Kimal inspected the maid's carts more closely, he would have noticed one of the cart's trashcans was filled with clean sheets and one of the carts was a hundred and ten pounds heavier than the other.

SALON MUSA

11:43 A.M.

"HOW ABOUT SOME RED HIGHLIGHTS?"

Berta looked at Trinity questioningly.

"Red is all the rage right now," said Lacy.

Susie nodded. "Oh, I think that would look marvelous."

Trinity ran her hands through Reen's hair and said, "And for you, I'm thinking platinum."

"Oh, yeah," Lacy cooed.

Berta and Reen looked at each other. They were both smiling. Then they both turned to Trinity and nodded.

This had been going on for the past hour. And again, Lacy was to blame. Conversation had been at a standstill—you can only fill the silence with expectations of death for so long before it becomes droll—and in fact, I'd been flipping through a magazine —*Sports Illustrated's* Swimsuit Issue—at the time Lacy decided to lift the lid on Pandora's box. I believe her exact wording had been, "So ladies, let's hear it, what were you going to have done to your hair?"

And everyone turned and listened as Berta announced she'd just wanted a couple inches off and Reen was going to get a bob. Yes, a bob. To which Trinity had exclaimed, "No, no, no, no, no," and proclaimed she *almost* completed cosmetology school and she was going to do their hair.

Again, this had been over an hour ago.

Susie and Lacy stood behind Trinity as she began washing both women's hair, which left Frank, Gilroy, Walter, Marge, and I in the back of the salon.

Taking up Susie's seat next to Frank, I said, "Welcome to *Extreme Makeover, Luxury Cruise Liner Overtaken by Pirates* edition."

He laughed.

I noticed Gilroy even cracked a grin.

Frank shook his head and said, "Women and weddings."

"You mean, women and civil union ceremonies."

"Right."

"Where did you and Susie get hitched?"

"Vegas."

"No!"

"*Chapel of Love*, baby."

"You're that couple."

"We're that couple," he said with a smile. "My parents were long dead and I only have one brother—who I barely talk to. And her parents are crazy hippies that live in Montana and they wouldn't come for the wedding. And Susie and I had just put our savings into the business and didn't have a pot to piss in."

While on the safari, Frank had recounted how he and Susie had made their fortune. They met Frank's junior year—Susie just a freshman—at New Mexico State University. Fast forward a year, and the two were living together in an apartment off campus. Both were working full-time—landscaping for Frank, waitressing for Susie—and going to school full-time, and they were barely scraping by. They were so poor, in fact, that Susie refused to let them run the heater in the winter. Whenever Susie would study she would wrap herself in a blanket, but she continually complained to Frank that each time she moved her arms to turn the page of her text book or take a drink of tea, she would let all the warm air out. Come Christmas, they made a pact not to buy each other anything but to make their gifts instead. Susie made Frank a couple mixed CDs. Frank, whose grandmother had forced him to knit with her every Sunday for ten years, knitted Susie a blanket. But not any blanket, a blanket with sleeves.

That's right, Frank invented the Snuggie.

It wasn't an overnight success. For the next two years, Frank worked during the day and knitted Snuggies at night. Susie was finishing up her degree in Finance and would join him on the weekends trying to sell door-to-door. Or in most cases, *not sell* door-to-door. Finally, Susie decided that they needed to do something drastic. So they pooled all the money they had, took out two loans, and made an infomercial. The rest is history.

"Sounds like a recipe for a Vegas wedding," I said.

He turned and stared at Susie's backside—which was blocking the hair washing stations, Trinity, Lacy, the salon entrance, and everything in between—and said, "If I could go back and do it different, I wouldn't change a thing."

"I got married in Vegas once."

Frank and I turned and looked at Gilroy. He was nodding. "Yep, wife number two. Sammy. Man, she was a looker. I was playing blackjack, the big table, thousand-dollar hands, and she was my cocktail waitress. First time she walked by, I hit on a nineteen, a fucking nineteen. Don't know what I was thinking. Lost my ass that night, like ninety thousand. Got hitched two hours later."

I said, "It's like a fairy tale."

Gilroy shot me a look. Frank fought down a smile, then asked, "What happened?"

"Oh, we were happy for a couple years. Then she got this thyroid thing and she just started packing on the pounds. She hit one fifty, and I hit her with the papers."

"She got sick and put on some pounds and you divorced her?"

"I can't walk into a room with a cow."

I thought Frank was going to pick him up and throw him through one of the glass dividers.

I was tempted to ask Gilroy about weddings one, three, and four, but I wasn't sure I could stomach any more of his megalo-mania without ramming my fist into his face.

Anyhow, I peered over at Marge and Walter and said, "How 'bout you old bats, did you guys get married by a woolly mammoth or what?" Actually, I said, "How did you two get married?"

Marge lolled her head to the side, already annoyed, and said, "We got married in Boston."

No shit.

"We got married at a Red Sox game," she supplemented. She had a twinkle in her eye that told me she was back on that day in 1935 or 1312. "Walter coached them back then."

"You coached the Red Sox?" Frank's eyebrows nearly jumped off his forehead.

Walter nodded.

Marge said, "He was a hitting coach, 1957 to '70."

"1956," Walter chimed.

"It was May 21st, 1959, a couple hours before the Sox played the Orioles. We got married on home plate."

"Was Ted Williams there?" asked Frank, taking up the seat next to Walter.

"Of course he was there," Marge scoffed. "He was Walter's best man."

This was almost too much for Frank to handle. This led to a series of tangents that I couldn't follow, nor cared to, and I went back to my *Sports Illustrated*. I had just mentally eloped and consummated with the cover girl when I heard, "Ta-da."

I looked up. Berta and Reen stood holding hands in front of Susie, Lacy, and Trinity, looking timid and meek. Berta's hair was light brown with red highlights. Reen's hair was platinum. I'd expected both girls to come back with crew cuts, but apparently

Trinity learned most of the ins and outs before she was dishonorably discharged from cosmetology school. I also suspected that while Trinity had been doing their hair, Susie and Lacy had done the women's makeup, and both looked for lack of a better word, heterosexual.

"Well, what do you think?" Susie asked.

Frank whistled.

"You girls single?" I catcalled.

The lesbians thought this was funny and Berta even struck a pose.

Lacy plopped down next to me and said, "I did the makeup."

"Oh, is that why they look like hookers?"

She slapped my leg.

"Who's next?" asked Trinity.

I looked around. Walter desperately needed to get his ears done and Gilroy needed to run some thinning shears through his chest hair.

Lacy pointed at me and said, "You could clean up around his neck."

"I'm fine," I assured Trinity.

"Real quick."

"Really, I'm fine."

But Trinity was already behind me with the clippers. She turned them on, stuck them to my neck, and then screamed, gouging me with the clippers.

I cringed, then saw what had made her scream. Lil Wayne was standing just feet from us. His gun was out in front of him. "Up. Wey move."

DECK 4

1:44 P.M.

THE PIRATES, two in front, two in back, marched the small group forward. To Thapa, they resembled a herd of cattle being funneled into the chop shop. Some of the hostages looked terrified, as if they knew exactly what lay ahead. Others, just numbly followed behind.

Thapa had been ordered to move all the hostages to two larger areas. He decided on Transvaal, the show lounge, on Deck 6 and Pretoria, the four-star restaurant, on Deck 2. Both were large enough to hold over two hundred people and had limited entry and exit points.

The group in front of them, one of the mini-groups from one of the Deck 4 double suites, approached the winding glass stairwell and began stumbling down. A lone woman at the back of the group, wearing purple pajama bottoms and a large white T-shirt, wasn't moving quickly enough for one of the pirates and he began screaming at her to move faster.

She wailed about having a bad hip, but this did nothing to appease the pirate. He jabbed the muzzle of his gun into her back and shoved her forward. She quickly took two steps down, tripped, and then fell forward the final three stairs, landing face first on the Deck 2 lobby.

Thapa watched as the two pirates laughed uncontrollably. Thapa couldn't understand how they could get so much satisfaction from the woman's fall. Thapa desperately wanted to help the woman to her feet, but he couldn't. The caring, compassionate Ganju was dead. No more.

After one of the people in the group had helped the fallen woman up, the group made their way past two pirates guarding the door to the nearly half-full restaurant. They entered the large room, scanned the individuals seated in the high-backed chairs surrounding the many white-tablecloth-clad tables, then quickly dispersed to seats of their own.

Thapa and the four pirates exited the room. There were still two more groups of cattle that needed herding.

———

Kimal had searched high and low. He had looked in every place imaginable. The girl was gone.

He took a deep breath. How would The Mosquito take the news? Kimal had thought The Mosquito was going to kill him earlier; surely he wouldn't survive another disappointment. Kimal had been the one responsible for finding the girl. That had been his only job. And he had failed.

Maybe he would plead with The Mosquito. Beg for his life. But he had heard stories of the man. He was ruthless. He had wiped out entire villages. Killed hundreds. Raped and beaten countless women. It was even rumored he'd executed a group of small children just for the hell of it.

Kimal looked out on the vast ocean, the softly rolling cobalt extending as far as the eye could see. The sun was directly overhead and had been beating down on him for the last twenty minutes. Sweat dripped off his forehead and ran down his cheeks. He looked down, his chin catching on the top of the orange life preserver. He pulled the black nylon straps tight as he'd been taught. He didn't want the life jacket coming off.

He picked the silver, blow-up lounge chair off the deck. It was surprisingly light. He thought of how he'd watched the woman floating on it in the pool, a bottle of beer held snug in one of the lounge's two cupholders.

He tossed the raft off the side of the ship and watched as it flipped and floated and fell the sixty feet, then stuck silently to the water, a sliver of silver tape on the rippling blue. The small waves carried the raft to the ship's hull where it rocked against the side.

Kimal wasn't stupid. He had packed a small survival bag, mostly water, some food, a blanket. He'd even packed a couple of magazines. Who knew how long he would be out there? He'd stuffed everything into trash bags, taped it secure, and then stuffed it into a large backpack. He slung the backpack over his shoulder, climbed up the railing, and before he could talk himself out of it, he jumped.

He surfaced, shaking the water from his eyes. He'd done it. The raft was a couple feet away and he swam to it, clutching it in his arms. He pushed away from the hull of the ship and paddled with his arms. The anchor was directly ahead of him and he pulled himself around the half-foot diameter chain.

The current picked up the raft and silently carried him free of the ship. He would live. Soon, when Baruti made his demands, there would be planes moving over the area, ships even. Kimal smiled. He would be picked up within the day. He clutched the bag to his chest. And if not, he had enough to survive for three or four days.

The current turned the raft slightly, and Kimal faced the ship, which was now a hundred yards away and growing smaller by the second. The water was fairly calm and he pulled the life jacket over his head and tied it to the backpack. He would put it back on if the waves began to intensify. He opened the backpack and fished out a bottle of water. He took a sip from the bottle, then placed it snugly in the cupholder. He almost laughed.

He squinted at the glistening white ship, specifically the nose of the ship. There was a man standing there. He was holding something large and black. Kimal could just make out the beret sitting atop the man's head.

The Mosquito.

Kimal flipped onto his stomach, dug his arms into the dark water, and began to paddle and kick frantically. He did so for a long minute, then turned and looked over his shoulder. The bullet hit him in the left eye. The young African's body slipped into the blue chasm, then slowly began to sink.

SHOW LOUNGE
2:52 P.M.

THE TRANSVAAL SHOW LOUNGE was located at the rear of the
ship on Deck 6. There were large ivory chairs, twenty to a row,
concentrically spaced outwards from the stage. The chairs were
arranged on a steep slope, with two aisles splitting the audience
into three sections. The sections funneled down to a brassy stage
being dusted by a heavy purple curtain.

Two days earlier, Lacy and I had been in the show lounge for
fifteen minutes. It would have been far less if I'd had any say in it.

Lacy had said, "We have to go watch this stand-up comic
tonight."

Now, J.J. Watkins might not be the worst stand-up comedian
on the face of the earth, but he was in the top ten, maybe even the
top seven. I mean, the guy did ten minutes on SPAM. And not the
e-mail type of spam. The actual, meat product SPAM. And then
he'd started in on the cruise ship. The last joke I'd heard before I'd
grabbed Lacy by the ear and drug her out was, "And how about
that breakfast buff-A? More like a breakfast buff-C-minus."

I'm serious. He said those words. In that order. If Frank had
been there, we might have had a man overboard two days ago.

Currently, the show lounge held roughly 140 passengers—

sorry, *hostages*—and three African pirates holding their automatic rifles at the ready. For some reason, I had an uncanny feeling that this stint in the show lounge would be a tad longer than my last and just *slightly* more painful.

The ten of us had been the first to enter the room and we had walked down the sloping red carpet and filed into the first three rows on the left side.

Berta, Reen, Gilroy, and Trinity were in the first row. Frank, Susie, Lacy, and I had taken seats in the second. And Marge and Walter had taken up seats behind us.

Over the course of the next hour, we watched as another small group and four large groups were ushered through the doors. Each of the large groups contained anywhere between twenty-five and thirty-five people. Most of the men were clad in underwear, mostly boxers and boxer briefs, with a sprinkling of embarrassing whitey-tighties. A couple of gentlemen wore shirts. One man was donning a robe. The women were a split between bra and panties or T-shirt and panties. Many of the women tried to cover their bodies as they walked into the room, then found their way to their seats.

At one point, Berta and Reen stood and joined a group of eight women that had taken up seats in the center section. The lesbians embraced each other, and I noticed when they sat down all of them were holding hands. A couple of people had joined a familiar face here and there, but apart from the lesbians, most had stayed with their initial group.

Keeping a watch on the lot of us were three pirates standing near the only entrance: Lil Wayne and two others. One of the others was wearing black jeans, no shirt. He was light skinned, with a shaved head and a beard. Sticking with the rap theme, I mentally named him Common. The third pirate was wearing a red shirt and a black bandana. Tupac. Behind the three pirates, two double doors were pulled closed.

Common walked up and down the aisles, his large gun held to

his chest. On closer examination, he had two matching scars running diagonally down his cheeks. They were perfectly symmetrical and I had a feeling they were self-inflicted. As he passed our group, I noticed he paid special attention to Lacy with his red stained eyes.

I mentally cut off his dick and shoved it up his ass.

Frank, who was on my left, jabbed me in the ribs and said, "Where do you think they're keeping everybody else?"

I thought about this for a moment. The logical thing would be to take everyone from Decks 5 and above to one place, and everyone from Decks 4 and below to one place. I was guessing this was exactly what they'd done.

Lacy said, "I bet the rest of the passengers and all the crew are in Pretoria. You just have that one entrance and the place could hold at least 250 people."

I agreed with her.

Frank said, "It's probably mostly crew down there."

He was right. Wherever they were holding the other hostages, there were fewer than seventy remaining passengers. The rest were cooks, maids, waiters, and the many other personnel that made up the crew.

The doors to the show lounge opened and two men walked in. Both were African. The younger of the two was wearing military fatigues, a beret, and dark aviator glasses. The older man was clad in a tunic that fed into a spongy beard. Square glasses were pushed down on his nose.

The Warlord and the Professor.

The Professor spoke to the three pirates. Lil Wayne and Tupac stayed at the door, but Common followed behind the Warlord and the Professor as they walked down the walkway and onto the stage.

The Professor removed a small device from one of his large pockets and handed it to Common. It was a video camera.

Common pointed the camera at the stage, and the Professor began to speak.

WASHINGTON D.C.
10:37 A.M.

PAUL GARRET DROVE through the southwest gate of the White House and presented the guard with his identification. He was escorted up West Executive Avenue and to the West Basement entrance. He was handed off to a second guard who led him down a flight of stairs, past the White House Mess, down a long corridor, then stopped at a thick white door. The guard knocked. The door was opened and White House Press Secretary Paul Garret entered the White House Situation Room.

This was not how he'd been intending to spend his Saturday.

The usual suspects were present and seated, and Garret did a quick round of hellos. He took a seat in one of the eighteen specially designed chairs and gazed across the oval table. There were nine empty chairs. The others were occupied by the President, Vice President, the Directors of the CIA, FBI, and NSA, the National Security Advisor, the Secretary of Defense, and the Admiral Chief of Naval Operations.

The National Security Advisor, also known as the Assistant to the President for National Security Affairs, was a tall, broad shouldered man with a commanding stare. A stare Paul knew only too well. The man had a thick mane of white hair and luminous blue eyes. The man peered around the room, holding his gaze just a millisecond longer on his only son, then said, "I'm sorry to see you all under these circumstances."

A folder was placed in front of Garret by an unknown hand. His father, retired Marine Corps General Roger Garret, cleared his throat and said, "Within this folder you will find a dossier on two men."

Paul opened the folder and looked at the top sheet. An aging black man with glasses stared back at him.

"Baruti Quaroni," affirmed his father. "Seventy-one years old. He was born in a small Zulu village in the KwaZulu-Natal province of South Africa. Raised by an uncle in Cape Town and eventually attended the University of Natal, but was thrown out after a series of anti-apartheid boycotts and later imprisoned at Robben Island. Quaroni undertook study at the University of London by correspondence through its external program, and received his degree in philosophy. In prison, he met Nelson Mandela. Quaroni and Mandela co-founded and commandeered the Umkhonto we Sizwe, or the MK, the active military wing of the African National Congress.

"After Nelson Mandela's imprisonment in 1962, Quaroni waged a guerrilla war against the apartheid regime in which many civilians became casualties. The MK was subsequently deemed a terrorist organization by the South African government and banned. In 1986, Quaroni was detained and convicted for his role in the 1983 Church Street Bombing, an explosion in Pretoria near the South African Air Force Headquarters, resulting in nineteen fatalities and two hundred and seventeen persons injured.

"After his release in 1996, with apartheid dissolved for more than two years, Quaroni turned his attention to the blossoming AIDS epidemic that had taken a stranglehold on his fellow Zulus while he'd spent thirteen years behind bars. In 2004, Quaroni filled twelve buses with infected Zulu villagers, drove them to a hospital in the coastal town of Durban and demanded the doctors treat them as patients. The doctors ignored his request. Six months later, Quaroni returned to the hospital, only this time he had six men at his side, each carrying a machine gun, and they took over the hospital by force. The hostage situation lasted thirty-six hours. After the dust had settled, two doctors and one nurse were killed and somehow Quaroni had escaped. He hasn't been heard from since."

Roger Garret took a breath and said, "The second man is Keli 'The Mosquito' Nkosi."

There was a pause as everyone shuffled to the second sheet. The picture showed a black man donning a beret, fatigues, and aviator glasses.

"Forty-three years old. Born in the Kono District in the Eastern Province of Sierra Leone, Nkosi was a leading member of the Revolutionary United Front. He was infamous during the Sierra Leone Civil War for his brutal tactics, which included amputation, mutilation, and rape. He earned the nickname 'The Mosquito' for his ability to attack when his enemies were off-guard.

"Nkosi made the move into the upper leadership of the RUF, and in January 1999 he planned and executed a devastating attack on Freetown, the capital of Sierra Leone. In 2006, he was indicted for crimes against humanity but fled before his imprisonment. It was rumored he joined with a terrorist unit in Liberia. On February 3, 2008, Nkosi was reportedly killed in a shootout with Liberian forces."

Roger Garret looked up and said, "It would appear the report was *inaccurate*." He paused. "What you are about to see was sent to my private e-mail account one hour ago."

Paul looked down at the angled monitor set under glass in front of him. Nkosi and Quaroni filled the screen. They were on a stage. Under the hand of a shaky camera, Quaroni began speaking. The words came in a clear, but slightly accented English. "I come to you with a heavy heart. A great deal of my people—my countrymen—are sick. A great many people. They are dying of a disease you call AIDS."

Garret looked up. He saw five or six others look up as well. They must have been thinking the same thing as him.

AIDS? This was all about AIDS?

He looked back down.

Quaroni continued, "Sixteen percent of South Africa and over a third of the adult population of the KwaZulu-Natal province have contracted this disease, this plague. How many people have to die before you intercede? How many children must lose mothers only to lose their own lives soon thereafter? Nearly two hundred thousand children were infected with HIV last year. Every one of these children will be dead in five years. You must help us. You *will* help us."

Quaroni looked around wherever he was, then said, "It shouldn't have come to this, but it has. I have control of a cruise ship off the coast of South Africa. I have over four hundred hostages. Their lives rest in your hands. Their lives rest in the generosity of the United States of America."

He took a deep breath, then stated, "I want every person in the KwaZulu-Natal province tested for AIDS. Every person. You will bring enough antiviral drugs for every person that is infected, over 1.6 million people. You will start in my hometown of Ptutsi."

Quaroni's hand disappeared into his jacket and he came out with something. Photographs. He said, "You will find these three children."

He held each individual photo up to the lens for a few seconds, two little boys and a little girl, then continued, "You will find these three children and you will bring them to the United States. You will give them the best medical attention money can buy. You have three days to meet these demands, three days to set up a testing site in the village of Ptutsi. You will remove these three children and send a photo of them at the airport in Johannesburg. If you do not comply. If you have not met these demands by noon three days hence, everyone aboard this ship will die. If any attempt at rescue is made, everyone aboard this ship will die. If we detect any vessel or aircraft within a five-mile radius of the ship, everyone aboard this ship will die."

Quaroni stared into the camera with deep set eyes, large behind his spectacles. He did not appear to be bluffing.

Garret let out a long past due exhale. These loony toons had taken over a cruise ship and were holding four hundred hostages. And for what? For the USA to help them with their AIDS epidemic? If the press got hold of this story, it would be a nightmare.

He looked down at the video. It wasn't over.

Baruti said emphatically, "Four hundred thousand lives were lost to this disease in South Africa last year alone. More than one thousand people die each day. I know you do not negotiate with terrorists. But this is different. I am not asking for money. I am asking for help."

The screen went black, but according to the counter at the bottom, there was still over thirty seconds of video left. He would have looked up had his father's booming voice not said, "Keep watching."

The screen remained black, then flickered back on. On-screen were six men. All in white officer's uniforms. Canvas bags covered their heads and necks. They were lined up, one beside the other, kneeling on the wooden deck of the ship.

Paul closed his eyes. He didn't want to watch. He opened them.

Keli "The Mosquito" Nkosi entered the screen. He turned toward the camera, his aviator glasses shimmering in the morning sun. He held a large silver gun in his hand. He walked down the line of men.

Pop.

Pop.

Pop.
Pop.
Pop.
Pop.
Finally, the video ended.

SHOW LOUNGE

7:15 P.M.

IT HAD BEEN hours since the Professor delivered his ultimatum via video camera, and I'm certain more than a few people in the United States received a phone call that went something like, "Um, yeah, sorry to disturb you, but it would appear some African pirates commandeered a cruise liner off the coast of South Africa and they are demanding, um, I hope I'm reading this correctly, 'A shitload of nucleotide analog reverse transcriptase inhibitors.'"

After the Professor finished his provocation, he'd said to the assemblage, "I have no intention of hurting any of you. Whether or not the United States complies with our demands, you will be released, unharmed, three days from now."

Well, that was encouraging. It was bullshit, but it was encouraging bullshit.

He added, "But if you do not behave, if any of you try to be heroic, I have no objection to letting my comrade here kill every last one of you."

He was about to step offstage when someone stood up and shouted, "Excuse me!"

The Professor and Warlord glanced at each other, then at the woman standing. The Warlord put his hand on his rifle and in a whisper-scream, I said, "Lacy, what are you doing? Sit down!"

She waved me off.

The Professor took a step forward, his eyes boring two holes through Lacy's chest. He said nothing.

Lacy pointed to Susie and said, "This woman is diabetic and if she doesn't get her insulin soon she could die."

Susie did her best to close her eyes and teleport to the nearest Department of Motor Vehicles. It didn't work.

The Professor smiled.

I relaxed just slightly. Maybe my sister wasn't going to die in the next three seconds after all.

"Where are you from?" he asked.

"I live in France but I'm from Washington."

"France. I have not been there. But, Washington, I have been to this place. Ah, the White House?"

"That's Washington *D.C.* I lived in Washington State. Seahawks, Mariners, and we used to have the Sonics. They're in Oklahoma City now."

He nodded. As if he had season tickets to all three. After a moment of silence, he said, "What is your name?"

Say Suri or Shiloh or Apple.

"Lacy Marie Prescott."

Or tell him the name on your birth certificate.

"You are brave Miss Lacy to stand up and speak." He paused. "Miss Lacy, when you were a child and you got sick, where did your parents take you?"

"To the doctor."

"And this man, this doctor, if you were sick, he would give you medicine. Yes?"

"Well, he'd write a prescription for medicine and then you'd go get it from a pharmacy."

"Yes, yes. I have heard of these *pharmacies.* Filled with every medicine imaginable."

He closed his eyes as if envisioning such a wonderful place. Like a kid conjuring Willy Wonka's Chocolate Factory. He opened his eyes and said, "We did not have these in my village. In fact, in my village, if you are sick, sometimes there is no doctor, sometimes there is no medicine. Sometimes you die." He nodded at Susie. "Your friend will see how it is to live in Africa." He swept his gaze over the entire room, then bellowed, "You will all see how it is to live in Africa."

Then he stepped off-stage and began walking up the aisle.

I pulled Lacy down and said, "What were you thinking?"

"What?" she scoffed, like she'd done nothing wrong, like this was a middle school assembly and she'd asked the principal why they stopped serving chocolate milk in the cafeteria.

A little about Lacy. She was tough. By far, the toughest woman I'd ever met. But that hadn't always been the case. As a kid, Lacy and I weren't very close. I was eight years old, a happy only child, when there was an accident. An accident that nine months later my parents named Lacy Marie. I can remember every second of her as a baby. I adored her. All my friends would be out playing in the street, and I was inside playing with my baby sister. Then I hit high school and suddenly I didn't have time for this super annoying little girl begging for my attention. When she was ten, I went off to college and I barely saw her for four years, even less when I started at the police academy, and even less when I was beat cop with the Seattle Police Department.

I can still remember seeing my sister the day it happened. My dad's accountant called and informed me about my parents. They'd been coming back from a concert in California, flying in one of the small Learjets used by my father's company. The plane had experienced catastrophic engine failure and crashed into the Sierra Nevadas.

Lacy was at swim practice and I drove to her high school. When she got out of the pool, I remember thinking, *When did my sister get tits?* Seriously, I'd just found out my parents were dead and I almost felt worse that I hadn't noticed my sister's tits. I wonder what Freud would have had to say about that.

Anyhow, I moved back home, and Lacy and I leaned on one another for support. I came to realize how fun and amazing she was. Her room was filled with paintings: sunsets, landscapes, murals, all done by her exquisite hand. Over the next two years, she became my everything. When it was time for her to go to college, she decided on Temple University in Philadelphia, which happened to have a world class swim team and boasted the Tyler Art School, one of the best art programs in the country. Coincidentally, after becoming the youngest detective in the history of the SPD, Internal Affairs was coming after me for allegedly, and I quote, "shooting a rape suspect in the balls." Actually, I'd shot him in the penis. His balls weren't what he was sticking in little boys' rears. I might have been able to weather the storm, but after I smashed a fellow detective's face—a not-so-friendly guy named Ethan who is now chewing Juicy Fruit in the great beyond—into a locker, I handed over my badge. It sounds better when I say I voluntarily handed it over and not that it took four cops, my sergeant, my captain, and the cleaning lady to get it out of my pocket.

Needless to say, I no longer had any reason to stay in Washington, and life without Lacy seemed utterly insignificant, so I tagged along.

We shared a nice two-bedroom loft near the college and Lacy soon became the star of the Temple swim team. As for me, I was now twenty-eight, happily unemployed, and slowly began to chip away at the seven-figure inheritance left by my parents—mainly giving it to Starbucks. Five hundred Pumpkin Spice lattes later, I ran into an old friend from the academy who was now a detective with the Philadelphia Police Department. He asked if I wanted to work a couple of cold cases. I'd just learned that there wasn't a fourth season of *Arrested Development* on Netflix, so I had some time to kill. I solved five cases the first year, seven the second.

That's when the FBI's Violent Crime Unit came knocking for me. And multiple sclerosis came for Lacy.

It was just fatigue at first. Lacy figured it was from her grueling schedule; up at 6:00 a.m., in the pool for two hours, classes from 9:00 until 4:00, and another two hours in the pool. When the fatigue persisted, she wrote it off as the flu, a bug that needed to run its course. But after six weeks, it had started to affect her swimming. She went from winning her events—the 100 back, the 200 back, the 100 IM, and the 400 butterfly—to getting second or third, and once she even placed fifth (something that had never happened in her more than ten years of competition). One day in February of her junior year, she came home early from practice. I was working my first case as a special contract agent to the FBI's Violent Crime Unit, packing for a trip to North Carolina —a suspected serial killer was going after elderly couples—and I asked what was wrong. She'd said that she was too dizzy to swim.

The dizziness lasted the entire week I was gone—we caught the suspect scouting a Perkins—and into a second week. The doctors said it was a virus. She would get better. And she did. The dizziness went away. She was fine for almost two months. Then her legs started tingling. Two weeks later it was numbness in her hands. She was sent to a specialist. There is no proof-positive test that confirms MS and the symptoms mimic many that could be from a variety of conditions, but after six months the neurologist felt confident diagnosing Lacy with multiple sclerosis.

I went on sabbatical, spending my time reading every piece of literature there was on MS. Lacy tried to take it in stride, but when Temple took away her scholarship, she crumbled. She went into a fit of depression, which easily could have been a side effect of any of the many drugs—Prednisone, Copaxone, Amantadine— she was taking daily. She quit school and spent her days on the couch. I took care of her, cooked her healthy meals, washed her clothes, and cleaned her room. From what I'd read, exercising was perhaps the most vital instrument against the disease and I tried everything in my power to get her to go for a run, or a swim (she scoffed in my face every time I mentioned swimming), throw the football, anything really. But she wasn't having it. After six months of watching her wallow and pack on twenty pounds, I told her that I couldn't do it anymore. I couldn't just watch her give up on life.

So I went back to work.

The FBI wanted me to assist a task force in Maine. A brother had mutilated his pregnant sister, then went on a killing spree. It would be the first time I had left my sister since she was diagnosed. A month earlier, I'd read a post on an MS blog from a woman whose son had been diagnosed and like Lacy, had become couch-ridden. She couldn't get him out of the house; she could barely get him to wipe his own ass. So one day she came home with a puppy. The kid was instantly revitalized, playing with the puppy, taking it outside for walks and within a couple weeks he was back to his old self.

I don't know why I bought her a pug. If I could go back and do it all over again, I would have gotten a Saint Bernard. As I was walking out the door, headed to the airport, I tossed the little guy on her chest—then no bigger than a hamster—and said, "When I get back, you better be off this fucking couch."

But I never made it back.

I was in Maine for close to a month, following Tristan Grayer's dead body cookie crumbs, when I was shot twice and took a fifty-foot plummet into the Atlantic Ocean. When I was released from the hospital, I decided I wanted to stay in Maine. I had fallen for one of the members of our task force, the medical examiner Dr. Caitlin Dodds, and I thought a change of scenery would be good for Lacy.

Lacy and Baxter joined me in a large house on the Penobscot Bay and suddenly the shoe was on the other foot. The combination of her love for her new dog—which happened to have a neurological disorder of his own, *Zzzzzzzzzzzzzzzzzzzzz*—and having to take care of me, propelled her out of her funk. The day she told me that she had decided to tackle this MS thing head on, that it wouldn't steal another second of her life, I cried.

She was a new woman. She got back into shape, she started to paint again, and she got involved in MS fundraising. Meanwhile, I mended my body and took a position teaching a criminology class at the local university.

Lacy met a guy—one of my students actually (and now her fiancee)—and her paintings, which were hanging in a couple local coffee shops, had started to garner much due praise. She was even slated for a gallery opening. But then the lights went off. As in, her eyesight. Temporary blindness is an uncommon flare-up, but not unprecedented. I half expected Lacy to revert back to her lifeless self, but it didn't slow her down a bit. She had her boyfriend or me take her places, she still painted, still swam each morning.

It was then that I realized my sister was tougher than me.

But sadly, MS wouldn't be her biggest test. The serial killer everyone thought dead—except me, of course—had come back for an encore presentation. And this time he was gunning for me personally. Women close to me started to die. I won't go into details. I can't. It hurts too much.

Lacy was kidnapped, duct taped, thrown on a boat, destined to become a science project once she reached the island her killer was taking her to. You can read about the story if you want, there are a couple books out there detailing the entire saga, but what's important is that Lacy escaped. She jumped off the boat and swam nearly a mile and a half to an island.

Compared to what Lacy had been through the last ten years, a couple of pirates were nothing. I was proud of her for her courage, but I was worried it was going to cost her nine millimeters of lead.

I said, "I'm not telling you to roll over for these dickheads, just don't paint a target on your forehead."

Gilroy turned around and stared at Lacy. Then he turned to

me and said, "You'd better tighten the leash on her before she gets us all killed."

Lacy cocked her head to the side and said, "Excuse me? Did you just say 'leash'?"

"Yes. You need to be trained better."

"First, I am not some dog you keep on a leash, you pig. And second, I was trying to help, and God knows you're too wrapped up in yourself to think of anyone else. And even if you weren't such a prick, you're too big of a pussy to say anything."

Gilroy leaned back. Trinity turned and gave Lacy a quick glance. I thought I saw a touch of a smirk hiding somewhere under her heavy lipstick.

"You better watch your mouth, young lady. You have no idea who you're talking to."

"Sure I do. You're Gilroy Andrews. Big ego. Little dick."

Gilroy flushed. He glared at her and said, "You just make sure you don't do anything stupid."

I'd been watching patiently, waiting for him to step over the line, whereby, I would slam my fist into his face. But, Lacy didn't need my help. And I didn't want to dent my knuckles on his huge incisors.

Gilroy turned, muttered something under his breath, and faced forward.

Lacy leaned toward me and said, "Can you believe that jerk?"

I shrugged and said, "He comes from a broken home."

She laughed.

"Try not to get in any fights while I'm gone."

"Gone? Where are you going?" she asked.

"To the bathroom."

She looked at the pirates and said, "You think that's a good idea?"

"There's only one way to find out."

WHITE HOUSE MESS
2:30 P.M.

PAUL GARRET SAT down with his Diet Cherry Vanilla Dr. Pepper and a heaping bowl of Frosted Flakes. The White House Mess never ceased to remind him of a college cafeteria. At thirty-nine, he should have started eating healthier; he couldn't go ten seconds without hearing about changing metabolisms or South Beach this or South Beach that. The truth of the matter was he weighed the same as he had his junior year of high school, 157 pounds. And he would die weighing 157 pounds.

He took a long swig of the soda—really his only vice apart from the occasional glass of scotch—and poured half the glass of milk over his cereal. He was still having trouble digesting the two-hour Situation Room meeting. An aging African civil rights activist living in exile and a *presumed dead* African warlord take over a cruise ship and demand medical aid.

But, the more he thought about it, the less surprised he was.

As Press Secretary, he was familiar with any number of World Health issues. For the past ten years, the World Health budget had been nearly a billion dollars—merely a sliver of the annual budget. And he knew the majority of the countries in the UN had similar programs, although not as heavily funded as the United States. It never ceased to amaze him how the United States had to be best at everything, from pollution to charity. What most people didn't know is that the United States borrowed most of this money from other countries. He once again thought of the national deficit and shook his head. In the five years he had been in the White House, the last year as Press Secretary, the deficit had continued to skyrocket with no ceiling in sight.

Anyhow, those were topics for another day.

Paul finished off his cereal, moved the bowl aside and picked up the stack of pages a White House intern had delivered to him ten minutes earlier. The top page was a color photograph of a cruise ship. It was on the water with hundreds of people scattered about the large vessel. Near the front, under a thick blue line running the length of the ship, stenciled in the same blue, was "Afrikaans."

The *Oceanic Afrikaans* had eight decks. Garret thought back to the cruise he had taken with his wife and two small boys only a year earlier. A five-day Disney cruise on the Caribbean. There had been over three thousand passengers on the ship and something like twenty-two decks. If Garret hadn't known he was on the water, he never would have suspected it. The cruise had been enjoyable, mostly because his boys had had so much fun playing with Mickey and Goofy and doing all the Disney stuff, but Garret had been disappointed by the food, as well as the atmosphere, and after five days he had been happy the cruise was over.

Garret flipped the page. There was a small blurb downloaded from *cruises.com*.

Five stars. Intimate in scale, but grandly outfitted, the Oceanic Afrikaans *hosts no more than 208 pampered guests. (Though most passengers are American and British, guests from Germany, Switzerland, Australia, and elsewhere sometimes spice up the mix.) Strictly upper-crust, the* Afrikaans *caters to guests who are well-mannered and prefer their fellow vacationers to be the same.*

*Generally, they aren't into pool games and deck parties, prefer-
ring a good book and cocktail chatter over champagne and
caviar, or a taste of the line's special complimentary goodies, such
as free massages on deck and soothing eucalyptus-oil baths
drawn in suites upon request. The dining can rival the finest on
the continent, most notably, Pretoria, the Michelin two-star
restaurant on Deck 2. An extremely high crew-to-passenger ratio
and a high standard of training ensure that service is both
personal and top-notch. Staff members greet you by name from
the moment you check in, and your wish is their command.*

Garret set the pages down. Now this sounded like a cruise he
could enjoy. Maybe in a couple months, he and Betsy would take
their own cruise. Get out of D.C. for a while. Garret envisioned
Betsy and himself sipping champagne and eating caviar. As the
doting waiter in his fantasy was refilling their glasses, Garret's
iPhone vibrated. He shook his head, picked up the phone, and
read the message. There were two words followed by a series of
numbers.

He looked at the phone number of the sender. He didn't recognize it. But of course, whoever sent it wouldn't want the number
traced back to them. And he had a good idea who sent it. He
memorized the series of numbers and then deleted the message.

He thought of the two words.

Call Gina.

BOLIVIA

2:41 P.M.

GINA BRADY MOVED the stethoscope down the small girl's back. The girl had complained of chest pain, cough, and shortness of breath. *Not another one,* thought Gina. The girl took a deep breath, and Gina heard the wheezing of air. Gina smiled. It wasn't tuberculosis. Thank God. She didn't know if she could deal with another one. Thirteen cases in the past four months. Four of them fatal. Three of those, small children.

Gina walked across the small hut and rummaged through a series of canvas bags. She pulled out an inhaler, pulled off the top, and told Dominga to open her mouth. The nine-year-old shook her head, her dark pigtails swishing around her brown face. Gina stuck the inhaler in her own mouth, pushed down the tab, and took a deep breath. Gina smiled, showing the girl the simplicity of the action. The young girl's anxiety abated, and she opened her mouth wide revealing a large gap where her two front teeth should be. Some things are the same no matter what latitude or longitude you're at. Gina stuck the inhaler in the girl's mouth and depressed the nozzle, sending the critical medicine into the girl's lungs. Gina walked over to a cabinet and returned holding a super-sized Sour Apple Blow Pop (which came once a year with her supplies). Probably not the best thing for a tiny girl with asthma, but hell, life is short.

The girl wiggled the enormous green sucker into her mouth, and Gina pressed the stethoscope to her back. The girl took a deep breath. No wheezing. Clean as a whistle.

Gina had a brief chat with the mother, who started into tears when Gina told her it was nothing more than a case of asthma. When the mother had first arrived with the child, it had been as though she were already grieving over the girl's death. Bolivia ranked third in the western hemisphere in number of tuberculosis cases and the "death cough," as the natives referred to it, struck a fear into the small village like nothing the doctor had ever seen.

Dominga jumped off the small exam table—if you could call a rickety table with a sheet over it an exam table—and stuck out her tongue. It was dark green.

Gina laughed.

The girl and mother left through the open door, and Gina smoothed out the small sheet covering the table. She heard footsteps approaching. She prayed it wasn't a child. It wasn't. It was Javier Kully, a fellow WHO—World Health Organization—doctor, and as of three weeks ago, a budding romantic endeavor.

The curly haired, self-proclaimed Peruvian-Australian—Gina still didn't know quite what that meant—smiled at her. He had an amazing smile, white and even. Gina noticed the satellite phone held to his chest. He said, "You have a call, my dear."

Gina raised her eyebrows. This would be her fourth call in three years. The first three from her best friend on her birthday.

Gina asked, "Who is it?"

"He wouldn't say."

"He?"

"Yeah. *He*."

Javier handed the phone to her and said, "Did you give your

number out to one of those naked gentlemen at last week's rain dance?"

"I would have, but I don't even know the number." In truth, she didn't. She had it written down on a scrap of paper somewhere. And her best friend had it. No one else.

Javier winked at her, handed her the phone, then turned and left.

Gina pressed the phone to her ear, which felt unnatural—she might have felt more comfortable holding a banana to her ear— and said, "This is Gina."

"Gina."

All it took was that one word. It was him. But why? And how? True, he was one of the most powerful people in the world, but it would still take some doing. "Paul?"

She could hear him pause. Maybe he hadn't expected her to remember his voice. He said, "The one and only."

"How did you find me?" *And why?*

"Well, actually you found me." He told her about the text message.

"Why would someone text you this number? And to call me?"

"I'll get to the *why* in a sec. As for the *who*, I'm leaning toward my father."

"As in the National Security Advisor to the President?" She was speechless. Why had one of the most powerful men in D.C., a man thought to have even more influence than the Secretary of Defense, tell his son to call her?

Gina's father, William Brady, and Roger Garret's paths had crossed in 1979 when both were stationed at Marine Corps Head-quarters in Washington, D.C. Both brought their families along for the ride, families that had followed them all over the map. Roger Garret and his wife, Prudence, had a seven-year-old named Paul. William Brady was a widower, his wife falling victim to a strange illness a year earlier, and he had a six-year-old daughter, Gina.

The children at the base were few and far between, and Gina and Paul had been inseparable from the second they'd met. Both their fathers had found a home in Washington D.C. and for the first time in memory, Gina was able to cultivate an actual friendship. Over the course of the next ten years, their friendship slowly evolved into a torrid love affair. Gina still remembered the night, three weeks after her sixteenth birthday, when they had first made love, sneaking off the base to a cheap motel just down the road. The memory still made the hair on her arm stand on end. When it came time for college, they both attended the University of Virginia, Paul studying political science, her pre-med. It had been four of the best years of Gina's life. After graduation, Paul had moved back to Washington. Gina enrolled in the University of Virginia's medical school.

At first, the mere two-hour drive didn't impact their relationship, one of them driving down to meet the other each weekend. But over time, it turned into every other week, then once a month if they were lucky. They tried it for a year. And then, three weeks into her second year, Paul called it quits. He couldn't do it anymore.

But Gina could have. She would have dropped out, moved to D.C. She would have done anything to stay with him. But she knew it was more than just the distance. Paul, her best friend, the love of her life, had fallen out of love with her. But in the back of her mind, Gina always thought they would end up together. Grow old together.

Over the years, Gina had tried to stay in touch with him. But it was too hard. Every time she heard his voice, the memories would come flooding back. By the time she started her residency, the two were lucky to trade e-mails twice a year.

The last year of her residency, Gina's father had died in a car accident. Paul had attended the funeral, a gorgeous redhead on his arm. Her current boyfriend, Tony, a fellow resident, had come with her but she still couldn't believe Paul had shown up with this *tramp.* Gina wasn't sure which was more painful, her father's death or seeing Paul with another woman. That had been six years ago. They hadn't spoken since.

But Gina still kept tabs on her childhood friend and the only man she'd ever truly loved. Paul married the tramp, who'd spawned him two boys, and he was recently named Press Secretary of the White House. And his father, the intimidating General Roger Garret, was now the top man in charge of National Security affairs. The Garrets were two of the most powerful men in the United States. And here she was, living in a remote village in Bolivia.

"What time is it there?"

Gina shook out of her reverie. "We're in the same time zone."

"Really."

"Look at a map sometime."

"No, I trust you."

There was something about the way he said these words, which almost brought tears to her eyes. Why after all these years? She swallowed hard, then asked, "Why did your father tell you to call me?"

"We have something of a situation on our hands."

Over the course of the next ten minutes, Paul briefed her on the terrorist situation in the Indian Ocean. After he recounted Quaroni's demands, she said in disbelief, "That's impossible."

"Actually, it's not. If we get the Red Cross involved as well as the National Guard, we could probably get it done."

"AIDS medication for a million people? Really?"

"Sure. We're the United States of America. We can do anything."

She laughed. His dry sense of humor rushing back at her. She asked, "So why don't you do it? Why not call the Red Cross and get over there?"

"We can't. We don't negotiate with terrorists, remember?"

"I forgot."

"If we cave in to this guy's demands, we'll be setting a dangerous precedent for the future. Then every crackpot with a boat is going to try to take over a ship."

He was right. If they caved, it would be like opening Pandora's box. She thought a moment and said, "So where do I come in?"

"The three kids."

"What about them?"

"Well, this is only conjecture but I think my father—and I agree with him on this—wants you to sneak in under the radar and rescue those three kids."

South Africa. A remote village. Three kids. Again, she asked, "Why?"

"A bargaining chip. To do something. To not just sit on our asses. Maybe it saves those four hundred people on that ship. Or maybe it just saves those three kids. I don't think anything bad could come of it."

"But won't you be caving to his demands?"

"Maybe. That's subjective. Hence, all the secrecy. No one else would know about this but you, me, and my father."

"Why not have a Special Ops teams sweep in and do it?"

"I'm guessing my father doesn't want this sanctioned by us in any way. He wants this done off the grid."

Well that was her. *Off the grid.*

Gina was silent for a minute. Deep in thought.

As if sensing her thoughts, Paul said, "Don't do this for me. Don't do this for my father. Don't do this for your country, if you even think of America as your country. Do this to save some kids and some innocent folks on that ship."

"Well, I'm not doing this for you. That's for sure. How's Betsy by the way?"

"She's good. So are the kids."

"And what would she think about your calling me?"

She could hear him take a deep breath through the phone.

"Look Gina, we were a long time ago. And like I said, no one knows about this but you, me, and my father. Nobody."

Gina looked around the small hut. Life was good here. A bit mundane at times. But good. And then she had Javier to think about. He was handsome and fun. And a good dancer. But then again, this would be quite the little adventure. And she could save three kids' lives.

She took a deep breath and said, "Okay. I'll do it."

SHOW LOUNGE
7:36 P.M.

THE BATHROOMS WERE against the far wall of the lounge. I could feel the nervous stares of my fellow hostages as well as the heavy glares of the three pirates, but the pirates didn't move nor appear to care that I was on the move. They were covering the only exit. They didn't have anything to worry about. I wasn't going anywhere.

I stepped clear of the chairs and took the ten steps to the bathroom. I pushed through the door, stopped at the faucet, splashed water on my face, and looked at my reflection. In six days, my skin had tanned to a light cinnamon. My hair was short, almost buzzed, the usually brown hairs lightened to an ash blond by the sun, and matched by the light dusting of beard I'd been growing since we first boarded. White slashes of crow's feet fringed steel blue irises set against sun-pinkened landscapes. Basically, I looked like a guy who was having a grand old time on a cruise ship when it was unexpectedly taken over by pirates.

After a long drink from the faucet, I did an appraisal of the bathroom. There were two stalls and five urinals. I jumped up and smacked the ceiling with my hand. Hard as a rock. No panels.

Looking for a way out wasn't the only reason I'd come to the bathroom, and I made my way to a urinal. As I let loose, I did some reflecting. I'd been in a number of tricky situations, but this one took the cake. Taken hostage by a band of African pirates who wanted nothing more than for the United States to help them with their little AIDS problem. My brain was having a hard time writing an algorithm for this one:

200 passengers + 160 crew / (10-15 Pirates) x (400,000 Deaths from AIDS + .013 [The probability the USA would meet these demands]) = why are they doing this?

Every time I tried to run the numbers I ended up getting an error message.

Of all the times not to pack my TI-82.

While I was running these numbers Base 2, I heard the door open. At first, I feared it was Lil Wayne and he was going to put a round in my spine leaving me holding a limp dick for all of eternity, but it wasn't. It was just a guy. There were five urinals—I was at the second one from the door—and the man nestled up to the one nearest me.

Bad urinal etiquette.

I glanced to my left. J.J. Watkins smiled at me. He was wearing a blue, green, and yellow Hawaiian shirt. He had this big gap between his two front teeth. He looked like a beaver. An unfunny, untalented, prematurely bald beaver.

In a thick New Jersey accent, he said, "Crazy shit, huh?"

"You could say that again."

"Crazy shit, huh?"

"Good one." I mentally plucked the blue urinal cake from my warm piss and made him eat it.

"Yesterday we were lying at the pool, sucking down piña coladas. Today we're fucking hostages."

This guy should work for the *New York Times*. I was at the halfway mark of my pee and I said, "You said it."

I wrapped things up, washed my hands, and then took another hearty drink from the faucet. J.J. Watkins was done with his piss, and as I turned for the door he stuck out his hand and said, "I'm J.J."

I looked at the hand he'd held his unfunny penis in six seconds earlier and decided against shaking it. I did say, "I'm Thomas. Nice to make your acquaintance."

"Acquaintance. I like that."

I didn't.

He laughed, then said, "I'm the ship comic."

"Fooled me."

He paused a second, then laughed. "Good one. We're gonna be buds."

Please no.

The door opened and two men entered. I nodded to both, then slipped out before the door closed. Men and women were coming toward the bathroom in droves. Apparently, I was a trend-setter. Take that, Timberlake.

I weaved my way back to Lacy, Frank, and Susie and plopped back into my chair. A hand darted over my lap, and I heard, "I'm J.J."

Lacy took his hand and said, "I'm Lacy."

He looked at me and said, "You with this guy?"

"I guess so."

He looked at me and said, "You're a lucky man."

"She's my sister."

He raised his eyebrows. "Oh."

"She's engaged."

"Got it."

J.J. introduced himself to Frank, Susie, Gilroy, Trinity, Marge, and Walter, then he said, "So do you think they're gonna do it?"

"Do what?" Lacy asked.

"*Do what?* Do you think the U.S. will meet the demands? You know, do all the stuff that guy asked for."

"They can't," I said, shaking my head. "That is called *negotiating with terrorists*. If I remember correctly, we don't do that."

Frank, who I hadn't heard utter a word in more than an hour, said, "Where does this guy get off? The United States does a ton for them. I mean, I can't buy a shirt, or jeans, or a box of cereal without some of the proceeds going to AIDS."

I don't know where Frank was shopping, but I hadn't heard much about AIDS in the past few years. But then again, he was from New Mexico which, from the stories Frank had told, appeared a bit behind the times. I mean, they were still using asbestos.

My sister said, "That money doesn't necessarily get in the right hands or help the right people."

Lacy of course knew this first hand. Since Lacy had been diagnosed with MS, I had attended more fund-raisers and written more checks than I cared to remember. A couple of years ago, Lacy held a fund-raiser at an art gallery raising more than two hundred thousand dollars for MS research. No small feat. The money, which she thought was going fully to fund research, didn't. It was given to a third party, then distributed among many hands. This weighed heavily on Lacy, prompting her to write a series of scalding e-mails to various people condemning the allocation of these funds.

Since then, Lacy and I have been more hands-on with our donations, seeking out a handful of those each year who had been diagnosed with MS —it usually hits at early adulthood, late twenties, early thirties, mostly women—but lacked the financial resources for the many necessary medications.

Lacy said, "Did you hear what he said? 'Two hundred thousand children were infected with HIV last year.' Obviously, all that money *The Gap* is raising isn't working. I mean, we've been hearing about the AIDS epidemic in Africa for twenty years now, and it's not getting any better."

I didn't put Lacy on my terrorist sympathizer list, but she *was* laying on the rhetoric a bit heavy.

She noticed my muse and said, "Listen, I'm not condoning what they're doing, but you have to admit the guy's got a point. I mean, what do these people have to do to get some help?"

Gilroy turned and said, "Give me a break. Tell these idiots to wear a fucking condom."

"It's not that simple." Lacy shot back.

"Sure it is. You open it up and roll it down your dick. It's pretty simple."

Lacy glared at him and he turned back around.

I think now would be a good time to disclose my philosophy on this whole AIDS thing. If Lacy was the far left, and Gilroy the far right, then I was somewhere in the middle. This may sound a bit naive, but for me it was simple: you screw around, you don't put on a condom, guess what? You might get AIDS. This didn't mean I didn't sympathize with people that contracted AIDS, I mean that would royally suck. But you reap what you sow.

Now, I know there are exceptions, but most people who had AIDS had Magic Johnson AIDS meaning they slept with the wrong person. Expanding on this, AIDS had all but disappeared in the United States. Yeah, it was big in the '80s and '90s, but you rarely heard about it anymore. And guess what, Magic Johnson is still alive. That's right, even if you have AIDS now, it's like it's not a big deal or something. But I was not *that* naive that I thought Africa AIDS and American—*You-Have-Thirty-Different-Varieties-of-Energy-Drinks-to-Choose-From*—AIDS were even remotely similar. Theirs was closer to the plague.

I was ready for a discussion change so I said, "Isn't there a cure for AIDS?"

Whoops.

"Nope," Lacy said, with a shake of her head. "It's in the same boat as MS. They have a bunch of drugs you can take to stop it in its tracks so it doesn't progress, but there isn't a cure. And the meds cost a fortune. They make my meds look cheap."

And Lacy's meds were anything but cheap.

Lacy continued, "It doesn't matter if there was a cure. There have been preventive immunizations for malaria for like fifty years and it still kills hundreds of thousands each year in places like Africa. Did you know tuberculosis is still around? We've had a vaccine for a hundred years and it's still killing people in Third World countries."

I didn't know my sister was so, oh what's the word? Greenpeace.

Susie screamed, "Who cares?"

We all looked at her. Including our three friends at the door.

"It doesn't matter," she sobbed. "These pirates have taken over our boat. It doesn't matter what they want. Who gives a rat's ass about AIDS? What are we going to do? What are we going to eat?"

We didn't have time to think about this. Or even answer. The doors opened and the Warlord entered.

This time he was alone.

"Uh-oh."

I looked at J.J. Watkins. "Uh-oh" was right.

The Warlord spoke briefly with the three pirates at the door, then all four walked down the angled walkway. I noticed the Warlord was holding an unfolded piece of paper in his hand. I had a feeling things were about to get uncomfortable. And not *The Office* uncomfortable. *The Sopranos* uncomfortable.

J.J. Watkins tapped me on the shoulder and said, "I think that guy with the beret means business."

I wasn't a huge fan of Mr. Watkins, but again, I had to agree with him. The Warlord continued down the walkway, leaving a pirate in his wake every twenty feet, sort of like Hansel and Gretel, but instead of breadcrumbs he was using African mercenaries. All bad metaphors aside, the Warlord made his way onto the stage and stopped. He looked around the room, then shouted, "All de wuman stan dup."

I looked around. Not a single woman had stood. Apparently, the Warlord noticed this as well. He pulled his gun from his waist, raised it above his head, and pulled the trigger three times. Spackle from the ceiling rained down onto the stage, and if there were any pirates sunbathing at the pool, they might want to check for an extra asshole.

"All de wuman stan dup!"

I looked over my shoulder. Still no one was rising. I think it was a combination of half the people not understanding what he wanted and the other half not wanting to be the first to stand should they take a bullet between the eyes.

Lacy stood.

I took a deep breath.

The Warlord stared at her, but said nothing. Lacy turned and yelled, "He wants all the women to stand up."

One by one, the women began to stand until all were upright, if not shaking.

The Warlord nodded. Then he cocked his head to the right— well, my right, his left—and said, "Aganst de wahl."

I looked up at Lacy. She gave me a smile and squeezed my hand. The smile said, "I'll be okay," the hand squeeze said, "But if I'm not."

I could feel all the women's eyes trained on Lacy. Without doing much, she had become the face of the group. As a hostage you wanted to blend in. Go unnoticed. You may already be aware of this, but going unnoticed isn't a strong suit for the Prescott clan.

Lacy looked at Susie, who was standing just in front of her, and said, "Do what he wants."

Susie gave Frank a pleading stare. Frank nodded at her, and after a couple calming breaths she stood. It was as if all of us were in a medium-sized movie theater, and all at once 70 women in the theater decided it was time to use the restroom.

J.J. leaned over me and said to both Frank and me, "This is bad. When this happened on *24*, the terrorists killed all the women."

I looked at him. The most important person in both Frank's and my own life had just left to go stand against a wall, and I didn't think the Warlord was going to make them stand there so he could give them each a bouquet of flowers and a box of chocolates.

I said, "You aren't allowed to talk anymore."

To his credit, he said nothing.

I watched as Lacy, Susie, Trinity, and Marge—Lacy in her tattered shorts and lime green bikini top, Susie in her rainbow vomit, Trinity in her two pieces of white dental floss, and Marge in her khakis and blue blouse—were lost in the large group making their way to the golden wall seventy feet away. As the women neared, one of the pirates would grab them, drag them to a certain spot, and then push them up against the wall. Berta, Reen, and los lesbianos were packed together near the bathroom door. Trinity and Marge were up at the top of the wall near the entrance, spaced four women apart. Lacy was smack-dab in the middle of the pack. She looked so small compared to Susie on her left and another large woman on her right. She made eye contact with me. She made a face she does sometimes, with her tongue out to the side and her eyes rolled up. I tried not to laugh, but it was impossible.

The Warlord walked to the woman at the far end of the line, closest to the door, and stood in front of her. He looked like an army sergeant doing a barracks inspection. The woman wearing a huge pink shirt that hung down near her knees. The Warlord lifted the piece of paper in his hand and put it next to the woman's face.

"I think it's a photo," I said to Frank,

"Looks like he's comparing her face to the face in the photograph."

"They must be looking for somebody," remarked J.J.

I thought I told him not to talk.

But he was right. They were looking for somebody. Not somebody. They were looking for a woman.

The Warlord glanced at Tupac, who was right behind him, and shook his head. Tupac grabbed the woman and shoved her down the aisle. She tripped and fell. When she made it to her feet, she ran back to her seat where her husband cradled her head in his arms.

This show went on for a while. Sometimes the Warlord would shake his head quickly and the woman would be dismissed straightaway. When it came time for Trinity, I glanced at Gilroy. I wondered if he was feeling the same thing Frank and I were feeling? Did his stomach feel like that big knot of Christmas lights Chevy Chase hands to his son in *Christmas Vacation*? Were his palms clammy? Did his heart feel like it was going to gallop through his chest?

The Warlord held the paper up to Trinity's face. He stepped back. He didn't dismiss her.

Frank and I cut our eyes at one another. *Was it her they were looking for?*

Without preamble, the Warlord reached out his hand and ripped away her bikini top. Her giant breasts leapt out and she screamed. The pirates all began to laugh. Tupac pushed her forward and she began stumbling back in our direction. She tried to cover her breasts, but her giant red nipples kept peeking out.

When she reached us, Gilroy said, "Dammit, cover yourself up!"

I really wanted to hit him in the face with a crowbar.

J.J. unbuttoned his Hawaiian shirt, he had a plain white V-neck underneath, and handed it to her. "Here."

She nodded her thanks, wiped her tears with it, and then put it on.

Marge was hardly given a second glance. Evidently, the woman in question was under two hundred. Marge started back toward us, then, thinking better of it, made her way to the bathroom (she would later say, "Since I was up").

The next five minutes passed in agony. Every so often the Warlord would make one of the women open their mouths, but each time he would shake his head and Tupac would send the woman rushing back to her seat.

When the Warlord was one woman away from Susie, Frank looked over at me. Written on his face, plain as day, was fear. Abject fear. I could feel the same fear crawling up my neck, climbing up my chin. What if the face on that piece of paper the Warlord was holding was Lacy's? And I'm sure Frank was thinking the same about Susie.

J.J. Watkins chimed in, "Ransom."

I turned. "What?"

"Ransom. They're probably looking for someone on the ship to ransom."

For the third time, I agreed with the annoying hack next to me. After hearing about the AIDS demands, I'd dismissed the idea of ransom altogether. I didn't doubt that the AIDS relief was their primary objective—you could see the conviction in the Professor's eyes as he spoke, a fury in his belly—but the Warlord was a different story. I couldn't see behind those aviator glasses, but my gut told me that when he'd been staring at Lacy, it hadn't been lust in his eyes, it had been dollar signs. As for Lacy, we had quite a bit of money, but it was all under my name, and since the majority of that money was tied up in stock I'd inherited from my parents' death, it wasn't liquid. It would take days, if not weeks, to get cash. And last I'd heard, the stock wasn't doing all that well, so I'd be lucky to squeak out a couple million bucks.

I looked at Frank, Mr. Snuggie. The guy had bundles of cash

on him at all times—thousands of dollars wrapped in a red rubber band—and after one too many Mai Tais, Frank confided in me that they had more money than they knew what to do with. Tens of millions of dollars. And who was in charge of all that money? Susie.

But, this didn't make sense. What were they going to do? Ransom one hostage from another hostage? No, the idea behind a ransom was to make an outside party pay for the release of the abducted individual. Although, I suppose they could force Susie to transfer the funds from their bank account to an account of the pirates' choosing. But if they were going to go this route, why not do it with everybody? No, they wouldn't single out one person. And they would be concentrating on the men. Susie was a rarity. She was probably one of the few women against that wall who controlled the family finances, and maybe that was her fat face on that piece of paper.

Talk about thinking in circles.

The Warlord dismissed the woman to the left of Susie, then took a step to the side and stood directly in front of Mrs. Camper. Frank leaned forward in his seat. I heard him sniffle. The Warlord's inspection—or comparison—of Susie was over before it began. Apparently, the women he was looking for had three chins or less.

Tupac pushed Susie down the aisle.

Frank beamed.

I watched in my peripheral as Susie wedged her way through the seats, but my main focus was on Lacy. The Warlord took two steps to the side and blocked my view of my sister. He held the picture up to her head and I could feel his eyes moving down my sister's body. He stood there for what seemed like an eternity. He stuck his left hand out and I knew he was running it through my sister's short blonde hair.

I saw his hand moved down to her neck. Then her arm. Then disappear. Although I couldn't see, I knew clear as day the

Warlord was holding onto my sister's breast. I looked down at the red carpet between my legs. This was too much.

And then it happened. A collective gasp. The Warlord crouched over, groaning. His beret fell from his head as he hobbled, holding his crotch.

Lacy had kneed him in the balls.

Um, *check please.*

The Warlord straightened. He leaned into my sister and I could hear his shouting. He pulled the knife from his pocket and it disappeared, its next stop my sister's throat.

This was it, I was going to watch my sister be gutted like a fish.

But it never happened. He whispered into her ear, then threw her down on the floor. She scrambled to her feet before Tupac had a chance to grab her and began wending her way through the chairs. When she was ten feet away, she raised her eyebrows and said, "How'd I do?"

"On a scale from one to ten? Minus fifty thousand."

She plopped down and said, "What did you want me to do? He grabbed my boob."

Oh, I don't know—*let him.*

I did say, "I thought he might have."

"Yeah, I don't like it when people grab my boobs." She cupped her breasts in her skimpy green bikini with her hands. "I know they're small, but I'm very protective of them."

Lacy turned to Susie and slapped her leg, "Good work, sister. You were great."

Susie gave a sheepish smile.

"Yeah, you were, babe," Frank concurred.

J.J. leaned over me and said, "What did he say?"

"I don't know, I couldn't understand him," Lacy said, shrugging.

I gave her a look. She knew exactly what he'd said. She looked at me and said, "He said he wanted to take me to Chili's when this whole thing blows over."

"You are a lying whore."

She laughed. "Dick."

"Did you get a look at the picture he was holding up?"

"I was too busy trying to keep my virginity intact."

I looked at Susie. She shook her head.

Lacy said acutely, "They must be looking for some girl. And the way he was looking at me, I'd say she's about my size. He kept looking at my teeth. Maybe she's a snaggletooth."

I looked at the Warlord as he moved down the wall. He wasn't going to find what he was looking for in this room.

THREE DAYS EARLIER

11:56 P.M.

"WANNA PLAY ANOTHER ROUND?" We'd been playing rummy for the past hour.

"I'm tired," Lacy said, batting her eyes open and closed. "And my vagina hurts."

We'd spent the better part of the afternoon on horseback. It had been Susie's idea to explore the white sand beaches of Mozambique astride the glorious beasts. My stallion, actually a mare, was named Bagru. He/she was brown and he/she acted more like a Roger, so that's what I called him/her. After seven hours astride Roger, my inner thighs burned, I could feel my heartbeat in my ass, and my testicles had officially put in for early retirement. In all honesty, the afternoon was considerably more fun than I'd expected. The four of us had tied up the horses at a number of small huts located up and down Praia de Zavala, sampling the local cuisine and lubricating with tropical offerings. Susie even to the point where she thought it would be a good idea to get her hair braided and beaded by an African woman on the beach. But the highlight of the excursion had been when Frank's horse, a white behemoth named Ratak, had decided he'd had enough of Frank's whistling and ran into the surf where he promptly and unceremoniously bucked Frank into the ocean.

"Put some ice on it," I replied.

"I just might," she said with a laugh, already halfway under the covers. "What are you gonna do?"

The Campers, who could barely make the trek back to the ship —both walking as if competing to see who could keep their thighs further apart—had called it a night an hour earlier. "I don't know. I'm not tired at all."

"I told you not to drink that Redbull."

"The first one or the second one?"

"The third one."

"Right."

She mumbled something else, but it was unintelligible. Baxter had materialized from wherever he'd been hiding and was already asleep on her chest, snoring away. I walked over and pulled the blankets up over the two of them and kissed Lacy on the forehead. I thought about renting a movie from the Blue-ray library and ordering room service, but I needed to expend some of this taurine or I was going to be awake until February. I slid into some casual duds; jeans, cranberry tee, and gray Chuck Taylors.

The casino was packed, and I remembered that it was some special night, and the band— a good enough quartet that played everything from reggae to country—was playing in the back corner. There was an empty spot at the baccarat table, and I changed a hundred. Baccarat was my new favorite game. If you've never played, it's like a complicated version of blackjack, but instead of twenty-one, you're trying to get nine.

I bet the entire hundred on the *banco* (banker) and won. The next hand, I bet all two hundred on the *punto* (player) and lost.

I was in the casino for exactly four minutes.

The arcade was a floor down. There were six or seven games, a pinball machine, and an air hockey table. There was a kid playing Miss Pac-Man. He was the only kid on the boat. Mika. He was from Greece and he was on the cruise with his parents, who appeared to be in their late sixties. I suppose they suspected there would be more kids on the ship. Lucky for Mika, there was plenty of booze and one extremely immature man/boy named Thomas. Aside from my sister and the Campers, I had clocked more hours with the pudgy thirteen-year-old than anybody else. I peeked over Mika's shoulder and said, "Eat that yellow dot...now that one... now that one...now that one...now that one...now that one...now that one..." until finally he started laughing, and the pink ghost got him.

"There are some beers behind the pinball table," he said.

I grabbed a beer and played a few games of pinball, impatiently waiting for Mika to die a couple of more times. After two beers, Miss Pac-Man accidentally came unplugged.

Mika's dark features creased. "What the fuck?" He shoved me in the arm.

I shoved him back.

Five minutes later, Mika tapped out.

Still got it.

We both dusted ourselves off, shot-gunned a beer, then played air hockey for an hour. He beat me four games out of seven.

After describing in detail how badly I was going to whoop his ass in pool basketball the next day, I walked out. I'd worked off about half the Redbull in my system, but I was still wide awake, and now I was hungry. I headed to Cargo, the late night cafe on Deck 7. There were three other people hanging out and I watched Sports Center and ate a delicious Johannes-burger with a fried egg and chased it down with a strawberry milkshake.

It was almost three when I walked into District 9. Only the diehards remained, thirty people spread between the bar and the dance floor. I sidled up to the bar and ordered Don Julio 1942, neat. I sipped the drink and watched the deluge of bodies grind to the electronic music blaring from the DJ in the corner.

I felt her before I saw her. A light squeeze on my right thigh.

She had light brown hair stacked high. Delicious cheekbones, pale skin, a face to remember, and one I did not. Light eyes that were hard to distinguish under the red lights. She was wearing black jeans that clung to a size-two body and a beige blouse with a drooped neck, revealing a hint of a cavernous shadow. Her face was stern and somehow sexier than any smile.

She took the drink from my hand, took a sip and handed it back to me.

"I want to dance," she said, in what I guessed was either a British or Australian brogue.

I was in love.

Again.

She took my hand and I let her lead me to the dance floor. She released my hand and began to move, her lithe body swaying, finding the music. She danced away from me, a cascade of fifty-something men closing in on her from every angle, but it was as if they didn't exist. Her eyes were closed. I danced, not good, not bad. Two women silently made their way in my direction. I danced with them for a couple of tracks. Again, I felt her before I saw her. She turned me around, pressed her body to mine. The one hundred pounds that comprised her were made of granite and fire. We moved against one another. She grabbed my shirt and pulled me into her, trying to melt our skin together.

A couple songs later, she took my hand.

We walked from the club in silence.

She pushed the door open to her room. She turned and licked my lips. She lifted my shirt and kissed my belly. She ran her mouth over the bulge in my jeans, blowing hot air onto my growing erection. I pulled her up and pushed her against the wall. She moaned. I bit her bottom lip, pulled it taut, bit it again. Slowly I kissed my way down her body. Unbuckled the clasp of her jeans. Pulled the zipper down, tooth by tooth. Her panties were black mesh. I put my mouth on her and returned the favor. She purred.

I picked her up, her legs interlocking behind my back, her tongue finding my neck and the edge of my ear.

The clothes did not come off fast.

Her body was petite but curvy, a body that was a gift to shadows. She took me in her mouth, kissing, and licking. I took her in mine. We probed, caressed, touched, and tasted each other's flesh. No words were spoken. None needed.

When I finally slipped inside her, her body trembled, her teeth clamped down on her palm.

The sun woke me up. I peeled the arm from around my waist and found my clothes. As I was leaving, I gazed back at the bed. Her light green eyes were open. She smiled. The sun reflected off the jewel set in one of her front teeth. A small diamond.

"I never got your name," I said, opening the door to leave.

She laughed lightly and said, "I'm Rikki."

SUITE 312

9:55 P.M.

RIKKI DROUGH SET down the book she'd found lying on the bed, *Fifty Shades of Grey*, and took a deep breath. Her back was starting to hurt and she thought about slipping out from her hiding spot and stretching a bit, but then again, why risk it? She didn't have to go to the bathroom yet. And she was enjoying the book. At least the sex scenes. She could hold out for another couple hours.

How long had she been hiding for anyway?

It felt like ten or twelve hours, but it couldn't have been more than seven or eight. She'd been in the maid's cart for at least three hours before coming here, and she'd been here for at least four. Plus, it'd taken her thirty minutes to find the hiding spot behind the TV. And now that she was here, how long would she have to hide for?

She thought about her attacker.

She wasn't sure who, but *somebody* had found her. How had they connected her to him? She'd never even met him. Their only connection was the money. But she never asked for it. She'd never asked for so much as a dime. Every so often he'd put a million dollars in her account. Was she supposed to *not* take it? Just let it sit there? She wasn't like her brothers and sisters—who probably didn't even know she existed—she had ambition.

She'd been forced to grow up early. More a mother to her mother than her mother ever was to her. When Rikki was eight, her mother had been stoned beyond comprehension—one of the many times Rikki was certain her mother would die from the drugs—and had purged the story of her father as if she'd gotten her hands on some bad Thai. Wanda Drough had been working at a small diner in London when he'd strolled in. He'd had an aura about him. Money and power. They'd had sex in the bathroom and nine months later, Rikki was the result.

Looking back, it all made sense. Twenty million dollars is twenty million dollars. Her mother had tried fervently to hide behind the hush money, tried to be the socialite, but she couldn't shake the husk of the ignorant waitress. Rikki had never asked where the money came from. She didn't much care. Anything she'd wanted, she'd had. That is until the money dried up, disappearing into a series of bad investments, aka, her many father figures—three to be exact—and the rest up her mother's nostrils.

When she was fourteen, Rikki had kissed her mother's pale, almost lifeless cheek, and set out on her own. She found a little restaurant in Scotland that hired her to wait tables, making enough to rent a room from the restaurant owner. She lived at the library. She soaked up everything she could get her hands on: Dickens, Voltaire, Machiavelli, Hemingway, anything and everything.

She still remembered the day it happened. It was three days after her sixteenth birthday. She'd gone to make her weekly deposit into her checking account, always exactly half of what she made that week, and had read her balance. She still remembered the number, $1,006,392.43.

Somehow she knew. He had found her. Maybe her mother had gone back to the well for more money, maybe blackmailed him even. It didn't matter to Rikki. Either way, he'd found her. And it's not like it would have been difficult. She paid taxes. Her mother could have found her. If she'd wanted to. Why not a multi-billionaire? It would be a cinch.

Rikki spent the next few years trying to put a dent in her account, but it continued to rise. She'd spend twenty thousand dollars on clothes, another ten thousand on rare books, only to find her account had risen by a million dollars.

But she vowed not to waste it. She transferred the funds to interest bearing accounts, she had an accountant, and she had a portfolio. She was going to do something with that money someday. But every day wasn't someday. It was that day. And she'd spend, spend, spend. But never frivolously, always on something amazing. She vowed to visit every country on the globe. By the time she was twenty-one, she'd been to nearly half.

She'd compiled some of the best works of fiction. Originals. She'd lost her virginity to a man in Brazil, danced on top of the Empire State building, hiked Mount Kilimanjaro, walked the halls of the Louvre, cheered at the Iditarod, watched a Bengal tiger run through the Indian jungle, and snorkeled the Great Barrier Reef. She did it all.

Now, at twenty-three, she was ready to put her stamp on the world, take the seven million she'd compiled over the years and put it to work. She'd already bought the restaurant she used to work at, and she had ideas of her own. Her vision was for a restaurant that was also a rare book dealer. *Rare*. That's what she'd call it. It would be grand. Big couches. Dark cherry wood. Books for menus. From there she would start her own clothing line. Maybe even write a book.

But she needed one last hurrah. A palate cleanser. Get it all out of her system. Put a check mark next to a couple more countries. A random person had sent her a link to the *Afrikaans* website on Facebook. It was the perfect cruise. It would stop at seven different countries. Seven check marks. It sounded wonderful.

And it had been. Until that man had attacked her.

After she'd kicked the guy in the balls, she'd run into the hallway. There had been a door open and Rikki had stuck her head in. There had been two maid carts and a dirty laundry cart in the room. She'd jerked the door closed, transferred all the sheets from one of the carts into the trash bag of the second cart and slipped into the small opening.

Five minutes after she'd hidden, the screaming had begun.

The yelling was followed by a stampeding of feet as if everyone on the floor had been herded past her door. The footsteps trailed away and there hadn't been a peep for over an hour. Then light footsteps. A single person. She could hear as the door to the room next to her was opened. They were searching. For her. And then it happened. The door to the closet opened. She'd bit her cheek for a long second, but after three breaths, the door closed.

She'd waited another hour. Then she'd made her move. She peeked out the door, then darted into the hall. She didn't want to hide in a room on her own floor, so she went to the winding stairs and listened. She crept up the stairs, ready to bolt back down, but she heard nothing. She made it up to Deck 6, ran down the corridor, and scurried into the first room with the door open.

The room was smaller than hers—she'd had a balcony suite—and the TVs were set into the walls. But the TVs were flat screens and there was plenty of space behind them. They must have had normal TVs sitting in the space before they'd upgraded to the flat screens.

She'd grabbed a bag of nuts and a Pepsi out of the mini fridge, snagged the book off the bed, and climbed over the television.

Rikki let out a long exhale, cracked her neck, quietly ripped the bag of macadamia nuts open, and flipped the page.

———

Ganju Thapa hadn't spent much time in Pretoria, preferring to eat his meals in his room, but he had eaten there on occasion. The food was always excellent, but each time someone would sit down next to him and strike up a conversation, Thapa found he didn't have much in common with these people. They were all rich. Rich beyond his wildest dreams.

Without him asking, they would tell of their travels, of their boats, their cars, and their many homes. He could not believe some of these people had three, four, or even more homes.

Thapa didn't want to hate these people. But he could not help it. Was it jealousy? Possibly. He hoped that isn't why he detested these people. Maybe it was because when they asked where he was from and he told them Nepal, they would look at him and say, "I've always wanted to go there."

Thapa wanted to tell them to stay away. Nepal was poor. And life was a struggle. They, in fact, did *not* want to go there.

Thapa looked around. Pretoria was the single largest room aboard the *Afrikaans* and took up more than a third of Deck 2. Two large chandeliers illuminated the considerable room. The many round tables were clad in white tablecloths with corners of white linens poking from wineglasses, and complimented by an array of dazzling silver. The chairs were cherry and sat on rustic brown carpet.

Usually, the room was filled with the clink and clatter of fork and knife hitting spoon, the white noise of a hundred different conversations, and the rhythmic sounds of whatever music softly resonated from speakers overhead. Waiters and waitresses dressed in red vests and black pants, would zoom in and out of the kitchen, delivering Chef Michael's daily delicacies.

But not today.

Situated around the tables were more than a hundred men including nearly the entire crew. He found Joe sitting at a table. Even from a hundred feet away, Thapa could see the dark bruising around his Adam's apple. As for all the women, they were lined up against the far wall, their backs to the many windows that ran the length of the ship on both sides of the restaurant.

Thapa looked at the four African pirates. He watched as one of them pulled down the shirt of one of the women passengers, revealing her small red nipple. The woman tried to cover herself up, but the black man pulled her arms away. Thapa wasn't sure what was going on, but he knew it was related to what he had seen at the bridge earlier with Ben or *Kimal.* They were obviously looking for a woman. But why? He'd been told this was about helping the poor South Africans with their AIDS epidemic. Thapa could relate to those people. That was his rationale in taking the money.

Thapa watched as the woman began to cry.

No, nothing good could come of this. Eight people were dead. The captain, his officers, and, of course, Stoves. Thapa had blood on his hands. He had taken a man's life. He was one of them. And for what? For money? So he could be more like these Americans? So he could become what he despised? But he was not a pirate. Or a killer. He was neither. He was something altogether his own. He'd once been a Gurkha. That was how he'd defined himself. Now he was something else. Something that did not sit well with him. He was a mercenary.

He shook his head and left.

WASHINGTON D.C.

4:50 P.M.

AFTER TWENTY YEARS, Roger Garret still wasn't comfortable behind a desk. He preferred being part of the action, but at the age of sixty-three he knew *being part of the action* now equated to *picking up the telephone.*

Garret's last active role had been in 1990 when he had participated in Operation Provide Comfort in Northern Iraq as Commanding Officer of the 24th Marine Expeditionary Unit. The first time he'd found himself behind a desk—a neat, utilitarian wooden desk, the only desk that seemed logical to the uber-analytical Garret—was when he was advanced to Brigadier General, J-3, U.S. European Command in Stuttgart, Germany.

Returning to the United States, Garret was advanced to the rank of Major General and was assigned as Commanding General, 2nd Marine Division, Marine Forces Atlantic, MCB Camp Lejeune, North Carolina.

As the titles grew longer, the desks grew bigger. Over the next decade, Garret carried such titles as Director, Expeditionary Warfare Division; Office of the Chief of Naval Operations; Military Assistant to the Secretary of Defense; Deputy Chief of Staff for Plans, Policies, and Operations; and now he was Assistant to the President for National Security Affairs, and his desk, situated in his office in the West Wing of the White House, was the size of a regulation pool table.

He remembered the first time he'd stepped foot into his new office five years earlier, his eyes immediately drawn to the massive, over-the-top, cherry desk. He'd found himself nearing hysterics. Why would anyone ever need a desk so large? It baffled him, but at the same time, it impressed upon him how important his job had become. The larger the desk, the greater the responsibility.

Today, that responsibility was four hundred lives.

Had the e-mail not been sent to him directly, the responsibility would still have fallen into his lap. Anything that was remotely related to terrorism—where U.S. lives were at stake—domestic or abroad, fell under the political umbrella of National Security Advisor. These days, ninety-nine percent of his focus was on the Middle East—as was just about everyone's in the national security community, all trying fervently to squelch the next 9/11 before it came to fruition—but every so often something from Africa would hit the radar. Nine out of ten times, it had something to do with Liberia or Somalia. However, there had been enough upheaval and infighting in South Africa which surprised no one. Least of all him.

The AIDS epidemic in Africa had raged for going on twenty years with no end in sight. It was only a matter of time before someone took things into their own hands. Roger Garret had no empathy for these men and he would have no qualms advising the President to kill every last one of them, but he understood them, understood that sometimes violence is the only answer.

The intercom on the phone squawked, "Your conference call is ready."

Garret hit the flashing button and said, "Admirals."

Both men chimed their hellos.

Garret said, "I trust your last six hours have been as uneventful as mine."

"I haven't finished the sudoku yet, if that's what you mean," came the sharp reply of Dexter Causic, the Chief Admiral of Naval Operations for the U.S. Navy.

His South African counterpart, Admiral Reggie Darcy answered, "Yes, I have been very busy."

"It's got to be nearly midnight over there, Reggie," spat Causic. Roger knew the two most powerful men of their respective naval programs were well acquainted.

"Yes, but I do not expect to get much sleep this evening."

Garret said, "So what exactly are we up against here?"

Admiral Darcy: "I had a recon team do a series of flybys—"

"Those cruise liners have pretty good radar," Garret interrupted. "I assume you took this into account."

"My guys didn't break fifty thousand feet. Plus, the radar on that ship has a ceiling of five thousand feet, its purpose is solely so the cruise ship doesn't run into other boats. Anyhow, it took the better part of four hours, but we finally located the *Afrikaans*. It dropped anchor roughly sixty-seven miles off the eastern coast of South Africa."

"Is it unusual for a ship to be out that far?"

"Not really. They're only a couple miles off their intended path. At any rate, when my guys finally located the ship, the sun had set, but we were able to snap some infrared shots. They aren't much help. We'll do another round in the morning."

"Don't worry about it, Reggie," said Causic. "Just give us the coordinates and we'll take some satellite images. These guys might have brought some of their own equipment aboard. I don't think it's worth the risk."

Reggie agreed.

"Do we have any idea how many pirates are aboard?" asked Garret.

"From the photos we can see three small fishing boats tied to the hull of the ship," replied Darcy. "Each of these fishing boats could carry up to six passengers."

"So there could be as many as eighteen of them?"

"Eighteen would be pushing it. Ten or twelve would be my best guess."

"What about other ships in the area?"

Admiral Dexter said, "Lucky us, we have a Virginia Class nuclear sub in the area, the USS New Hampshire, which just so happened to be asleep thirteen miles off the Somali coast."

Reggie gave a laugh. "Thirteen miles, huh?"

"Yep."

The first twelve miles off any coast belonged to the respective country, after that it was international waters. The international waterways off the coast of Somalia were infamous for their treachery and their piracy. There had been more than fifty attempts to hijack vessels moving through the area in the past three years and a number of them had been successful. There were still nine ships that remained under the control of Somali pirates. A year earlier, there had even been an attempt on a cruise ship, but the cruise liner was able to outrun the fishing boats, using their LRAD to ward off the pirates' attack.

"I take it the sub is no longer asleep?" probed Garret.

"She's headed due south at twenty-five knots. She could be parked there by late Monday."

"Monday night? That's two days from now."

"Sorry, she's the only ship in the area. But it's the best of our fleet. We have a Los Angeles class sub halfway between Africa and Antarctica, but she probably wouldn't get there any faster."

"How 'bout you, Admiral Darcy?"

"We don't exactly have the budget of the US Navy, but the few subs I do have in the water are doing a training exercise off the coast of Angola. They are headed south as we speak, but my girls don't move as fast as yours. We'd be lucky to have one there by daybreak Tuesday."

"All right. Admiral Darcy, what are the odds of keeping this thing quiet?"

"Right now, I'd say pretty good. Only a handful of my best men have been briefed."

"Good. Do your best to keep a lid on it. If this finds its way back to the States, this thing will explode." Roger Garret thought about his son, standing in front of the podium of the White House Press room, doing his best to dodge the reporters' darts. He added, "This is just the beginning. I want to make sure we have our asses covered. If this guy puts us in a position where we feel these people's lives are in imminent danger, I want to be ready to move at a moment's notice."

Admiral Darcy asked, "Have they tried to contact you yet, General?"

"No. They haven't."

"I don't know how much you know about these two men, but both have done unspeakable things in the past. I saw the after-math of the hospital Quaroni took over several years earlier. He executed three doctors and one nurse. All four shot between the eyes. This man does not think of himself as a killer, he thinks of himself as a crusader. He will not blink twice before he kills every person aboard that ship. And I can only hope that Quaroni kills them all before The Mosquito gets hold of them. If he does, everyone aboard the ship will pray for death."

"HERE YOU GO." Lacy handed the small cup of water to Susie and she gulped it down. "How are you feeling?"

"Just a little shaky," replied Susie.

"Do you want more water?"

Susie nodded—the beads in her hair clacking off one another —and the two headed back to the women's bathroom to refill the small cup.

I looked at Frank and said, "You ever have to deal with her not having her insulin?"

"Once the pharmacy gave her the wrong kind and it took a day and a half to figure it out. She wasn't doing very well by the end."

I knew diabetes took a while to do its damage and most people ultimately died from kidney failure. But, I also knew diabetes could kill on a whim. And being that Susie was the all-time worst diabetic on the planet, I didn't see her lasting more than another day. Two tops.

"She'll be all right. We'll figure something out."

If Frank felt encouraged by my words, he didn't show it.

Lacy and Susie returned. I patted Lacy's leg next to me and said, "How are you feeling?"

"Fine."

Lacy had missed three sets of pills already, and in three more hours, it would be four. She said, "More hungry than anything."

The last meal I had was lamb chops with a mint pesto and rosemary mashed potatoes, followed by a pumpkin crème brûlée, but that had been more than twenty-four hours earlier. There had been a point when I could feel my stomach growling, but it didn't last long. I think my brain saw what Susie was going through and told my stomach to stop being such a pussy.

"Good," I responded, knowing full well that if Lacy had felt anything, she would keep it to herself. In the case of her temporary blindness two years earlier, she'd kept it to herself for an entire day (close your eyes and see how long you last).

This made me feel better about having not told Lacy about Rikki. When I'd gotten back to my room that morning, Lacy was still asleep. I joined her and we both slept until past noon. Once awake, she asked me how my night had gone and I told her about the casino, and Mika, and the cafe, but I'd left out the part about my tryst. As for the trystee, over the following days, I kept a lookout for Rikki, scouring the boat for her, but to no avail. I even went to her room once and knocked. I could have sworn I heard her walk up to the door, could feel her looking through the peephole, but she didn't answer.

Then I realized that she didn't want to go back to the well. I'd been a one-night stand.

Needless to say, I was not accustomed to this sort of behavior and I started to have grave concerns about my sexual prowess. Had I not delivered sexually? We'd only had one go, but it was quite the go, and she'd been the one to fall asleep afterward. What could I have done differently? Should I have moved this leg here? Should I have gone counterclockwise with my tongue? Should I not have done my Rodney Dangerfield impressions?

This is what I was thinking about when I heard, "How you guys holding up?"

Berta and Reen were standing in the walkway. They were both looking at Trinity.

"Better now," said Trinity. She had cried for about two hours after being molested by the Warlord. Gilroy was more sympathetic than I expected, only telling her to "Oh, quit your crying" six different times.

"How about you guys?" asked Lacy.

"We're doing alright," said Reen. "Starting to get a little restless, but we're a tough bunch."

Most softball teams are.

"You look familiar," Berta said, looking at J.J. Her face lighting up, she added, "Oh, you're the comic."

"That's meeeeeeeeeeeeee."

"You were so funny!" cried Reen.

Did these two see the same show I did?

"What was that bit you did on dinosaurs?"

J.J. took a deep breath and said, "And what's the deal with dinosaurs? Seriously? I mean, how old are they? A gazillion years old? A million gazillion? They're so old that they were around when *they* were around. [*Laughing at his own joke.*] They're so old that dust collects them. They're so old that they think the *Big Bang Theory* isn't just a TV Show. [*Laughing at his own joke.*] They're so old that they went extinct."

Berta and Reen were laughing uncontrollably. Walter and Marge were both smiling. Even Frank was chuckling.

Was there something that I wasn't getting? Why did these people find this stuff funny while I wanted to put J.J. through a wood chipper like in *Fargo*.

When Berta got her breath back, she asked Lacy, "Did you really knee that guy in the balls?"

Lacy smiled coyly and said, "You don't mess with Queen Latifah and Amelia Earhart." That was what Lacy had named her tits.

The lesbos got a kick out of this. When they settled down, Reen asked, "So what do you think our government is doing?"

For all the alphabet soup of government agencies I'd worked with, I didn't know much about the bureaucracy of the U.S. of A. As an act of terrorism, I was sure this situation either fell under the jurisdiction of the CIA or NSA, maybe even Homeland Security. But being on the water, I had a hunch if any sort of rescue was to be attempted, it would be at the hands of the U.S. Navy.

On this note Frank said, "It's still pretty early on so they're probably still gathering information. Trying to figure out who these guys are, how dangerous they are, how credible the threat is. But I'm sure the Navy has been alerted and at least a theoretical rescue plan is taking form."

"By who?" Trinity asked.

"The Navy SEALs. This is their bread and butter."

I visualized a bunch of guys in black suits crawling up the ship and taking these pirates out one by one. But the SEALs weren't plan A, or B, or even F. The SEALs were plan Z. We still had a long way to go before we got there.

But Frank knew an awful lot about the SEALs and he spent the next ten minutes telling a story about how the SEALs had rescued a group of anti-whaling activists who had been taken hostage aboard a Japanese whaling ship. Frank was an excellent storyteller and everyone, even Walter, was glued to the narrative. When he was finished, the many smiles circling me spoke to the confidence my hostage friends felt that we would be saved in the same climactic fashion.

I was a bit more cynical.

Anyhow, after a short lull, Reen asked, "Do you guys believe this is all about AIDS?"

Well, it wasn't all about AIDS. It was also about a young British girl, but I wasn't sure how that factored in yet and until I did, I was keeping that information close to the vest. But Gilroy, proving he wasn't as big of a blockhead as he appeared said, "This isn't about AIDS."

I wondered if he'd seen Rikki around the boat. Heck, maybe he'd had his own tryst with her.

He scoffed and said, "It's about hydrocarbon."

Okay, so he was a *bigger* blockhead than he appeared.

Who or what was *hydrocarbon?* Was he one of the Avengers?

"Hydrocarbon?" asked Lacy, with a wrinkled forehead.

"Oil," clarified Frank.

"Yes, oil," scoffed Gilroy. "Everything always comes down to oil."

Except a hijacked cruise ship off the coast of *South Africa*. But maybe Gilroy thought he'd signed up for an eleven-day Middle Eastern cruise.

Come join us for a spectacular 11-day cruise as we voyage around the Middle East. With stops in Saudi Arabia, Yemen, Bahrain, Qatar, Kuwait, Iraq, and Iran, you'll think you died and went to sand heaven. Brush up on your Farsi as we travel to one of the beige-ist places on earth. Don't have a nice camera? Don't worry, there's nothing worth taking a picture of here. Scared of harmful UV rays? Well then, this is the cruise for you as you will be forced to wear a burka at all times. And don't miss out on the world famous falafel in our Weapons of Mass Destruction cafe. With three mosques and even a tiny chapel for you infidels, the Oceanic Ali Al Salem Harijjibad Mesahieed *is the ship for you.*

All kidding aside, Gilroy was an oilman, and in his world everything probably did come down to oil. But I'd been around enough narcissists, present company included, to know that Gilroy was simply trying to swing the conversation into his area of expertise.

He added, "There's more oil in Africa than anywhere else in the world. They just haven't found it yet."

"Doesn't matter to me," I said. "I just bought a Chevy Volt."

He flipped me off.

Lacy shook her head and said, "No, I'm pretty sure it's about AIDS and whoever this girl is that they're looking for."

All the ladies nodded.

"Any idea who it could be?" asked Berta.

No one had any idea.

"Did he look at your teeth?" asked Lacy.

"Come to think of it, he did," said Reen.

Berta shook her head and said, "Not mine."

"I wonder what he was looking for?" asked Lacy.

He was looking for a diamond set in the left bicuspid.

Reen and Berta left soon thereafter. And soon after that, the doors to the show lounge opened and two men in white—they looked to be the cruise ship cooks—pushed in three room service carts brimming with covered silver trays. The cooks disappeared and the pirates flocked to the carts, pulling off the silver tops, unleashing a barrage of steam. The three looked at one another, breaking into smug smiles. They probably hadn't seen such beautiful food in their lives.

Lil Wayne grabbed a turkey leg and tore off a large bite of meat, the juices running down his chin.

"Now that's just cruel," quipped Lacy.

"Do you think they'll share?" asked J.J.

The comic was *not* joking.

"Why don't you go ask them," said someone named Thomas.

J.J. raised his eyebrows, stood, and headed in that direction.

Lacy slapped me on the shoulder and said, "You're going to get him killed."

"Hopefully they just remove his larynx so he can't tell anymore jokes."

She gave me a look. The same look she'd given me when I'd said it wasn't fair the guy in the wheelchair was allowed in the limbo competition.

J.J. Watkins started up the incline. The pirates stopped eating and stared at him. I don't know if they were shocked or mystified by this idiot. I saw J.J.'s mouth move. The pirates laughed. Seconds later, almost in unison, all three began throwing food at him. Fruit smashed him in the face. Potato salad rained down on his head. The pirates were nearing hysterics.

J.J. started back, head down. He rejoined our group, flopping back down in his seat. He said quietly, "They don't want to share."

Lacy leaned over me, picked a couple pieces of potato salad and a piece of errant pineapple out of his hair, and popped them in her mouth.

GINA WIPED the sleep from her eyes, then flipped on the small light above her. She wondered how long she'd been out. Five hours? Six? She knew tomorrow, or *today*, was going to be long and she needed to be rested. She checked her watch. It was 11:01 p.m. in Bolivia, but she had no idea what time it was in whatever time zone the plane was moving through. She hadn't been able to sleep on the three-hour flight from Santa Cruz to Sao Paulo, nor during the two hours while she waited to board the ten-hour flight from Sao Paulo to Johannesburg.

She pulled the folder from the seat pocket in front of her. The folder had been waiting for her at the check-in desk of South African Airways. Gina had thumbed through it quickly. It contained a series of faxes from Paul: a handwritten note, a couple maps, a couple pictures, and a few internet downloads on various subjects. Knowing she had a ten-hour flight ahead of her, she'd decided to leave the reading for the flight, but once aboard the plane, her eyes had grown heavy, and minutes after the plane leveled off, she was out.

Gina placed the red folder on her lap and opened it. The top sheet was a handwritten letter in Paul's neat all-caps script.

If you are reading these words, I trust you made it safely to Sao Paulo. Sadly, this will have been the easiest leg of what lies ahead. When you reach Johannesburg, there will be a satellite phone and twenty thousand USD waiting for you. I have set up an e-mail for you: DR.GinA113@GMail.com. Your password is Bolivia (I know, it's stupid, but it's all I could think of). The phone is state-of-the-art. It will work anywhere on the planet. Very cool stuff. Very expensive. Do not lose it!!! Make sure you exchange at least five thousand USD for South African Rand. You might need to shop around, make sure it's trading above 10. Below and you're getting screwed.

Gina shook her head. What a tightwad. She remembered once when they'd taken a trip to Mexico and Paul had spent three hours at the airport looking for the best exchange rate. He'd found some guy at their hotel who'd gotten a little bit of a better deal, whereby, Paul had taken a taxi back to the airport, exchanged the pesos back to dollars, then hunted out the place the man had spoken of. Gina had found this annoying, albeit refreshing, and somehow she had come out loving him even more.

Anyhow, as Paul had said, "That was a long time ago."

Gina continued reading the letter.

The name of the village is Ptutsi. I have attached a map. (The map isn't very good. FYI...I could not find any listing of the village, but I made a couple calls and it does exist.) The village is in the South African state of KwaZulu-Natal. We have hired a guide to take you to the village. He does not know why. Only that he is being paid handsomely. (Do not tip him. He has already been paid.) His name is Timon (Like from "The Lion King"). I told him that if he gets you back alive he gets a little bonus so don't be alarmed if he is a bit protective of his cargo.

Ptutsi is a Zulu village. I have downloaded some info on Zulus from the internet. Please read. I have also included some AIDS Demographics for South Africa. Very depressing stuff. Most people in the area speak Zulu, but most have a passing understanding of English. I have attached the photographs of the three children. They are still-shots of the video close-ups and they aren't perfect, but they should be distinguishing enough. When you find the children, take pictures of them with the camera (there's one on the phone) in front of the airport. E-mail them immediately. Best of luck. I will call you.

Regards,
Paul.

Regards? She scoffed.

She turned the page. It was a map of South Africa. And he was right, the map did suck. *How about a map with roads?* There was a thick red line that led from Johannesburg southeast through a town named Ladysmith, then east toward Ptutsi. She used the key at the bottom and decided the trip was somewhere around 450 kilometers.

She flipped the page. There were three pictures. One picture of a small black girl, braids in her hair, most of her top teeth were gone. She reminded Gina of Dominga. Then, there were pictures of two little boys, both at that adorable age around five.

She flipped the page. It was a Wikipedia download for Zulus. She read the opening paragraph: "The Zulu (isiZulu) are the largest South African ethnic group of an estimated 10-11 million people who live mainly in the province of KwaZulu-Natal, South Africa, fairly distributed between urban and rural areas."

The article went on to talk about the Zulu's origins, conflict with the British, the Apartheid years, the KwaZulu homeland, the Inkatha Freedom Party, their food, their clothing, and their religion. It was information overload, and Gina decided she would have to read it a couple more times before she took anything other than "The women wear lots of beads and their attire is very revealing" away from the article.

The two following pages were far more interesting. They were downloaded from a book titled *The Zulu of Africa* by Nita Gleimius. She read:

The typical Zulu village has between twenty and fifty family groups, or anywhere between two hundred and six hundred persons. The Zulu village is round or oval. It has two fences, one inside the other. The Zulu build huts between the two fences. Traditional Zulu huts are beehive shaped huts called iQukwane. The roof is made of strong branches, and its walls are built using bricks. The largest hut is built opposite the entrance to the village. This hut belongs to the mother of the chief. The chief's hut sits to the right of his mother's home. Unmarried teenage girls live together in a large hut on the left side of the entrance to the village, unmarried teenage boys in a hut to the right. Small huts sitting on poles serve as watchtowers. The chief's two eldest sons work as the village gatekeepers. They welcome important visitors and send unwanted visitors away.

The Zulu like to build their villages on large hills. They build the entrance to the village at the low end of the hill. That way, rainwater will run down the hill through the cattle kraal, cleaning it quickly without soaking the ground and huts. The cattle kraals are located in the center of the village, within the inner fence. The cattle kraal is the safest and most important area in the village. It is used for religious ceremonies and sometimes a burial place for chiefs.

Gina said quietly, "I can't wait."

She turned the page and looked at the first of four pages detailing the AIDS crisis in South Africa. Being with the WHO, Gina was well aware that the AIDS crisis in South Africa was bad.

But for some reason, she'd been under the impression the blossoming epidemic had been quelled, that the rate of new infections had been dropping exponentially for the better part of half a decade. And for most countries of Africa, this was true. But according to the statistics in her hand, this could not be said for South Africa.

There were nine provinces that made up South Africa: KwaZulu-Natal, Mpumalanga, Free State, Gauteng, North West, Eastern Cape, Limpopo, Northern Cape, and Western Cape. Five provinces had an HIV prevalence over 10 percent. KwaZulu-Natal had a prevalence of 16 percent for the general population. That meant that one out of every six people living in the providence of KwaZulu-Natal was infected with HIV, and over 40 percent of people ages fifteen to forty-nine were. Two out of five.

Gina shook her head, turned to the next sheet, and began reading. She stopped and reread the downloaded paragraph from AVERT.org:

> *It is thought that almost half of all deaths in South Africa, and a staggering 71 percent of deaths among those aged between fifteen and forty-nine are caused by AIDS. So many people are dying of AIDS that, in some parts of the country, cemeteries are running out of space for the dead.*

Gina shook her head. No wonder these guys took over a cruise ship. Someone had to do something.

DAY 2

I CRANED my head over my shoulder and opened one eye. Lacy was lying on her back, using the *natural* curves of my butt in place of her orthopedic pillow. I wiped the sleep from my eyes and turned over, Lacy's head slipping to the soft carpet.

"What are you do—" she murmured, but feel back asleep before finishing the thought.

Late last night, Lacy, Susie, Frank, J.J. and I had made the move to the carpeted floor near the men's bathroom. Susie and Frank— their chubby limbs intertwined, looking like two felled redwood trees—were ten feet to Lacy's and my right. J.J. was perpendicular to the four of us, curled up near our feet. He was in the fetal position, his hands steepled in prayer and wedged between his knees. He looked like a three-year-old. All that was missing was the Batman pajamas. Gilroy and Trinity had remained in their seats, and they were both fast asleep. I noticed a spittle of drool running down Gilroy's chin and into his chest hair. Two rows behind them, Marge and Walter both sat upright, both eyes wide open. I doubted if they'd slept a wink. As for the other 130 hostages, a few other couples had decided to make the move to the floor, but it appeared the majority had fallen asleep in their chairs or hadn't slept at all.

I didn't wear a watch, but Frank did, and as I'd started to drift off last night, I remembered him saying something about it being, "Ten after two." Or maybe he said, "Ten till two." But, I guess in the grand scheme of things, when you haven't showered in a couple days, haven't eaten in nearly two, are in desperate need of a toothbrush, your contacts feel like little shards of glass, you could pole vault 17'3" with your morning wood, and you are a hostage, then I guess it doesn't matter the exact moment you fell asleep.

But I was curious what time it was now. I crawled over to the snoring Campers and tried to ferret out Frank's left wrist in the aforementioned fat pretzel. I finally located it and read the time on his watch, 8:05 a.m.

Hmmmmm, what to do today?

Maybe I'd get a massage, or a bite to eat, or a smoothie, or maybe I'd just hang out in a chaise lounge by the pool all day reading *The Game of Thrones* and knocking back Coronas. Or, I suppose I could just sit in the show lounge for, oh, I don't know, until I got shot.

Anyhow, I was going stir crazy.

I spent the next twenty minutes doing some push-ups, sit-ups, and light stretching. And after splashing some water on my face in the bathroom and grabbing a long drink from the faucet, I felt almost human. As I exited the bathroom, I noticed the doors to the show lounge were open. Lil Wayne and Common were each holding a big cardboard box. They looked at each other, then heaved the boxes. They crashed to the floor, their contents spilling out. Bottled water. The water bottles rolled down the incline, some coming to a rest behind chairs, others rolling down and crashing into the stage.

The people who were still asleep—including my four friends—stirred, while the mass of people already awake, found their way to a water bottle. Another box of water bottles was thrown, followed by three white cardboard boxes with plastic wrap. One of these boxes cartwheeled down near the stage and I noticed it was one of those Frito-Lay variety packs. From my golf course snack cart driving days, I knew these boxes contained Doritos Nacho, Doritos Cool Ranch, Ruffles Potato Chips, Fritos, Lays Potato Chips, Lays Sour Cream and Onion, and Cheetos.

Cheetos. Yum.

I'm not going to say I sprinted to the stage, but I did. I didn't want to get stuck with some fucking Ruffles.

A bunch of people beat me to the pack, mostly men. Some of the men took one bag, or two—which I presumed was for their better half—but I noticed a handful of men leaving with a third or even a fourth bag which, as you could imagine, irked me. There were 50 bags in each box, so a total of 150 bags of chips, and at last count there were 140 of us. At this rate, there wouldn't be enough chips to go around.

I watched as Sour Cream and Onion, and Doritos Nacho, and my good friend Cheetos were pulled from the bag. As I was about to stick my hand into the box, myself and two other individuals were pushed aside by the hulking frame of Gilroy Andrews.

I should point out that I am by no means a small individual. I had lost a considerable amount of weight the months following the wolf attack, but when I was finally able to start rehabbing, sometime in late April, I had done so with gusto. For the better part of the last four months, I had spent at least an hour a day lifting weights, and I was the strongest I'd been since college, so I was no slouch. That being said, Gilroy had me by six inches and fifty pounds, and the guy's bicep was the size of my thigh, and if we went toe-to-toe, my money would be on him. So, for the time being, I let the jerk slide.

The three of us watched in utter disgust as Gilroy dipped his hands into the box repeatedly.

"Hey, why don't you leave some for the rest of us?" complained one of the guys behind me.

Gilroy turned. He was holding six bags of chips in his hands. He smirked and said, "Survival of the fittest."

"Then I suppose you need all the help you can get," I said.

He cocked his head to the side. I think he was trying to figure out if I had insulted him or not. Finally, deciding that my comment had in fact been an affront to his manhood, he replied, "I can assure you, that if and when this situation turns ugly, I will still be standing."

And he sauntered off.

I was pretty sure that if you looked up "dick" on Wikipedia, right under male reproductive organ would be a picture of Gilroy Andrews. In all truth, I hoped when this whole thing was over, Gilroy was left standing, because if that shithead survived this mess, then I had a feeling all of us would survive. But, I had an odd sense of foreboding that Gilroy's superiority complex was going to rub one of these pirates the wrong way and possibly get us all killed. And I sure as shit wasn't going to allow that to happen.

When I made it to the box, there were seven bags left. Miraculously, there was one bag of Cheetos. The other six, Ruffles and Fritos. I grabbed the Cheetos, two Ruffles, and two Fritos.

I walked over to where my four friends were beginning to show signs of life. Susie, however, was still lying on the ground. She didn't look good. Her face was a pasty white and drenched in sweat. Her breathing was heavy, labored. Susie looked at the bags of chips in my hands and her eyes began to water.

She leaned up and I said, "You get first pick, my dear."

She took Fritos.

Frank took Ruffles.

J.J. took Fritos.

Lacy took the Cheetos.

I looked down at the bag in my hand. Ruffles.

Man.

One of the male hostages was walking around with one of the boxes of water and we each dipped our hands in and grabbed a warm *Afrikaans* Spring Water. There was a picture of the cruise ship on the front. I could see the bright red lifeboats hanging off Deck 6.

We'd been so close.

I watched as Susie took a chip from her bag and took a small bite. *Savoring* is the word that comes to mind. Lacy caught my eye and laughed. Then her face dropped. I followed her gaze over my shoulder. She was staring at the Kohns. Both dinosaurs had a water bottle in their hand, but no chips. They looked around at the people eating around them. Why hadn't I thought to get them any?

Lacy looked at me.

I nodded and handed her my unopened bag. She knew my affinity for Cheetos and opened her bag and handed me two. Then she walked over to Walter and Marge and gave them our chips. At first they wouldn't take them, but Lacy talked them into it, probably told them she'd already had a bag, and walked back. I handed her one of the Cheetos. We touched them together and threw them in our mouths.

Lacy threw her head back and let loose an orgasmic moan. Meg Ryan would have been proud. She tossed her hair. Then she stumbled, using the wall to hold herself up.

My breath caught. "You okay?"

"Yeah."

But she wasn't. I could tell. Something had her scared.

"Dizzy?"

"It was just from throwing my head back," she said with a shake of her head. "It was nothing."

I knew when my sister was lying. And my sister was lying.

I said, "Let's go sit down."

She nodded.

I led her back to our chairs—it's funny that they had become *our* chairs in such a short duration—and sat next to her. I kept giving her little glances. Trying to see something in her eyes. I had been shot twice, I had lost my parents, and I had seen terrible things as a cop with the Seattle Police Department and far worse as a Special Contract Agent with the FBI, but nothing was even remotely close to the pain my sister's disease caused me. It gnawed at my insides. A hive of yellow jackets stinging at my heart.

My sister stuck out her hand and she said, "Paper, rock, scissors."

"You're on."

I did scissors. She did rock. I stuck my arm out. She licked two fingers and swatted me on the forearm. It was a good one. It would leave a mark. We did it a couple more times. I won one. Then Lacy won the next two. We played for fifteen minutes until both of us had raised red welts covering our forearms. At one point, J.J. leaned over and stated that he wanted to play.

My arm was tingling and I switched seats with Lacy.

I could hear her explaining the rules to him. At one point he asked, "Can I do a tornado?"

Moron.

I took a deep breath and let it out. What would the day bring? I could only imagine. I looked out on the stage where the Professor had videotaped his rant. What was the United States doing, if anything? He'd said they had three days, until noon two days from now. Were we supposed to sit here and wait? Wait to die? Waiting wasn't one of my specialties. And dying. I wasn't good at that either.

I thought back to my last close encounter.

I could see the other wolves standing around, waiting for their turn. I only had a second. Half a second. I pushed myself up with a grunt. My left leg and right arm were useless. I took one step, and three of the wolves came at me. One hit me on each arm. Another went for my ankle.

They dragged me down. I let them. The fight had drained out of me. And then I saw him. The big black wolf. He was jetting forward, about to sink his inch-long daggers into my throat and rip—tear—the life out of me. I saw his eyes. Saw him zeroed in, just like that first day I'd seen him. I could feel his breath. I could feel him run his nose on the back of my head and sniff my wet hair. I felt his teeth scrape my neck. His jaw open, the joint stretched to its absolute breaking point. And when his brain sent the signal to those muscles to clamp down, then I would be dead.

My reverie was broken by a small movement in the curtains. If I hadn't been staring at them, I never would have noticed it. I leaned forward. Where the curtains met in the middle, there was a small black finger peeling back the curtains a half inch. Just above the finger was an eye. The tiny eye swept across the room, then settled on me. The lone finger was joined by another, and the curtain was peeled back another inch. A tiny black nose peeked out.

I turned to Lacy. She was still playing with J.J. I looked at Frank. He was holding Susie in his arms. She was still pulling chips from her bag, still savoring.

I wanted someone to corroborate what I saw, tell me that I wasn't seeing little black children. That I wasn't crazy.

I looked back at the curtains, but the fingers were gone.

SUITE 319

THERE WAS LESS than a foot of clearance under the bed, but it was still light years more comfortable than her spot behind the TV. Rikki slid herself from beneath the box springs and lifted the bed skirt. Light cascaded through the windows, painting hot white rectangles on the plush blue carpet.

Rikki tiptoed into the bathroom. When she was finished, she instinctively reached to flush, then caught herself, thinking better of it. She looked down at her bright yellow pee. At one point when she was young, Rikki and her mother had taken to sleeping in a series of run-down motels. The toilets rarely worked, and there was always urine leftover from the previous guests. That coppery yellow pee that always seemed to be a trademark of the poor. Ever since, Rikki couldn't stand urine. Even her own. She couldn't stay in this room knowing her pee was only a few feet away. She would either have to flush or move rooms.

Rikki walked to the door and cracked it open. She listened for a good minute and heard nothing. The door across from her was open, and she scampered across. She pulled the door closed and turned around. Sitting on the end table were a trashy gossip magazine and a box of Wild Berry Gushers.

Jackpot.

Rikki picked up the gossip magazine and two packs of gushers. Then she climbed over the TV and settled into her little nook.

The gossip magazine was *OK!* In the top right corner it read, "UK Edition." Rikki decided her new boarders were from the United Kingdom. What luck?

She looked at the magazine in her lap. Did she dare?

She took a deep breath, tore the top off a pack of Gushers and poured half the pack into her mouth. She bit down, squishing out the Wild Berry syrup. Delicious.

The headline of the magazine read, "Guy Likes Guys." It was a picture of Guy Ritchie holding hands with a young man. Rikki laughed. Madonna turns another one. Rikki flipped through the pages. Dirt, dirt, and more dirt. Keira Knightley's latest love interest, Kate Beckinsale's divorce, Hugh Grant's drunken outburst, Colin Farrell's new look, Prince William and Kate Middleton's new baby, Prince Harry's latest binge.

Rikki turned to page 32 and stopped. There was a picture of a man with white curly hair, blue tinted glasses, and an orange scarf. The headline read, "Track Bowe Turns 60." There was a photo of a bunch of people on a gigantic yacht.

Rikki read the blurb beside the photo:

Travis "Track" Bowe celebrated his 60th birthday in style. The Alidi Indy team owner and famed economist partied with friends aboard his yacht, the seventy-two-foot Track III. *Among his one hundred-person guest list were Sir Michael Caine, Elton John, Dame Judi Dench, Ben Kingsly, Bono, Josiah Wedgewood, Rod Stewart, and Ringo Starr. The lavish party lasted until sunrise and was said to cost a staggering $800,000. A trifling amount for the 11th richest man in the world.*

Rikki closed one eye, held up two fingers, and squished Travis "Track" Bowe's face between her fingers.

Alidi Indy team owner.

Squish.

Famed economist.

Squish.

11th richest man on the planet.

Squish.

Her father.

Squish.

LONDON

9:32 A.M.

TRACK BOWE GAZED down 96 stories at the London streets below. He liked the view from the top floor of the Alidi building. The tiny people and cars moving down the thin streets. Almost as if he was God looking down on His kingdom. He laughed. Sometimes he was appalled at his narcissism. Whenever this happened, whenever he was feeling invincible—which was often—he would look at the photograph on his desk. It was a picture of the number thirteen car in shambles. Track had been in second place coming into the final lap when it'd happened. His inside rear tire blew out, sending him into the wall at 212 mph. Six long seconds and nineteen flips later, his car—or what was left of his car—came to rest.

Three cracked vertebrae, two skull fractures, a broken leg, a broken arm, seven broken ribs, massive internal bleeding. As he was airlifted away in a helicopter, it was said one of the technicians working on him started crying. Nicknamed "Track" in his early teens for his precocious driving skills, he was worshipped by thousands. Millions. The most beloved Indy car driver in three decades. And on May 24th, 1986, his driving career and most likely his life, would be over.

But miraculously, he held on. He recovered and rehabbed. Even tried his hands at a few races. But he was never the same. His best finish, tied for twenty-first. But over the years he had stockpiled millions upon millions in winnings, made some sound investments, and endorsed everything from Gillette to Old Spice to window washing fluid. By the age of thirty-nine, Track was a millionaire several times over and decided to make the move to owner. Team Alidi wasn't an overnight success, but by the late 1990s, they had a stranglehold on the competition. In the last twelve years, one of Track Bowe's drivers had won the circuit all but twice.

But racing had become secondary. Track had slowly found his niche in the stock market, and before his 50th birthday he was worth over four and a half billion dollars. He was the largest holder of stock in all the UK, his buys and sales sending the market into frenzies. By fifty-five, he was the 30th richest person in the world. By fifty-eight, the 23rd. And as of two months ago, he'd been named the 11th richest person in the world, with a net value of twenty-two billion dollars. He had his eye on Buffet. Gates even.

The phone on his large cherry desk buzzed, and Track set the framed picture down. He pushed the intercom, and his secretary Judith said, "You have a call. A man. Says it's about one of your kids."

Track leaned back. Which one was it this time? Emily? John? Sam? Eleanor? Daisy? Quinn? Roger? How many was that? There were nine in all. Did they overdose? Were they in jail? How much was one of his monsters going to cost him this time?

Track let out an exasperating sigh and said, "Have Jonathan deal with it. Tell him to call me if it's a lot."

A lot, meaning money. If the price was under a quarter million, his lawyer, Jonathan Strom, would deal with it. Usually, they could pay somebody to keep it out of the papers. Track didn't much care what his kids did as long as it didn't affect his stocks.

And it always did. Somebody—someone on his payroll—did a study that each time his name showed up in the tabloids at the expense of one of his stupid kids, his net holdings would drop a quarter of a percent. It had become so predictable there were said to be thousands of people who bought and sold stocks based directly on his children's antics.

The last one had come at the hands of Adrian, his second youngest. Pictures of her with another woman, both blowing coke, both nude as the day they were born. Track had tried to pay to keep the photos out of the press, but three million dollars? He couldn't bear to do it. But in hindsight, the photos had cost him 500 million when his holdings plummeted more than a percentage point. That had been nearly seven months ago. And his holdings still hadn't recovered from the blow.

Judith answered in her predictable, "Will do."

After a half minute, the door to his immense office opened and Judith strolled in. She had once been a stunner, and in her mid-forties she still turned heads. She was the one woman who had never let Track sleep with her, which was probably the reason she was still around, and why she was the only person Track trusted.

She walked toward him, her knee length tan skirt swishing, and said, "I gave the guy Jonathan's number. He didn't seem to care for that much."

"Who was he?"

"Didn't say. He sounded foreign. Anyhow, he said he was going to call back in ten minutes."

Track grimaced. The nerve of some of these people. He said, "Well, when he calls back, give him Jonathan's number again. Or tell him to go to hell. I don't care."

And he didn't. His kids had caused him more agony, and by agony, he of course meant money, then he dared to think about.

"Who is Ricky anyhow?" asked Judith. "You've never mentioned him."

Track thought for a moment. Ricky? Did he have a Ricky?

Judith took her boss's deep thinking for a cue to leave and turned around. It hit Track, almost like the wall had thirty years earlier. Not Ricky. *Rikki.*

He cleared his throat and said calmly, "When this man calls back, why don't you send the call back here. I'll take care of it."

Judith nodded, then left.

Track Bowe paced his large office for the first time. He hadn't paced when he'd been awaiting word on a six-billion dollar merger of two of his companies. He paced now. Last he'd heard, Rikki was in South America. He had a private agency he paid handsomely to keep tabs on his only bastard child. He often thought about the hypocrisy in that the only child he cared for he'd never met—well, officially—nor had he married her mother.

He had nine kids by five different wives. His latest was Olive, a twenty-six-year-old dance instructor. She spent seven hours a day in the gym and it showed in her long, toned muscles. He'd had his tubes tied after his fourth marriage flopped. Olive and he had a three-year-old, Abram. Track had tried to sue the doctor who had performed his vasectomy. The judge had laughed at the case and told him to go buy two baseball gloves.

Abram was already a hellion and Track had the premonition he was going to cost more than the other eight combined. But Rikki, she was different. She'd had a job when she was 14. Waiting tables at a restaurant in Scotland. He'd stopped in once for lunch. He'd watched as Rikki moved about the small room with a wide grin and a graceful step. Once, she passed his table and he'd asked her for some butter, which he didn't really need. Rikki had smiled, brought back the butter, and patted his back on her departure. Those two soft pats had filled him with something he'd never felt before. He'd put a million dollars in her bank account the next day. He'd gone back to the restaurant later that month, but she was gone.

The phone buzzed.

Judith said, "He's on the line. Want me to patch him through?"

"Please."

The phone rang and Track picked it from the receiver with a sweaty palm. He said, "Hello."

"Is this Travis Bowe?" The English was slightly accented, but crisp.

"This is."

"Is Rikki Drough your daughter?"

He had never told a single person about Rikki. Not even his beloved Judith. He took a deep breath and said, "Yes, she is my daughter."

He could feel the next words, "Your daughter is dead." He just knew. He could feel it in the man's voice. Something horrible had happened to her.

Track couldn't hold it in. "Is she dead?"

"Not yet."

Not yet?

The man said, "I have your daughter."

Have her?

"Do you have a cell phone?"

His mind was reeling. "Yes."

"Give me the number."

He gave him the number. Meanwhile, he was trying to grasp what this man was telling him. This man had Rikki. Track's cell phone chirped. He picked it up off his desk. He had a photo message. He brought up the picture. It was a photo of a blue card. *Oceanic Afrikaans* ID. Rikki Drough. Rikki's face—blonde hair and green eyes, timid smile—took up the left half.

Rikki was on a cruise?

"This photo was taken seven days ago," said the voice, then added, "Write this number down."

Track instinctively wrote down the numbers the man recited.

"The first is an account number, the second a routing number.

You will transfer two billion dollars to this account by end of business tomorrow, or Rikki will die."

Track stared at the phone. Unable to speak. Did he say two *billion* dollars?

The man added, "And she will not die painlessly."

The phone went dead.

JOHANNESBURG

12:11 P.M.

SOUTH AFRICAN AIRWAYS flight 218 taxied down the runway of OR Tambo International Airport—formally Johannesburg International Airport and renamed after former President of the African National Congress Oliver Tambo—coming to a halt at gate 20b.

"After you."

Gina looked up. An old African gentleman with white hair and a white goatee was staring down at her. She was confused for a moment, then it registered he was holding up the line so she could step out and get off the plane. She nodded politely, pulled her backpack over her shoulder and walked down the airplane aisle.

She walked through the gate and stopped by the check-in desk. There was a well-coiffed black woman behind the computer, and Gina said, "There's supposed to be a package waiting for me."

After taking a quick look at Gina's passport, the woman nodded and said, "Oh, yes."

She bent down, then stood, and handed over a small brown package. Gina thanked her and then walked over and plopped down in a chair. Inside the package were a phone, four spare phone batteries, and an envelope filled with crisp one hundred dollar bills. Gina looked down at the phone in her hand. It'd been seven years since she'd had a cell phone, her last one a bulky Nokia. She tried a few different buttons, but she was unable to get the phone to turn on. There was a Starbucks kiosk across the corridor, and after sticking the money and extra batteries in her backpack, she made her way over to the green Starbucks parapet.

There was a line of five in front of her, and directly in front was a young girl around fourteen. Gina tapped her on the shoulder. She smiled and said, "I'll buy your Starbucks if you give me a crash course in Blackberry real quick."

The girl was American, with a thick southern accent. She said, "I have an iPhone but my buddy Billy has a Blackberry. It's super easy, ma'am."

Ma'am? That was a first.

She mentally sighed and said, "How do I turn it on?"

The girl looked at her warily, took the phone, and said, "You hold down this button." The girl held down a red button and two seconds later, the phone was showing signs of life.

"Can you show me how to check my e-mail?"

The little girl showed her the simplicity of the operation and said, "You really need to know this kind of stuff, ma'am."

Gina thanked her, then ordered and paid for both her and the small girl's drinks. Her caramel Frappuccino and fruit and cheese plate in tow, Gina made her way to the opposite wall and slid down to her butt. She popped a grape and piece of cheddar in her mouth and logged onto Gmail. There was one e-mail. It was short and to the point. "Hope you got to South Africa okay. I have attached a better map. It will get you to Ptutsi. Send an e-mail when you arrive. P."

She clicked on the attachment. It loaded. It was a detailed map with roads that showed the exact route to the coordinates that she assumed were those of Ptutsi. At the bottom it read, "Distance 487 Kilometers. Estimated time: 8.57 hours."

Gina saved the map, then clicked the reply button. She typed, "Just got in. G."

She finished off her food, sucked up the last of the Frappuccino, and stood. She passed one of many currency exchange windows, the Rand was trading at 9.54, and she traded in five thousand dollars. She imagined the look of disapproval that would have washed over Paul's face. After she stuck the money back in the envelope, she found herself at a loss. Should she make her way outside? Or just stroll around the small airport? Was this Timon character just supposed to find her? With just Paul's description to go by? Good luck.

Gina wondered how Paul had described her.

You know that journalist lady from Blood Diamond, she looks like her, but bitchier.

In fact, Gina did look a bit like Jennifer Connelly. She was thirty-seven, but most people thought she was thirty, or even in her late twenties. Not that she was complaining. But as a young doctor it had proved difficult to be taken seriously when everyone thinks you are a first year undergrad. Timon had probably heard, "5'5", 120 pounds, hazel eyes, long coffee-colored hair—probably pulled back in a ponytail—jeans, T-shirt, *Asics*, perfect rack."

She looked down. Unfortunately, the last two were two of her most defining traits. An avid runner, she would not stray from her beloved *Asics*, sometimes waiting months for them to arrive in whichever hard to reach place she was calling home. As for her rack, they hadn't come until she was 18, but they had come in a hurry. And they *were* perfect.

Gina noticed a sign for the women's bathroom and, as if waiting for the cue, an imaginary vice tightened around her bladder. She went to the bathroom, washed her hands for a good minute, and pushed back out into the airport lobby.

"Gee-na?"

Gina turned. A handsome black man was staring at her, arms crossed, shaved head reflecting the white airport light. He was smiling, his teeth three shades whiter than Javier's against his beautiful black skin. She took a step forward and said, "Timon?"

He nodded and said, "Eveybody go pee."

She shook her head.

"Afta long plane, eveybody go pee."

She smiled. "Yes, after a long plane ride, everybody does have to go pee."

"We 'ave a long way, we must hurray."

Gina followed him. They walked through the busy airport, through the doors, and walked toward an illegally parked Jeep Wrangler. The sky was a perfect cobalt blue.

Timon jumped into the driver's seat and Gina climbed into the passenger seat, throwing her backpack into the backseat. Timon put the car in gear and zoomed from the airport lot. He took a left turn and said, "Ladysmith is four hours away."

"Then how long to Ptutsi?"

He let up on the gas. "*Ptutsi?*"

Gina nodded. It was evident Timon had not been briefed on this. She said, "I must go to the village of Ptutsi."

Timon took a deep breath. Gina noticed him gaze at a necklace dangling from the rear view mirror. There was a charm at the end. Timon stared at the necklace and uttered silent words under his breath. He was quiet for over a minute, the speedometer stuck on 33 kph. Timon threw the Jeep into third, pushed down hard on the gas, and said, "The road to Ptutsi is bad. Very bad."

Gina took *road* to mean *the trip*. The trip to Ptutsi is very bad.

Timon said, "It will take half day if no trouble."

If no trouble?

Timon gave Gina a sideways glance and slammed the Jeep into fourth gear.

SHOW LOUNGE
2:11 P.M.

"WHEN CAN I expect those Navy Seals you were talking about?"

Frank shrugged. In fact, I don't think the question even registered. He was too preoccupied with Susie. Susie was lying on the floor in front of Frank and Lacy, who had been dozing for the last half hour herself. Susie's breathing was shallow, like she was trying to breathe in and out through a straw. Every once in a while Frank would pour water into her mouth. I'd been trying to take his attention off his progressively sick wife. Apparently, I'd failed. I should have outsourced the job to Mr. J.J. Watkins.

Speaking of which, I turned to my left and said, "So, how did you get into stand-up?" Yes, I was this bored.

"You ever heard of *The Last Comic Standing?*"

"Maybe. I don't watch a whole lot of television."

"It's like *American Idol*, but for comedians."

"Gotcha."

"America votes the comedians off each week until there's a winner."

"I'm familiar with *American Idol*. I get it."

"You do like a three-minute bit and then people call and vote."

I wondered if I could vote him out of this conversation. I said slowly, "I understand."

"Season three, baby."

"You won?"

He shook his head.

"You come close?"

"Not really."

"How did you do?"

"I was the first person voted off."

I couldn't hold back a snicker.

He shrugged. "But, I mean, like twenty thousand people tried out for the show and they only picked like fifteen of us."

Well, that was something. I said, "So your claim to fame is that you were the first person voted off Season Three of *Last Comic Standing*."

He nodded.

"And how is that working out for you?"

"Not too bad. I mean, this is the third cruise I've been on this year. Free room and board. Lots of pretty women. Not really on this cruise. Bunch of yuppies."

"What about when you aren't on a cruise. You get a lot of gigs?"

"It fluctuates. I sell cars on the side. Do a show every now and again. Not a bad life."

"Doesn't sound too bad."

"How about you? What's your story?"

I wasn't in the mood to reminiscence and went with my usual, "That could take awhile."

He looked around and said, "Where am I gonna go? I'm a fuckin' hostage."

Touché. "I grew up near Seattle."

"No shit. I'm from Jersey."

"I would have guessed Texas."

"Really?"

"Or one of the Dakotas?"

"Yeah?" he laughed. "North or South?"

"South."

"Naw, Jersey."

If I hadn't mentioned earlier, Andrew Dice Clay would have done a bit on how bad J.J. Watkins' Jersey accent was. *Dis moderfuckas moderfuckin accent is soooo moderfuckin bad....*

"You go to school up there in Washington?" asked J.J.

I nodded.

"Yeah? I did a couple semesters of community college, but it wasn't for me."

"It's not for everybody."

"What did you study in school?"

Here we go. "Criminology."

"No shit." He hit me on the arm. "You a spook?"

"That's classified." I hit him back.

He found this amusing and through a hacking laugh, he said, "I'm gonna use that. *Classified.* That's priceless." He paused. "What are you really? A Fed?"

"I'm nothing. But I worked with the Feds for a couple years."

"Doin' what?"

"Homicides."

"No shit?"

I told him about how they would contract me out weeks or months at a time to help them augment a homicide investigation. He heard about the case I'd worked up in Maine and couldn't believe that was me.

He said, "Weren't you on the cover of *Time?*"

"Yep." *Time* and *People.*

Gilroy, who had been listening to our entire conversation, turned around and looked at me. I did my best Ice Man impression, chomping down my teeth at him. He turned back around.

J.J. asked, "Then what? You retired?"

"Tried to."

"Yeah? What happened?"

"I moved back home to Seattle." I told him how my parents' house—well, it was my house, but I couldn't ever think of it as mine—backed up to the Puget Sound. "I wasn't there more than an hour when I saw a woman's body floating in the water."

This case had also made huge headlines, and he said, "I remember that shit. The governor. Wolves or something?"

I rolled up my sleeve and showed him the inside of my right arm where one of the wolves—I think there had been a total of four—had latched on.

"Holy shit. You got any others?"

I showed him the nickel-sized scars on my left shoulder and right thigh.

"You got shot twice?"

I nodded.

"Fuckin' a."

We were quiet a minute. It was a great minute. J.J. broke the silence with, "Hey, you know how a Porsche and a porcupine are different?"

"Other than in every possible way?"

He laughed. "A porcupine has the pricks on the outside."

How again, did this guy beat out 20,000 other people? Did the other 19,999 all tell stupider jokes than the Jersey beaver to my left. Anyhow, we got back to talking about the case in Washington and I said, "Actually, the governor's husband gave me this cruise as a thank you gift."

"Really?"

I looked around. The fact that I was a hostage flooded back. "Sadly, yes."

"So you're not rich like the rest of these yuppies?"

I didn't think J.J. Watkins wanted to hear about my seven-figure inheritance so I went with, "Nope. I'm just like you."

He hit me on the arm again. "Me and you. Long lost brothers I tell you."

I thought about telling him it was closer to step-long-lost-twice-removed-third-cousins-by-marriage-who'd-found-each-other-by-accident-on-Facebook.

That's when it happened. I'd heard a soft moaning and turned. It was coming from Susie. Frank knelt down and dabbed at her face with a wet cloth, telling her she would be okay. As I turned my head in Susie's direction, the stage curtains had moved into my line of sight. He could have been there for a while. Just waiting for me to notice.

I squinted at the lone eye trained on me. A finger slipped out. One finger. It wasn't like the last time. This time it was extended. He was pointing.

"You okay, man?" prodded J.J.

I waved him off and said, "Fine, give me a second here."

"Yeah, sure man, whatever you want."

I acted as if I was stretching my neck then looked back to the curtains, but the fingers were gone. What was he pointing at? His finger had been pointed straight across the curtains to my right. The only thing over there was the women's bathroom. Did he want me to go into the women's bathroom?

J.J. leaned into me and said, "What are you looking at, bro?"

I ignored him. I nudged Lacy with my elbow. She stirred. She looked at me. She wasn't happy.

"Since you're awake," I said.

She slid upright and said, "How long was I out?"

I stared at the women's bathroom. The curtain stopped four feet from the walkway leading to the restroom. "About an hour."

At the far right edge of the curtain the tiny black finger appeared. It was pointed down. And then it disappeared.

"Are you all right?" asked Lacy.

I nodded. Then I stood. That's when I saw it. At the far end up the stage, just below where the curtain stopped, there was something. Something small and white. I guessed it was a folded piece of paper.

I looked around. If he would have put it on the opposite side by the men's bathroom, I could have easily plucked it off the stage unnoticed. But if I were meandering over by the women's bathroom, one of the pirates was sure to take notice. And the last thing I wanted to do was blow this kid's cover who was hiding behind the curtains. But if he'd gone through all the trouble to write me a message, it must be important.

I looked at Lacy. She was staring at me like I was a rabid dog. She asked, "What's gotten into you?"

I leaned toward her and whispered in her ear.

Over my shoulder J.J. muttered, "Secrets don't make friends."

I ignored him.

A moment later, Lacy yawned and said, "I've got to pee."

"Where's she going?" asked J.J.

"To pee," I said, my eyebrows raised. "She has to go *pee*."

"Oh."

I watched Lacy walk to the bathroom. She pushed through the doors and disappeared. Easy as pie. I noticed movement out of my right eye and turned. Tupac was headed in the direction of the women's bathroom.

Rutt-Ro.

I thought Tupac was going to go in the bathroom, but he didn't. He stood with his back to the wall just outside the door. This wasn't good. Where he stood, Lacy might not see him before she went for the paper. And if he saw her pick up the piece of paper he might take it out on both Lacy and the little boy. I stared at the door, waiting for it to open. I could see small pockets of others were watching things unfold. Two seconds passed, three seconds, five, ten, twenty. The door opened.

Tupac grabbed Lacy and threw her up against the wall. I stood. But before the door swung closed, it opened again, and Lacy strolled out. The woman the pirate had pinned against the wall wasn't even Lacy. Lacy saw the two of them and reeled backwards onto the stage. Tupac threw the other woman on the ground and headed toward Lacy. Lacy flipped over on her stomach. Tupac flipped her over onto her back and started yelling at her. I watched his hands waiting for him to pull out his knife.

He leaned over her and stuck his face in hers. I saw his tongue come out and run down her cheek. Lacy said nothing. Didn't open her mouth. It wasn't like her not to fight back. Not to scream.

Tupac stood and began laughing. He looked at his two comrades near the door. They too were laughing. He walked to them, and one of them handed him something. Money maybe. They'd probably bet whether he could lick her face without getting kicked in the balls. Whatever the bet was, Tupac had come out victorious.

I turned back to Lacy. She'd composed herself and was walking back. She didn't take her eyes off the three pirates. Daring them to try her again.

I willed her to settle down.

She sat down next to me. She didn't speak, not for ten seconds, not for twenty. Her mouth was clenched tight. Then she turned to me and smiled. Within her teeth was the folded note.

She coughed into her hands and seconds later slipped me the tiny piece of paper. I made my way to the bathroom and sat down on the pot. I unfolded the note and read the message, then tossed it in the toilet, and flushed.

In large brick lettering, written in red crayon were five words.

There is a way out.

WASHINGTON D.C.

8:33 A.M.

A LITTLE BOY in a red jersey kicked the ball. It went three feet. Another little boy with a red jersey kicked the ball. It went four feet. Two little boys in green jerseys reached the ball at the same time. They both kicked it. It went ten feet. The ball was now twenty feet from the goalie. A little boy with red hair three shades lighter than his jersey and a face plastered in orange freckles—both inherited from his mother—sprinted toward the ball. His brown eyes—he got these from his father—were wide. This could be his first goal. He ran hard, planted his left foot, and took a massive swing with his right. His foot missed the ball and the little boy fell flat on his back.

Most five-year-olds would have lain on the ground, tears streaming from their eyes. Not Ben Garret. He popped up, turned toward the sideline, located his father among the many parents wearing painful expressions—and smiled.

Paul Garret laughed. It would take quite a bit more than that to make his son cry. Ben had fallen off the jungle gym when he was four and never made a peep. Betsy had taken him to the hospital three days later due to the swelling, and X-rays revealed the bone was broken in two different places. Paul wished he'd been half as tough when he was little. Hell, he wished he were half as tough now. Sometimes when he was standing in front of that podium taking rapid-fire questions, he thought about when his little boy broke his arm.

Paul watched as his son threw him another smile, then sprinted off in pursuit of the ball. He looked away from the game —the scrum of little boys had moved down near the opposite goal —and down at the iPhone in his hand. He had a new message. He took a deep breath. *What now?*

He'd been in and out of meetings for the last twenty-four hours. He'd tried to beg off the soccer game, but he knew how important they were to Ben. Paul was yet to miss a game. And if he missed his son's first career goal, he would never forgive himself. Plus, there wasn't much he could do at this point. So far, they'd kept a lid on the hostage situation in South Africa.

The message was from Josh Ritter, the White House Chief of Staff. It read, "This just ran on SABC3, which runs most of South Africa Broadcasting Corporation's English content. It's only a matter of time before the story breaks in the U.S. Be advised. GBHN."

GBHN.

Get Back Here Now.

He clicked on the attachment. A video window popped up. It showed the clip was three minutes and nine seconds. The play button faded away leaving an attractive African woman with a microphone. She was standing outside, a two-lane road behind her. Groups of twos, threes, and sometimes larger walked into the screen, then disappeared. A line of cars moved slowly but steadily in the background. The woman spoke in accented English. She said, "You might ask why this lightly traveled road is overflowing with people on a bright Sunday afternoon. You might be wondering why all these people are flocking to a small village known mostly for its sick and its sadness."

She held up a newspaper. "This full-page ad ran in last week's

Isolezwe, KwaZulu-Natal's largest Zulu newspaper." The text was in Zulu, but there were four letters that circumvented the language barrier, *AIDS*.

The anchor said, "The ad reads in Zulu that the Red Cross will be distributing lifetime supplies of AIDS medication in the village of Ptutsi this coming week."

There was a map beneath the text. Then the Red Cross symbol.

The woman said, "The Red Cross denies placing the ad, but as you can see—" the anchor turned and looked over her shoulder at the people walking in droves, "this is not affecting the thousands of people who have already picked up everything to go to the small village of Ptutsi. We are stationed three miles east of Lady-smith, the last town before forty miles of dirt road and heavy brush. It will take these people more than a day to reach the small village, but what awaits them might not be death, but life."

The video paused—Garret had an incoming call: Sally-CNBC. He clicked Ignore. Another call, Ted-CNN. He pushed Ignore again. He ignored five more calls: Bill-ABC, Joan-CBS, Monica-MSNBC, Craig-FOX, Monique-NPR.

He checked his e-mail. Twenty-seven. Then it moved to forty-one.

Shit had officially hit the fan.

Paul walked over and tapped Sam Tillen on the shoulder. He wasn't crazy about Sam, but Sam's son Trevor was Ben's best friend. Sam looked at Paul and said, "Hey, quite the fall Ben took a couple minutes ago."

"Yeah, it was. Hey, listen, you think you can drop Ben off after the game?"

"No problem. Something happen?"

Paul raised his eyebrows.

"Terrorists?" Sam was always looking for the inside scoop. He was also the only person Paul knew, well outside of the President, who had his own personal bomb shelter.

"Nothing like that."

Sam eyed him quizzically, then asked, "It okay if I take them for some pizza after the game?"

"Of course."

Paul turned to leave.

Sam yelled, "Will I need my gas mask?"

Paul ignored him and ran to his car. Seven minutes later, while Paul was on speakerphone with Josh Ritter, Ben scored his first goal.

LADYSMITH

4:33 P.M.

HOUSES STARTED TO POP UP, sparsely at first, then every thirty feet or so. They were small, the size of a typical shed, with thatched roofing. Each bungalow had a minute porch, two small windows, a perfectly centered door, and a prominent chimney. They looked sturdy, but it wouldn't necessitate a wrecking ball to knock one over. Every once in a while they would see a woman, usually with a bandana on—white, blue, black—either sweeping the small porch or rocking in a chair, needle and thread in hand.

Timon looked at Gina, raised his eyebrows, and yelled, "Ladysmith."

They hadn't spoken much on the four-hour drive. Mostly because Timon drove fast and the hot wind churned through the open Jeep like a poor man's cello concerto. And because Gina had fluttered in and out of sleep the entire trip. She was a bit jet-lagged after all. When she *was* awake, she gaped at the beautiful landscapes. Wide valleys. Lush tropical green forest. Rolling hills. She once thought she'd seen the long neck of a giraffe, but she could not say this with certainty.

Timon let up on the gas, and in an octave just below a scream, Gina asked, "Can we stop?"

"You need pee?"

She laughed. "Yes, I need to pee."

"Hungry?"

"Starving."

"Good. I know place."

They drove for another five minutes. Many people were moving in the small village. Gina noticed a large group, twenty or thirty people walking on the side of the chalky street. Many of the women carried large wicker baskets balanced on their heads. Gina noticed the baskets appeared full, heavy. They were walking toward the heart of town. Presumably to do some shopping. Or trade their wares.

They drove past a football field stretch of small stores, an outside market. Fresh produce. Different goods. Gina noticed a handful of white folks mingling with the store owners. Women held up large colored hats. Small African children zoomed in and out of their legs like tiny fruit flies.

Timon pulled off the road and parked in front of a small restaurant. They walked through the open door. There were ten small tables, each with a different colored tablecloth. Half the tables were occupied. A beautiful African woman met them near the door and spoke to Timon. She smiled at Gina, then led them to a table.

Gina whispered to Timon, "Pee."

He smiled and said something to the African woman. She took Gina's hand and led her around to a small room. Boxes filled half the room, but the other half was filled by a sparkling white toilet. After Gina finished, she washed her hands in a pristine sink. There was no mirror and she was glad; she didn't want to know what she looked like after thirty hours of traveling. But she'd be lying if she said she wasn't concerned about her appearance.

She returned to the table, a bottle of water awaiting her.

Timon said, "I have ordered for us both. We cannot, what do you whities call it? Dilly-dally?"

Gina laughed. It was a combination of *whities, dilly-dally*, and the enchanting smile that had accompanied the remark.

"Yes, we must not dilly-dally."

He asked, "You are a doctor?" Gina was having an easier time understanding his English, but the question still came out, "*You aw docta?*"

"Yes. How did you know?"

"The man call you Dr. Gina."

"He did?"

Timon nodded. "He also say, you very pretty."

Gina's cheeks flushed. At him calling her *very pretty* or Paul having called her *very pretty*, she wasn't certain.

Timon asked, "Is this man your husband?"

"Just a friend."

"No husband?"

She wiggled her fingers in front of him to show she didn't have a ring. "How about you?"

"Yes. I have woman I am to marry," Timon said, his face lighting up. He pulled out his wallet. "I have picture."

He passed her a neatly clipped picture of a striking woman. She made the hostess look drab and plain. Gina handed the picture back to him. "She's beautiful."

He smiled once more.

"When are you getting married?"

"In sixteen days. I am very excited."

Their food arrived. Timon explained the various dishes. *Biltong*, dried, salted ostrich. *Bobotie*, South Africa's version of Shepherd's pie. And *boerewors*, handmade farm sausages.

Gina picked up a piece of biltong, which resembled something of jerky and tore off a piece. It was salty and delicious. Timon did the same, then asked, "Where were you doctor?"

"I went to school in the states, practiced medicine for a couple years, got bored, then I joined the World Health Organization. I spent three years in Romania doctoring rural villages, then I spent the last three years in Bolivia fighting an unending battle with tuberculosis."

"I have heard of this illness. It is very bad."

"It is also very treatable."

"Where were you born?"

"My dad was in the Marines and we moved around a lot when I was little. I spent a lot of time in Europe, then when I was six my mother died. My dad decided it would be best if he settled down and he took a job in Washington D.C. I basically grew up on the marine base there."

She took another couple bites of food, then asked, "How about you? Were you born in South Africa?"

"I was born in Mozambique. A small town called Kepo. My mother died when I was very young. My father died later in mining accident. I lived with my Auntie until I was ten, then moved with another Auntie in Johannesburg. I have been here ever since."

They ate in silence for a moment. Timon was in deep contemplation. He peered at her over his food, then asked, "Do you go to Ptutsi to help these people?"

She thought about the question. "Yes."

"Many people are sick. Many people die. Very sad place."

She remembered something he said and asked, "You mentioned trouble at the airport, what did you mean?"

"We have no trouble. I pray. We have no trouble."

Gina didn't know what to say to this so she asked, "So you are a guide?"

"Among many other things. I am also fisherman. And artist."

"Artist?"

"I make things."

"What kind of things?"

"Clocks."

"I would like to see one of these clocks someday."

He smiled.

They finished eating and Timon took out his wallet. Gina waved him off. She took out a stack of rands and handed it to him. She asked, "Is this enough?"

He laughed. "That is enough to buy the restaurant."

"Give her half."

He counted out half. She told him to keep the rest for himself. He tried not to take the money, but Gina wouldn't budge. He finally put the money in his pocket, thanking her repeatedly. She said, "Think of it as an early wedding present."

They walked back to the car, and Timon said, "We will go buy some food for the rest of the trip."

They drove back to the market and bought fresh fruit, more biltong, bread, cheese, and other snacks. While Timon haggled with shopkeepers, Gina perused the goods, buying three small wooden toys and some candy she thought the three children might like.

Back at the car, Timon pulled out a large duffel bag. He began ridding the bag of its many items. He removed something gingerly and handed it to Gina.

Gina looked down at the clock in her hand. It was made of brass and stone. The detail and markings were some of the most precise she'd ever seen. The second hand swept silently past each small stone. It was a sight to behold. The clock would go for upward of two hundred dollars at any high-end shop in the states. She asked, "You made this?"

He nodded.

"It's beautiful."

"I give to you."

Gina tried to resist. But he was more stubborn than she'd been about the money. She thanked him with a hug, then wrapped the small clock in a shirt, and stuffed it in her backpack. Timon packed the duffel bag with the food, and they both hopped into the Jeep.

They drove out of Ladysmith and came to a fork in the road.

Droves of people walked along the side of the road. They passed the group they'd seen earlier, the women holding the wicker baskets on their heads. The road was filled with cars. They took a left onto the beaten road, falling in behind a truck filled with men and women. The passengers all looked war-torn and frail, as if they'd traveled millions of miles to find themselves on this chalky, windswept, dirt road.

Gina looked at Timon and asked, "Where are all these people going?"

He looked at her and said solemnly, "The same place we are."

SHOW LOUNGE
4:56 P.M.

I WAS SKEPTICAL. It didn't sound like it would work. And I hated to bring J.J. into the loop, but there was no other way. I said, "An hour?"

J.J. nodded. "I have two or three hours' worth of material."

"No SPAM jokes."

"What's wrong with my SPAM bit?"

"Other than it not being funny."

He shook his head. "I got all sorts of great stuff. Don't you worry."

But I was. I was worried one of the pirates would kill him the second he grabbed the microphone. And although it appeared the pirates had a passing understanding of English, I was worried they wouldn't grasp enough English to understand his jokes. But mostly, I was worried they *would* understand him completely, find him quite unfunny, and put a bullet in his forehead.

I was banking on the fact the pirates were as bored as the rest of us. They might be up for a little entertainment. Plus, it wasn't like anyone would, or could, go anywhere. Although, if my little friend was telling the truth, there *was* an exit other than the one the pirates were guarding. I would soon find out.

I'd wanted to wait until the pirates' dinner came. But I couldn't wait any longer. Susie was nearly comatose. She no longer would open her mouth to let Frank pour water in.

I nodded at J.J. He took a couple deep breaths. Then he stood and headed toward the stage. Lacy's hand found mine and she gave it a timid squeeze. She hadn't been fully on board with me going, and insisted that if I did go, then I had better bring back her dog. I told her I'd do my best. For all I knew he was asleep at the bottom of the Indian Ocean. Anyhow, the entire plan hedged on the lights. According to J.J., there were several buttons under the microphone that controlled the lights. He could dim the lights in the show lounge, then turn on the spotlight. But, if the pirates had messed with the main lighting grid at the back of the room, then all bets were off.

J.J. clambered up the small stairs. All conversation stopped. I peeked over my shoulder at the pirates. Lil Wayne tapped Common on the shoulder and pointed at J.J. They seemed curious. Not angry.

J.J. took a couple steps on stage, then fell in behind the microphone. He started messing with the buttons. I looked upward. The lights were still blazing.

Shit.

J.J. looked panicked. Then, the lights began to dim.

Whew.

Soon Transvaal was pitch dark, save for the bright white ellipse that shone down on J.J. Watkins like a beam from a UFO. I looked at the pirates. I could make out their outlines near the door. One pirate took a step forward. Another grabbed him by the shoulder and drew him back. So far so good.

J.J. gazed at the crowd. He didn't say a word. He kept blinking his eyes. Don't tell me this asshole was freezing up. Lacy glanced at me. My eyes hadn't adjusted to the dark, but I knew she was looking at me with eyes wide, eyebrows high up on her forehead. I'd wanted to be on the move already. I'd wanted to take advantage of the sixty seconds before the pirates' eyes adjusted. But if this idiot didn't start talking soon, they were going to walk up to the stage and drag him off.

J.J. continued to blink. He looked straight ahead. His Adam's apple danced in the white light.

Come on.

I looked over my shoulder. One of the pirates had started marching down the walkway. Two long strides. Three. He was nearing the back row of chairs. It was Tupac.

"You want to know the top ten reasons why a gun is better than a woman?"

Tupac stopped.

"Number ten. You can trade an old .44 for two new .22s."

Tupac smiled, then laughed. I had a feeling J.J. Watkins had decided to go with an old but reliable safety net. David Letterman.

"Number nine. You can keep one gun at home and have another for when you're on the road."

I watched the pirate. Tupac laughed again, then plopped down in one of the large chairs in the back row. I looked at the two pirates by the door. Both of them were also laughing. I shook my head at J.J. He rattled off two more. All three of the pirates were laughing. One of the pirates was doubled over. J.J. was hitting on the two things our pirate friends could relate to, guns and women.

Genius.

"Number six. If you admire a friend's gun and tell him so, he will probably let you try it out a few times."

There were a couple low chuckles from some of hostages. I could even hear Lacy give a stifled laugh. One of the pirates near the door hit the other one on the shoulder. Maybe he was asking if he could borrow his wife sometime. Anyhow, this was my cue to start moving. I gave Lacy's hand a soft squeeze.

J.J. was starting to feel the energy from the audience, and it showed in his delivery. "Number five. A handgun doesn't take up a lot of closet space."

There was quite a bit of laughter and I slid down in my chair. All eyes were on J.J. Even Gilroy, who I had worried would call attention when I made my move, seemed to be enjoying the show. I slowly slid to the floor. Then I crawled past the seven empty seats leading to the small walkway opposite the men's bathroom.

"Number four. Handguns function normally every day of the month."

Loud laughter.

I slithered up near the last chair. There were six feet of space from the chair to the wall. Then another ten feet to the edge of the curtain. There would be a moment when I would be fully exposed. There was a small amount of residual light cascading off the stage, but if the pirates kept their attention on J.J., I would go unnoticed. As if sensing this, or perhaps he'd seen my approach out of the corner of his eye, J.J. took the microphone from the stand and walked to the edge of the spotlight, as far away from me as possible.

Maybe he was smarter than I gave him credit for.

"Number three. A handgun doesn't ask, 'Do these bullets make me look fat?'"

Uproarious laughter.

I darted to the edge of the stage, flattening my body against the two feet of raised wood. The laughter faded and J.J. said, "Number two. A gun doesn't care if you fall asleep after you use it."

I scurried to the back edge of the stage, the heavy curtain brushing against my buzzed head. I made my way under the curtain, climbing up the wall with my hands. The curtain was thick and the space behind the curtain was as black as the widest reaches of space. I put my hands out in front of me and took a step forward.

Through the thick curtain, I heard, "And the number one reason that a gun is better than a woman…"

I felt pressure on my shirt. Someone was tugging on it. I lowered my hand. Felt the soft spongy hair of a child.

"…you can buy a silencer for a gun."

I could hear the laughter. Even a little stomping. I hoped J.J. had enough Letterman Top Tens to fill an hour.

A hand intertwined with mine. The little boy led me through the blackness. We turned. Where there should have been a wall, there wasn't. I'd only been to the show lounge once, to see J.J. and they'd kept the curtains closed, but it made sense that there would be more stage behind the curtain, and I recalled a picture in the hallway leading to the show lounge of a full twenty-piece orchestra. The full stage must stretch back thirty or forty feet beyond the curtain.

"Three steps," whispered the child.

We ghosted down three steps. A tiny red light glowed ten feet ahead. I heard as the boy swiped his card. The light turned green. The door was pulled open.

"I shut the lights off," he said. "There are sixteen steps."

I let him guide me down the steps, then a door at the bottom was opened, and we emerged into soft light.

He couldn't have been more than six. He was caramel brown with six inches of spongy afro.

I said, "That was very brave what you just did."

"I know." He spoke perfect English.

"I'm Thomas."

"I'm Bheka." He pronounced it, *be-HEEK-ah.*

"Are you here with your parents?" I asked, already knowing the answer.

"My mom works on the ship," he said, flashing the card. "She's a maid."

"And you live on the ship?"

"Yes."

"Where is your mom now?"

"She got off in Mozambique to see some people. We're picking her up in Cape Town."

I told him that he spoke excellent English.

"Most people speak English on this boat."

I nodded.

"I understand them, too."

"Who?"

He cocked his head upward. "The bad guys."

"You speak African?"

"Zulu. Two of those men are speaking Zulu."

Lil Wayne and Tupac.

"My mom is Zulu. And my dad, he is like you."

"Like me?"

"White, like you."

That would explain his caramel coloring. I was putting two and two together. "And your dad, who is he?"

"My mom won't tell me. Some guy on the ship." He didn't specify whether this was a passenger or crew. Better left unknown.

"And everyone knows that you live here on the ship with your mom?"

"Yes."

"But they don't know that you didn't go with her." It was more of a statement than a question.

"No."

"How did you escape the bad guys?"

"I hid."

I nodded, then for the first time, I surveyed my surroundings. The red lights. District 9.

I guessed four minutes had elapsed since the lights had gone off in the show lounge. I had a nagging suspicion J.J. Watkins wasn't going to buy me more than a half hour. I said, "I'll be back in twenty minutes, stay here."

Bheka looked at me solemnly and said, "Be careful."

DECK 6

5:06 P.M.

SUBISISO WAS GROWING tired of the man on stage. His first bit about guns and women had kept his attention, but now he had other things on his mind. He could feel it crawling up through his chest. Behind his eyes. He needed it. He needed it now. He looked at Mausi sitting in the chair. He was still laughing at the pudgy man's jokes. Although Subisiso was a couple years older than Mausi, technically Mausi was his commander. But he wouldn't be missed. And if he was, he would say he wanted to take a look around.

Subisiso turned to Caj and said in stilted English, "I be back soon." Mausi and Caj both spoke Zulu, but Subisiso was from Namibia and spoke a dialect of Oshiwambo.

Caj shook his head and replied, "Mausi say not leave."

"You be fine. I not be gone long."

Subisiso unlocked the door and slipped out before Caj could protest. He walked through the large walkway. He had never been surrounded by such decadence. For twenty-five years he had known only poverty. Recruited when he was ten years old, a gun in his hands by eleven, smoking marijuana, drinking, having sex by the same age. He'd killed his first man when he was twelve—a traffic stop. The black man in the jeep refused to give them any money. Subisiso had shoved his gun into the man's neck and pulled the trigger. Then shot the passenger as well. That night his commander had taken his knife and made two long slashes across his cheeks. Reminders of the two men he'd killed. That was also the first night Subisiso had plunged the beautiful nectar into his veins. He'd never felt anything like it. So peaceful. A blanket of tranquility.

He noticed the sign for the bathrooms and pushed through the door. He had the syringe in his hand before his image appeared in the mirror over the sink. He pulled out the small corroded spoon. He'd found the spoon many years ago. It was his crucifix. He pulled the small pouch from his back pocket. He cooked the white powder until it boiled. He bit his lip.

He pulled back the plunger, the syringe drinking up the dark liquid like a wild animal at the edge of a brook. He brought the syringe up. Watched himself in the mirror as the needle moved passed his glowing red eyes. A drip of nectar clung to the edge of the needle. He stuck out his cragged tongue and soaked up the drop. He swallowed hard. His pants felt tight around his loins. His heart crunched against his chest.

He pushed the tip of the needle against the large throbbing vein in his neck. His stomach muscles tightened. His jaw clenched. He eased down with his thumb. He leaned against the wall, slowly sliding to the floor. His head fell back and his glowing red eyes hid behind their thin black curtain.

———

Rikki stood in the bathroom doorway. She had her heel pressed awkwardly against the bottom of the door jamb, her arms pushing in the opposite direction. She twisted her body, her spine emitting a series of small cracks. She let out a deep satisfied sigh.

She repeated the movement on the opposite side of the doorway, giving way to another series of pops. Now all she had to do was empty her bladder and she'd be good to go. She lifted up the seat and sat down on the toilet.

———

Subisiso's eyes snapped open. He pushed himself up and off the wall. He pushed through the small doorway. He felt massive, like he could barely squeeze through the wide hall.

He walked past the winding glass stairwell, past a room filled with plush couches, tables, large TVs, and a bar at back. He passed the elevators, then stopped when he came to the passenger suites. He pushed into the first room. He was getting paid well for his services, but a little bonus could never hurt. He rifled through the owner's drawers, pants, and luggage. He found a watch and a wallet with over three hundred dollars in it.

He exited the room. He thought about going back to the large room with the large stage. He would be missed soon. No, he would check a couple more. Then go back.

———

Rikki finished peeing, stood, and flushed.

———

Subisiso pulled his hand out of the large duffel bag and cocked his head. He scampered to the wall next to him and pushed his ear against it. He could hear water moving. Someone was in the room next door.

He exited, ran to the room directly left, and tried the door. It was locked. He rammed the door with his shoulder. It budged a little. He stepped back and gave it a hard kick. The door splintered slightly. He gave it two more hard kicks. The door flew open. He ran into the room. He saw nothing. He walked into the bathroom and stared at the toilet. He lifted the lid. The water was still. He pulled the shower curtain back with his left hand. Nothing. The sink too, was dry.

Was he hearing things? It wouldn't be the first time the White Lady had played tricks on him.

He walked out of the bathroom. He opened up the closet. Looked under the bed. He looked everywhere. There was no one in the small room. He grabbed a suitcase and heaved it onto the bed. He began rummaging through it. He found a wad of cash, not dollars, Euros, and began counting it. He'd heard somewhere the Euro was worth even more than the dollar and he was holding close to five grand. He thought how much sweet nectar he would buy.

He glanced at the TV. It was wide and thin. Maybe he would buy one of those. He noticed something white dangling over the edge. He took a step forward and looked at it more closely. It was a shoelace. He grabbed the TV and threw it to the floor. He stared at the small girl curled into a ball. He was no longer thinking about money.

WASHINGTON D.C.

10:30 A.M.

"THERE IS a man on the phone, he said you would be expecting his call."

Roger Garret pressed a red button on the phone, which would record the following conversation, and pressed the speaker. He said, "Hello."

"General Garret?"

Roger recognized the ominous accented English from the video. "Yes."

"Do you know who this is?"

"I do."

"Then I trust you received my e-mail."

"I did."

"What did you think?"

"What did I think about you taking over a cruise ship? Or what did I think about you threatening the lives of over four hundred hostages? Or what did I think about your demands?"

"My demands."

"Oh, no problem."

He was silent. "Are you being condescending, General?"

"No, not at all. You ask and you shall receive."

"I advise that you be careful, General."

"With all due respect Mr. Quaroni, what did you expect? You know the United States doesn't negotiate with terrorists. If we comply with your demands, we will open the door to any number of terrorist threats."

"I understand your position, General. But you must understand mine. Every one of my brothers and sisters, my mother, my father, every relative I ever had, is dead. Every one of them died from AIDS. If I had not left my village when I was a young man, I too would be dead."

"I am well aware of the crisis in your country. I sympathize for the loss of your family and friends, but there are other ways to go about things. What you have done, what you are doing, is not the way."

"You are naive, General Garret," he scoffed. "You have been living on American soil far too long. This is the only way. For the past twenty years, this epidemic has raged through my country. Twenty long years. I have tried to reason with the South African government. Do you know that our last minister of health denounced the treatment of AIDS by western medicine? She promoted beetroot, garlic, lemons, and African potatoes as a way to fight AIDS. Our current president still expresses doubts about the connection between HIV and AIDS and the effectiveness of antiretroviral drugs in treating the disease.

"South Africa is the only country in Africa whose government is still obtuse and negligent about rolling out treatment. It is the only country in Africa whose government continues to promote theories more worthy of a lunatic fringe than of a concerned and compassionate state. My government refused to provide AIDS drugs until forced to do so by a 2002 court ruling. And yet, little progress has been made. More than 5.5 million of my countrymen are infected with HIV. Most will die before I do. If there is another way, please tell me."

Roger found himself saying, "Let me make some phone calls."

"It is a bit late for phone calls, General Garret. If I am not witness to an overwhelming surge of doctors, medical supplies, and antiviral medication to the village of Ptutsi noon two days from now, every single person aboard this ship will die. There is no room for negotiation. You either help us or you pull four hundred bodies from the Indian Ocean."

There was a pause, then Quaroni said, "About the three children."

"Yes. I was going to ask."

"They are my grandchildren."

Roger couldn't help but ask, "Do they have AIDS?"

"Yes, they do."

"How do I know you will release the prisoners if the United States complies with your requests?"

"You have my word. No one aboard this ship needs to die. If by noon, two days from now, I am sent footage that the United States has begun testing and distributing medicine in the village of Ptutsi as well as a photograph of the three children, I will give myself and my men up to the authorities."

"Where do I send this footage?" The question surprised Garret. He hadn't intended on asking it.

"The address from which I sent the e-mail."

"Is this your private e-mail?"

"No, it is not. But, it should suffice."

Roger mulled things over for a moment, thinking, then he said, "We may need more time."

"You've had twenty years, General. Your time has run out."

The phone went dead.

AS LACY HAD ATTESTED EARLIER, District 9 had been decorated for the lesbian wedding. Rainbow streamers. Cardboard cutouts of Ellen and Portia. A pink foam arch. They must have gotten it all from some lesbian superstore. I half expected Rosie O'Donnell to jump out and tackle me. The tables were set with wine glasses, candles, place cards, gift bags, and rose petals. It looked like it would have been one hell of a—well—of a civil union ceremony.

Halfway across the dance floor, I stopped. Directly overhead were Lacy, and my new friend Frank, and the quickly declining Susie. They were all counting on me. I had maybe twenty minutes to locate Susie's medicine, retrieve Lacy's fanny pack from the lifeboat, and find some sort of weapon. I'd also pondered finding the computer center and trying to get a message out. That being said, I'm sure one of the first things the pirates had done was to shut down all communications. But, *they* needed to communicate somehow; the Professor had sent that video to someone. If I could get an e-mail out, I could pass along pertinent details that would help someone to rescue us. And they needed to know about Rikki. Something fishy was going on there.

At any rate, I had a lot to accomplish in a small amount of time.

I hurried across the dance floor and pushed through the doors and into the wide lobby. I swept my head backwards and forwards as I walked. I had a strong feeling I was the only person on Deck 5, but you never know.

There was a sign with arrows and listed destinations, one of which was the Computer Center on Deck 4. If I returned soon enough, I would duck in and try to send a quick e-mail. But I'd sent maybe two dozen e-mails in my life, most of them coming during my tenure teaching a criminal justice class in Maine and a handful to Lacy when she fled overseas, and I had no idea who I'd send it to.

Barack@gmail.com?

Sally@hostagehelp.org?

Andersoncooper@whyismyhairsofuckingwhite.net?

I suppose I'd cross that bridge if I came to it.

I came abreast of the brass stairwell. I looked up and down. The coast was clear. I crept up the stairs. When I was near the top, I peeked over the edge. I could see the walkway that led to the show lounge, but there was nobody out there. I scampered up the remaining stairs and made it to the safety of the opposite hall. This led to a wide room with large couches, TVs, and a bar.

I passed the room, filed past the elevator lobby, and entered the corridor leading to the guest suites. Frank and Susie's room was Suite 06, one of the Presidential suites. I walked briskly through the tight halls. Then I stopped dead. I turned to my right and stared at door 319. The lock was mangled, the door slightly off its hinges.

From inside, I heard a girl scream.

SUITE 319

5:12 P.M.

RIKKI HEARD the TV crash to the floor and she knew she was in trouble. She peeked through her fingers. An African man with a shaved head and red eyes stared at her with a wide grin. He had two large scars running diagonally across his cheeks, feeding into a mangy beard.

She could feel his hot acrid breath move through her wispy blonde bangs. The man reached out and grabbed her by her hair. He pulled her off the ledge, and she fell to the floor.

She looked up at the man and said, "I'll do whatever you want. Just don't hurt me. I'll do whatever."

"You betta," he laughed

He pushed down on her chest with his foot, leaning her backwards onto the sharp edges of the broken TV. His eyes ran up her compact body. The top button of her small white shorts had come undone and Rikki knew he was staring at the top of her pink underwear when he licked his bottom lip. He lifted up her gray tank top with the tips of his dirty black boot. She wasn't wearing a bra and the man pressed the tip of his boot into her left nipple. Her stomach tightened and she held back a scream. No one would hear her. Better to let him have his way.

She said desperately, "I will give you as much money as you want!"

"Monay?" he asked questioningly. He pulled a large roll of bills from his pocket and said, "This?"

She nodded. "A million dollars."

He was quiet.

"Just don't kill me," she begged. Her eyes began to water. She had never begged for anything in her life.

He grabbed her by the hair and walked her on hands and knees to the bedroom. Then he yanked her upward and pushed her down on the bed. She looked up at him. He pulled a gun over his head. Her breath caught. How had she not seen the gun yet? She quivered. Her mind raced. Could she fight off this beast? She had a hard time carrying four hardback novels; there was nothing she could do.

She felt a tearing near her groin and opened her eyes. The man was cutting off her small white shorts with a large knife. "PLL-LEAAASE…," she cried.

He didn't even look up. He cut the shorts off and tossed them on the ground. Rikki felt her panties pulled down and a tiny pinprick. She looked down. The knife nestled in her thin patch of light brown pubic hair. She instinctively tried to bring her legs up to her chest. The man grabbed at her foot and twisted her. Then putting all his weight on top of her, he stuck his face in hers. He said nothing. His hand was around her throat. Rikki wanted to keep her eyes closed, but the man's hand was tight around her windpipe and her eyes bulged. She sobbed.

The man let up on her neck. Rikki lolled her head to the left. What fight she had was gone. Tears poured down her cheeks onto the bed.

She felt the man's hand. Inside her. She whimpered. His touch disappeared for a moment and Rikki heard a soft rustling, the unbuckling of pants. Rikki bit down. Blood ran from her bottom lip, mixing in with the stream of heavy tears, forming a pink river of anguish, hate, and hopelessness.

DECK 6

5:15 P.M.

THE MUFFLED scream of a woman stopped me in my tracks. I took a step toward the blistered door and listened closely. I could hear the low moans and shifting body of a struggling woman. Instantly, I thought of Lacy. Maybe my plan had failed me already. Maybe the pirates had hit the lights. Noticed I was gone. Taken Lacy and dragged her to this room.

I pushed the door inward a foot. It was a small stateroom, with a wall that jutted out into the living room blocking any view into the bedroom. On this note, from the bedroom, I could hear soft whimpers. I visualized Lacy underneath one of the dirty pirates, and my stomach churned.

I quickly surveyed the suite's foyer. The bathroom was off to the left. I poked my head in, but didn't see anything I could use. I looked at the closet off to the right. If it was similar to the closet in my suite, it contained an ironing board and a nice heavy iron. I slid the door open half an inch, waiting for some sort of screeching. None came. I opened the door another foot and spotted the large steel Sunbeam high up on the shelf.

I grabbed the iron and took three silent steps into the living room. On the ground, near the large wall, was a shattered flat screen TV. I was barefoot and I gingerly stepped around the jagged pieces of black plastic. The bedroom had two large doors and they were pushed in halfway. I could see the back half of the pirate. He was standing at the edge of the bed. Dirty black pants. A pistol held in a holster. A bare foot draped over the edge of the bed. It could have been Lacy's foot. On the ground, near the door, I could make out the pirate's shiny AK-47.

I took a deep breath. I angled my head so I had a better view. I could see the pirate in his entirety. It was the man with red stained eyes. Common.

Motherfucker.

I thought of his fondness for Lacy and my head spun. I could only see the bottom half of the girl, who was fully nude, and I guess it was a good thing, but from this view alone, I couldn't ascertain if the girl was Lacy.

I could hear a low murmur. Then silent sobbing. It took almost everything I had to keep myself from crashing through the doors. But in the man's right hand, holding the woman's legs open, was the deadliest knife I'd ever seen. If he caught my advance through his peripheral, he would slice and dice me. No, I had to wait. Just a bit longer.

I pulled my head back. I heard rustling. I took another peek. Common was unbuckling his pants. I watched as they fell to his knees. The pistol in the holster thudded as it hit the floor. His huge slong stood at full salute. His right hand opened and the large knife fell to the soft carpeting. He grabbed his penis with his right hand, his lips turned upward in a wide grin.

I went.

I threw the door open. Common's head turned toward me, his red eyes open in surprise. He let go of his penis and started to bring his arms up. It was too late. I smashed the iron against the right side of his face. The sound of splintering bone filled the room. The momentum sent the pirate reeling, hitting the wall, then crumbling to the ground.

I stole a quick glance at the woman in the bed. It wasn't Lacy. I grabbed the thin comforter from the edge of the bed and tossed it to the woman. She covered herself, her eyes never straying from mine. I turned away, glancing at the fallen pirate. He wasn't moving. I knelt down, grabbed the knife off the carpet, and knelt over him. Blood gushed from the side of his head where I'd connected with the iron. For all I knew he was dead already. Then his eyes snapped open. Glazed over and neon red.

I was glad. I was glad he watched as I slammed the large knife down hard into his chest.

SUITE 319
5:19 P.M.

THE BLOOD POURED from the pirate's convulsing chest and his red stained eyes flickered, then closed for the last time.

I peered up from the dead pirate to the woman on the bed. She was still staring at me. At first glance, I had only cared the woman *wasn't* Lacy. I hadn't cared who the woman *was*. It took me a moment to recognize her. Her face was red, her eyes puffy. Blood and tears clung to her cheeks. I smiled and said, "There are a lot of people looking for you, Rikki."

She didn't smile, but her face changed at the sound of her name. She nodded.

I said, "Get dressed. We have to hurry."

She nodded again.

I looked down at Common. I had a feeling when he came up missing they would search the ship for him. And I didn't want them to know one of their own was dead. I knelt beside him, wiggled the knife from his chest, and then rolled him under the bed.

"You don't think they'll look there?"

Rikki was standing over me. She was wearing large yellow athletic shorts, a gray tank top, and appeared remarkably composed all things considered. She said, "They're going to see the busted telly and the blood. You don't think they'll check under the bed?"

She was right. I looked around. We could stash the body in the closet or somewhere else in the master suite, but they would eventually find him. And when they did, I had the feeling people would start dying. And fast. I peered at the thick glass windows. I wondered if I could shatter one, then heave the body overboard. But these windows were made to withstand high winds and hard seas, it would take quite a bit of effort to break one of them. Of course, I could use the gun. But I didn't want to risk being over-heard. I said, "You have a better idea?"

She nodded.

I took the 9mm from the pirate's holster and tossed it on the bed. I then pulled the pirate's pants up and buckled them. We then hefted the pirate up—me on the arms, Rikki on the legs—and waddled over the broken *telly.* We set him down near the door, checked the hallway, saw all was clear, then dragged him fifty feet to a closet. Rikki opened the door and wheeled out a large cart filled with towels. We pulled out the towels, tossed the dead pirate in, then covered him.

"Do you moonlight as a maid?" I asked.

She smiled, the diamond in her right bicuspid flashing a bead of light. She quickly recounted how she was attacked and how she had hidden in a similar cart for three hours. On this note, I asked, "You have any idea why they're after you?"

"Money."

I would have pried more, but I had bigger fish to fry. I told Rikki to sit tight for a second. I ran back to the room, tried to cover most of the blood with the comforter, slung the AK-47 over my shoulder and jammed the gun into the waist of my shorts. I thought about taking the knife, but it was too bulky and I stashed it under some clothes in the dresser. Then I ran back to where

Rikki was leaning against the wall. She was standing two doors from the Camper's room.

I signaled for her to follow me into the room, then said, "We are looking for insulin and syringes. I know she keeps them in a leopard skin fanny pack."

"Got it."

The Camper's room had been ransacked. Or they were just slobs. The room was strewn with Frank's huge flowered shirts, whitey-tighties, opened bags of chips, salsa, Pepsi, Dr. Pepper, Mountain Dew, macadamia nuts, Three Musketeers. I picked things off the bed and tossed them on the ground. I opened up the top drawer of the dresser and spotted the fanny pack. I opened it. It contained Susie's diabetes kit, a waxy chunk of cheddar cheese, a bag of gummy worms, and a prescription bottle. I opened up the kit. Inside were her tester, test strips, and needles. No insulin.

I almost screamed.

Rikki came up beside me. "Find it?"

"Yeah. But there's no insulin."

Her eyes lit up. She ran to the mini fridge and pried it open. She removed her hand and revealed three vials. She said, "This old guy who let me rent a room from him had diabetes and he kept his insulin in the fridge."

I threw the vials in the fanny pack.

There was some cheese and other goodies in the fridge and I realized how hungry I was. I opened three string cheeses and ate them in six bites. I spent the next minute throwing all the Campers' snacks into a backpack. There was a giant bag of trail mix, and I took a handful and ate it, then washed it down with a yogurt smoothie and a Three Musketeers.

Exiting the room, we walked briskly down the hallway, back through the sports bar, and found our way outside. The crisp ocean air felt amazing, cleansing. I peered over the side of the ship and looked down. Swaying in the small waves were three fishing boats. They appeared to be tied to the ship with rope. Rikki and I could have easily jumped the sixty feet into the ocean, climbed into one of the boats, and zipped away from this nightmare. If Lacy had been with us, I might have given the idea a second's thought.

But it was good to know the boats were an option. I was thinking that if worst came to worst, the boats could be crammed with ten people each. Thirty of us.

Anyhow, the fishing boats were a moot point. I wasn't going anywhere. I ran up the walkway to where our failed lifeboat experiment dangled off the edge of the railing. Rikki watched idly as I climbed up the railing and jumped into the swaying boat. I grabbed my backpack and the fanny pack and gave a cursory inspection for Baxter. "Hey, you little shit. Where are you?" I whispered. "Baxter, seriously, get the fuck out here." I spent three more minutes searching every nook and cranny. He wasn't on the boat.

I climbed back over the railing and Rikki asked, "Who's Baxter?"

"Uh, nobody. Let's move." I handed the backpack to Rikki and said, "Hold this."

She took the backpack and slung it over her shoulder. We were near the stairs leading up to Deck 7 and I wanted to take a quick peek around. It was risky, but I wanted to learn as much as possible while I had the chance. Rikki followed me as we crept up the stairs. But we had nothing to worry about. The back bar, the hot tubs, the pool, they were all empty. Not a pirate in sight. I was set to go back down the stairs when I noticed something glimmering in the late afternoon sun on the large open area of deck. I took a couple hesitant steps forward.

There were six pools of blood.

"Oh my God," Rikki muttered from behind me.

I looked down at where six men had been executed, then their bodies presumably thrown overboard. I thought back to the Professor's words, "None of you will be harmed."

Liar.

I turned, grabbed Rikki by the shoulders, and prodded her back toward the stairs. "Let's go."

She nodded, her face ashen.

We made it to Deck 5 with no problem. I had the gun out in front of me, just in case, but we didn't encounter any trouble. Since I still had ten minutes of the thirty I'd allotted myself, we continued down the stairs to Deck 4 and the Computer Center.

As the room came into view, paneled wood and foggy glass windows, I asked, "How fast can you type?" I was a woodpecker when it came to typing.

"Fast enough."

I pushed through the door and slid a chair out from one of six flat screen Toshibas and Rikki plopped down into it. The computer was on, which was a good sign, and the clock in the bottom right corner read, 5:22 PM. I asked, "Do you have any friends you could e-mail and tell them to forward it to the police or call the authorities?"

"I guess." She tried to log onto the internet, but the page wouldn't load, and she said, "Bollocks."

"Did they shut off the internet?"

"No, it's getting a signal, but really weak—oh, here we go," she said, Google finally loading.

She logged into her Gmail account and said, "I'll just e-mail it to everyone I know."

Fair enough.

I started dictating and she started typing. "Tell them you are aboard the *Oceanic Afrikaans* where an estimated ten pirates have taken the ship hostage." I described the Professor and the Warlord best I could and Rikki's fingers clattered away. "Write, 'The pirates made a video of their demands and they may or may not have sent the video to high ranking officials in the U.S. They are demanding the United States help them with their AIDS crisis, especially in some small village.'"

Rikki looked over her shoulder at me and said, "Really?"

I'd forgotten that she hadn't been with us. "Really, although I suspect this is simply a cover and that their main objective is to hold you for ransom."

She nodded.

"You said something about money earlier."

She took a deep breath and said, "My biological father is Track Bowe."

Track Bowe was some European billionaire. England's Warren Buffet.

"One of his other children was captured ten years ago and held for ransom," she said looking up. "He didn't pay."

"Did they kill them?"

"They were dragging him into the woods, probably to kill him, but he got away. It was big news. It was even bigger news that my father had decided not to pay."

"And this happened to one of your brothers?"

"He isn't my brother. He doesn't even know I exist." She spent the next minute regaling me with the ins and outs of her relationship to Track Bowe. "What I don't understand is how whoever wants to ransom me knows that he's my father."

Curious, curious.

But we needed to finish this e-mail and I needed to get back to the show lounge. "Tell them that we have reason to believe six men have already been killed. And then tell them that they are trying to hold you for ransom. Tell them to contact your mother and to contact Track Bowe, and if they haven't heard the story on the news to make sure to call the media."

I wanted as many people to know about us as possible. If that video the Professor made had been sent out, then I was guessing only a handful of people knew about us and I had a feeling those people would want to keep this thing quiet. The more people that knew about our plight, the better. "Send it."

She clicked Send.

A progress bar popped up, then after five seconds it disappeared, replaced by the message, "Unable to connect to the internet right now."

Rikki tried sending it one more time. Same error. She tried to get on Facebook, but the page wouldn't load. She tried sending the e-mail again. Three more times. *Bollocks*, which I'm pretty sure translates to, *Fuck you, you stupid computer*, was said frequently.

After several more attempts, she said, "I might just need to reset the router. I bet the servers are in that closet."

There was a large closet at back with sliding doors. Rikki opened the doors and gasped.

I stood up and joined her. In the far corner were two large black computer-ish looking things, which I guessed were the servers Rikki was searching for. Lying on the ground next to them was a large black duffel bag.

I found myself gasping as well.

The duffel bag was partially unzipped. An opaque yellow baggy poked through the small opening. It appeared to be full of a chalky pink substance. I'd attended enough conferences on terrorism that I knew that I was looking at some sort of plastic explosive. I was guessing Semtex. A half-pound of the stuff was enough to blow up a small passenger aircraft as was the case in Pan Am Flight 103. There had to be over fifty pounds filling the duffel bag. Enough to send the *Afrikaans* to the bottom of the Indian Ocean in pieces roughly the size of a Rubik's cube.

There was an iPhone atop the bag connected to an assemblage of wires. Numbers filled the screen.

41:38:11.

41:38:10.

41:38:09.

I thought about the Professor's words, "If you have not met these demands by noon three days from now, everyone aboard this ship will die."

It wasn't a threat. It was a countdown.

RURAL ENGLAND

WITH THREE LAPS left in the 1983 Monaco Grand Prix, Track Bowe's' yellow number thirteen car was running in fifth place. After the left-right turn of Casino of Monte-Carlo, he was in fourth. With two laps to go, Track had moved into second place. When he slowed for the left turn at the Tobacco Shop, he was thirty yards behind the bright green number six car running in first place. As he came into the stiff right Rascasse, Track gave the six car a friendly nudge. The two cars flew past the 45,000 cheering fans in the Quay stands at over 230 mph, separated by a mere two thousandths of a second. As the two cars approached the treacherous Sainte Dévote curve, the six car slowed, the thirteen car did not.

Track Bowe exhaled deeply. He put the Maserati in fifth gear and flew up the long country road. He'd thought nothing could ever compare to the day his racing career had ended. Now, it didn't seem all that bad. He would rather take the Sainte Dévote at 500 mph than fork over two billion dollars.

Track was an hour outside London, driving through a road that wended through western England's many farms. Next stop Scotland. The last time he'd driven this road, he'd been on his way to Rikki's restaurant for the second time in two weeks. He'd been so excited. He'd wondered if she would pat him on the back again. He'd hoped so. Maybe he would ask her name. Try to get her chatting. But she hadn't been there, and when he'd asked the owner about her, he'd said that she'd quit the week before. He'd never seen her again. And if he didn't fork over two billion of his hard earned dollars by close of business tomorrow, he never would.

If he paid the ransom, he could kiss his title of 11th richest person in the world goodbye. Plus, where would he get the money. It's not like he had a bank account with two billion dollars in it. He had a couple different accounts with a hundred million or so, but 95 percent of his money was tied up in stock, real estate, or other various investments. He looked at his phone and thought about how the conversation with his accountant would go. "So Will, I was thinking about selling some stock."

"Oh yeah?" Will always said "Oh yeah."

"Yep."

"How much?"

"Oh, I don't know. How about two?"

"Oh yeah? Two mil?"

"Billion, Will. Two *billion*."

At this point the conversation would be over because Will would be having a coronary. If he somehow survived his third heart attack, he would say, "You do know this isn't the best time to sell stock. You'd lose, well, billions."

"Just do it."

And that would be it. And Will would do it. And the money would be in a bank account of his choosing within the day.

Track pulled the car over on the side of the road. A plume of dust kicked up and was carried west by the prevailing wind. He took a deep breath. Why was he even considering this? Was he out of his mind? Two billion dollars? Who cared if she was his flesh and blood? If it had been any of his other children, he would have laughed at the idea. When his first son was kidnapped, they asked for a hundred thousand dollars. The idea of paying the ransom didn't even cross his mind. Not for a second. And the kid got away. If he hadn't gotten away, if he had been killed, Track might have felt guilty, but then again, he might not have. His children were lepers. Parasites.

Track knew he wasn't a good father. Hell, he could hardly be called a father. But, he'd done his fatherly duty. He'd given each of his children five million dollars on their eighteenth birthday. A going away present. It wasn't his fault that all seven of them had run through the money before their twenty-first birthday. None of them had ever had a real job. And now he had another one he would have to deal with: Little Aiden. Damien himself. The kid was going to cost him a fortune.

But Rikki. Such a sweetheart. Track thought about the pirates. What were they doing to her? He'd said she would not die painlessly. How would they kill her? Did she know that they were ransoming her for money? Would she know if he didn't pay? Would her last thoughts be about her old man who she'd never met not coming through?

Save Rikki.

Two billion dollars.

He went round and round. If he paid, his life as he knew it was over. If he didn't pay, well, his life might be over as well. He might not be able to live with himself. But he would still be fabulously wealthy. Maybe even make it into the top ten within the next couple years. Then maybe take a crack at the top five.

That was it. His mind was made up. He put the car in gear, checked for oncoming traffic, and did a U-turn.

COMPUTER CENTER
5:33 P.M.

I THOUGHT about picking up the duffel bag, scooting outside, and dropping it in the ocean. But, I didn't want to mess with the bomb. I knew iPhone batteries only lasted a day, so this thing was connected to a secondary energy source, probably buried somewhere in the plastic explosives. And I also knew that iPhones could be set as antitheft alarms and when it was moved, it went crazy. For all I knew this guy downloaded a *Time Bomb* app and when I picked it up, I turned Rikki and myself into hot dust. In the end, I decided to leave it alone. My plans did not include being on the *Afrikaans* in forty hours anyhow. Plus, I needed to get back to the show lounge before J.J. Watkins started telling knock knock jokes—which he did.

We made our way back up the steps and started back toward District 9, cutting through the lobby bar. We were three steps into the soft brown carpet when I heard the unmistakable ding of an elevator opening. I shoved Rikki, and we dove behind one of the tan leather couches. After five long breaths, I inched upward and peeked over the top of the couch. A pirate was behind the bar, making himself a drink. I could only see his profile, but from the misshapen ear, I knew it was the pirate who had jumped overboard. I'd assumed the pirates had left him to die after he'd done his *forward one and a half tuck*, but apparently these were very considerate pirates.

I ducked down and put my finger to my lips. Rikki nodded. Hopefully, Greg Louganis would just make himself a cocktail and continue on his merry way.

I leaned backwards against the couch. I was left staring across the lobby and down the corridor that led to the aft passenger suites. There was something in the middle of the hallway. It was getting bigger each second. I squinted.

NONONONONONONONO.

I tried to hide behind Rikki, but he'd already seen me. And if history was any indicator, he was going to sprint up to me and start barking his head off, then lick my face until his tongue fell off. That was if Greg hadn't already blown my face off.

Baxter was now in the lobby, two and half seconds away from giving away our hiding spot. I fingered the gun. I was going to have to put Louganis down. I just prayed nobody overheard the shots.

I could see Baxter's ears flopping, his brown eyes wide with recognition. *There's that guy who is always telling me to shut the fuck up. I love him.* He had something pink in his mouth. I'd just made the move to my feet when I saw Baxter's eyes close. He nose-dived, slid for a foot, then his forward momentum flipped him once, twice, then a third time.

I let out a long exhale. Thank God for narcolepsy.

Baxter's seven-pound tumble hadn't made as much as a peep on the thick carpet, but he was now in the middle of the lobby—on his back, drooling into his eyes, the pink thing in his mouth now wrapped around his curly-cue tail—in plain sight of the pirate.

I slowly peeked over the couch. The pirate was searching through the bottles. I watched as he finally picked two. One clear, one brown, then walked out from behind the bar. He snapped his head in my direction and I sunk down, gripping onto Rikki's leg. If he was still looking in our direction, Baxter would be hard to miss.

But we soon heard the open and close of the elevator.

I crawled forward and looked at Baxter. He was in dreamland. I pulled the pink thing off his tail and started laughing. The little guy had been on a panty raid.

"Let me guess. This is Baxter," said Rikki.

I nodded, picked him up, and started toward District 9.

———

"Bheka," I whispered.

Bheka came out from behind the door that led to the stairs.

Rikki gave me a sideways glance.

I said, "Friend of mine."

I introduced Bheka to Rikki, and laid the machine gun, the 9mm, the fanny pack, and my backpack on a table. Rikki was holding Baxter, who was now wide awake, and licking her neck. This was the first time I had a really good look at Rikki, even counting the night we'd shared. It's amazing how little you remember when you're thinking with your dick. There was no question she was beautiful, but she was young. Far younger than I'd previously thought. I'd put her in her early twenties. Very early twenties. Not that I was complaining. But I'd been down this road before and it never ended well. I was 34 going on curmudgeon. I couldn't keep up with a girl like Rikki. I didn't want to.

I'd been meaning to ask her why I hadn't seen her again, why she didn't answer when I knocked on her door, and what that thing was that she did to my prostate. That conversation was penciled in on my Remax pad. Just not at the top.

I focused back on the items on the table, staring at them for a couple long minutes, visualizing my plan of attack. I opened up Susie's diabetes kit and extracted three syringes. I'd watched her administer her medicine on two separate occasions and I recalled that she'd filled the syringe up a third of the way. I inserted a syringe into the small vial of insulin and pulled back on the plunger until it was over a third full. I filled the other two syringes, then capped all three. I put them back in the kit and placed it in the fanny pack, to which I also added my sister's meds, some snacks, and the 9mm.

"I'm gonna leave you guys the machine gun," I said.

"I'm going with you," spat Rikki.

"No you're not. You're going to stay hidden." My tone didn't leave any room for debate.

After showing Rikki how to use the gun, I said, "Don't fire it unless you absolutely have to. But if your life is in danger, kill every last one of them, then the two of you jump off the side of the ship and steal one of the fishing boats."

Bheka looked at me wide-eyed. "Jump off the side of the ship. Are you crazy?"

I don't think he was a big fan of heights. Or maybe water. Or maybe it was a combination of the two. I looked at him and said, "Promise me you will jump into the water if you have to."

He thought about it, then said, "Okay, but only if I *have to*."

"Can you swim?"

"Like a dolphin."

So it was the heights.

"Stay on your toes, you two," I said, moving to the door. "If you hear me coming down those steps, be ready to run."

They both said they would.

I swiped Bheka's mother's maid card and opened the emergency exit door.

"Thank you."

I turned.

"Thank you," Rikki repeated.

I nodded, then started up the stairs.

LITTLE CREEK, VIRGINIA
1131 HOURS

TORREY ROYAL—*ROYAL* to anyone that mattered—circled around the large stone statue of an eagle standing stoically on an anchor, checking the sleek Luminox snug on his left wrist. It usually took him thirty minutes to traverse the nine kilometers that comprised the Naval Amphibious Base in Little Creek, Virginia, but the running numerals of the dive watch showed he was slacking by two minutes. He slapped Eddie, the name everyone called the noble eagle, turned around, and quickened his pace.

At 30 years old, Royal was still in his prime, but he was on the outside looking in. Growing up in inner city Philadelphia, he never would have thought, nor even dreamed, that his life would turn out as it had. But Royal had always been a tad different. While his brothers were at the park playing basketball, he was flipping through college calculus books on the dusty floor of their third story apartment in the Philly projects. And while all the other kids in the neighborhood were either selling crack, or smoking it, he was hunkered in the corner of the bedroom he shared with his three brothers, playing the saxophone.

Oddly enough, the sax had saved his life. At the age of eleven, on a cold November evening, Royal was waiting for the bus outside the public library where he went nearly every Saturday and Sunday. Royal had pulled out his saxophone—which due to the alarming rate of burglary and the fact that one of his brothers would most likely pawn it in his absence, was never out of his reach—more to keep warm than anything else. By the end of his first song he was surrounded by several curious onlookers. By the end of his third song, a throng of people were leaning over one another to glimpse the small black prodigy. One of the onlookers asked if he could contact Royal's mother. Royal told her that they didn't have a phone. Nor did he want this strange white woman talking to his rarely coherent mother.

A month later, at the same bus stop, the same woman approached him, and asked if she could take him home. Royal wasn't one for charity, but it was one of the coldest days in memory and he didn't hesitate to climb into her white Lexus. As she drove him home, she told him about a school she wanted to pay for him to attend. Royal asked why, and she said that it was a special school for young, gifted musicians like himself.

The woman's name was Margaret O'Leary. Over the course of the summer she would often visit Royal at the library. She was smart and had traveled the world and would tell him all about her adventures. Her husband had died earlier that year of a heart attack. She often spoke of her son, telling Royal that he reminded her of her Nathan. Nathan had also played the sax. He was in the Navy. Had been at any rate. He'd died three years earlier.

Over the summer, Royal and Margaret spent many days together, and Royal found himself staying the night at her large Victorian home on weekends, then five times a week, and soon he was living with her full time. His mother and siblings didn't seem to notice or care in the slightest.

The following autumn, Royal was enrolled at Perkimen School of Music in Pennsburg, Pennsylvania. One of only five black students, and one of only two students on third-party scholar-ships, Royal wasn't sure what to expect. But he found the kids in

the school shared his same interests—music, reading, learning—
and he soon found his niche.

His fourth year at the school, he was pushed into the swimming pool by one of his friends and nearly drowned. When this
information found its way to the swim coach, he took Royal
under his wing, and slowly forced him to learn to swim. To both
of their surprise, Royal had a natural gift for the water, and soon
found himself the star of the swim team. Margaret was there at
every meet to cheer him on. Over the course of the next two
years, he broke every school record, won the state championship
in three events, and still held the Pennsylvania state record for the
200 fly.

Royal was offered countless scholarships as he was a straight-
A student, a talented jazz musician, and one of the best swimmers
in the country. Music had always been his one true love, and after
a tearful goodbye to Margaret, he enrolled at Berkeley College of
Music in the fall.

He could still remember that September morning in 2001. He
sat transfixed in front of the TV. How could this have happened?
Two planes sent hurling into the Twin Towers? Who? And why?
Then just three weeks later, during their weekly phone call,
Margaret confided to Royal that she had pancreatic cancer.

Royal took a leave of absence from school to care for
Margaret. She died eight weeks later.

He returned to school. But he wasn't the same. The 9/11
attack combined with the passing of his dear friend Margaret had
changed him. He withdrew from school and enlisted in the Navy.

It didn't take long for his commanders to take notice. He was
bigger, stronger, faster, and smarter than those around him. He
was quickly plucked from the masses and entered into SEAL
training. Two years earlier, Royal had been picked to be part of an
elite platoon, the best of the best, SEAL Team Six, commonly
known as DevGru. Short for Naval Special Warfare Development
Group, *DevGru*, was the top secret United States Naval Special

Warfare Command's tier-one special missions and counterterrorism unit. Its size, structure, operations, weapons, equipment, training, missions, and personnel remain top secret. DevGru was one of the two U.S. primary counterterrorist units, the other being Army Delta Force. Six had done any number of missions, from boarding hijacked freighters to placing explosives on the hulls of submarines to a special op aboard a Japanese oil tanker.

As Royal's feet pounded into the gravel, he felt a vibration on his hip. He stopped, slipped the matchbook sized pager from the waistband of his pants, and looked at it. He puffed his cheeks, slipped the pager back onto his shorts, and took off back to the base. He covered the distance in record time.

STAIRWELL

5:38 P.M.

I PUSHED the door open to the garbled noise of J.J.'s voice.

Good, he was still going.

As I tiptoed across the back of the stage, I patted the fanny pack in front of me, feeling the weight of the gun. There was a full magazine and one in the chamber. Fifteen rounds. Two that at some point in the near future were going to put an end to a couple of rap careers. After two deep breaths, I made my way to the edge of the curtain. When I was halfway there, the lights flipped on. Someone had just decided J.J.'s set was over.

Son of a biscuit.

I had a decision to make. Did I attempt to sneak back to my seat or did I head back down the stairs and take my chances with Rikki and Bheka? But the whole reason I'd left was to get Susie's medicine, so if I aborted now the whole seek and recover mission would have been in vain. But my getting caught would help no one. The pirates would confiscate everything, and I might get myself killed in the process.

I decided to take a quick peek, take stock of the situation, then make up my mind. I pulled the curtain back a half-inch and peeked out. My eyes immediately found Lacy's—who must have been staring at my exact location—and she shook her head with tight lips. I heard a door open and pulled my head back, flattening myself against the curtain. From my peripheral I watched as Lil Wayne walked from the bathroom.

I waited a minute, then snuck another glance. Gilroy and Trinity were arguing in the front row. J.J. Watkins had found his seat next to my sister and was staring in my direction as well. Frank was staring down at where Susie lay on the ground. Walter and Marge were asleep against one another.

J.J. poked Lacy in the ribs. Lacy glared at him.

I looked over the top of them to where Lil Wayne had joined Tupac. There were only two of them now. Although, to be fair, I *had* smashed an iron into the side of their buddy's head, then jabbed a seven-inch blade into his heart. The two were engaged in a heated discussion, no doubt wondering where their fellow mercenary had absconded. They were distracted, but if I darted from the curtains to my seat, they would see me.

I turned my gaze back to Lacy. She flashed her hand at me.

She flashed it again and I understood. Five. Five seconds. I nodded. I pulled my head back, leaned up against the wall and counted. *One Mississippi . . . two Mississippi . . . three Mississippi . . . four Mississippi . . . five Mississip—*

There was a loud *CRUNCH* on the far side of the curtain and I knew that Lacy had chucked her water bottle across the room. That was my cue. I shot from the curtains, army crawling to the edge of the seats and to the second row. I slinked past J.J., past Lacy, then slid upright into my seat, and tried to play it cool.

After a couple seconds, I asked Lacy, "How is she?"

"She hasn't moved since you left."

I glanced to my right, where Tupac was holding up a dented water bottle and gazing in our direction. The water bottle in his left hand, his AK-47 in his right, he started toward us. As he passed the other hundred hostages, not a single sound was made.

Stopping in the walkway just off Frank's shoulder, Tupac lifted the water bottle and said, "Who throw dis?"

I half expected Lacy to raise her hand. She didn't.

Tupac glared at me. Maybe unconsciously he'd noticed I'd been missing when he'd made his way to the bathroom. And now I was back. But if I wasn't in the bathroom, then where had I been?

He cocked his head to the side and said, "Where go?"

"Me?" I pointed to myself, then shook my head. "I didn't go anywhere."

He barked at Frank and Susie to stand, then took three steps into the row. He stood, straddling Susie's body as if it were a crack in the sidewalk and said, "New shit."

New shit.

He poked me in the chest with the barrel of the machine gun and repeated, "New shit."

New shirt.

"Same shirt," I lied. The black shirt I was now wearing was baggier than its predecessor, allowing room for the bulge of the fanny pack. And unlike the plain black tee I'd been wearing, this one had NMSU written on the front. New Mexico State University.

"No. New shit."

"Same shirt."

He poked me in the chest, then the sternum. He was checking to see if I was hiding anything. Which I was. I held my breath. He poked me in the stomach. There was a rustling.

"What is?" he barked.

I took a deep breath and pulled out the bag of trail mix. I'd taken it out of the fanny pack before I'd stashed it under the first chair in the row.

I handed the bag to him.

"Where get?"

"I had it in my pocket the whole time."

Lil Wayne had been the one to pat me down initially, so he was a bit confused by how I'd come to smuggle a big bag of Trail Mix. But I'd figured he was smarter than he looked and he needed to find something to satisfy his curiosity, otherwise, he would always be hovering around.

He took the bag, smelled it, then poured some in his mouth. Then after patting me down extensively, lifting my shirt, even cupping my boys, he made his way back up to the entrance.

Oh and he might have poured the rest of the water out on my head.

"Nice of you to share," said Trinity, wiping water splatter off her face. I wasn't sure if she was talking about the water or the Trail Mix.

"No, really, I mean, what else have you been hiding? You got a satellite phone, too?"

Nope, I couldn't find one.

"Be quiet," I said.

"Don't you fucking tell her to be quiet," Gilroy huffed, leaning over his seat. "She's got a point. Where do you get off hoarding all that trail mix for yourself, you selfish prick?"

Said the guy that took six bags of chips.

I almost head-butted him. But I probably would have knocked myself unconscious in the process, so I reeled in my anger. I took a cleansing breath, leaned forward, and said, "Listen you stupid ape, here's what you're gonna do." The words came out like lava. "You and your dingbat are going to turn around and have a staring contest for the next five minutes. Because if you don't, then one of those pirates is going to come back over here and Susie is probably going to die. So turn around and shut the fuck up."

Gilroy breathed in and out through his nose. Then he jerked Trinity and himself around.

I whispered to J.J., and he went to the bathroom. When he came back, he tied his shoe near the first chair. Moments later, he slid the fanny pack between us. Without looking, I unzipped it, and found the pre-loaded syringe.

I glanced at Frank. He was staring blindly ahead of him, and I doubt he knew I'd ever left. It was as if his dear wife was already dead. Maybe in his head, she was.

As I leaned forward and pulled up Susie's shirt, I noticed Frank staring at me. I winked at him. I jabbed the syringe into her stomach, pushed in the plunger, then sat back down. Even when his wife sat up, stared at me, and said, "Hey, that's my shirt," Frank never took his eyes off me.

THE ROAD TO PTUTSI

6:05 P.M.

EVERY ONCE IN a while a car would pass them, usually a truck, and usually full of men and women who had seen better days. Skinny to the point of emaciation, their eyes glazed over, skin yellow with jaundice. Gina knew every one of them was infected with AIDS. And not the early stages. Even if these people where given the best medical attention money could buy, they wouldn't last more than a year, their immune systems all but decimated by the HIV virus.

The road before them had become uneven, strewn with large rocks, and the Jeep was bumbling along at a crawl. According to Timon, the village was less than 50 kilometers away, but at the rate they were going, it would be half a day until they reached Ptutsi. Over the course of the last couple hours they'd passed flocks of people making their pilgrimage to the village. These people might not have been as far along as the people in the back of the trucks, but there could be no doubt these people had AIDS.

Gina couldn't believe these people had the energy, or the fortitude, to walk fifty, even a hundred miles. And for what? According to Paul, no medical treatment would be available to these people for the foreseeable future. But it couldn't just be coincidence. Could it? And speaking of Paul, how much more difficult had the task he'd asked her to do just become? It would have been hard enough to find three children in the small settlement, now it would be nearly impossible. Who knew how many sick had already flocked to the village? Hundreds? Thousands? By this time tomorrow, the number could be in the tens of thousands. A modern day Woodstock unfolding before her eyes.

She looked at Timon. She wanted to tell him everything. She'd gone back and forth a hundred times. What could it hurt? What did Timon care if there was a cruise ship filled with hostages and she needed to rescue three children to try to save their lives? This impacted him none whatsoever. He was being paid handsomely regardless. But something was keeping her from telling him. A promise to Paul that she would tell no one. Not her guide. Not her priest. No one.

There were two large rocks strewn in the thin road ahead of them. Timon brought the car to nearly a complete stop, then maneuvered around the first with ease. Gina watched his face, contorted in concentration. His eyes widened and Gina followed his gaze to the road where a small army of young men had materialized from the brush. There were seven of them. Three had cigarettes dangling from their lips. Two had their shirts off. Another two were wearing black bandanas. All were holding some large firearm.

Timon put the car in park and said, "Do not speak."

Gina couldn't understand why Timon didn't just drive over them. The boys—that's all they were—would scatter. But she'd forgotten about the second large rock. The rock was somewhere behind the band of misfits, and if they ran over it, they would run aground.

The seven boys collectively strode toward the stopped Jeep. The sun was hovering in the tall limbs behind the road, and the machine guns held tightly in the black fingers of the small children glistened. Even with the guns, Gina was yet to find herself frightened. *Kids with toys* is all she kept thinking. Kids with toys. Timon stared at the charm dangling before him. His lips moved silently. Sweat had formed on his heavy brow and his fingers would grasp then release the steering wheel. Grasp. Release.

As the children neared, he said, "They will just want some money. A tax for using their road. I will give them money. Do not speak."

Six of the children stood in front of the Jeep, twelve eyes locked on Gina's chest. The seventh child, the tallest, made his way to the driver's side door. His black head was shaved. He had yellow teeth, like he'd smoked a pack a day for fifty years, hidden beneath large swollen gums. He was one of the two wearing black bandanas. He shouted at Timon in African.

Timon nodded. He took out his wallet and handed the boy a stack of bills. The boy took the money briskly, then nodded at Gina. He spoke in African, then smiled.

Timon shook his head.

The boy barked in African once more, and again Timon shook his head.

The boy smashed the butt of his gun against the side of Timon's face, emitting a loud crunch. Gina knew instantly Timon's cheekbone had just been shattered. She reached over him and yelled, "No!"

Roars, shouting, and thunderous gunshots rang from the six who had slowly surrounded the Jeep. African was being screamed at her from every angle.

Timon tried to cover her mouth. She pulled his hands away and screamed, "He gave you money. What do you want? We'll give you anything you want." She looked at Timon and begged, "Tell them. Tell them we will give them anything they want."

Timon, blood gushing from his face, said, "They want you."

PRESS BRIEFING ROOM

PAUL GARRET STOOD behind the podium in the newly renovated James S. Brady Press Briefing room. The story had leaked two hours ago. Well, the fact a cruise ship off the coast of South Africa had been taken over by a band of pirates had leaked. It could have leaked in any number of ways. The cruise line, the South African Navy...there were hundreds of possibilities. But the identities of the pirates and their demands had so far been kept quiet.

Garret took a sip of water and said, "I can't get into any particulars, but I can tell you that within the U.S., the Pentagon, the Navy, the Coast Guard, the Department of Homeland Security, the Department of Transportation, and the State Department all have a stake in the day-to-day activities of maritime security. Obviously, because of the nature of the threat on the *Afrikaans*, the United States Navy is the lead agency."

A reporter for the *Washington Post* and one of the few information vultures Garret didn't mind, stood and asked, "What is the U.S. Navy doing to combat the terrorists?"

"I can't give you any tactical information," answered Garret. "But rest assured, if any rescue mission is attempted it will be headed up by the best America has to offer."

He smiled inwardly. He knew the quote would be plastered on every front page in the country and repeated *ad nauseum* on every news station.

Paul peered out on the group of fifty or so reporters. For the most part, the press conferences were civil, and the reporters waited to be called on by Joe—a man in a black suit off the wing—who ran the show.

A man in jeans and a white T-shirt stood. Tyler something or other from MSNBC. Garret couldn't stand the pretentious asshole. He asked, "Have the families of the passengers onboard the *Afrikaans* been notified?"

"Oceanic Cruise Line, the company that owns the *Afrikaans,* has contacted each passenger and crew's emergency contact and notified them of the situation."

"How many Americans are on board?"

He swallowed hard. "154 Americans."

There was a soft murmur.

"Has anyone been killed?"

"Not that we know of," he lied.

Another murmur.

"What are the pirates demanding?"

"No comment."

Seeing that it was a futile effort, the man finally took his seat. The questions went on for another fifteen minutes. *Do we know the identity of the pirates? Do we know the nationality of the pirates? How were they able to board the ship? What security measures did the ship take? How much money do they want? Will this impact oil prices? How has the South African government reacted? Is Al Qaeda in any way connected? What are the coordinates of the ship?*

If he didn't answer "No comment," Garret answered vaguely. The only information he'd been *permitted* to reveal was that, yes, there was a cruise ship that had been taken over by pirates. And, yes, the United States was doing everything in its power to insure all 400 people on board the ship survived. He'd probably overstepped his boundaries with his U.S. Navy quip and he no doubt would receive a tongue-lashing for it.

The press conference was nearing its finality when Joe said, "Final question."

Joe pointed at a man in the front row. He was a relatively new appointee, but Garret was pretty sure his name was Karl.

Karl asked, "How will the crash of the London Stock Exchange impact the United States?"

Garret looked at Joe, who shrugged as if to say, "News to me." A number of reporters had pulled out their phones and were scrolling wildly.

Garret leaned forward and said, "I wasn't aware the London Stock Exchange had crashed."

The London Stock Exchange was the fourth biggest stock exchange behind New York, Nasdaq, and Tokyo. Closing auction was at 4:30 p.m. their time, roughly seven minutes earlier.

Karl smiled. It appeared he was the only one in the room privy to the information. He said, "It happened ten minutes ago, right before closing auction. The largest single shareholder in the London Stock Exchange sold a hefty number of shares, it created a panic, and the entire market collapsed."

Garret absorbed this. He hoped the collapse of the London Stock Exchange wasn't in some way connected to the *Afrikaans*, but in his gut, deep down, he knew it was. Garret asked, "Why would that have anything to do with the topic at hand?"

"The shareholder was Track Bowe," Karl said with a smirk. "And he is the principal shareholder of Oceanic Cruise Lines."

THE ROAD TO PTUTSI

6:22 P.M.

GINA WATCHED in horror as the six boys surrounded the vehicle. They couldn't have been more than ten or eleven. One boy stuck his hand in and grabbed her breast. Then another hand darted in. Timon leaned over her and slapped one of the kids in the face, earning himself another blow to the head by the tall boy. Soon Gina was being groped from every direction. She covered her face. How had she been so naive? Kids with toys? These were monsters. Monsters with machine guns.

The door to the Jeep was wrenched open. One of them had her right leg. Then her left. Another grabbed her arm. She was being dragged from the car. She imagined what the next hour would hold if they successfully pulled her from the Jeep. She saw herself lying naked in the brush, the seven of them taking turns putting their tiny black dicks inside her.

Gina screamed. She kicked her legs frantically. Thrashed and squirmed. One of her legs connected hard with something and her leg was free. Then she got an arm free. She opened her eyes and saw Timon having a fight of his own. He smashed his forearm into the tall boy's face. He too would not go without a fight.

Gina leaned over him and pushed down on the gearshift. It wouldn't budge. She screamed, "Clutch! Step on the clutch!"

She watched Timon's left foot, it was headed for the pedal, but then her head was ripped backwards. One of them had two handfuls of her hair and was yanking with all his might. Another had crawled on top of her and was ripping at her shirt. Tiny hands fondled her breasts. She let loose a terrifying scream. Her earlier scream had been a scream of fright. This was a scream of anger, a scream that sent every animal in South Africa scurrying for cover.

Probably scared senseless, whoever had hold of her hair, let go. The others were more resilient, but Gina had turned into a bucking bronco. Not even the best cowboy in the land would have had a chance. She slashed at faces, hacked away with her fists, kicked in every direction. She grabbed the kid on top of her, hands holding onto her breasts like cup dispensers, and threw him into the windshield. The windshield spider webbed and she kicked the kid in the head, sending him tumbling out of the car. And then she was free.

She dove to the gearshift and smashed it down. It moved. She yelled, "GAS IT!"

The car lurched forward. She had one hand on the steering wheel and was trying to visualize where the rock lay on the road. She yanked the wheel toward her, the car crunching over what she thought was probably the kid she'd kicked out of the car. Good, she thought. Then the car stalled.

They had gone sixty feet. They had maybe a second to spare before the kids were back. And after they'd probably just killed one of them, she doubted they would give a second's thought to using their guns. The tall boy had somehow stayed with Timon and was smashing his gun into Timon's stomach. Gina turned the key in the ignition and the engine roared.

"Clutch!"

Timon's left foot found the clutch. Gina rammed the car into first gear, then reached down with her right hand and pushed the gas pedal down to the floor. The car shot forward. She couldn't see, but she pulled the steering wheel to the right. Gunfire erupted. The windshield shattered, the glass cascading into her hair. She kept her hand down hard on the gas, then pulled the steering wheel back to the left. The car rose, bounding, and she knew they'd cleared the large rock. Bullets zipped through the air, clanking off the side of the Jeep.

Timon yelled, "Stay down."

The jolt from the rock had sent the tall boy reeling. Gina heard the beautiful sound of a car door slam then felt Timon's foot slide over her hand on the gas pedal. She slid her hand out from under his foot. She could feel him shift into second gear, the car zooming forward. Timon was leaning over, holding her head down, when a final barrage of gunfire ripped through the still air.

Gina felt Timon's body lurch next to her. The gunfire stopped and Gina rose. Timon had his left hand limply holding the steering wheel. His right hand was clasped down on the inside of his left shoulder. Blood gushed over his fingertips.

Gina instructed him to switch seats with her. She climbed over him into the driver's seat. For the next ten minutes she traded glances with the wounded Timon and the curving road. When she thought they were a safe distance away, Gina pulled the car over to the side of the road. Timon was leaned against the passenger side door. He was a bloody mess. The cut on his cheek was two inches long and half an inch deep. It had already swollen to the size of a tennis ball, pushing his left eye closed. His right hand was resting lightly on his left shoulder, the blood trickling freely down his shirt to a blossoming puddle on the seat. His Adam's apple moved slowly in his throat.

Gina pushed two fingers to his neck. His pulse was a strong 85. She whispered, "Timon." She ran the back of her fingers lightly over the top of his unscathed head. "Timon."

He stirred. He tried to sit up, then cringed. He took a deep breath and said, "How do I look?" He forced his face into a smile.

For all the punishment his face had taken, he'd kept all his beautiful teeth. Gina said, "Like shit."

He laughed. Cringed again.

Gina said, "I need to look at your shoulder."

"Yes, docta."

She found herself smiling. Docta. Docta Gina. She moved his hand from his shoulder. She found the bullet hole in the red shirt and ripped it open. She jumped into the backseat, grabbed her backpack, and pulled out the supplies she would need. She told Timon to stick out his tongue. She asked, "Are you allergic to any medicine?"

He said placidly, "I don't know. I've never taken any."

Well. Okay, then.

She placed two Vicodin and two Cipro—a wide-spectrum antibiotic—in his mouth, then brought a water bottle to his lips. Next, she poured iodine on the wound. Timon never flinched as she scrubbed the wound. As for the gunshot, it was a clean shot. If the bullet had been an inch lower it would have clipped the brachial artery, and Timon would have already bled out.

After cleaning the entry and exit wounds, Gina spent the next twenty minutes stitching them up. Then she went to work on the gash on Timon's cheek. After bandaging all three wounds, Timon began snoring. The Vicodin had taken hold. He would be one hurting puppy in the morning, but he would live.

Gina kissed Timon on the forehead and stowed her backpack. The sun had long ago set, and as Gina flipped the lights, her eyes were drawn to the charm dangling in front of her. She wasn't sure what Timon had said, or who or what he'd prayed to, but she thanked them.

She put the car in gear and eased back on the road.

SHOW LOUNGE

11:10 P.M.

I THINK I finally understood how those people aboard Flight 93 felt. They knew two planes had been hijacked and crashed into the Twin Towers. They knew their flight was destined to have a similar fate. They couldn't let that happen. They had to do something. Even if it cost them their lives. Now, don't get me wrong. I'm not saying I was ready to die to save 400 people, because I wasn't. And maybe in hindsight, plucking *Flight 93* from the Blue-Ray library on the first night wasn't the best idea. But, after seeing the blood spatter from the six executed individuals and the ticking bomb, I knew no one was getting off this boat alive. Not unless somebody did something. And as I looked at my fellow hostages—heads down, dejected, coming to terms with their fate, or maybe just coming to terms with waiting it out—I knew the responsibility had fallen in my lap. Like it or not, I had to be the one. Thomas Dergen Prescott was the only chance these people had.

Needless to say, we were fucked.

Over the course of the past hour, Susie had continued to improve. When she uttered the words, "I want some beef jerky," her full recovery was made official. Frank, too, was back in rare form. At one point he leaned over Lacy and kissed me on the cheek.

As for Lace, after swallowing down twelve of her pills, I asked how she was feeling. She said she hadn't felt any weird sensations since the dizzy spell. I wanted to believe her, so I did. But, if we did come out of this thing alive, it could be weeks or months before she incurred a flare-up because of the missed dosages. On a side note: at one point, Lacy had noticed her favorite pirate had gone missing. I'd tried to act surprised, but Lacy knew better. Other than a suspicious wrinkle of her nose, she hadn't pried. And as far as Baxter went, I told her that I didn't find him. No use getting her hopes up. For her to be reunited with the little guy, a lot of chips had to fall into place.

J.J. had peppered me with questions about the hour I'd been gone. The questions came out like a Gatling gun—a weird New Jersey-accented question-shooting Gatling gun. *Where did you go? Did you see any pirates? Did I give you enough time? Did you see me look at you behind the curtain? What did the Catholic priest say to the altar boy?*

I tried to downplay things. Told him it was a piece of cake. Told him I couldn't have done it without him. I think I said those exact words seven times, and each time, J.J. would beam like an eight-year-old winning the egg toss.

In fact, I hadn't disclosed much information about the hour I'd been gone to anyone. Even Lacy. I'd made it sound as if it was a breeze. No mention of Rikki, the dead pirate, or the bomb. I was too busy trying to formulate a plan.

Sadly, my plan only considered the people in this room. Well, along with Bheka and Rikki.

But back to my plan. It was a work in progress, but here is what I had so far:

1) Kill the pirates.
2) Get off this stupid fracking ship

No, it was more complex than that. Killing Lil Wayne and Tupac would be the easy part. It was the next part that would get tricky. The gunshots would attract unwanted attention and there would be a short window to coordinate an escape plan. Best-case scenario, the gunshots weren't overheard, and all of us got off the ship, and none of the pirates were any the wiser. Worst-case scenario, the gunshots were overheard, and the pirates cut down every last one of us in cold blood.

The true outcome would probably be somewhere in the middle.

I looked over my shoulder at the entrance. Only Tupac remained. Lil Wayne must have been patrolling the ship for the now deceased third wheel. Hopefully, he wouldn't stumble on the towel cart holding his dead comrade and would come back shrugging his shoulders. That's when I would approach them, pull the gun from my waist, and put a hole in both their foreheads.

As for the present, with only one pirate on guard, this was a perfect time to reveal my plan to Lacy, Susie, Frank, and J.J., all of whom, the plan would rely heavily on. And as much as it pained me, I would need Gilroy's help as well. I tapped him on the shoulder, and he turned around. Walter and Marge had been with us since the beginning, and I decided they deserved to know the truth too. They both leaned forward. I told everyone to act cool, but listen closely.

I didn't hold anything back. I told them about Bheka and the note. About Rikki and her connection to Track Bowe. About how I'd killed Common. About the six puddles of blood on Deck 7. And about the bomb. To say the group was shocked would be an understatement. They were like eight deer in headlights.

"There is no way they're letting anyone off this ship alive, is there?" asked Susie.

"No, there is not," I answered.

I needed them to be scared. They would be more open to my

plan if they knew—if they accepted—that our backs were against the wall.

"What does the gun look like?" asked Frank.

I thought about opening the fanny pack and showing him, but it would cause too much of a stir. Tupac might even come back over. And I had an inclination Gilroy wouldn't stop until he had the gun. Or at least a couple of the energy bars.

I told him it was a 9mm semi-automatic.

"Good and accurate. Plus, after we kill these two assholes, we'll have two machine guns."

I would have preferred a couple grenades, a dozen light sabers, Wolverine, the Predator, an invisibility cloak, and a couple of the Real Housewives from Orange County, but a 9mm and two machine guns wasn't shabby.

I informed them about the fishing boats and if it came to it we could jump overboard and use them to escape. A selfish act, but a selfish act we would be able to tell our children about. And Katie Couric.

We spent the next half hour going over the small details. The second I took the first shot, the wheels would be in motion. J.J. and Frank would jump up and coax every man to pick up their chairs and carry them to the stairwell. Susie, Trinity, Marge, and Walter, would usher all the women to the lifeboat and get them inside. And Lacy would run behind the curtain, down the stairs, and retrieve Bheka and Rikki.

Of course, the only person who didn't like the plan was Gilroy. He said, "That plan is shit. Why do I have to carry you?"

I said, "You're the only one who can do it. Frank will pass out halfway up the walkway."

Frank nodded. "There's no way."

"Why don't you carry *me*," spat Gilroy.

Now I was strong. But, the odds of my carrying Gilroy's 260 pounds up a 120 foot incline ramp were about as good as Mike Tyson winning the Nobel Prize.

I shook my head. "I can't."

It appeared to appease him that he could do something I couldn't. At that precise moment, the door opened and Lil Wayne returned. I watched out of my peripheral as he reported his findings to Tupac. From his body language, I inferred he was saying, "I didn't find Swahiliahishisi," and not, "I found Swahiliahishisi and half his face has been steam pressed."

That was our green light.

DISTRICT 9

12:09 A.M.

THEY HAD BEEN PLAYING hangman for the last couple hours. Rikki couldn't believe how smart the little guy was. He'd guessed correctly on Afrikaans, Captain, and even Star Wars. But two hours of hangman was about her limit, and her mind was starting to wander. To her attack. She could only imagine what would have happened if *he* hadn't shown up. Would she be dead right now? Or even worse, she might still be alive. She couldn't bear to think about living a single second after that man had been inside her. The idea made her shudder in horror. But she wasn't dead. He was. She thought about Thomas, about those blue eyes that looked like two pieces of sapphire, his hard body, the muscles long and lithe, his smell, an intoxicating musk. She'd been with many men; she collected them much like she collected books, and Thomas had been a first edition Mark Twain. The second she'd laid eyes on him that night in the club, she'd instantly craved him. He was different than the other men aboard the ship, the rich banker from Austria, the real estate mogul from Hungary, the tall oiler from Georgia. They just expected her to jump at the chance to sleep with them. But Thomas had been so aloof, as if he didn't even know every woman in the club had cut their eyes at him as he sat down at the bar.

Then after their night, their amazing night, he had come knocking on her door the next day. She'd wanted to answer, but she also didn't want to ruin the perfect memory. To find out that he was the same as the others, some accountant, and forever tarnish the delicious memory.

But he wasn't an accountant. The way he'd killed the pirate, the way he'd handled the gun, the way he'd moved. She felt another shudder, this one pleasant.

"How about we try something else?" she said to Bheka.

He shrugged.

"Why don't we go see what's going on up there?"

He shook his head disapprovingly.

"We'll just take a peek. You said yourself that you've been up there before." And that's all she intended to do. Take a quick peek around. See what all the hubbub was about. Maybe see Thomas.

"I think we should stay here."

"Do you?"

Bheka nodded.

"Suit yourself. I'm gonna take a peek."

Rikki nodded to Baxter, who was asleep on the table and said, "Watch him." She walked to the door, then realized she needed a card to open it. She smiled at Bheka and said, "He took the card, didn't he?"

"Yep."

"But you've got another one." She eyed him. "Don't you?"

He shook his head. But he was smiling. She ran toward him, then started tickling him until he finally gave up its location in his back pocket.

A moment later, she ran the card through the reader and eased the door open.

Bheka came up beside her holding the sleeping pug like a football and said, "Just a peek, then we're going back down."

She nodded.

SHOW LOUNGE

12:12 A.M.

I STARTED COUGHING. Just once. Then another. Then another. Then two together. Then a series of three. Then a string of five.

I pushed myself out of my chair and stumbled past Lacy, Susie, and Frank, meanwhile coughing up a storm, then falling into the walkway. The plan was for me to lie there for a long minute, hacking away, then Gilroy would come and pick me up and carry me up to the pirates with a concerned look on his face. I would continue to cough as though no man has ever coughed before until said time when I would pull the gun out and give each of the pirates a third eye. As I'd already been lying there for going on two minutes and my throat was starting to hurt from my forced hacks, I wondered why I wasn't being hefted up in the massive arms of Gilroy Andrews.

I opened one eye and peered up. Gilroy was still in his seat. I looked at Lacy. She shrugged with her face. Then I watched as she leaned forward. I could almost hear her whisper into Gilroy's ear, "Stand up you prick and go pick him up."

Whatever she said had no effect. I guess he'd had a change of heart. I made a mental note to kick him in the balls if I didn't get myself killed in the next minute which, without his help, would be more than likely.

I could feel a hundred heads glancing in my direction, praying for me to shut up.

I pushed myself up with a groan and gazed up at the pirates. They were both staring at me, but they seemed more entertained than anything else. I braced myself with the nearest chair, which was one chair from where Gilroy sat, and continued hacking away. Gilroy looked at me with a deadpan expression as if to say, "I don't take orders from God himself, let alone your little twink ass."

But I wasn't a Twink. I was a Bear.

I leaned forward and let loose the mother of all gut-wrenching, spittle flying, mucus-enriched, almost on the verge of puking, 15 mph coughs directly into Gilroy's face and said, "Pussy."

He whipped his head around, but I didn't get to see his face—which I'm sure looked a lot like when that Ghostbuster got slimed in the first movie—as I was already on the move. Still coughing away, and more or less doubled over, I started up the lengthy incline. I could feel the heaviness of the gun in my waistband. I should mention when I was a detective in Seattle I'd been a decent enough shot—not one of those standouts who could put it between the perp's eyes every time—but my paper man's face and chest usually resembled a block of Swiss cheese. But the shooting range was one thing. Real life was another. Now, without the aid of Gilroy, I had a feeling the two pirates would be a bit more circumspect if I tried to get any closer than twenty feet. That meant I had maybe one second to get the gun out of my waist and get off two shots. Two kill shots. If I didn't stop these guy's hearts with one bullet, I was going to end up looking like a Connect 4 board.

As I gingerly made my way up the incline, hundreds of eyes bore into me as I walked. Some of the eyes urged me on. Some begged me to go back. Others were disconnected, like a TV whose cord has been yanked from the wall.

I made sure my breathing was labored. I squinted my eyes. I licked my lips. I wanted these idiots to think I was barely holding on. That I didn't have the strength to put up much of a fight if it did indeed come to that. When I was thirty feet from the pirates, both reached for their guns. I thought about abandoning the mission, but it wasn't like I could just turn around and walk back down. I had a friggin' gun stuffed down the back of my pants.

I took five or six more strides, then stopped. The pirates had each taken a hesitant step forward, and there were less than ten feet separating us. Both had their guns dangling at their sides, barrels pointed at the ground, fingers on the triggers.

Tupac barked, "What you want?"

I'd planned on this being the last words the pirate ever spoke. I reached behind my back.

When they reached the back of the stage, Baxter's eyes snapped open. He wiggled, flipped, and flopped his way out of Bheka's grip. There was a sliver of light poking through where the curtains met in the middle, and Baxter darted in that direction. Rikki ran after him. Just before reaching the curtain, Baxter stopped short, turned around, and shot through Rikki's legs causing her to lose her footing. As Baxter headed back down the stairs, Bheka chasing after him, Rikki was reeling toward the curtain.

As my fingers wrapped around the barrel of the gun, both pirates' faces dropped. But they weren't looking at me. They were looking over my shoulder.

I released my grip on the gun and looked over my shoulder. Splitting the curtains, on all fours, frozen like a wedding ice sculpture, was Rikki.

Before I could react, Tupac had pulled the radio from his belt and began talking into it excitedly. Lil Wayne rushed past me and down toward the stage. I thought about pulling the gun and popping two shots into the back of his head, then taking out Tupac, but if he'd relayed his message about Rikki, then this party was about to get a whole lot bigger real fast. I decided my best bet, my only bet, was to get back in my seat as quickly as possible.

I let loose one last cough, pulled my shirt out, fluffed it— hoping it would cover the gun—then turned and started down the walkway. If Tupac noticed the outline of the gun or that after two steps I had miraculously recovered from my tuberculosis as if touched by the hand of God, he let it slide.

As I made my way down the decline, I watched as Rikki tried desperately to get back behind the curtain. But she couldn't find the opening and when she finally did, it was too late. Lil Wayne clasped his hand on her shoulder and whipped her around. Her face was ashen. I watched as her eyes scanned the many faces staring at her, then found their way to mine. Tears dribbled down her cheeks. I thought I saw her mouth, "Sorry," but I didn't want to look directly at her. I didn't want the pirates to connect the two of us.

Lil Wayne pulled her off the stage.

I didn't want the gun on me when this party doubled in size, so I continued coughing and pushed into the bathroom. I pulled the gun from my waist and looked for a place to hide it. I thought about hiding the gun in one of the toilet tanks, but there weren't any tanks.

There was a paper towel dispenser, one of the automatic ones, against the far wall, and I appraised it. I wondered if I could hide the gun inside it. But I couldn't even figure out how to open the thing. I had decided just to go back to my seat and hide the gun under my chair when the door to the bathroom opened.

"What you doing?"

My back was to the door, but I could tell it was Tupac. He hadn't forgotten about me after all. I held the gun close to my chest with my left hand. I could have turned around and shot him, but there was a decent chance he had his gun leveled at my back this very second. And if I was somehow able to kill him, then I would be killed soon after by any number of pirates that were en route to the show lounge this very moment.

I moved my left hand near the paper towel dispenser. It whirred and six inches of paper towel appeared. I waved my hand again. Then coughing, I ripped the foot of paper towel off, then coughed hard three times while wrapping the gun in the paper towel. Then I sidestepped a foot to the trashcan and pushed the gun through the opening. I waited for a loud clunk, but it never came. There was enough padding from past paper towels to cushion the gun's fall into a soft thud, one that I hoped the pirate was unable to hear beneath my ragged coughing.

I turned around, wiped my forearm over my mouth, and said, "I had to go to the bathroom."

Tupac leveled his gun at me and cocked his head to the side. I think he knew I was full of shit, and I could tell he was deciding whether to just get rid of me then and there.

He waved the gun at me and yelled, "Ged out!"

He kept the gun trained on me as I moved past him, pushing through the doors.

I plopped down next to Lacy, who probably hadn't taken a breath since she'd watched the pirate walk into the bathroom, and patted her leg.

J.J. said, "What do we do now?"

I shook my head. I had no idea.

The door to the bathroom opened and Tupac emerged. He wasn't holding an extra gun, so I assumed he hadn't gone through the trash. He joined Lil Wayne who was holding a kicking and screaming Rikki near the entrance.

Moments later, the doors opened and five men walked through. The Professor, the Warlord, Ganju, and two pirates.

The Warlord appraised Rikki. He cupped her chin in his hand and lifted her top lip with his finger, and smiled at the sight of the small jewel. He looked at the Professor and nodded. Both smiled. Then they dragged Rikki from the room.

SOMEWHERE OVER THE ATLANTIC
1103 HOURS

THE BOEING E-6 Mercury operates as an airborne command and communications center. Adapted from the Boeing 707 commercial airliner, the E-6 Mercury is half the size of a football field, but with all the electronics equipment on board, the capacity is just twenty-three passengers. As the gray hull of the large Mercury cut through the night sky above the Atlantic Ocean at five hundred miles per hour, it carried only nine passengers. Nine very important passengers.

Torrey Royal sat upright in the tall black chair in the command center and scanned the faces of the seven other men that had comprised SEAL Team Six. To his left were Chase, Reed, Frost, and Sanchez. To his right were Sam, Pollock, and Deeter. There wasn't a set of brothers on the planet that were any closer. Each would take a bullet for the other.

So far, they knew little about Operation Water Moccasin, only that it would take place in the warm waters seventy miles off the coast of South Africa and they were to rendezvous with a Virginia Class sub at 0800 hours.

Royal turned his attention to DevGru Commander Lawrence Fuller. Fuller had been in the inaugural class of the United States

Naval Special Warfare Development Group, so when Fuller spoke the words, "Before we talk specs here, I just want you guys to know I'll be accompanying you on this mission," Royal knew Operation Water Moccasin would be unlike anything they'd seen in their previous ops.

Glenn Sanchez—a Colorado kid who was the best shot in the Navy, capable of putting a bullet through someone's pupil from fifteen hundred meters—sat upright and said, "You serious?"

"You think I would kid about this?"

Fuller wasn't exactly the kidding type.

Pollock, a lanky white kid from South Beach who had beaten Royal by two hundredths of a millisecond in the 200 Free at Nationals and had never let Royal forget it, asked, "You sure you'll be able to keep up, old man?"

At the age of fifty-six, Fuller could swim farther and drink more than each of the eight men sitting down before him. "With you fucking pansies? No sweat."

All eight of them laughed.

Fuller flicked a switch, and a three-dimensional hologram of a cruise ship hovered over the oval glass table in front of them. This was Royal's third time aboard the Mercury, and each time he got the sense he was sitting on the *Starship Enterprise*.

"This is the *Afrikaans*," said Fuller. "It's a luxury cruise liner. Two hundred and eight passengers, a hundred and sixty-four person crew. Yesterday the ship was hijacked by African pirates."

Over the course of the next hour, Six was brought up to speed on the situation, the opposition, and the layout of the *Afrikaans*.

The plan was laid out and drilled into each of them for the next hour. When Fuller was finished, Deeter, at twenty-four the youngest of the SEALS by three years, started clapping his hands together. Sanchez soon followed suit. And within seconds, all eight of them were thumping in unison.

THE BRIDGE

1:33 A.M.

NEITHER MAN HAD SAID a word to her as they dragged her up the stairs, but she could tell from the smirks on their faces—especially the gap-toothed one with the beret whom Thomas had referred to as the Warlord—that finding her was the equivalent of finding a Monet at a garage sale.

Once they'd reached Deck 7, the Warlord had made her walk to the front of the ship and into a control room of sorts. On the glass door it read, "Bridge."

They pushed her down in a chair and both stared at her. The man on the left, the one Thomas had referred to as the Professor, looked like just that. In his high-collared gown and expensive glasses he looked like he should be teaching Anthropology at Georgetown University.

The Professor said, "Rikki Drough."

Rikki found herself nodding.

"Where have you been?"

In any other situation, this would have been a simple question. She decided against a narrative of her last day and a half and simply said, "I've been in the hot tub."

To her surprise the Professor laughed. Then he said, "Well, I highly doubt that." He paused. "No matter. We have you now."

Yes. Yes, they did. They *had* her.

Rikki wondered if their plans included letting her go. But then she remembered the bomb. No one on the ship would be let go. Including her. Unless. Unless her dad—Track—was smart enough to make them release her. Maybe this wasn't so bad after all. Maybe she would be the one person who would survive this mess. Track hands over a couple hundred thousand and they put her in one of those boats and say, "Bon Voyage."

But as she glanced up at the Warlord, all hope of her survival vanished. She did not have one iota of doubt this man was going to kill her.

"Will your father pay?"

She turned her gaze back to the Professor. She thought about the question. How could she know? She didn't even know the guy, had never laid an eye on him. Once, she thought she'd seen a man at her restaurant that resembled the pictures she'd seen of him in the tabloids, but if it were him, he would have said so. Right?

She asked, "How much?" She hadn't expected the question coming out. It just had.

"Two billion dollars."

"Two *billion* dollars?"

He nodded.

Rikki didn't even know if her father had two billion dollars. In truth, she hadn't wanted to know. But then she thought back to the article that she read. He *was* the 11th richest man on Earth. She didn't know what that computed to. She'd heard in passing that Bill Gates was worth something like sixty billion, but she didn't have the slightest idea what her father was worth. Now, thinking about it, he must have billions. Her gut told her Track Bowe would not pay, but she couldn't just laugh and say, *Are you kidding me? Two billion dollars. You'd have a better chance drinking the ocean than getting my old man to fork over a hundred dollars, let alone two billion.*

If she said this, she might already be dead. Or even worse, the Professor might just nod at the Warlord and tell him he might as well have some fun.

She looked the Professor hard in the eye and said, "Yes, he will pay."

He smiled.

"How did you know he was my father?" she asked.

The Professor leaned back. He appeared reluctant to answer the question. But then, either deciding it didn't matter because she would soon be dead or because he thought in some way maybe she deserved to know, he answered. "We have been looking for the right person for three years. We pay very expensive people to investigate prospective—" he paused, thinking for the right word, then apparently finding it, added, "—clients."

She found this hard to believe. There were only three people on the planet that knew of her connection to her father. One was her. The other was him. And the third, her mother. If anyone else had made the connection, it would have been plastered on the front page of every tabloid on the planet: *Track Bowe has Illegitimate Child.*

But then again, she wasn't sure what *very expensive people* were capable of. Maybe they were able to hack into her bank account and somehow connected the large deposits to Track. Still, it was one thing to find a connection to a millionaire, it was another to find a connection to the 11th richest man on the planet. Too big of a coincidence for Rikki.

"Well, you hit the jackpot, didn't you?" she said defiantly.

The Professor shrugged with his face, then said, "We shall see."

He then turned and walked to one of the many control panels behind him and popped open a beautiful briefcase. From fifteen feet away, Rikki could make out a laptop computer among other electronics. He returned with a small video camera. He stopped five feet shy of her and pointed the camera in her direction. Rikki watched as he adjusted the zoom and framing. When he was satisfied he gave a slight nod to the Warlord.

The Warlord smiled, reared back, and smashed his fist into the side of her face.

PTUTSI

1:52 A.M.

"WE'RE HERE."

Gina lightly shook the resting Timon, and said again, "We're here."

Timon leaned up, his eyes flashing intense pain. He gazed around, his eyes opening even wider. A small smile seemed to appear on his face, but it was hard to tell because his face looked like a punching bag. He said, "Yes. Yes we are."

But they weren't the only ones. For the last ten miles, it had been bumper-to-bumper traffic. The hundreds of vehicles that had been in front of her now filled the expansive plains on both sides of the road as far as the eye could see. Hundreds of buses and rusty sedans were now empty, their passengers somewhere up ahead. And that wasn't to mention the exponentially increasing foot traffic.

The Jeep was parked off the battered road, slipped between two rusty cars, situated at the crest of a large hill. A three-quarter moon lit the small village at the base of the hill five hundred feet below in a soft glow. Two sets of fences, as the literature had promised, surrounded fifty small thatch huts. Gina understood why Timon had smiled. It was beautiful.

But the beauty of the small village wasn't the reason Gina was leaning forward, almost standing behind the wheel. On the long expanse of hill in front of them—maybe a half mile of open field—there were well over a thousand people. Many of the truck beds were still littered with the sick and feeble. Others sat in circles in the grass. Others cooked over an open fire. Gina was prepared to see a vast assembly, but the sheer number of people was remarkable.

Gina turned her attention to Timon, giving him a quick evaluation. His blood pressure and pulse were good. She checked the wounds, and save for a small amount of bleeding, they looked better than she expected. She cleaned them, then changed the bandaging. She put another couple of Vicodin on Timon's tongue and after taking them he mumbled, "I like medicine."

Gina laughed.

She then grabbed Timon's backpack and took out some food. She ripped a banana into small pieces and fed it to the quickly fading Timon. She gave him another dose of Cipro, and minutes later he was snoring through a swollen nose.

Timon's snoring was broken by a low chime. It took Gina a moment to find the phone. She answered the call, "South African Child Rescue, Gina speaking."

"Good one," Paul said.

Gina could tell from the two words alone the man was exhausted. She imagined the deep crease between his two dark eyebrows. After a moment's pause, he said, "Are you there?"

"Yeah, we actually got here about fifteen minutes ago."

"Any trouble?"

She decided against telling him about the *trouble* and said, "Nothing we couldn't handle."

He let out a breath. She knew he wouldn't push her. He asked, "How are the roads?"

"The roads leading into Ladysmith were okay, but after that they were pretty rough. The last fifty miles were all dirt."

"And the village?"

"It's there." She paused, then added, "I think you should know that thousands of Africans have made their way to the village."

"I heard."

She listened as he recounted the news report.

"We didn't see any news vans."

"Yeah, well, if you're surrounded by ten white vans when you wake up, don't be surprised."

Gina asked him about the Red Cross and the promised AIDS relief.

"They deny any responsibility. We're having trouble tracing the ads, but it would appear—to me at least—that the ads were paid for by the pirates. They think if they can get a couple thousand sick Africans to that village, it will force our hand."

"And will it?"

"You know we can't cave to their demands. It would be one thing if these Africans just came to the village, it is entirely different when they are threatening the lives of four hundred individuals."

"And what are the other countries doing?"

"Well, all the countries in the UN have the same policy, so at this point they're all standing down. Our biggest problem is private organizations. Even yours."

"The World Health Organization?"

"Yeah, they want to send in a team of doctors and tons of medicine. The order had to come from the President himself that they would do no such thing. He threatened to court martial any party that interceded on behalf of the United States."

"And organizations from other countries?"

"So far so good. Most of the other organizations aren't heavily enough funded to do any real damage. Plus, I just got word the South African army will be setting up roadblocks sometime tomorrow. They will continue to let Africans in, but I hardly think a team of doctors will get through." He hesitated, as if remembering something, then asked, "Did the South African Rand trade above ten?"

"Yeah, just over," she lied. No sense getting into an argument over currency at a time like this. She added, "You sound exhausted."

"I was exhausted five hours ago. There isn't a word for what I'm feeling right now. I probably sat in on twenty hours of meetings the last two days and I've held eight press conferences. At this point, I'm not at liberty to disclose anything so the press is getting restless. They're ripping me to shreds."

There was probably no person on Earth that knew Paul as she did, not even his wife. Paul was too sensitive, he cared too much. He didn't have the thick skin necessary to work in Washington, let alone at the tip of the sword. She never knew why Paul had decided on politics; even his father had tried to push him away from Washington.

Paul said, "Well, it's probably getting pretty late over there so I'll let you get some rest."

It was almost as if Gina hadn't known just how tired she was until Paul said these words. She found herself yawning. "Yeah, I should get to sleep."

"Goodnight then."

"Goodnight."

There was a pause. Then Paul said, "And Gina?"

She tensed. "Yeah?"

"Thanks."

She laughed. To expect to hear those three words after all this time. How naive. She said, "Don't mention it."

The phone went dead.

Gina ate the other half of the banana and listened to the soft drumming reverberating from somewhere on the hill. Slow and rhythmic. The sounds made her eyes heavy. Even so, her mind raced. Somewhere in that sea of people were three small children. Three tiny ants she needed to find and somehow persuade to come with her. Yes, tomorrow was going to be a long day. Longer than today even. But today. Today was over.

Gina pulled up the handle and laid back the seat. A minute later she was asleep.

SHOW LOUNGE
2:35 A.M.

AFTER RIKKI HAD BEEN DRAGGED from the room, the security officer, Ganju, was left with Lil Wayne, Tupac, and one additional pirate, my friend Greg Louganis. If the Warlord or Professor had been informed or cared about the missing Common, I didn't have the foggiest idea. My instincts told me that Common's drug use was no secret and they probably all assumed he was off doing smack somewhere. As for Ganju, I would describe his mood as distraught. He'd stormed down the walkway and ripped the curtains open. As security officer, he should have known about the exit behind the curtains. But evidently, he hadn't. Or had he? Or had he thought that since you needed a crew ID to open the door, it was useless? Regardless, the clumping down the aisle, the throwing open of the curtains, it was a bit too showy for me. It easily could have been a reproduction of *Streetcar Named Desire*, the brown security officer in the role of Marlon Brando in an all-out rage. What I'm getting at is this: the whole charade didn't fit the quiet, well-tempered man I'd chatted with for five minutes. But, then again, I hadn't pegged him as a savage pirate either.

Ganju disappeared and I assumed he'd gone down the stairs. I silently prayed Bheka had been smart enough to change hiding places. But I knew he had. He was a smart little bugger.

"What the hell was she doing?" asked Gilroy.

I was curious as well, but I also knew that if Gilroy hadn't sat on his ass and had done what he'd ensured me he would, then both pirates would be in line at the fiery gates and it wouldn't have mattered why Rikki had fallen through the curtain. "Maybe she heard there was this guy in the front row acting like a total chicken shit coward and she had to see it for herself."

He scoffed. "Seems to me we were doing just fine until you went on your little fucking treasure hunt." And then he added, "And who the fuck put you in charge anyhow?"

How thick was this idiot's skull? First and foremost, if I hadn't sneaked out, Susie could very easily be dead by now, not to mention the unspeakable things that would have become Rikki. I didn't expect Gilroy to care about either of these. But the bomb was another thing. Very slowly, pausing frequently, I said, "If *we*—do *not* find—a *way*—*off* this ship—in the *next*—*thirty-six hours*—*we are* going—*to die. What*—don't *you* understand—about *that?*" And then I added, "And I wasn't in charge before. But I *am* in charge now. And if you do anything else to jeopardize anyone's chance of getting off this boat, I swear to the gods of Winterfell I am going to feed you your own dick."

Gilroy didn't say anything, he simply lunged. I pushed him off and he came at me again. He took a swing at me and I just barely escaped his giant fist. Frank was trying to get between the two of us, but Gilroy shoved him, sending him into Susie and Lacy, and the three tumbled into the hallway. I picked up my chair and threw it at him. As he deflected it, I noticed Ganju had returned, pushing through the curtains. He was empty-handed. No Bheka. No machine gun.

My brain made half a dozen computations in less than a second. *The conversation I'd had with him. The act. The look on his face when he watched Rikki dragged away.*

Gilroy picked up his chair and threw it at me. I shoved it up and away and it came crashing down two rows behind us. Now there was nothing between Gilroy and myself. I knew the pirates were probably on their way down to see what the commotion was. I had to get to the stage quick. And Gilroy was directly in my path. It was a goal line stand. I was a running back, and he was the middle linebacker. A white Ray Lewis. There wasn't enough room for me to go around him. I would have to go through him.

I was getting ready to take a knee when I felt Susie getting to her feet next to me. But she didn't stand, she darted forward, a two hundred and forty pound Rainbow Brite of a fullback. Gilroy didn't know what to do until it was too late, and Susie simply clobbered him. The two went down with a loud, "OOF." I ran behind her, leapt over the two of them, and hit the stage. Ganju's eyes opened wide. I put my shoulder into his chest, flattening him into the thick curtain. I could hear the wind knocked from his lungs. Our combined weight—300 pounds, 180 of them mine—ripped the curtain from its fastening. The curtain engulfed us, and when we finally came to rest, it was in complete darkness.

I had maybe twenty seconds before the pirates could make it to the stage and untangle us from the curtain.

The thin man wrestled in my grip, but he was no match for my strength. I squeezed his body between mine, then said, "Listen, I don't know what the fuck you're up to, but I know you aren't one of them. If you don't remember, let me refresh your memory, *you're one of the good guys.*"

He continued to squirm. I took a deep breath. "I don't know how much they're paying you and I don't really give a shit. If you keep helping them, you will never be able to live with yourself. You'll never be able to look your kid in the eye again."

He stopped fighting.

"Do you even have any idea what these guys are up to? This isn't about AIDS. It's about the girl. A young British girl whose father happens to be rich as hell. They're ransoming her."

He probably figured this out earlier, but I could tell from the deep breath he exhaled that he didn't know she was British.

"And guess what, the whole ship is loaded to the gills with plastic explosives."

Thapa's body tensed.

"That's right. In about thirty hours they're gonna blow this ship to smithereens. They're going to kill every last person on this ship. Every person in this room. Me and *you*."

He closed his eyes.

Loud footsteps surrounded the stage. I had five seconds left. "If you don't believe me about the bomb, check the closet of the Computer Center."

The curtain was being wrestled out from under me. Light darted in from somewhere and I could see Thapa's eyes. I stared at him. He stared back.

One of them had my legs and yanked me free of the curtain. They flipped me on my back. My eyes wouldn't focus. When they did, it was too late. Something slammed down on my right eye and white light seared through my brain. Then a blinding pain shot through my ribs. I brought my knees up to my chest. Something rained down hard on my leg, probably the stock of one of their guns, but it could have been a bullet. The last thing I remember was the acrid taste of my own blood.

DAY 3

PTUTSI

5:55 A.M.

GINA STIRRED FROM A DREAMLESS SLEEP. She sat upright and rubbed the kink in her neck. The kink may have come at the hands of her odd sleeping position, or possibly it was the result of the mauling she'd taken the previous day. Probably a combination of the two. At any rate, she was doing far better than her traveling companion. In the rising sun, Timon's face didn't resemble much of a face. His cheek was the size of a cantaloupe, pulling the skin taut. A couple of the stitches holding the large gash together had slipped out, giving his face the look of a misshapen football with broken laces.

She lifted the bandage on his shoulder. For as bad as his face looked, the bullet wound looked far worse. It was red, swollen, and crusted over. Yellow pus oozed from every opening and heat radiated off his shoulder like a light bulb. An infection had already taken hold.

Gina closed her eyes.

Any doctor at any hospital in the world would have taken one glance at Timon's shoulder and been immediately concerned, both for his arm and his life. They were dealing with a quickly propagating bacteria that needed to be wiped out. And fast. They would have put him on an IV drip with powerful antibiotics and would have checked in on him every hour to make sure they had impeded the infection's growth. So to say Gina was concerned would be an understatement. She was scared.

She thought about her options. Did she abandon the mission at hand and try to get Timon to a hospital? Did she take a quick look around for the three children, maybe an hour, try to get lucky, and then take him to the hospital? Was she even being rational? Was Timon's life worth more than any of the 400 people on the cruise ship? No, of course not. But she didn't know any of those people. None of those people had taken a bullet trying to save her life. Didn't she owe Timon that much? And what about the three children? The odds were stacked against her from the get-go. It would have been a miracle if she did pull it off. It's not like Paul could hold it against her, could he? And what if he did? Who cared?

She found herself laughing. Why was she even having this conversation? Of course she would turn around. She would turn the Jeep around right this instant, and get Timon to a hospital. She turned the key in the ignition.

The engine turned over. Then died. She looked at Timon. He was holding the key between his fingers. Timon's good eye was trained on her. He said, "Do not worry 'bout me. I will bey fine."

She shook her head. "Your shoulder is infected. We need to get you to a hospital."

He put the key in his pocket. He took a deep breath and said, "You find doze children. I will bey fine. I'm strong like bull."

Gina let out a nervous laugh.

"But I will take more medicine."

She nodded. She made him eat another banana, then fed him a couple more Vicodin, and then a double dose of antibiotics. After he'd eaten, she cleaned the wound—Timon didn't breathe for an entire minute while she scrubbed away the pus—applied a generous amount of antiseptic, then redressed the wounds.

She hardly noticed the constant flow of people making their way past their Jeep. She turned and looked over her shoulder. As far as the eye could see there were men and women holding baskets walking down the long dirt road.

She stood up in the driver's seat. The sun had risen over the rolling hills and illuminated the waking village. But the village wasn't what put the slack in Gina's jaw. She attempted to coax Timon out of his seat with little more than unintelligible syllables in response.

Timon fluttered his eyes, then somehow found his way to his feet. He followed Gina's gaze to the rolling hills behind the village. The hills, going back a mile or maybe even two, were overflowing with people. Thousands upon thousands upon thousands of people.

"They must come from opposite side," said Timon.

Gina nodded.

They were both silent for a couple minutes trying to digest the sight. Timon looked at her and said, "When we get new President Motlanthe, I go hear him speak. So many people." He pointed out on the rolling hills and said, "That more people."

He sat back down. The strain of standing up had exhausted him.

Gina's brain could hardly put the sight into context. There had to be over fifty thousand people surrounding the small village with a steady stream joining the group every second. By this time tomorrow that number could double. Or even triple.

She took a deep breath. She needed to get down to that village while she could still part the masses. She looked at Timon. Her task would have been much easier if she had him at her side to translate, but it was out of the question. She patted him on the thigh and said, "Okay, I'll go." She added, "But don't you go anywhere."

He opened his one eye. Then closed it just as quickly. Gina thought maybe he'd tried to smile or roll his eyes, but spotting an expression on Timon's battered face was like trying to see the wave right *behind* a tsunami.

Gina readied him some food, then set aside a couple more doses of Vicadon and Cipro. She put them on his lap and said, "When you wake up, take these. I'll be back as soon as I can."

She pulled on her backpack, gave Timon one last look, then fell in with the sea of people. She heard her name and turned. She was five or six feet from the Jeep by this point, but she had no doubt what Timon had yelled to her.

"Do not come back alone."

SHOW LOUNGE

I WAS ALIVE, but I was one hurting puppy. I was pretty sure I had Ganju to thank for the *alive* part. It was all a bit foggy, seeing as I was getting my ass kicked at the time, but as I faded away into unconsciousness, I thought I'd heard the word, "Stop."

At the time, I'd assumed it was the guard at the pearly gates telling me I couldn't pass through, but a more logical answer was that Ganju had risen to his feet and yelled at the pirates to stop killing me.

Presently, I was confined to a chair near the entrance. Not only was Greg Louganis a skilled diver, he was gifted with duct-tape and I couldn't as much as wiggle. Even so, every ten minutes either Greg or Tupac—Lil Wayne was now sitting in a chair at the center of the stage, guarding the staircase—would walk over and double check that my sticky silver restraints were intact. Each time they would gaze at me, I knew how badly they wanted to put a bullet in my skull.

Every so often Lacy, Susie, Frank, J.J., Marge, Walter, Trinity, or even Gilroy would turn around and peer in my direction. They must have been shocked beyond belief when I'd run on-stage and tackled the security officer. But, I had to do it. If I could go back and do it all over, I would do it all the same. Maybe I would have rummaged around the attic for my old high school football gear first, but hindsight's always twenty-twenty. Regardless, I would call the mission a success. I'd seen it in Ganju's eyes. I'd gotten through to him.

Why else would my heart be beating this very moment?

As for Ganju, when I'd awoken from my imposed slumber, he'd been gone. That had been hours ago.

I couldn't help but think about Rikki. What were they doing to her? They needed to keep her alive; she wasn't any good to them dead. But from firsthand experience, either inflicting it or absorbing it, I knew there were several different levels of alive. Right now, I was at a level four. There was a good chance my right eye socket was busted. I had at least a couple broken ribs, probably some degree of a concussion, and every so often I would be hit with a wave of nausea so intense I would have to bite my lip to fight back throwing up. I'd been at a level three a half dozen times and a level two twice. Level two is when you're just conscious enough to wish you were dead. Level one isn't so bad. You don't remember level one, but it usually includes paddles, the words "Code Blue," and people with masks on.

I had a feeling Rikki was probably on the elevator headed for level three as we speak. But to stay with the analogy, my future plans included putting the Professor and the Warlord at a level zero.

I'm a *glass is half-full* type of guy.

At any rate, there wasn't a damn thing I could do at this point. I would just have to sit and wait.

LONDON
6:25 A.M.

TRACK HAD BEEN on his way back into town when it happened. Stopped at a stoplight nonetheless. A father and daughter walking across the street. The little girl, no older than four or five, riding on her dad's shoulders. The father was dressed in a business suit, probably just gotten off work, probably just picked his daughter up from daycare. He had his hands clamped down on his daughter's tiny shoes, some black sparkly numbers, with this huge grin on his face. But his grin was nothing compared with the little girl's. It was so wide it looked almost like a caricature.

Before the light turned green, Track had sold two billion dollars' worth of stock.

Now, as he sat in the study of his twelve-million-dollar loft, sipping a single malt scotch made in one of several distilleries he owned, he wasn't sure. He wasn't sure if he could go through with it. For one, he didn't know for certain these whack jobs had Rikki. Anyone could have gotten their hands on the photo they had sent him. They could have gotten it from any cruise she'd been on. Or they could have made the picture. It was easy to create documents and forgeries. You could become a completely different person, or conjure a person from thin air, for about five hundred dollars.

The phone had rung nearly an hour earlier. It had been William, Track's accountant. Track thought he'd been calling to ask about the two billion in sold stock. He hadn't. He informed him the *Afrikaans*—the cruise ship Rikki was supposedly on, and which was all over the news for having been hijacked by African pirates—was owned by Oceanic Cruise Lines. OCL was one of his holdings; he owned a 32 percent share in the company which made him the principal stock holder.

Was this a coincidence?

William had promised to call back when he had more information.

Track plopped an ice cube into his scotch and stirred it around with his finger. The phone rang and he stiffened.

He punched the speaker button and said, "William?"

It was silent for a beat, then in a voice that did not belong to his friend William came the words, "Good morning."

Track leaned forward, "How did you get this number?"

"Why do you worry about such things? You should worry about your daughter."

Track had to admit the man was right. As he'd rehearsed earlier, he asked, "How do I even know you have my daughter? You could have sent that picture from any computer in the world. And if you do have her, how do I know she's still alive?"

"Do you want proof?"

Track did not like how the man said, *proof.* He said it as a man who is holding four aces might say, *Check* at the poker table. The man didn't wait for his answer. He said, "Check your e-mail. I will call you back in three minutes."

The phone went dead.

Track picked up the scotch and took a long sip. He flipped open his laptop and logged onto the internet. Track logged into his private e-mail. He had one new message. It was sent two minutes earlier. The man had sent it before he'd called. He'd expected to provide proof. The sender was registered as 56723129437@gmail.com. No doubt untraceable.

Track clicked on the message. A video box popped up. The date and time in the corner showed the time to be 2:07 AM, 09/25/2012. Today. If they were off the coast of South Africa, then they were a couple hours ahead of him, and if he could believe the date and time—which was easy to manipulate—the video was shot six hours earlier.

Track pushed the play button. The room on-screen was all metal and glass. There were a bunch of computers in the background. In the center of the screen was a young woman in baggy shorts and a tank top sitting in a chair. She looked older, and her hair was lighter and shorter, but there was no doubt the woman on the chair was his daughter.

They had her.

They had Rikki.

Rikki looked at the screen, then her head whipped violently to the left. Someone off-screen had slammed their fist into the side of her face. Rikki righted herself, shielding her face with her hands.

Off-screen a voice asked, "What is your name?"

She didn't answer and she was hit again.

"Rikki Drough," she sobbed. "Rikki Drough."

There were a couple seconds of silence, then the same voice he'd heard over the phone asked, "Where are you?"

"Um. A cruise ship?"

"What is the name of the cruise ship?"

"The *Afrikaans.*"

"What day is it?"

She shook her head.

"What day is it?"

"Uh. The eighth day of the cruise. So, um, that would make it September, um, 25th?" She said this questioningly.

Whoever was off-screen must have nodded that she was

correct. Track knew this was no act. This wasn't some low budget production taking place in a garage somewhere. This was real.

"Who is your father?"

Rikki choked. "Um, Track. Track Bowe."

"And how do you know this man is your father?"

No answer.

"How do you know this man is your father?"

No answer.

The fist hit her in the stomach this time. Rikki fell off the chair. The camera angle moved over her. She wheezed in and out, then yelled, "My mom said so!"

"That wasn't too hard. So your mom told you Track Bowe was your father?"

Rikki was in the fetal position, but still managed to nod.

"Does he love you?"

Rikki looked up at the camera. Her eyes were brimming with tears.

"Does your father love you?"

"I don't know." Rikki looked up at the camera. "I've never met him."

Track leaned back in his chair. He thought about flipping the laptop closed. He didn't know if he could stomach any more. A tear dripped down his cheek. Probably the first tear his body had made in twenty years.

Back on-screen, the voice asked, "Is your father rich?"

Rikki wiggled onto her butt, then pushed herself back onto the chair. The camera operator backed up to where he'd started.

Rikki nodded and said, "Yes, he's rich."

"How rich?"

"Rich, rich."

"How much do you think he will pay for you back?"

She shook her head. "I don't know?"

"A million?"

"I don't know."

"Ten million?"

"I said, *I don't know.*"

Rikki's eyes opened wide. A long silver knife, three inches thick—far bigger than any knife Track had ever seen—entered the screen. The blade nestled up against Rikki's throat.

"How much are you worth to your father?"

Rikki took a deep breath, her throat flexing against the blade. "I don't know. I have no idea how much I'm worth." She was sobbing. "I've never met him. He's just a name. He's always just been a name. I don't even know him."

"But he's given you so much over the years?"

"He hasn't given me squat."

"You mean your father has never given you any money?"

Her eyes opened wide. As did Track's. How did they know about the money? Rikki didn't answer. She choked back tears.

"How much money has he given you over the years? A couple hundred?"

She shook her head.

"A couple million?"

She nodded.

The blade was retracted by an unseen hand.

The voice said, "Your father has given you millions of dollars over the years and you don't think he'll pay a million dollars to get you back."

Rikki sniffled, then shrugged, as if to say, I have no idea.

It was silent for a moment, then the man said, "If you had a message to give to your father right now, what would it be?"

She looked down.

"What would you say to this man who you've never met? What would you tell him?"

She shook her head.

The blade returned. Pushed hard against her throat. Tears ran down Rikki's face and onto the blade of the knife.

The man off camera screamed, "What would you tell him?"

The blade moved along Rikki's throat, blood trickling down her soft neck. She began convulsing. Her eyes closed. She looked like she was on the verge of going into shock. Then her eyes flashed open. She stared into the camera and screamed, "I don't want to die. Please. Please, pay these men. Please. Don't let them kill me. Please. All you've done is let me down. My whole life, you've let me down. I would give all the money you've given me, every dollar, just to have met you. I would. Every penny. Please, daddy, don't let them kill me." She took a deep breath, then said quietly, "Save me, daddy. Save me."

The video stopped.

Ten seconds later, the phone rang.

THE LOUD MECHANICAL VOICE CHIMED, "Twenty seconds."

Torrey Royal looked directly at the back of Fuller's helmet. He wasn't sure if Fuller had any rituals like the rest of them did. Royal knew that Sam, six men behind him, had moved his wedding ring to his opposite hand and was massaging the ring with his gloved thumb. He knew three back, Sanchez was patting the Rosary underneath a thick layer of neoprene and saying the Mother's blessing. Chase did some weird thing with his parachute he refused to tell anyone about. Reed had the bullet that nearly took his life in the mountains of Afghanistan in the tip of his left shoe, and Royal could hear him lightly tapping his foot on the cold surface of the cargo hold. Deeter was at the back, doing whatever crazy people do, probably thumping his chest and paying homage to Rambo. Frost was directly behind Royal, and he knew his closest friend was reciting one of Robert's poems from memory, which is how he acquired his moniker. And Pollock was some-where back there, doing some deep breathing thing. Yeah, they all had something. They all had a ritual. Royal, too, had his own. He rubbed his left wrist, where he'd gotten a saxophone tattooed on his eighteenth birthday, and whistled his favorite jazz tune. Lou Reed's *Walk on the Wild Side*.

With the door fully open, the nine men disappeared one after another thirty thousand feet above the Indian Ocean. Four minutes later, nine parachutes opened. Two minutes later, there were nine silent splashes.

Royal surfaced, shaking the water off his helmet. He saw the flare outstretched in the black form of Fuller and swam in that direction. The nine men tread water for thirty seconds, then watched as the dome of the USS New Hampshire silently rose from the water.

The nine men swam to the sub, climbed up the netting the officers had thrown in the water and were pulled aboard.

Royal pulled off his helmet and found himself standing next to Commander Fuller. Royal threw him a wry smile and said, "Can I ask you a question, Commander?"

"Shoot."

"You have a pre-op ritual?"

Fuller sniffed, wiped the moisture from below his nose, and said, "Sure. Doesn't everybody?"

They were about to climb down the hatch and Royal asked, "What's yours?"

"I scratch my balls."

A minute later, the sub was again submerged.

PTUTSI

10:52 A.M.

IT TOOK Gina over an hour to make it to the small village. The settlement was no more than a mile away, but negotiating the mass of people had proven both tricky and time consuming. It was like trying to get up to the stage at a Rolling Stones concert.

There appeared to be two separate camps, a modern day caste system. At the first camp Gina encountered, high up on the hill, the Africans were dressed respectably in shorts and a T-shirt for the men and a colored dress for the women. These people wore shoes, drank from bottled water, read books. A few cooked on gas stoves. Gina guessed these people were responsible for the parking lot from hell. Men and women congregated in small groups. The overall mood was somber, but not forlorn. In each family—or pair, or faction—sprawled out on a large blanket, were the sick, more often than not being attended to by one of the women. A damp towel, the rubbing of feet, a soothing prayer.

As Gina moved through these people she would receive an odd stare here, or the stopping of a conversation there, but mostly these people didn't give her a second's glance. These were the people they'd seen in the cars and walking on the streets. From the cities.

The second camp was located at the base of the hill, separated from the top camp by a football field expanse of high yellow grass. If the first camp was the size of Rhode Island, the second camp was the size of Colorado. The Africans wore little. The men had loincloths covering their genitals, their ribs poking through their tight skin. The women were topless, their large brown breasts sagging into whatever colored material was wrapped around their waists. These people had no doubt come from the surrounding villages.

The Africans sat or laid on the grass. None had blankets. A few of the people chewed slowly on small chunks of bread or drank from large bowls of cloudy water. As Gina gingerly moved around the people and over them, she couldn't help wondering how these people had survived the journey. Some had possibly traveled by bus, but Gina knew the majority had walked. Walked perhaps hundreds of miles. Some must have left over a week earlier.

Gina stepped over countless unmoving bodies. No one attended to anyone. Every single one of these people was sick, some more than others. But within a year, if none got treatment, and sadly even with treatment, every person in this camp—other than their caregivers—would be dead.

Their eyes—blood red in many cases and yellow in others—bore into her as she wended in and out of the tightly cramped groups. Their stares were pleading. Gina might as well of had "Doctor" inscribed in Zulu on her white skin. She could feel their questions floating around her, hovering over each African's head like a halo. *Is she the first doctor to arrive? Will there be more? Where is all the medicine they speak of? Will this woman be the one to save my life?*

In all her travels, Gina had never seen such despair. It was heart-wrenching. She suddenly found herself angry. How could they let this happen? Not how could *these people* let this happen. How could the *world* let this happen?

Gina thought of America. Why didn't they send help? Who cared about the terrorists? Paul said they manufactured enough medication to treat every person with AIDS on the planet. Then why didn't they? So the fat cats at Pfizer could drive bigger cars. So some scientist could have a house in the Bahamas.

She was furious with Paul. He expected her to come to this forsaken village, sweep up these three little children, and haul them back to the States. What about the other hundred thousand people? Was she just supposed to forget about them? Forget about them like every other person on the planet had. Like their own government and her own government and the government of countless other countries had forgotten about them.

Of course these nations had problems of their own—deficit, recession, unemployment, health care. And of course many of these nations were trying to help these people. And yes, she knew the United States—who had to be the best at everything—gave the most money to battle the AIDS effort, but that was no excuse. There was no excuse for the sight before her.

And she hadn't even arrived at the village yet.

Gina turned and looked over her shoulder up the hill. She wanted to run up the hill, sprint up the hill, jump in the Jeep, and drive as far away from this place as possible. She didn't want to see the village. At least these people were still alive. She had a feeling this wouldn't be the case within the fence.

Gina turned back around. She mentally and physically gritted her teeth. She would be tough. She would go to the village, she would find the children, she would get them to the States, then she would spend every last breath trying to get help for these poor people.

By the time Gina had cut through the lower camp and approached the crisscrossed, six-foot high fence made from sticks, it was approaching 8:00 in the morning. The village was beginning to stir, and several Zulus were peering through the fence at the swarm of people surrounding them. They must be wondering why all the people had flocked to their small village. Gina wondered if they'd seen what was unfolding on the hills behind them. They were in for a real shock. If the facing hill was the population of Colorado, the hills flanking the settlement were North America.

The villagers were dressed similar to their brethren at the lower camp, with some small additions. The men wore head-bands, mostly light blue, some white, and had matching material wrapped around their calves. Their bodies were muscular and strong. Their limbs were covered in white chalk. The women wore colorful beaded skirts, colorful beaded necklaces, and were covered in golden jewelry. A couple of the women held small babies in their arms, the babies suckling away at their nipples. Some of the men held long wooden spears.

Centering the village was a second fence—the cattle kraal—enclosing maybe fifty cows chewing their cud.

Gina approached the entrance. There were two men standing just outside an opening in the fence. She thought back to what she'd read, *the chief's eldest sons?* She wasn't sure how these people would react to her presence. Would they be friendly? Or would they tie her up and cook her for dinner?

She took a step forward. Then a couple more. The two young men eyed her suspiciously, then let her pass. Clearly, the lone white woman with the backpack wasn't as threatening as the thousands of visitors camped on the hill before them.

As she moved into the heart of the village, Gina noticed the huts resembled giant coconuts cut in half and stuck in the ground, light brown and husky. There was a four-foot opening in the front of each hut. Some were bigger than others, ranging from the size of, say, a large teepee to the size of a two-car garage. In front of many of the huts, women were cooking. They had large bowls out and were mixing some sort of grain. A small boy and girl sat next to their mother and ate the chalky meal from a bowl with their hands.

Gina surveyed both children. Gina had memorized the pictures down to the last detail and neither of the children on the ground fit the profile.

Gina wasn't sure where to start. The settlement was much larger once you were inside it. She suspected there were more than fifty of the small thatch huts. Was she just supposed to poke her head into each one? Surely someone would take offense to this. Two villagers, both men, both with spears, crawled out from a hut. Both walked up to her, eyed her for a moment, then walked past.

Gina figured she was not the first white woman to enter the village. Maybe there had been missionaries before her or other doctors that had visited. She knew the WHO had many doctors stationed in towns throughout sub-Saharan Africa. It was possible she would meet a fellow doctor. Gina thought about what she would say. Would she tell them why she was here? Or make up some absurd story? She decided she'd cross that bridge when she came to it.

For the first time, Gina noticed the smell of the village. For all its brightness, it smelled dark. Dank. Just underneath the wafting aroma of whatever the women were baking was the smell of decomposition. Decay. Firm and musty. Gina took a couple steps to her left and drew in a breath from her nose. Yes. It was there. And it was strong. It was the smell of death.

Gina quietly walked the small settlement. As she strode past the many villagers, they would quickly glance up, but only for a moment before going back to their task at hand. Many of the women were now sweeping the dirt away from their huts. Sweeping dirt off the dirt. The men were few, and Gina wondered if they were having a secret meeting somewhere or if they were out in the surrounding hills hunting and pillaging. Each time Gina came across a small child—usually running past her or engaged in some game, something resembling hopscotch for the girls, wrestling for the boys—she would appraise them intensely. Most of the children she encountered were either toddlers or teenagers. In fact, Gina saw only three children that could have been the children she was searching for, but none was the right one.

Gina didn't want to think why there were no *children*, but she had a theory. If the toddlers were in fact infected with AIDS, it was silently ravaging their insides, and they would fall victim to the disease in another couple years. As for the teenagers, they had so far escaped the reaches of the disease. But according to the statistics, of the ten teenagers standing in a circle taking their turn wrestling, nearly half would contract the disease when they became sexually active. And the children—the four-, five-, six-, seven-, eight-, nine-, ten-year-olds—they were all dead.

But again, this was just a theory.

When Gina reached the far edge of the village, she noticed six thatch huts far off in the distance. She began hiking in that direction. After a half mile, the dirt stopped and dense grass began. The effervescent chamomile of the grass was unable to mask the stench wafting in from the huts. Gina knew immediately what she was looking at. The village quarantine.

When she was within a dozen steps of the first hut, she stopped. The perfume of death was so overpowering she could no longer take it. She opened her backpack and pulled out a small tube of mentholated chapstick. She ran the stick underneath her nose and drew in the satisfying fumes of menthol.

The opening to the hut was much larger than in the heart of the settlement. Flies and other insects darted in and out of the darkness. Gina took a deep breath, swatted away at the insects, then pushed inside. The sun poked through the thatching in a couple different areas, and the space was surprisingly well lit. The hut was filled with tables, twenty or so. Sprawled out on each table was either a very sick person or a very dead person. The hut was filled with the sound of wheezing, coughing, and groans.

Gina walked to the nearest bed. Gina peered down at the young woman, no older than twenty, on the bed before her. Her skin was pulled taut against her face, her red eyes glaring upward. Even against her dark black skin, the typical Kaposi sarcomas were visible, purple blotches and mush-like deep bruises on the body's surface. Gina peered in her mouth and saw another tell-tell sign of AIDS: bulbous growths—oral carcinomas—inside and around the mouth. The lymph nodes on the woman's neck looked like walnuts hidden beneath the skin.

Gina knew the progression of AIDS was not pretty. The young woman probably contracted the virus four to seven years earlier, but noticed no ill effects until a couple years earlier. Her T-cell count—her fighter white cells—would begin to plummet, activating the virus. The virus would begin sweeping through her body, infecting her spleen, skin, lining of the abdomen, and lining of the lungs. The stem cells in her bone marrow would die. The virus would invade the nerve and brain cells. The young woman would notice a lower level of cognition, mental precision, and motor skills. Going about her usual routine, she might experience growing apathy, tremors, gait unsteadiness, slowing of the reflexes, and loss of hand-eye coordination. Her speech would become slurred. She might even become mute.

In the final stages, the woman likely experienced a dry cough, severe weight loss, shortness of breath, high fevers, night sweats, diarrhea, fatigue, and skin rash. The virus would open the way for the opportunistic infection of other organisms resulting from the weakening of the immune system, often pneumonia.

She watched the chest of the woman before her rise and fall. Her open eyes pleaded to Gina.

Gina pulled one of three bottled waters from her backpack and poured water into the woman's mouth. It gurgled down her throat. If the water appeased the woman, she didn't show it.

Gina suddenly felt angry. Had this young woman been born in the United States she would have led a normal life. She would have had access to antiretroviral drugs—"the cocktail" as westerners called it—that would have kept her T-cell count in check. But in a nation where the average life span is 75 years, this could be said for many different ailments. In Los Angeles, you might have to worry about the occasional earthquake or getting killed on the interstate, but you didn't have to worry about twelve types of snakes, thirty species of spiders, thousands of viruses, unfriendly tribes, malnutrition, and a thousand other things Americans take for granted that can kill you in an instant. In the remote village of Ptutsi, where you were probably lucky to see your thirtieth birthday, things were different.

Very, very, different.

Gina slowly walked through the tables. It was the same sad story. Women, men. In the hut, there were twenty people. Eleven were dead. Nine were well on their way. There were two children, both dead. Gina scrutinized both, almost like a mother gazing down at their offspring on the cold steel table of a morgue. At each bed, she readied herself to see one of the children she was searching for. But she never did. She moved on to the next hut. Then the next. It was all the same. Every single one of these people had either died or was dying of AIDS.

In the fourth hut, Gina encountered a man moving in and out through the tables. He wore a heavy beaded headdress. He laid beads on some of the people and spoke in low tones. Gina wondered if he was a shaman. Regardless of whether he was a witch doctor or an actual doctor, he wouldn't be able to save any of these people. The man didn't even register her presence and she exited the hut.

Gina was about to turn around and head back to the village when she noticed a small dip in the landscape between the final hut and the outside fence, as if they were digging a hole for a swimming pool. She cocked her head to the side and started in that direction. As Gina approached the drop-off, the unmistakable sound of buzzing insects resounded in her ears. She edged to the sheer artificial cliff and peered down. Through a thick cloud of humming insects, Gina could make out the outlines of hundreds of dead stacked one on top of the other.

Gina fell to her knees.

Why didn't the villagers burn the bodies? Why would they want this constant reminder of death? Maybe it had something to do with their beliefs. In Bolivia, they believed that if they burned the bodies, their souls wouldn't ascend to heaven. Gina wished she had Timon by her side to ask questions, or at the very least translate her questions to the villagers.

Gina stood. And then she heard it. A long, hollow wailing. A child's cry.

Gina ran back to the hut closest to her and ducked through the entrance. The screaming was coming from the back corner. The young girl was naked, sitting upright on the bed, her mouth open, giant tears streaking down her face. The girl couldn't have been more than four of five. How had Gina missed her? Gina picked the girl up and started rubbing her small back.

The child relaxed in her arms and Gina carried her from the hut and into the hot sun. She sat the young girl on a rock in the grass and gave her a thorough inspection. She had a rash on her neck and chest, a fever, her glands were swollen, and her liver and spleen were larger than normal. This child was sick. But not from AIDS. Some of the symptoms were the same, but the swollen spleen told the story. AIDS destroyed the spleen, it did not make it swell.

The little girl had mono.

She would feel lousy for another week or two, but she would be as good as new in a month. Gina couldn't blame the villagers for believing the child had AIDS, but she could blame them for simply casting the girl aside. Just leaving her to die. How could the mother let this happen? Did the mother have any control? Or was the death of a child such a common occurrence that it just was?

In her haste to inspect the girl, Gina had failed to get a good look at her. Now, the girl sitting up on the rock, her tears drying in the afternoon sun, Gina noticed the large dimple that danced in her cheek.

Gina smiled.

One down, two to go.

SHOW LOUNGE
12:17 P.M.

"I HAVE TO PISS."

Tupac gave me a sideways glance, smiled, and said, "So peas."

As if being duct taped to the chair wasn't bad enough, now this asshole wanted me to stew in my own urine. Not that I could blame him. If I'd come from where he'd come from, seen the things he'd seen, I wouldn't hesitate to make a rich westerner piss in his pants.

Anyhow, I did have to pee. But, I could hold it. What I wanted was for one of these idiots to untie me and take me into the bathroom. If I could get into the bathroom, I thought there was a good chance I could get my hands on the gun, then either hide it on my person, or do my impression of Billy the Kid.

That was starting to look like a pipe dream.

From my seat near the entrance, I had a commanding view of all the hostages, well, at least through my left eye. My right eye was almost swollen shut. But I wasn't the only one who was hurting. We had entered day three of this nightmare, and it had taken its toll on the passengers. Other than a bag of chips over twenty-four hours earlier, no one had eaten anything. Apart from Susie, it didn't appear anyone was in any danger of actually dying, but the sense of dread in the room was palpable. And yet, these people had no idea what they were up against. In less than twenty-four hours, this ship was going to explode, and every single person in this room would be incinerated.

Part of me wished that I was among those in the dark. Yes, most of these people were miserable and scared, but at this point, I think most felt they would survive this mess. They would just have to wait it out. And before their brains could even comprehend what had happened, they would be dead. Vaporized. But for nine of us, that wasn't the case. We were on death row. We were waiting for the chaplain, waiting for that last meal. We would slowly tick away the seconds to the explosion that would ultimately end our lives.

I peered at Tupac with my good eye and yelled, "You know what time it is?"

He ignored me.

I tried another approach. "Yo, shithead. I'm having dinner with your mom in her hut. She's making zebra stew, and I don't want to be late. Could you tell me what time it is?"

He found this humorous, gazed down at the thin black watch attached to his wrist and said, "Twel-twenny." The way he said it, you would never have thought the man had run through a list of different ways that he wanted to kill me.

I smiled my thanks.

12:20.

I did the math. It took me a minute, but I finally got there. 86,400 seconds to live. Well, now it was 86,040.

86,039.

86,038.

86,037.

Wasn't this going to be fun?

I looked at Lacy. She was looking over her shoulder at me. I wondered if she was doing the same thing. Probably not. She was probably praying. Or maybe thinking about her fiancee. She wasn't counting down the seconds until she died.

The door opened, and Ganju walked through. I cut my eyes at him, then faced front, trying to act frightened, which wasn't a complete act. Maybe over the course of the last ten hours, he'd seen the light. The light being he was being paid handsomely to do a job, and he'd come to kill me. He said something under his breath to Greg and Tupac, then made his way over to me.

I tensed, pulling the duct tape taut.

Ganju stood over me, then I felt a heavy sting across the left side of my face. He'd slapped me. I felt my head wrenched backwards and his brown face nearly touching mine. His face was contorted in a sneer. He whispered, "I visited the computer center."

I saw it in his eyes. He had officially defected. Or had defected again. Either way, he was on our team now.

He gripped my chin between his hand and squished my mouth together. I murmured, "Bathroom."

He cocked his head, then reared back and slapped me again on the side of the face. He turned to the pirates and said, "Cut him loose."

They looked puzzled and Ganju walked over to them and spoke in a hushed tone for several seconds. When he finished, both pirates were smiling ear to ear.

What had Thapa told them?

Greg walked behind me and I could hear as his knife cut through the thick tape. After several seconds and 652 hairs ripped from my flesh, I was free. Ganju walked toward me, grabbed me by the ear, and began dragging me down the walkway. I could hear the pirates' laughter resounding from behind me.

After several feet he released my ear, then shoved me in front of him. I knew without looking that his gun was trained between my fourth and fifth vertebrae. I stumbled down the aisle way, feeling the sympathizing stares of my fellow hostages. Or maybe they felt that I had this coming for my heroically foolish stunt. If only these people had a clue.

As I approached Lacy and friends, I tried to give a wry smile, nothing that would betray too much. With my left hand, I pulled my three middle fingers in, leaving my pinkie and thumb outstretched. Lacy was the only one that caught the gesture and I saw her fight down a smile.

Hang Loose.

Frank looked like he was thinking of doing something stupid, like jumping up and getting himself shot. I shook my head at him and said, "Don't."

He took a deep breath, and we moved past him.

As I passed Gilroy, he threw me a smirk. I had the sudden urge to scissor kick him in the neck. I didn't.

I could feel Lil Wayne's eyes on me from the stage, and I wasn't surprised when just feet from the bathroom, I was thrown forward, and I guessed that Thapa had decided a swift kick in the butt needed to be part of our act.

I slammed into the door of the bathroom, doing my best Vlade Divac impression, making it seem much worse than it actually was. Thapa followed me into the bathroom. I made my way to the trash-can. From behind me, I heard him say, "I am sorry. For everything."

I turned around and said, "Sorry about tackling you earlier."

"I understand. You had to."

I lifted the lid on the trashcan and began rifling through the trash.

"I saw the bomb," said Thapa. "It is more than enough to destroy a ship twice the size of the *Afrikaans*."

"These guys don't fuck around."

"No. They do not."

"I think they're going for the dramatic. Huge explosion. Maybe they have scuba gear or something. Get picked up by a boat a couple miles away and no one notices."

"I am not sure of their getaway plans. But I am sure they do not include myself or any of the other pirates for that matter."

My body was halfway down into the trash, my fingers combing the bottom, and my voice echoed through the plastic, "Where is the girl?"

"They are keeping her at the bridge."

"Is she okay?"

"They beat her up pretty bad, but she'll live."

My hands found the gun and I pulled it out. I was out of breath. It was still wrapped in paper towel and I peeled this off. Ganju's eyes grew large. He asked, "Where did you get that?"

"We have one less pirate to worry about."

He nodded. I thought I saw a twinge of a smile. If I didn't know better, I'd have thought he was proud of me. He said, "We must hurry."

I nodded. But I did have to piss. I quickly peed, then stuck the gun in the waist of my pants.

We spent the next thirty seconds going over a plan. Then he said, "Go. Before they get suspicious."

We walked from the bathroom and headed back toward the entrance. I kept my eyes focused straight ahead. If I made eye contact with Lacy or Frank or even J.J., my face would show some iota of encouragement, something I couldn't allow the pirates to notice.

Ganju led me back to the chair, then shoved me down into it. The gun jabbed hard against my back and I had to bite my lip in order not to flinch. Greg Louganis started toward us, excited for an encore duct-taping, but Ganju waved him away. He shrugged and walked back to his position at the door.

Ganju picked the roll of duct tape from the ground behind the chair and began wrapping it tightly around my arms and legs. After a couple minutes, he was done. He'd done almost as good of a job as Greg had done earlier. Key word being "almost." There were a couple areas where the tape was much looser than it appeared to be, especially when I flexed against it.

The pirates were close to thirty yards away and I said under my breath, "What did you tell them?"

Ganju looked at me sternly and said, "Tell them what?"

"What did you tell the pirates earlier that had them smiling, then had them cut me loose."

He cupped my chin in his hands and brought his face inches from mine. From far away it must have looked like he was telling me that I was a dead man. Instead, he said, "I told them if they cut you loose now, then later tonight they could kill you however they wanted."

Touché.

Ganju punched me in the solar plexus, the wind knock from my lungs. As I gasped for air, I could hear his fading footsteps, then the door open and close.

WASHINGTON D.C.

10:38 A.M.

PAUL GARRET PULLED the pink bottle from the bottom drawer of his desk and took a long pull. It had been nearly two hours since his morning press conference and his stomach was still in knots. Over the course of the last twenty-four hours, the entire world had gotten wind of the story, down to every last crumb, and a once dormant volcano had erupted, spewing hot lava down the side of the mountain, destroying everything in its path. Unfortunately, at the bottom of the volcano, directly in the path of the flowing red-hot lava, was Paul Garret's career.

Garret flipped on both small flat screen televisions situated in the wall of his den. The television on the right was tuned to CNN. The one on the left MSNBC.

CNN was at commercial. MSNBC was broadcasting a live press conference. The man behind the podium had a thick neck, reddish skin, and a face that wasn't meant for television. He spoke in accented English. At the bottom of the screen a banner read, "Isaac Crown. President Oceanic Cruise Lines."

Isaac was in midsentence, "…the families of the passengers have been contacted. Of course we cannot release any of these names."

"How many are American?" a reporter shot.

Isaac looked off-screen, perhaps at the OCL's lawyer, and seemingly getting the nod, answered, "According to our manifest, there were—sorry, *are*—154 Americans aboard the ship. The remaining passengers are mostly European, with a few Australians. The 164 person crew is international."

Paul already knew of all these details and he wasn't interested in what else Isaac had to say. Anyhow, CNN was back on, and Paul flipped off the other TV.

Wolf Blitzer was on-screen in front of a map of southern Africa. Over the course of the next couple minutes he used the telestrator to show the world where the *Afrikaans* was located seventy miles off the eastern coast of South Africa and where the small village of Ptutsi was located two hundred miles northeast of Durban.

CNN had a correspondent at the small village. They flashed to a young man with a hooked nose. Behind him was a blockade of military vehicles, and yards behind them a thick wall of Africans could be seen. He said, "We're about a quarter mile outside the heart of Ptutsi where the South African Military has set up a blockade. They are no longer letting anyone pass through, but for the past week, Africans have been flocking to the small village after being promised AIDS relief by several Zulu newspaper ads as well as an ad that has been running on a local Zulu television station. And somewhere behind these blockades are rumored to be close to a quarter of a million people."

A quarter of a million people?

For a split second, Paul's stomach clenched, but for a different reason altogether. Last he'd heard it had been a couple thousand. And now there were a quarter of a million Africans all supposedly infected with AIDS? Paul couldn't help thinking how Gina was in that mess of people somewhere. And he put her there.

Wolf Blitzer said, "It would appear the terrorists aboard the *Afrikaans* had prompted these people to flee to the small village in an attempt to elicit help from the United States. Have you seen any sort of medical tent or anything that would indicate help is on the way?"

"No, I haven't. There has been an influx of news vans and reporters, and of course the military presence, but nothing that would suggest medical relief of any kind."

"Thanks, Mark. We'll check in with you later."

Mark signed off. Wolf was standing in front of a large flat screen television and said, "If you're just joining us, two days ago a luxury cruise liner off the coast of South Africa was boarded by African pirates. The pirates, yet to be identified, have demanded AIDS relief be sent to a small village forty miles southeast of the town of Ladysmith, or about two hundred miles northeast of the coastal city of Durban. Ptutsi currently carries the highest prevalence of AIDS in the world with close to fifty percent of their inhabitants infected with the virus. The Zulu village's population is just under four hundred, down from more than eight hundred only five years ago. Earlier, the White House Press Secretary spoke about the incident. Here is the scene everybody is talking about."

The large television behind Wolf flashed to Garret standing behind a podium, the White House seal emblazoned on the blue wall behind him. Garret—the Garret watching himself—tipped the pink bottle back once more and took a healthy pull.

On-screen a reporter asked, "Why did the White House attempt to keep this quiet for so long?"

This had been fifteen minutes into the press conference. Paul watched himself take a deep breath on-screen, then say, "Our main focus was, and still is, the four hundred people on the *Afrikaans*. By keeping the story quiet we were giving those hostages the best possible chance to survive."

"What is the U.S. doing to combat the terrorists?"

"Obviously I can't tell you that. But I can assure you the President and the United States Navy are doing everything in their power to ensure the survival of everyone on that ship."

"You said the Navy is involved. What are they doing?"

Paul knew this was the question that had started the slide. On-screen, Paul gritted his teeth and said, "Do you really think I am about to divulge the United States Naval strategy to you? The act of piracy aboard a ship carrying American passengers falls under the jurisdiction of the United States Navy. This is why they are involved. And this is all you need to know."

"It's been rumored the pirates demand the United States send medical aid to South Africa to help combat their AIDS epidemic."

The pirate's demands had leaked at some point the previous night. No one knew exactly who was responsible for the leak. It could have easily been someone in the White House, but no one had discounted the pirates making a couple calls themselves. The more airtime their demands received, the more shots of tattered Africans lined up for miles to get AIDS medicine, the more pressure on the United States to send relief.

"This is correct."

"Is the US sending aid?"

"For those of you who haven't lived in the United States, or have never watched a *Die Hard* movie, or are just plain stupid we do not negotiate with terrorists."

There was a brief quiet in the room.

A brave reporter asked, "But don't you think we should send help?"

"The United States is already the single largest contributor to AIDS relief in the world. It's not like we are just sitting on our asses watching millions and millions of people die of this disease. In the two years since the President has been in office, relief to South Africa has more than doubled."

Garret peered at the reporter and said, "Craig, how much money have *you* contributed to AIDS relief?"

"Um."

"That's what I thought. You and your pals sit here with your fifty-dollar haircuts and your four-dollar lattes, and you point fingers at the President, his staff, and the military for not helping. Or in some cases helping too much. We can't win. Well, let me tell you something. We can't save the world. We have the highest level of unemployment in history. Our own healthcare system is in shambles. Our national deficit is at an all-time high. And we are expected to take care of the entire world. Well, that costs [bleeping] money."

There was an awkward silence. Then a reporter stood up and said, "Give us a break Garret, we're just doing our job."

"Yeah, well, I'm [bleeping] sick of it. You're a bunch of [bleeping] sensationalist lepers for all I'm concerned."

Garret stormed off the stage. Then he stormed from the White House. And he'd been in his den for the past hour. He looked down at his cell phone. He had over a hundred missed calls.

Garret tipped the pink bottle back and finished it off.

PTUTSI

4:04 P.M.

WHEN GINA REACHED THE JEEP—SHE'D slid the small girl through one of the openings in the fence, then climbed over—she had half expected to find Timon dead. She was surprised to see his fever had broken and the gunshot wound to his shoulder looked markedly better. The infection had gone down, and the blood flow had all but stopped. He would live.

This had been around noon.

Gina had eased the small frame of the child into the backseat of the Jeep, and given Timon strict instructions on how to care for her. She explained the young girl was infected with a virus, but not HIV. The virus would run its course in the next couple weeks, they just needed to keep her pumped with fluids. Gina cracked open a bottled water and slowly poured the tepid water into the young girl's mouth.

Gina wondered how long it'd been since the girl had a drink of water. She gulped the water down, then opened her mouth for more. "Keep filling her up," Gina said, handing the bottle to Timon. "And see if you can feed her a banana."

Timon nodded, then said, "Go. We will be fine. You have two more children to find."

From her perch high up on the hill, she peered down on the village. At the center of the village she noticed a small gathering. Between eight and ten small boys. She couldn't make out their faces, but her gut told her the two boys she was searching for were part of the small group.

After what seemed like an eternity, Gina once again found herself at the bottom of the hill, and she once again approached the two young men at the entrance to the gates. They looked far less friendly than they had on her earlier expedition. Almost as if they had been instructed no one was allowed to enter.

Gina put her head down and tried to walk past them nonchalantly. When she had taken two steps past the guards, she felt a hand clasp around her left biceps.

So close.

The young men dragged her through the village. Gina wondered where the men were taking her. To see the chief? What would she say? Surely he didn't speak a lick of English. And if he did, what would she tell him. *Oh, no biggie, I just came to steal three of your children and take them with me. Take a chill pill.*

The guard dragged her past the many smaller huts, and they began to approach a larger hut Gina hadn't noticed earlier. It was on the far right edge of the village, opposite the quarantine, nestled up to the fence. It was nearly three times the size of the other huts and there was a large boulder blocking the entrance. Whoever was in the hut was not permitted to enter and exit freely. If the boulder, which was enormous, was not a deterrent in and of itself, there were two sentries posted on either side of the large rock.

Gina immediately knew the purpose the large hut served.

It was a prison.

DECK 7

5:52 P.M.

THAPA HAD SPENT the last three hours making one final sweep of the ship, making certain there were no unaccounted-for enemies meandering about. He was astonished at how quickly his mindset had changed. At first the hostages had been his enemy, now it was the pirates. He had always known something was amiss. He'd been told he would be helping millions of sick people. And if ten people had to die—Stoves, the Captain, and his officers —to help save the lives of a couple million poor Africans, Thapa could deal with that.

Finding out the boat was rigged with explosives and the pirates were secretly ransoming a young British girl hadn't set well with him. As a Gurkha for twenty years with the British Army, Thapa had come to think of England as his second home. Yes, the people were nearly as corrupt and capitalistic as the Americans he'd encountered, but they were *his* people. He had sworn to protect them.

Thapa thought of the mantra the British Army had bestowed on the famed Gurkhas: "He is brave, tough, patient, adaptable, intensely proud, and has unwavering loyalty."

Loyalty? What did he know about loyalty?

He was loyal to the almighty dollar. He was no different than any person on this ship. What had the man with blue eyes, this Thomas, said to him, "You will never be able to look your children in the eyes again"?

And he was right. If he took the money, his son might one day walk again, but it would cost him a father. Thapa would never be able to look him in his deep brown eyes ever again.

Thapa had decided then and there to do everything in his power to save all the people on the ship. He might not be loyal. But he was *adaptable.*

In Thapa's sweep of the ship, he'd spent most of his time in Pretoria. The powers that be must be more concerned an insurgence would occur down here with all the crew than with the passengers in the show lounge. There were six pirates, all heavily armed. Of course, Thapa would have the element of surprise, but there was no way he could take out all six. If they were standing shoulder to shoulder, Thapa was certain he could put a bullet in each man's heart before one of them reached for their gun. But the pirates were stationed far from one another: two at the entrance, then four positioned in various places throughout the restaurant. And of course, between them all, two hundred hostages.

An idea had struck Thapa, an idea that had brought him up to Deck 7. The radio room was situated directly behind the bridge. Thapa looked at his pistol. He could put a stop to this whole thing right this second. Cut the tail off a snake, and it will live. Cut the head off the snake, and the snake will die.

He approached the glass door to the bridge and peeked inside. Both men were staring at the screen of a laptop computer. Both wore large grins. Thapa watched as the men looked at one another, then back to the screen, then back at one another. Thapa would describe their look as disbelief. Or wonder.

In the back of the room sat the girl, slumped down in a chair, her swollen eyes staring ahead, open but unseeing.

Thapa turned his gaze back to the two pirates. The Mosquito was staring at him, the mirrored glasses hiding what Thapa assumed must be cold dead eyes. For as much as the other man trusted Thapa, he was aware this man was a bit more cautious. As he should be.

Thapa pulled the door open and stepped inside. The older man turned and looked genuinely pleased at his presence. "Ganju," he said. "Ganju, come here, let me show you something."

Thapa took a couple hesitant steps forward. He could easily take his pistol out and get off a couple shots. But the other man had moved and was situated behind the girl. A wise tactical move. If Thapa were to put a bullet in the older man, the young warlord would no doubt use the girl as a hostage or simply pull out his machete and gut her here and now.

No, The Mosquito would have to live. For now.

Baruti waved him forward and said, "You must look at this."

Thapa walked forward until he was a couple feet from the laptop. He was familiar with computers; he had been trained on them extensively, and he kept in contact with his family through e-mail when he was at sea. He looked at the screen. It was a bank's webpage. Thapa didn't have a photographic memory, but numbers always seemed to stay with him—he could recite pi going back nearly a thousand decimals—and he committed the IP address to memory.

He assumed this meant Monaco International Bank. Thapa had heard Monaco was the new Switzerland. The safest place to hide money outside the Caymans. But transferring money to the Caymans took days. In Monaco, he'd heard it took minutes.

There were several places that information needed to be filled in. An accountant number, a password bar, a second password bar, and then a third field marked "RGP."

Thapa had heard banks were using these now. RPG. Random Generated Password.

Baruti typed in a long account number, then two separate 20

digit passwords. Thapa watched his fingers move deftly across the number pad. When it came to the RGP field, Baruti pulled something from around his neck, a tiny capsule on a silver chain, and peered down at it. He then entered in an eight-digit code.

Baruti noticed Thapa's curiosity and said, "The number changes every minute."

Thapa nodded.

The screen refreshed and showed the account balance. Thapa had never seen so many zeros. Just under 747 million dollars.

The man smiled and said, "Think of all the good we can do with that money. Think of all the lives we can save."

Thapa appraised him skeptically. He was certain the man would live lavishly until he took his last breath—who wouldn't who had just inherited, or stolen, a billion dollars—but Thapa had no doubt the majority of the billion would be money well spent. The man would probably make more of an impact with that money that any government in the world could.

Baruti said, "I want to show you something else."

He clicked on the recent transaction button and the screen refreshed. There were several transactions on the page. There were three transactions that had just occurred. One was for 250 million dollars. Something very expensive. There was another for one million, and a third for two million. He noticed the two-million-dollar withdrawal was to a numbered account. His numbered account.

Baruti patted Thapa on the shoulder and said, "I thought you deserved a bigger piece of the pie for your efforts."

Thapa knew there wasn't a sum of money that could buy his loyalty back. Not two million, not ten billion. His loyalty wasn't for sale. He tried to appear overcome with gratitude and said, "Thank you. Thank you."

Thapa then retraced his steps and left. The Mosquito never took his eyes off him.

Thapa couldn't help thinking that now that these men had

their money, they no longer needed anyone on this ship. The countdown on the bombs would be at just over eighteen hours, but he knew they would have a remote detonation switch. They could blow the ship at any second. Thapa pondered their getaway plan. Did they have scuba gear or a mini sub stashed somewhere? Would they get a mile or two away from the ship, then blow it? That's how he would do it. In the confusion of the ship exploding, it would be an easy getaway.

Thapa decided he wouldn't let that happen.

He made his way into the radio room and slipped the key into the steel door. He went to the safe at the back and entered in a code. If what Thapa came for had been found during one of the routine inspections, it would have been confiscated and Thapa would have had a lot of explaining to do. He extracted the small compact object from the safe and hurried out.

SHOW LOUNGE
7:07 P.M.

HITCH. Independence Day. Men in Black. Men in Black II. I, Robot. Both the *Bad Boys. Hancock.* How many was that? Seven. No, there had to be more.

It was a game my sister and I played often. You went back and forth saying how many of an actor's movies you could name. For example I would say, "I can name seven Johnny Depp movies," and my sister—who was obsessed with Depp, part of the reason I think she moved to France—would say, "I can name thirty Johnny Depp movies." And I would say, "Name those movies."

It's a tad different when you're playing with yourself. Currently, I was trying to name ten Will Smith movies, what should have been an easy enough task, but I was stuck on eight. *Enemy of the State.* Make that nine.

I remained stuck on nine. I am confident I would have been able to conjure up a tenth film had Gilroy not stood up.

I noticed it out of the corner of my right eye, which still throbbed, but had opened about halfway. I was staring at Lil Wayne on the stage, mostly because I was trying *not* to stare in the direction of my sister and the gang. I didn't want to give them false worry. Or false hope. Oddly enough, Gilroy was the one I'd been most concerned about. He didn't seem like the type that would sit idly by while death inched closer and closer to him. No, he was a man of action. And I was surprised it had taken him this long. But, again, I couldn't blame him. And if I were in his shoes, I can't say I wouldn't have done the same.

As Gilroy strolled up the aisle, part of me wanted to signal him that I had things under control. That if he just sat his hairy ass down for a couple more hours, he, along with everyone in this room, would survive this mess. But another part, a sinister part, wanted to see what this idiot had planned. Now, don't get me wrong, I didn't want to see the guy get killed, but I wouldn't mind if he lost a couple of those dazzling white teeth in the process of pulling whatever stunt his genius bravado had come up with.

Tupac and Greg watched as Gilroy approached, his wide chest pushed out, his shoulders back, the enormous bulge in his swim trunks growing larger every step. Part of me wondered if the pirates were impressed by Gilroy's package, but another part, the part prone to a racial generalization every now and then, thought otherwise. I'd played basketball almost all my life. I'd seen things.

Gilroy shot a look my way. On any other face, it might have read, "Don't worry, I'll get you out of this," but on his face it screamed, "You got yourself into this mess and I'm sure as shit not going to stick my neck out to get you out of it!"

As he approached the pirates, he put his hands up, the international way of saying, "Hey, I come in peace."

Greg and Tupac eyed each other warily. I knew they would see what he had to say. I mean, they had to be bored out of their minds. Even if they'd been playing the movie game as well—*I can name seven Tiagalo Dgegea Mateila Saminella Protaatsue Cialis Tutatloo movies*—it was only good for an hour or so.

Tupac waved Gilroy forward with his gun, then motioned him to stop when he was five steps away.

Gilroy took a couple steps forward, then glanced at me. I knew he would prefer to have his little powwow with the pirates in private, and he was weighing the options of my overhearing his conversation. Evidently, he decided the chances of my dying in the next half day were infinitely better than anyone else's, and began speaking. He flashed that smile of his and said, "How are you doin'?"

I imagined Gilroy saying this to a little old lady whose house he wanted to tear down so he could drill for oil.

The pirates didn't respond.

Undeterred, Gilroy asked, "I just want to know how much you guys are being paid?"

"Monay?" asked Tupac.

"Yes. How much money are you being paid?"

"Many monays."

"Good, good. I'm glad you boys are being well compensated for your efforts. It would seem to me that you gentlemen are the one's doing all the heavy lifting while your bosses reap all the rewards."

The pirates didn't respond and Gilroy pushed on, "Here's the deal. In my room I have some money hidden." He looked at me, then said, a bit softer than his previous statements, "Ten thousand dollars."

I smiled behind the tape. What happened to the other one hundred and ninety thousand dollars? Plus, I didn't think ten thousand dollars was going to spark much interest in these guys. For one, this whole operation was ironclad which means there was a lot of money backing it. Two, they were ransoming a young girl for what had to be millions of dollars. Surely these men had been promised a share of this money. And third, the pirates probably already had his money. I'd seen the rooms. They'd been ransacked. Everything remotely valuable in each room was sitting in a garbage bag on this boat somewhere. Pardon the cliché, but these pirates were making out like bandits.

"Ten thouzand dollas?" repeated Greg.

"Yes. And it's yours. All I ask in return is that you provide me with a small life raft and a couple day's rations. That's it."

The pirates looked at each other. Tupac asked, "Jus you?

"Just me."

The pirates huddled together. It appeared they were considering his plan. Maybe I'd been wrong. Maybe these guys were getting paid jack shit. Maybe the Professor and Warlord would get all the money and jewels, along with the millions in ransom, and these guys were being paid in old T-shirts.

Finally, after what seemed like an eternity, Tupac said, "Okay."

Gilroy smiled.

"Bud furst we shood you."

"Shood me?" Gilroy looked confused.

"Yes. Shood you."

Tupac pulled his gun up and shot Gilroy in the left leg. Greg shot him in his right leg.

Gilroy's screams filled the small room.

I noticed many of the hostages covering their ears as not to hear his moans and cries. He reminded me of that horse who broke both his legs during the Kentucky Derby and they had been forced to kill him. I was glad I didn't have access to my gun at this moment in time. I would have pulled it out and put him out of his misery. Yes, I despised the guy about as much as a closed-caption typist despised Charles Barkley, but I still felt bad for the guy.

At least a *little* bad.

I watched as Gilroy opened his eyes and stared at his bleeding legs. He looked up at the pirates and screamed, "My legs! My fucking legs!"

I looked over at my sister. She had her hand covering her mouth. Susie was holding Trinity's head in her arms. I turned and looked at Gilroy. The first shot hit his left knee. The second his right shin. There are not words on this Earth to describe the pain he was feeling.

I shook my head. If Gilroy somehow survived, and with the

amount of blood pouring out of his legs, the odds were slim, he would probably never walk again.

Gilroy's only hope was for Ganju to come barging through those doors in the next twenty minutes or so. His life depended on it. All of our lives did.

THE BRIDGE

8:03 P.M.

"THIRSTY?"

Rikki nodded.

The older gentlemen walked over to her and handed her a bottled water. She cracked the top and pressed the bottle to her lips. She winced. Her bottom lip was cracked from where she'd been hit. She tilted the bottle up and poured the water down her throat.

She drank the entire bottle. She set it on the ground.

The older gentlemen said, "Well, as you may have overheard, your father has transferred one billion dollars to an account of my choosing."

Rikki eyed him suspiciously,

He continued, "Unfortunately, we require two billion dollars for your safe return. So we have two options. We could just throw you overboard and keep the one billion. Or we press your father for the second billion. Or we could release you and hope your dad follows through."

"Follows through?"

"Yes, just before the money was wired to the account, we

received an e-mail from your father." He paused a moment, then said, "Would you like me to read it to you?"

Rikki was sure she would be listening to the e-mail regardless of what she answered. "Sure."

The older gentlemen walked over to the laptop, fiddled for a couple moments, then began reading, "In one hour, I will transfer a sum of one billion dollars to the account you have requested. But I am no fool. The only chance you have of getting the second billion is for you to send me video footage of my daughter in a lifeboat set out to sea. When I get this footage, I will transfer the remaining one billion dollars. Travis Victor Bowe."

Rikki raised her eyebrows. She was surprised. Her father did care. She found tears begin to well up in her eyes.

The Professor said, "Tomorrow morning at daybreak, we will not put you in a lifeboat, we will do one better. We will put you in one of our fishing boats. There are many boats stationed just five miles away, and you will have no problem finding your way to one of these ships."

Rikki cocked her head to the side and said, "You're really going to let me go?" She had tried to trick herself into thinking she might survive this mess, but deep down she knew she was headed for certain death. She asked, "What about all the others?"

He smiled, but didn't answer.

The next moment was a blur. The door crashed open and someone yelled, "Don't move!"

Rikki looked toward the voice. It was Bheka. He was holding the machine gun in his hand. He swung it back and forth between the older gentleman and the man with the beret.

The older gentlemen said, "Be careful."

Rikki bit her lip. She couldn't believe it. She yelled, "Shoot them!"

He nodded, but did nothing.

"Shoot them!"

The man with the beret began advancing toward Bheka. He didn't seem to know what to do.

Rikki screamed, "Shoot him, Bheka!"

Bheka pointed the gun at him and pulled the trigger.

Click.

Bheka looked down at the gun. Pulled the trigger again.

Click.

The man with the beret began laughing. He ripped the gun from Bheka's hands and said, "De safety."

He looked at the older man, who let out a deep breath. Then the man with the beret kicked Bheka in the stomach. Bheka fell to the floor groaning.

The older man walked to Rikki. She leaned back in her chair. He leaned down and said, "Didn't I just tell you that we were going to let you go and this is how you repay us, by telling him to shoot us."

He slapped her in the face and said, "You can die with the rest of them."

WHERE WAS GANJU? Had he gotten cold feet? Had he decided the money was more important than looking his son in the eyes after all? Had he been caught? Had they gotten wind of his traitorous activity and put a stop to it? Was he even alive? And if he was alive, what was he waiting for?

These questions were running through my head in a continuous loop, a dog chasing its tail.

I looked at Gilroy ten yards from me, his ruined legs lying in a tepid pool of blood. He was laying on his back, his eyes closed, his face ashen. I would have thought him dead had his hairy chest not rhythmically moved up and down still. It was a miracle he'd survived this long. But he wouldn't survive much longer. There were six quarts of blood in the human body. At least two quarts of Gilroy's were soaking into the thick carpet.

There was a creak and I turned toward the door.

It was time.

Ganju walked past Tupac and Greg, then stopped. He peered down at Gilroy's askew body. He turned toward the pirates as if to ask a question, but then thought better of it. He walked around

Gilroy and started down the main aisle. He did not glance in my direction.

My heart was pounding against my chest, and I attempted a couple calming breaths, pulling as much air through my nostrils as humanly possible. By the time Thapa had reached the halfway mark to the stage, my heart felt like it was going to implode. Over the course of the last six hours, I had loosened the restraint around my right forearm to the point I would be able to slip it from beneath the tape.

I turned toward Lacy. She was trading glances between Ganju and me. I could see it in her eyes. She knew. She knew shit was about to hit the fan.

I watched Ganju. Lil Wayne stood onstage, making it appear as though he was hard at work guarding whatever he was supposed to be guarding. I wondered what was going through Ganju's mind. It would have been much easier if all three pirates had stayed together. And if this wasn't bad enough, Tupac had decided to make his way into the main aisle and was standing on the outskirts of the first row of chairs. I noticed he was holding his gun in his hand. Maybe he'd seen something in Ganju's eyes. Maybe he'd seen what Lacy had seen. Either way, he was on guard, and the chances of our success had just been cut in half.

Ganju yelled something and started for the women's bathroom. When he was halfway there, a loud crack filled the auditorium, and Lil Wayne fell backwards onto the stage.

That was my cue.

I slipped my arm from the tape. There was another loud crack, and I hoped Ganju had hit Greg with his second shot, but I could see Greg ducking behind the row of chairs on the far right.

I wrenched my arm behind my back, my fingers finding the stock of the gun. Pulling it out, I swept the gun at Greg, who was leveling his gun at Ganju.

I had shot a gun from a sitting position a couple times, but never with three of my four appendages securely fastened. I aimed the gun at Greg, but some of the hostages were now standing, and I didn't have a clean shot. Meanwhile, Tupac had moved behind me and continued down the right hand wall.

I tipped the chair forward, then fell face first, softening the blow with my hand holding the gun. I could bend my knees just slightly, and I used my toes and the barrel of the gun to propel me forward.

Greg had started down the decline, and I heard three shots.

Gilroy was situated exactly where I needed to be to get a clean shot. I more or less scooted to him, then dove on top of him, my knees sinking into his belly.

Sorry, buddy.

Greg was fifty feet in front of me and down twenty vertical feet. By now all the hostages were duck-and-covering, and the place looked empty. I lined up the gun with Greg's spine and pulled the trigger twice, turning him into a paraplegic. I could see the top of Ganju's head peeking out over the top of the first row of empty seats in the center section. I gazed to my right. Tupac was crouched low, making his way to the stage. Once he made his way onto the stage, Ganju would be a sitting duck.

He took three crouched steps, then stood. I could tell by the smirk on his face that he had a clean shot at Ganju.

Using Gilroy's chest as a support, I lined up the shot.

Gilroy began to move and I yelled, "Sit still!"

I tracked the moving Tupac with Gilroy's inhales and exhales, my gun moving up and down with the rise and fall of Gilroy's chest. As his chest fell, I pulled the trigger twice.

The first bullet skimmed over Tupac's head. The second bullet blew out his brains.

I let out a long exhale though my nose, dropped the gun, and rolled off Gilroy. A couple moments later, I felt a body kneel beside me. I craned my head upward, and said matter of fact, "Hey, sis."

"Nice shooting."

"Anybody get hurt?"

"Just those three assholes."

Lacy began ripping the duct tape from the chair. A moment later she was joined by Frank, J.J., Susie, even Walter and Marge began helping rip away the tape.

"That was fucking awesome," spat J.J.

"Glad I could entertain you."

The tape was removed, and Frank pulled me to my feet. He wrapped his huge arms around me. I hugged him back. Then pushed him off. There was no time for long-drawn-out man affection.

I scanned the room. All the hostages were staring at our little group. Most were dumbfounded, not sure what to think about the mini OK Corral they'd just witnessed. I told Lacy I needed her to round up our lesbian friends. She nodded, then headed to where they were seated.

Ganju was limping up the inclined aisle.

I looked down where Trinity was kneeling over Gilroy, caressing his face. I wondered if she knew he'd tried to sell her out. Probably not.

I ran to where the roll of duct tape was on the ground and ran back. I knelt beside Gilroy's bloodied legs. Bone splintered through his shin and his knee looked like someone had smashed it in with a hammer. Blood continued to ooze from the wounds and I again wondered why this man still had a pulse.

Trinity looked at me and asked, "Is he going to be okay?"

"If we get him to a hospital soon enough, he should be. But we're going to have to move him and we can't risk him losing any more blood."

I began pulling off long strips of duct tape and made two tourniquets. Each time I would wrap the tape around one of his legs, Gilroy would whimper. When I finished, I stood.

Ganju let out a long exhale and said, "Nice shooting."

"You too."

I looked down at his left foot. His shoe was red. I asked, "You get hit?"

"Just a scratch."

Lacy returned with Berta and Reen.

J.J. asked, "So what's the plan?"

I told them.

DECK 5
9:55 P.M.

THAPA MADE his way across the stage, hesitating slightly as he clumped past both pirates' corpses. After he'd shot and killed the pirate on stage, he had turned to see that one of the pirates who should have still been near the door, had moved halfway down the ramp and was pulling his gun up. Thapa couldn't risk a shot in the pirate's direction, for if he missed, he would surely hit one of the hostages. As the pirate's gun had come up, Thapa dove for cover, trying to roll under the curtain. He'd been successful, but the pirate had unloaded on him and one of the bullets clipped his left foot. Thapa had never been shot before, his worst injury having been a broken forearm, and his foot now felt like someone had dipped it in gasoline and lit it on fire.

For an instant, he wondered if what he felt at the moment was what his son felt every time he took a step. Thapa pushed his son's crippled leg from his mind. There would be plenty of time for self-loathing later. Right now, he had a job to do.

Thapa clambered down the steps at the far back of the stage and down to District 9, then out the doors and to the galley that housed the food for both District 9 and a small cafe at the rear of Deck 5. He pulled open the enormous walk-in cold storage and stepped inside. Sadly, this refrigerator, one of a half dozen on the ship, was probably the safest place to be if the ship did explode. Of course, the ship would sink quickly thereafter, but nestled next to the hundreds of hamburger patties and the large plastic bags of chicken tenders, and cornucopia of fruits and vegetables, one might survive.

But Thapa wasn't interested in the burgers, he was interested in the four-tier wedding cake sitting on the wheeled table at the back. Thapa had stumbled on the cake when he'd done a thorough inspection of the ship the first day. Atop the cake, were two small figurines. Thapa couldn't help but notice both figurines were women. Maybe someone had goofed.

Thapa pushed the cart holding the cake from the walk-in and toward the elevator opposite District 9. As he pushed the cart— his left foot stepping, dragging, stepping, dragging—into the lobby, he surveyed the winding staircase. It had been blocked off with dozens of the large chairs from the show lounge. He imagined a giant wall of fifty or sixty of the large leather chairs. The pirates would not get to Deck 6 by stairway.

He wondered if they had started to lower the lifeboats. He hoped they were being careful. They were relatively safe from attack or gunfire from below, but one man with a gun on the above decks could lean over the railing and unload a barrage of bullets. But the only people above Deck 6 were Baruti and The Mosquito and the girl. They were at the opposite end from the lifeboats and they were preoccupied. Hopefully.

Thapa pushed the cart through two more rooms, then into the elevator shaft. This would be the elevator's last voyage. The ride should have lasted only a couple seconds, but Thapa had a bit of cake redecorating to do, and it took well over a minute. The elevator door opened for Deck 2, and Thapa inserted a key, shutting all the elevators off.

He pushed the cart into the lobby and started toward Pretoria. As the two pirates sitting in chairs outside the restaurant doors came into view, Thapa gritted his teeth. As much as it hurt, he needed to walk as normal as possible. He couldn't risk one of these guys looking down at his foot, which looked as though it had been dipped in strawberry syrup.

The pirates stood as he approached: one had short, matted, black hair, the other a red bandana.

Thapa smiled and said, "I brought you guys a present."

The two pirates smiled. The one without the bandana took a step forward, dipped his finger into the top tier of icing and stuck it in his mouth.

Thapa hoped the two pirates didn't notice the second tier of the cake was slightly lopsided. He pointed to the spot where it appeared a fist had driven into the cake and said, "I'd stay away from there. I think they might have dropped that part on the floor."

The pirates laughed.

"Why don't you go get your buddies?" said Thapa. "I'll watch over things for a while."

The pirate with the red bandana nodded, pulled Pretoria's large double doors open and walked in. Thapa stared through the doors at the dejected people huddled around the tables. He made an oath to himself that every person in that room would survive.

Thapa walked to the door and peeked inside. There was probably a minute to spare, maybe less. Two pirates were walking in his direction, cutting through the tables. Both looked excited at the promise of cake. A moment later, they strolled past Thapa and joined the other two in their gluttony. The pirate with the bandana was across the room talking to the two pirates on the opposite side. Neither pirate appeared enticed. So either these guys didn't like cake or they were a bit wary of what was going down. *And since everybody likes cake...*

Thapa counted the seconds as the pirate with the bandana wended his way through the tables. Thapa couldn't help but stare at the two large pirates across the room. They would be a problem. But there was no turning back now.

Thapa was starting to get antsy. The clock in his head was down to thirty seconds and the pirate with the bandana was still at the halfway mark of the room. It was going to be a close call. With ten seconds left, the pirate was only steps away. He said, "They no want."

Thapa forced a smile. "More for you."

The pirate nodded, then joined his three buddies whose hands were covered in the thick yellow cake. Thapa began pulling the doors to the restaurant closed. He didn't want any of the hostages to end up with a head or an arm on their table. When the doors were about to close, one of the pirates yelled, "Yo food."

Thapa turned.

The man pointed down with the cake in his hand and said, "Food."

Food? Did he mean the cake?

Thapa looked down. Not *food*. Foot.

All four pirates were looking at his left foot.

"One of your buddies shot me," Thapa said calmly.

The pirates looked at one another.

"But don't worry. He's dead now."

Thapa pulled the doors closed. Then dove to his left. Before he hit the ground, he heard the earsplitting explosion of the timer-grenade. The heavy doors shook as sixty pounds of cake and the bodies of four men were torn to pieces.

ZULU PRISON

10:00 P.M.

GINA PRESSED her ear to the inside of the hut. She could hear the drumming coming from the heart of the village. She could picture the natives dancing, the women's breasts bouncing wildly as they thrashed their bodies to and fro, the men circling around one another, preparing to wrestle.

She wondered if the two boys were there watching the spectacle, or perhaps even taking part.

Gina turned back around. She loosened her arms from around her knees, which she had pulled tightly to her chest, and brought her hand to within an inch of her face. She tried to make out the outline of her fingers, her palm, or even her wrist, but she couldn't. Pitch dark was an understatement. It was as if light simply did not exist.

She'd been able to see for the first few hours. Tiny specks of light poking through an insignificant hole here, a crack there, the faintest of clefts over there. There were five small cots, arranged on one side of the enclosure. Although Gina could neither see nor hear them for they didn't make any noise, she knew there were two men across from her.

Gina wasn't sure if either man was alive. Both were bone

skinny, eyes shut, lying face down. She thought she'd seen the rise and fall of one of their chests, but she wasn't sure. The doctor in her wanted to attend to the men, help them. But both men were covered in oozing sores. Not from AIDS. They had been lashed and the wounds had grown infected. Possibly from sitting in their own feces or from festering bugs.

All of these, of course, accounted for the stench.

It was horrific. A porta-potty baked in the sun for eight months. Gina was lucky she had her vial of Mentholatum with her. And even still, she kept her nose buried under her shirt, and only allowed herself to breathe every so often.

A noise coming from the entrance startled Gina. She couldn't help thinking optimistically they had come to release her, drag her from the village, and tell her not to come back. And she wouldn't. She would get as far away as possible. She did not belong here. What did she think would happen? That these people would look blindly as she invaded their village and took three children. Yes, the village was more of a hospice than a village, but it was still theirs, and they did not know otherwise. She was an intruder. No, the more she thought about it, she would not be released. She would die here.

The noise intensified and Gina realized it was the sound of the enormous boulder being moved.

Soft light shone into the cavernous room. A man poked his head in. He was holding a primitive tray with three bowls. There was the tiniest of candles burning in the center. He set the tray just inside the entrance, then exited. The boulder was rolled back in place.

Gina looked at the two men across from her in the soft light. One man hadn't moved. The other had opened one eye, then quickly closed it. It was almost as if he knew the food wasn't going anywhere. When he wanted it, he would get it. There was no rush.

Gina crawled forward on her hands and knees, until she was

hovering over the bowls of white, oatmeal-like mush. She didn't know how hungry she was, thought she was too scared to be hungry, until she'd seen the food. She hadn't eaten since that morning. She had a couple of energy bars in her daypack, but the men had taken it from her.

She thought about her options. If there were any chance of her escape, she would need her energy. And it wasn't like the food was going to kill her. She had eaten worse things for the past three years in Bolivia. She dipped her finger into the mush, and stuck them in her mouth. It was bland, but not unpleasant.

She crawled back to the edge of the hut and slowly ate the food. Twenty minutes later, the candle flickered, then died.

Gina silently crawled back to the tray and grabbed a second bowl.

USS NEW HAMPSHIRE

"BRING US UP TO PERISCOPE DEPTH."

Royal looked up at the speaker the voice had resonated from, then stared at his brethren sitting against the walls. One by one, they slowly began to climb to their feet. It was go time. There was a knock at the door, and Commander Fuller entered. With no preamble he said, "We're three miles out. I tried to convince the Captain to get us closer so we wouldn't have to use the submersible at all, but this is as close as he's willing to get. He said we should be at depth in three minutes. Then we rock and roll."

And he left. Probably had to make one last phone call. Make sure nothing had changed. Make sure they still had the green light.

Royal slipped the specially-molded plastic earpiece in his left ear, then pulled on his black neoprene mask. He then picked the quarter-inch Kevlar vest off the ground and slipped it over his head. The vest doubled as a life preserver and there were two strings at the bottom which, when pulled simultaneously, would inflate the jacket. The vest tripled as an oxygen tank. A flat tank of compressed air was hidden in the back of the jacket, weighing roughly eight pounds. The digital readout on his left shoulder told him the tank was at 98 percent and held fifty-six minutes of air.

Royal lifted the hose and attached mouthpiece snaking out from the right shoulder of the vest and stuck it in his mouth. He took a deep inhale of the crisp synthetic air. Delicious. He picked up his mask, which he had spent the last hour making sure did not carry a single blemish, and pulled it on, leaving it snug on his forehead.

Now for the good stuff.

He reached into the small backpack and pulled out a plastic box thirteen inches long, eight inches wide, and two inches thick. He entered a twelve-digit digital code and the titanium case popped open. He pulled out the seven-inch dive knife, the blade's silver alloy glistening in the cabin's white light. Just six months earlier, Royal had used the knife to slit the throat of a North Korean scientist, and the blade had glistened in red.

The op hadn't even had a name as it was completely unsanctioned, authorized by one of the highest government officials. Three months earlier, there had been an explosion in a hotel in Istanbul, killing 183 and nearly destroying the seventeen-story structure. The explosive compound used was new, nearly one thousand times more powerful than C-4, and the technology was traced to an underground lab in North Korea. Six had infiltrated the lab, killed the four guards and the fourteen scientists, recovered more than two hundred pounds of what was now being called LDX, and transported it back to the States.

Royal forced himself back to the present, pulling his gun from the case. A SIG SG551 semi-automatic. Jenny. Jenny's magazine held fifteen rounds, and Royal clipped a second magazine to his belt, then slipped Jenny into the holster on his right thigh. Finally he picked up two small flash grenades, each about the size of a Red Bull can, and slipped them into the specialty designed pockets of the vest.

Royal pulled out his small, eight-inch fins and pulled them on.

Lastly, he pulled on a pair of paper-thin, webbed gloves.

He looked up. Each of them had a different routine, none had taken the same ten steps, but all of them finished within the same minute. The door opened and Fuller strode in. He was dressed identically.

He smiled and said, "Go time."

The nine men made their way through the narrow confines of the sub. The officers aboard stopped and stared. Royal thought he saw tinges of jealousy in their smiles.

The plan was to exit the submarine through the escape hatch in the forward torpedo room. Once outside of the sub, the SEALs would use ropes and grips that had been prepared to find their way back to the conning tower—a raised, enclosed, observation tower—and to the Zodiac inflatable boat stored there.

Royal made his way to the cramped room, filled with eight unarmed torpedoes. The men lined up single file. One by one, the men pulled their masks down over their face, chomped down on their regulators, laid down in the escape hatch, arms and legs crossed, and were shot into the ocean.

Human torpedoes.

At the surface, the Zodiac inflated itself in eight seconds, one less than the nine men who clambered aboard. The Zodiac moved across the water, the low hum of the twin 300-horsepower motors propelling the small boat across the ocean at a speed of forty knots, roughly fifty miles an hour. The USS New Hampshire, with its state-of-the-art radar-jamming software, was jamming the *Afrikaans* from three miles away. If the pirates were looking at the radar, the Zodiac wouldn't so much as make a blip.

The tiny Christmas tree that was the *Afrikaans* slowly began to grow, and when it was the size of a quarter, the motor was cut and the Zodiac fell in with the slow ocean current.

The nine men fell backwards off the Zodiac, and the boat deflated.

It would never be seen again.

DECK 7

10:03 P.M.

IT WAS DARK, the lights of the ship just barely able to illuminate the water seventy feet below. I leaned over the railing of Deck 7 and peered down at Deck 6. Lacy and Susie were below me, shouting out instructions as the lifeboat was lowered. Berta and Reen were doing precisely the same on the opposite side of the ship. J.J. and another man were acting as sentries, posted at two strategic places on Deck 6. Both had machines guns, as did I, and I instructed them to shoot anything that moved. And wasn't a hostage. And looked like a pirate.

Speaking of triggers, I looked down at the Uzi held in my right hand. I had shot a machine gun a couple times in Washington with a guy from the force who was a gun nut. We had driven to this remote spot in the woods and unloaded for a couple hours. The thing about machine guns is they're good if you are up against an army—I mean if General Custer had whipped out a couple machine guns there probably wouldn't be a hundred medi-ocre hotdogs stands named after him—but if you are trying to put a couple well placed shots into a pirate's forehead, they weren't exactly ideal. What I'm getting at is I would have preferred a nine-millimeter with a laser scope.

As for Ganju, he said he would take care of the hostages in Pretoria. I wasn't clear how he planned on taking out six pirates by himself, but he'd simply said, "Not to worry." And I wasn't.

And then you had Frank. With Frank's technological prowess and a thirty-second crash course given by Ganju, Frank was the logical choice for the covert mission on Deck 8. It was only a matter of time before the pirates caught on and either started shooting or blowing things up. "Things" being the ship. Frank's objective was to scramble their brains so they could do neither.

I yelled Lacy's name, and she looked up. She said, "Be careful."

I winked at her. "Always."

I held the machine gun out in front of me and started up the walkway. The bridge was located at the foremost tip of the ship, and I hoped it was far enough away from the action that the pirates hadn't heard any of the gunshots. The acoustics of the show lounge were designed to keep sounds in, but essentially the odds of the pirates taking notice were about the same as a neighbor three houses down overhearing a domestic dispute. Then you had the radios. In the three days I'd observed the pirates, I'd only seen them use the radios a handful of times, and I had yet to hear the squawk of Lil Wayne's radio, which was attached to my hip. But they could easily have switched channels if they suspected their communications had been compromised.

That being said, I still felt I had the element of surprise in my corner. But let's just say that when Roy's tiger clamped onto his neck, he was probably more shocked than I'd be if I walked into a trap.

I neared the door to Salon Musa. From my previous stay—which felt like a month earlier, but in actuality was just over a day and half—I knew there was a walkway inside that ultimately led to the bridge. I'd seen the door. But the odds of the door being unlocked were slim. That meant my best bet was to stay outside and try the door that led directly to the bridge. There was also the possibility of climbing out on the glass dome of the bridge and shooting my way in. I'd penciled this in as *last resort.*

I stayed in the shadows just outside the reaches of the lights. I could see the slanting glass dome that designated the front of the ship. I inched closer. The white noise of the vessel and the ocean, a low hum under a gentle splashing, was the only sound. If Lacy or Susie was still shouting commands, they were either carried away by the soft wind or simply too far away to be heard. I hoped they had at least one of the lifeboats already in the water. I couldn't risk waiting too much longer, but I wanted my sister and the other hostages to have a head start before the shooting began.

The lights of the bridge came into view, sharp and white. The dome glowed white against the blackness of the night. I bypassed the door to the radio room. I peered through the small window. No one. I thought about darting in real quick and trying to relay a message, but I knew this was foolish. The hostages aboard the *Afrikaans* weren't a secret. I'm sure the entire world was following every second of the story. If they only knew what was really going on.

I took three more steps. I could see the door to the bridge. Two more steps. I could see into the room through the small window. Metallic controls and gadgets. No pirates. But then again, they wouldn't be standing near the controls. Would they? One more step. Keeping my head down, I reached out my left hand and grasped the doorknob. Ever so slowly I turned it. The door was unlocked. I pulled back my hand.

Just then the radio squawked, followed by frantic African. I didn't understand the words, but I didn't have to. The jig was up.

I had to go.

Now.

I turned the knob on the door, ripped it open, and burst into the room. My finger itched the trigger of the Uzi. In the center of the room sat a metal chair. It was covered in droplets of dried blood. This is where Rikki had sat. I was too late. I let out a deep exhale. But the room was empty. At least I thought it was. There was someone in the Captain's chair: Baxter.

He was on his back, sawing logs.

"Dude," I said.

I flicked him and he woke up. He smiled at me and started licking my hand. On the table next to him was a laptop. The screensaver was on and I hit the mouse pad. The screen refreshed.

There was a large red missile on-screen. I read the blurb underneath.

An ATMIP, Russian made Aviation Thermobaric Missile of Increased Power, is the most powerful non-nuclear weapon in the world and openly referred to as "The Father of all Missiles." The missile, which does its destruction by shock wave and extremely high temperatures, has a blast radius of a half mile and will kill everything within two. Laser-guided or beacon-guided, it has an operational range of two thousand miles, is capable of supersonic speed, and is delivered by a portable VLT, Vertical Launch Tube.

"Fuck."

Baxter started barking. I looked at him, then turned and looked out the large glass dome. The Warlord was glaring at me through the glass, his automatic rifle pointed directly at me. I grabbed Baxter and dove to the floor as the sound of gunfire erupted. The dome shattered, sending a couple thousand pounds of glass raining down on me. As I covered my head, a hundred bees stung me as the small shards of glass embedded in my skin

The gunfire ceased. There was a thump as the Warlord jumped down, then the crunch of glass as he walked over to me. Something sharp pinched the side of my neck and I knew this wasn't glass, but the tip of the Warlord's machete.

I slowly opened my eyes.

The Warlord was holding a radio in his right hand. He lifted it to his lips and began speaking. There was no mistaking it was the same voice I'd heard just seconds earlier.

Only one word was spoken. Only one word need be.

"Gotcha."

PRETORIA

10:07 P.M.

"GOTCHA," came the voice through the radio held in the pirate's left hand. In his right hand, the pirate held a pistol. The pistol was pressed to Thapa's forehead.

After the explosion, Thapa had scrambled to his feet, as had all two hundred of the hostages in the room. It was chaos. Thapa tried to locate the two pirates across the way through the scattering of people. Then he saw one of them. Huddled against the door, pulling his radio up.

Thapa clambered up onto the closest table and unloaded three shots across the room. The pirate slumped against the wall, the radio crashing to the soft carpet floor. Thapa's gunshots silenced the hostages, and Thapa scanned the large room for the second pirate. He saw him nowhere.

Thapa heard a loud crash, and the double doors burst open. The doors were covered in orange goop, a combination of the yellow cake and blood. The goop dripped down the sides of the door to the floor. Through the doors, Thapa could see the wreckage left by the grenade. The table the cake had been sitting on had been turned to confetti, as had three of the pirates. But somehow the pirate with the red bandana had survived, the red bandana clinging to what was left of his head. His face was almost gone and his right arm was a nub, but he was alive. He was covered in the same orange goo. He stood in the doorway, wobbling, trying to remain on his feet. His tongue dangled from his mouth, and he emitted a ghastly noise, a whimpering.

He didn't appear to be much of a threat. Thapa pointed his gun at the man's forehead and was set to put the man out of his misery when the table beneath Thapa was heaved upward. The other pirate had crawled from the opposite door, darting from table to table underneath the cover of the many hostages. When Thapa had turned his attention to the zombie-pirate at the door, the other pirate had made his move, crawling under the table Thapa was standing on, then heaving it upward.

Thapa fell backward. As he fell to the ground, he felt a shooting pain in his side. Immediately, Thapa knew what happened. The knife on his waist had turned during the fall and punctured his side. He moved his hand across his lower abdomen, coloring it a deep crimson.

Thapa watched out of the corner of his eye as the pirate walked over and picked Thapa's gun from the floor. The pirate walked over to his comrade, who was still in the walkway, but had fallen to his knees, and put a bullet through the man's heart.

Thapa was struggling to his knees when he felt the icy cold barrel of a gun pressed to the side of his head. Thapa was sure the man was about to pull the trigger when the radio on his side had erupted in frantic African. The pirate walked in front of Thapa, pulled the radio up, and held it to his ear. Then there had been a silence, followed by the single word, "Gotcha."

The pirate smiled, and Thapa knew Thomas' mission had also failed. The pirate had alerted his superiors of the uprising, and Baruti and The Mosquito had taken action. They had played some sort of trick, enticing Thomas to act, and it had apparently worked.

"You kild my brodders!" the pirate screamed at Thapa. "Now it is yo turn."

Thapa wanted to picture himself holding his wife and his son in his arms when the bullet came. But as he was set to close his eyes, a bright light moved over his left pupil. He blinked, then opened his eyes. Directly in front of him on the pirate's leg, there was a glowing red dot. Thapa recognized it immediately and said, "Look."

The pirate looked down at his leg and saw the red dot. His eyebrows rose. Thapa watched as the red dot moved up the pirate's leg, up his stomach, crawled up his neck, and settled between his eyes. Then the red dot turned into a small black hole.

DECK 2

2209 HOURS

ROYAL LOWERED HIS GUN, stood from his kneeling position, and gingerly stepped over the cake-covered limbs.

The half-mile swim had taken approximately seven minutes. They had reached the hull at exactly 2203 hours. Each SEAL had silently removed the suction plungers that were affixed to their fins and began the methodical climb up the forty feet to the lowest deck.

Four of the SEALs—Royal, Pollock, Deeter, and Sanchez—pulled themselves over the edge of Deck 2. The other four would continue up to Deck 6, where hostages could be seen lowering a lifeboat into the water.

Royal and the other three silently pulled their masks up and slipped their laser scoped SIGs from their holsters. Royal pushed his finger to his ear and said, "Landed. Beginning Sweep."

According to the layout of the ship, the largest single room was a restaurant on Deck 2, Pretoria, and it would be the most logical place to hold a large majority, if not all, of the hostages. Royal held up two fingers behind him and Deeter and Sanchez silently disappeared. They would go around and approach from the opposite side.

Pollock pulled open the heavy metal door leading to the interior of the ship and Royal darted through, scanned for enemy targets, then waved Pollock in. They moved through a series of walkways, which led to the officer's quarters. They peeked into a couple rooms, but saw no one.

They passed a room marked "Medical," then moved into a foyer that would lead to the restaurant. Royal peered around a corner, and his eyes took in the site. Body parts were scattered everywhere. A mess of blood and limbs. Two doors where partially open. Between the two doors, two men were visible. One man was on his knees. The other man was standing over him, pressing a gun to the man's forehead.

Royal didn't even think. In the time it takes to swallow, he planted his left knee, stabilized his right leg, pulled the gun up with two hands, tilted his head to the left, and closed his right eye. He didn't need the laser scope, but it didn't hurt. He moved the red dot up the black man's body, settled it right between his eyes, and pulled the trigger.

OBSERVATION DECK
10:11 P.M.

EACH TIME I would slow down, the tip of the blade would push into the small of my back. I took a couple steps forward, then stopped. I reached my right hand over my left shoulder and tried to find the alien presence that was causing me so much agony. The blade pressed into my back, but the pain barely registered compared to the throbbing emanating from my left shoulder blade. My fingers combed the area, then stopped when they hit the jagged piece of glass. I pinched the glass with my thumb and forefinger. It didn't budge. My eyes began to water as I wiggled the glass back and forth, loosening it in the skin, then slowly pulled it out.

"Wak."

I took a couple more steps and inspected the quarter-inch thick, half-inch long shared of glass that was one of many embedded in my flesh. I shook my head and tossed the glass over the side of the ship.

The Warlord marched me forward until I had eclipsed the bridge's shattered dome. I could see three people standing on the nose of the ship where there was a small observation deck. Illuminated by the bridge's lights were the Professor, Bheka, and Rikki.

Rikki looked like she'd been through war. Her shorts were torn and covered in droplets of blood. Her shirt was gone and she had her arms crossed, covering her breasts. Tears dripped down her cheeks as she watched me hobble toward her. And Bheka. His body was rigid, his face tensed, as he white-knuckled the railing in front of him. I think he was more frightened of being on the edge of a seventy-foot plummet than of the man holding the gun next to him.

The Warlord joined the Professor. He slipped the machete back into its sheath, then pulled a pistol from the small of his back and pointed it at my chest. He motioned me to put my hands on my head.

I did.

The Professor appraised me, then asked, "Are you the one I need to thank for this rebellion?"

"Rebellion?" I scoffed. "This isn't apartheid. We are merely trying to survive. Wouldn't you be doing the same if the tables were turned?"

He appeared to be deep in thought. Then he said, "What makes you think I ever had the intention of hurting anyone?"

"Oh, I don't know. Maybe because you killed the captain and all his officers in cold blood."

He smiled.

I added, "And maybe because you plan on blowing up the ship. None of us were meant to survive."

"That may be."

I looked down at my watch. I had a minute and a half I needed to stall. I asked, "Did you get the money?"

He looked at Rikki, then turned to me and said, "Unfortunately, we were only able to get some of the money. I had plans to get the rest, but it appears that is no longer an option. Anyhow, a billion dollars can do a lot of good."

"Did you just say 'a billion dollars'?"

"Yes."

"And that was only *some* of the money?"

"Yes. A down payment. Tomorrow morning, I was to put this young lady on a raft with a radio, and her father was going to transfer the remaining funds." He added, "But now…"

This of course meant he had intended on letting her live, *but now* he didn't.

I peered at both Rikki and Bheka. I willed them to jump overboard, take two steps backwards and simply fall over the railing and into the ocean. At least one of the lifeboats had to be in the water by now. They might survive.

"How do you know my mother?"

The Professor gazed at Rikki, and asked, "Why do you ask?"

"I'm not buying that you found me by accident. Either Track is behind this or my mother. And I doubt it was Track."

"I met your mother while living in exile," he said. "One night, after too much vodka, she began to open up. About you and about your father. From there, the plan started to take shape."

"She could no longer milk the well that was my father, so she had to find another way to hit it big. I guess I was the answer."

"Yes. You were."

"How much are you giving her?"

"A million dollars."

Rikki wrinkled her nose, deep in thought, but remained quiet.

"How do you plan on getting away?" I asked.

The Professor and the Warlord looked at each other. Determining that me knowing of his getaway plan when I had little time left on this Earth was of little consequence, the Professor said, "Over the last couple months, my good friend Keli and I have been doing a lot of scuba diving. When the ship explodes tomorrow, we will be miles away. I have another friend in the South African Navy, who for the small price of one million dollars, has agreed to pick the two of us up. It will be easy."

It sounded easy. And I probably would have done it just the same. I was curious about something the Professor had said earlier and asked, "What did you mean by one billion dollars can do a whole lot of good?"

"Well, not a billion. Keli here gets a big share, and a couple other people, but what's left will still be a small fortune. And by good, I mean, I will be able to help many of my countrymen."

"You mean this whole AIDS things was legit?"

He looked at Keli. I thought I saw him smile. "I have devoted the last twenty years of my life to the AIDS epidemic that is destroying South Africa. You have no idea how many of my Zulu brothers and sisters have been stolen by this disease. And the children. The orphans. Millions of them. And half of these orphans are infected with the disease. It is a never-ending cycle. We need to start over."

I wasn't exactly sure what he was getting at. "What do you mean 'start over'?"

"There are too many sick. Even with the best treatment, my countrymen will continue to spread this disease. And the numbers will not decrease as people think. They will continue to get worse. Think of the plague. It killed millions of people, so many in fact, that it wiped itself out. There was no longer anyone alive who could pass the disease along. But with AIDS, it takes so long to kill, we will never get rid of it."

I was starting to see where this was going. I stuck my hands in my pockets. It seemed like a good time to do it. Before either of them could yell at me to put my hands back up, I said, "So you plan to do God's work for him."

He nodded. "Nearly a quarter million of my countrymen—men, women, and children infected with AIDS—have converged in one spot."

"And let me guess. You are going to kill every last one of them."

"Think of all the lives I will be saving. Each of these people would have passed the disease to countless others. By killing these quarter million, I will be saving possibly tens of millions."

I imagined a square mile of sick Africans who had been promised medicine and would be vaporized instead. "You're sick."

"Misunderstood."

"Who did you get the missile from? China? Russia?"

"No matter, it cost a quarter of a billion dollars. And as we speak, there is a beacon broadcasting a silent signal from the small village."

"Beacon?"

"Yes. An electronic device that pinpoints exactly where the missile will detonate."

"Let me guess, this is happening at noon tomorrow."

He looked impressed. "Four hundred hostages killed aboard a cruise ship, another quarter million vaporized in a small village. Who is going to be searching ships looking for stowaways?"

I couldn't help myself and said, "For everyone who you plan on killing, I just want to say, fuck you."

I looked down at my watch. Five seconds.

I slowly pulled my hands from my pockets and put them back on my head. I positioned the foam in my fingers. I could see the Warlord staring at my hands, trying to figure out what I was doing. I moved my fingers down to my ears and shoved in the specialty-designed earplugs Ganju had handed out to everyone before we'd left the show lounge.

The Warlord began screaming at me, but I couldn't hear him. Then he buckled over, his hands clapping to his ears. The Professor, Rikki, and Bheka did the same.

Frank had come through. Positioned at the bow of Deck 8, was an anti-attack device called an LRAD. A Long Range Acoustic Device. It had been Ganju's idea. He knew the chances of my taking out the pirates by myself were slim. So he'd brought everyone earplugs and given Frank a half-minute instruction on how to use the device. It sounded simple enough. Point the LRAD where you want the sound waves to go and everyone within the line of sight will be crippled. And everyone within a hundred feet of the sound waves wouldn't be able to hear for a week. Maybe two.

Even with the earplugs, my head ached. It felt as though I was standing with my ear to the speaker at a Rage Against the Machine concert. As for the Professor, the Warlord, Rikki, and Bheka, all four were now on the ground, hands clapped over their ears, writhing on their backs.

I ran forward and picked up both Bheka and Rikki in my arms. They should have been heavy, but they weren't. "Heavy" wasn't in my vocabulary at that moment in time. I jumped off the nose of the ship and lugged both their squirming bodies to the walkway on Deck 7. I pulled four of the earplugs from my pocket. I pried Rikki's left hand from her ear and crammed in one of the earplugs, then another. Then I did the same with Bheka. Both looked dazed, like they had been struck with lightning, but both were able to walk. I yelled as loud as I could, "Take Bheka and go by the hot tubs. Wait there."

Nodding that she understood, she took Bheka by the hand, and both hobbled forward.

I should have gone with them. But first I had two people I needed to kill.

I climbed back onto the nose of the ship, both men still on their backs. The Warlord, *Keli*, had thrown his gun, and it was twenty feet to my right. I calmly walked over and bent down. I noticed movement in my peripheral and turned. The Warlord had somehow made it to his knees. He had one hand clamped down on his left ear. With his right hand he reached down and pulled the machete off his back. Then without hesitation, he placed the blade behind his ear. His bloody right ear fell to the ground. Then his left.

I was too stunned to move.

Did this crazy fuck just cut his ears off?

The Warlord stood, blood dripping down the sides of his face, running together on the bottom of his chin. He charged toward me. I reached out for the gun, but somehow ended up knocking it three feet further. I dove for the gun, wrapped my hand around it, but out of the corner of my eye, I could feel the Warlord reach me. I could almost see the glimmer of the machete as it came down on the back of my neck.

I closed my eyes.

The blow never came.

Just silence.

I opened my eyes. The machete was lying two inches from my face, its proud owner next to it, lying at an awkward angle, an enormous hole where his left eye once was.

Someone was standing over me. I looked up. It was Ganju.

The gun that was in his hand silently fell to the ground. I watched as he staggered to where the Professor lay writhing on the ground. Ganju knelt next to him and I watched as he dug his hand down the man's shirt and tugged. I was waiting for Ganju to shoot him, but he didn't. He hobbled back to me and fell to the ground. He held his stomach with his hands. I knew that beneath that bloody shirt was something awful. Something beyond imagination. And something beyond medical help.

I sat up and knelt next to him.

His eyes were closed.

He thrust his hand out. In it were a silver necklace with a small electronic capsule and a small piece of paper. He said, "The account information."

I took both items and shoved them down into my pocket.

I held the small man in my arms as he struggled to breathe. He began to cough. Blood spilled down his chin. His small body convulsed. He was dying. He whispered, "Tell them I love them."

Then he went still.

I let out a long exhale. And I would have maybe said a prayer and given the little brown man the proper thanks for saving my life had the Professor not been struggling to his feet. In all the commotion, I hadn't noticed the LRAD had been shut off. Either

Frank thought he'd turned it on long enough, or someone had made him turn it off. The Professor held Ganju's gun.

I dove over Ganju and rolled off the nose of the ship, falling five feet to the walkway. A bullet whizzed by my head as I ran past the wall that separated the bridge from the nose.

I ripped the earplugs from my ears and threw them. Two more gunshots erupted. There was a loud clump as the Professor jumped down. I probably had a twenty-foot lead on him. I rounded past Salon Musa and into the expansive deck splitting the pool and the hot tubs. Across the way, Rikki and Bheka stood against the opposite railing, both staring at me at wide-eyed. Rikki was holding something gray. Baxter.

"Jump!"

Neither moved. Both probably still had their earplugs in and they wouldn't be able to read my lips from thirty yards.

"Jump!"

I could hear the loud steps of the Professor start on the deck. The sight of the man holding the large gun prompted Rikki and Bheka to start clambering up the railing. Another bullet whizzed by my head. I saw the sparks as it clipped the railing just a couple feet from where Rikki was climbing up.

When I was ten yards away, Rikki jumped.

But Bheka didn't.

He looked back at me. Tears ran down his cheeks.

"JUMMMMMMMMMMMP!"

Another gunshot. Wayward. The Professor was having trouble aiming and running.

I was two strides from the railing, and Bheka was as still as a gargoyle on the edge of a Paris hotel. I leaped into the air, wrapped my arms around his small body, and the two of us plummeted to the ocean seventy feet below.

ROYAL AND POLLOCK had walked into the restaurant and found nearly 200 hostages, primarily crew members, huddled beneath the many round tables. A small brown man, the man Royal's pinpointed bullet had saved, rose to his feet. He was holding his stomach. Royal knew the man before him was in the process of dying.

Without preamble, or even a simple thank you, the small man shouted, "There is a duffel bag filled with plastic explosives and rigged to go off at noon tomorrow!"

"How much plastic?" Pollock asked,

The small man said sedately, "Enough to blow up a ship three times this size."

Pollock whistled.

"Where?" asked Royal.

Ganju took a deep breath, then said in a shallow whisper, "I have to show you."

He started out the door. Royal told Pollock to get the hostages to Deck 6 where they could be lowered into lifeboats, then followed the hobbling brown man.

They entered into the elevator shaft, which Royal noticed was dark. Almost as if it weren't working. The tiny man inserted a key and the elevator light flickered on. The man pressed Deck 5 and the elevator doors closed. Neither man said a word. The doors opened and the small man spoke, the words hardly audible, "Go through that lobby and you will find the computer center. The bomb is in the closet."

Royal asked, "Aren't you coming with?"

The man shook his head and hit the button for Deck 7. He said, "No. There's still something I need to do." He held out his hand and said, "Give me your gun."

Royal looked down at the gun in his hand. It was the way the man said it. There was no way Royal could have refused. He handed over Jenny, stepped from the elevator, and watched as the doors closed.

That had been three minutes ago.

Royal watched as the numbers on the iPhone resting on the duffel bag ticked down from 13:38:42 all the way to 13:37:07.

He still couldn't believe his eyes.

"STOP SQUIRMING."

I looked up at Lacy with daggers in my eyes. I said, "That's easy for you to say, you didn't just pour saltwater into a thousand gashes on your body."

If the salty Indian Ocean finding its way into sixty different places on my body in the way of sulfuric acid was bad enough, Bheka and I had turned over in the air, and I had done a seventy-foot back flop. I more or less cushioned Bheka's fall, but it was going to take a team of chiropractors to fix what was left of my spine.

We hadn't been in the water long, maybe two minutes, before Rikki, Bheka, and myself were pulled aboard a lifeboat. At seeing Baxter in Rikki's arms, Lacy had screamed, then began to cry. And Baxter, he was so excited to see his mom that he'd now gone 12 minutes without falling asleep. A new personal record.

Everyone had made it safely aboard. Amongst forty others were J.J., Susie, Frank, Trinity, Walter, Marge, Berta, and Reen. Even Gilroy had made it and was still conscious. How much blood did that guy have in his body? He probably kept half of it in his dick, which accounted for his still breathing.

Lacy, Rikki, and Susie had been doctoring me for the better part of ten minutes. Picking the pieces of glass from my body, then wiping away the saltwater with shirts dipped in bottled water. I no longer felt like I'd been stung by a thousand angry wasps. Now it was more like fire ants.

Susie and Lacy recounted how they'd lowered the lifeboats in the water, how they'd made everyone put in their earplugs, and how the sound had been nearly unbearable. The most intriguing detail was the sudden appearance of four men in black suits after the second lifeboat had been lowered: Navy SEALs. At this, Frank looked at me, and I even allowed myself a smile.

They had come after all.

Presently, we were about a half-mile away from the *Afrikaans* and we had a commanding view of the last lifeboat being lowered into the rolling surf. I scanned the boat and noticed most people were euphoric. They had stared death in the face and survived. Yet, most of them had no idea how close they'd come to dying.

I was happy for these people. For them, it was over. But not for me. Not by a long shot.

There were still a quarter of a million people in a village somewhere who were going to get vaporized sometime tomorrow if I didn't alert the proper channels. Now, it wasn't as though I knew any of these people. To me, they were simply sick Africans, but to one person in this lifeboat, they were anything but.

As Bheka and I had surfaced from our plummet, the small boy had clung to my neck as I trod water and waited for the approaching lifeboat. His face was wet. But not from the ocean. Large tears were running down his cheeks.

"It's okay, little man," I'd said softly. "It's over."

He'd shook his head. "What that man said," he'd said, sniffling. "All those sick people. How they're going to be killed."

"Yeah. What about them?"

He'd stared at me. Broken. Unable to say the words. And then it hit me. His mom. That's why she'd gotten off at the last port of call. She'd heard about the village where help was headed.

"Is your mom sick?" I'd asked

He'd nodded.

Now, as the women tended to me, Bheka sat on my lap. And as the two of us watched the eighth and final lifeboat touch the water, I knew he was thinking about his mom, wishing she was on this boat.

I patted Bheka's leg and promised him that his mom would be okay. A promise I intended to keep.

Then I began thinking about the Professor. I was curious if the SEALs had stumbled across him and filled him with bullets. Or even better, slit his throat. But I would know soon enough. The SEALs, or maybe the Navy, would need to debrief us. Then I could tell them about the village.

But for now, I was going to allow myself a moment of satisfaction. The last lifeboat was five feet from the water. The last of the hostages were seconds away from being free. The second the lifeboat touched the water, it was New Year's Eve. Everyone started clapping, kissing, hugging.

The celebration was shattered by the loudest sound I'd ever heard. The fireball that was once the *Afrikaans* lit up the night sky, a white sun on the dark horizon.

Susie and Lacy said it simultaneously.

Oh, dear God.

THE DOOR OPENED and Roger Garret's daughter-in-law smiled. After they embraced, she said, "He's holed up in his den."

Roger laughed and said, "I thought that might be the case."

After a second's pause, Betsy Garret, asked, "Is Paul's career over?"

"In Washington? Probably."

Betsy nodded.

"But I don't think Paul was cut out for the White House. All the bullshit. The lies. Pulling the sheets over everyone's eyes. That's not him." He almost added, "The opposite of his old man."

"No, it's not."

Roger pulled Betsy to him once more and said, "Don't worry. You guys will be fine. I've already had five people call me with job offers for Paul. Job offers that pay triple what he's making right now."

"Really?"

"Really."

Roger stepped into the foyer and asked, "Where are the kiddos?"

Betsy informed him that his grandkids were out playing, and after a quick rundown on how both were doing and promises for the zoo the following weekend, Roger excused himself and made his way to his son's den. He didn't knock. He opened the door and strode into the beautiful wood-paneled room.

His son was sitting behind his desk, a large snifter of scotch held in his right hand. Paul appraised his father, then laughed. "I wasn't expecting you this soon."

"I have to make sure my baby boy is okay."

Paul shook his head with a smile. Then he stood, walked over to the wet bar, and poured his dad a gin gimlet. He walked around the desk and handed the glass to his father.

"That was quite a show you put on," said Roger, fighting back a smirk.

Paul puffed out his cheeks and raised his eyebrows.

"Reminded me of Lou Piniella in his prime."

Both men laughed.

"It was only a matter of time," Roger said, with a shake of his head. "I'm surprised it took you this long."

Paul took a sip of scotch and swished it around. His father had told him countless times that he didn't have the personality for politics. He cared too much. "Yeah."

Roger told him about the job offers. One job in particular was for Paul to be the new face of US Steel. It would pay seven figures.

"No shit."

After a lengthy pause, Roger said, "But that's not why I'm here."

They stared at each other in silence. Finally Roger said, "The ship exploded."

Paul cut his eyes at him. "How many dead?"

"The last lifeboat was being lowered when it exploded. So however many that holds. Fifty from what they tell me. Plus an entire team of SEALs."

Paul let out a deep exhale. "What about the pirates?"

"Apparently, all the pirates are dead."

"Do you know anymore?"

"Nope. All the passengers are being transported to Durban as we speak by the South African Navy. We'll track down the passengers within the next couple days and get the story."

"What about Gina and all the Africans in that village? I haven't heard from her in nearly a day."

"Nothing we can do. The South African Army isn't letting anybody else in. Soon enough the Africans will up and leave. And Gina, she'll be okay."

Paul walked over to the bar and poured himself another couple fingers of scotch. He turned to his father and said, "Has the press got wind of it yet?"

"Not yet. But it's only a matter of time."

Paul nodded. It was always just a matter of time. For the first time he wondered who his replacement would be. Of course, there was a chance he hadn't lost his job, but he didn't want his job. He had publicly resigned on live television.

His father took up a chair in the far corner, and Paul took the chair next to him.

They were silent for a while.

Finally Paul said, "Tell me something, dad."

"What?"

"If you could do it all over, would you have played it all the same?"

Roger took a sip of his drink, rattled around the ice cubes. "I guess it's always natural to second-guess your decisions. If you're asking would I go back and cave to the pirate's demands? Would I send medicine for all those people and hope they gave up the hostages unharmed? Maybe those fifty hostages would still be alive. Maybe that team of SEALs would survive to see another mission."

Paul smiled. "You didn't answer my question."

Roger finished off the last of his gin, stood and walked to the doorway. He thought about everything that had led to this moment. He turned, stared down at his only son, and said, "If I could go back and do it all over, I would do it exactly the same."

DAY 4

DURBAN NAVAL BASE

RIKKI, Bheka, J.J., Lacy, and I had been sitting in a locked room for the past three hours.

By the time the SAS *Isandlwana*—a South African Navy warship—had loaded all the passengers from all seven lifeboats, what was left of the *Afrikaans* was comfortably asleep on the ocean floor. Everyone was in a state of shock, including myself. Though there were times during the ordeal when things looked grim, I never imagined that people would actually lose their lives. Yes, I know the Captain and his officers had been murdered in cold blood, and I know Gilroy was in the process of dying, and I'd always known there was a good chance I would get myself killed playing Batman, but the other 370, the inconsequentials, I'd always figured they would make it out okay.

But fifty of them hadn't.

As for Gilroy, he was airlifted from the ship to King Edward VIII hospital in Durban, which I hoped had better surgeons than it had a naming board. Trinity was so shaken that Susie and Frank had accompanied her on the helicopter. We promised to meet them at the hospital as soon as we could.

Meanwhile, after scouring the ship to make sure Mika was

okay (he was), I spent the two hours it took to reach shore trying to get someone to take me seriously about the impending genocide of a quarter-million sick Africans. I was repeatedly told that the South African Army had had a presence in *Ptutsi* for the past 36 hours and that it was most assuredly safe from attack. Yes, but *not* from a huge fucking missile. After being laughed at by several officers, then nearly getting in a fist fight with two officers who refused to let me see their commander, then being handcuffed when I tried to make my way to the bridge of the ship, I gave up.

Currently, the five of us were in a small briefing room. When the warship docked, a kaleidoscope of media lights could be seen on the outskirts of the naval base a half-mile inland. The five of us were the first off the ship, and once the handcuffs were removed, we were ushered through the gray stucco naval base and to a room with four walls and no windows. On his departure, the officer promised that we would be heard *momentarily*, which he was obviously confusing with *not for a really long time*. Over the course of the last hour, I'd purged everything Baruti had told me to the others, and the collective theory was that someone was going out of their way to make sure we were not heard.

Twenty minutes ago, Lacy had banged on the locked door and said that she had to pee. I was beginning to worry when the door was ripped open and Lacy stuck her head in. "Let's go," she yelled.

The four of us popped up from our seats and made our way to the door. Lacy was holding keys in her hand. Keys the guard had held twenty minutes ago. "How did you get those?" I asked.

"I told him to come into the bathroom with me. Then I let him play with Queen Latifah and Amelia Earhart for a couple seconds, then I handcuffed him to the toilet."

I couldn't stop laughing.

"Who are Queen Latifah and Amelia Earhart?" asked Rikki.

"My boobs," she confessed. "Now let's go."

The five of us began a slow trot down a long gray corridor. "Where are we going?" I asked.

"We're going to that village, stupid. We're gonna save all those people."

Oh.

"We need a car," I said.

"How about a bus?"

Idling perpendicular to the walkway was a compact bus. Army green with SAN stenciled in white on the side.

"Do I even want to know how you got the keys to this?"

Lacy looked down at the ground in mock shame and said, "No, you do not."

This made me laugh.

I composed myself, looked at Rikki, Bheka, and J.J. and said, "You guys don't have to come."

"My mom is there," said Bheka sprinting onto the bus.

"I'm bloody well not staying here," spat Rikki and followed suit.

J.J. just shrugged and said, "Why not?"

That's the spirit.

I shook off my grin, ran up the steps and sat behind the wheel. I was good with a stick shift and rammed it into first, then did a tight U-turn in the lot, testing the laws of physics. Lacy ran up from the third seat back and said, "Don't forget this," and slapped the little hat her boyfriend had been wearing on my head. I told the four of them to duck and started making my way through the labyrinth of side streets. Because of the media, there was increased security, officers everywhere, but they seemed overly concerned with who was coming in and not at all concerned about who was going out. We were stopped at the exit to the base and the guard asked, "Where are you going?"

"Gotta get this boy cleaned up and ready to transport some of the hostages. Matthews will have my ass if I don't get back in a snap." I may have done an Australian accent.

He looked at me like the idiot I was, then raised the gate to let me pass.

Three minutes later, the media vans were a mile back and I was taking a left turn at a stoplight.

"Alright, all clear. First one to find a map wins a South African Navy hat."

No one found a map, so I kept the hat on.

We had to stop at a gas station and since we didn't have any money, I told Bheka to steal a map. He did. He handed it to Lacy, and back on the road, I said, "Patootsi."

"How do you spell it?"

"I don't know. P-A-T-U-T-Z-E." I added, "Triple word score on the z. And I used all my letters. That's gotta be worth like ninety points."

"I challenge."

"You always challenge."

"Cause you always make up words."

"You're being qzivkpl again."

She ignored me. "God, there are like a million small villages . . . Oh wait, here it is. Ptutsi."

"How far?"

"Give me a second."

I could see her measuring the scale with her fingers, then plotting them along the path from Durban to the village. "About three hundred and fifty kilometers."

I looked at the dash, I was going 55 kilometers an hour. That would put us there in seven hours. The clock on the dash of the bus read 5:54 a.m. We'd be too late.

"Take this right," Lacy directed. "Then stay on this road for two hundred kilometers."

I took a right onto the two-lane road and punched down the gas.

We had six hours to save 250,000 lives.

ZULU PRISON

9:19 A.M.

WHERE WAS SHE?

Gina lifted her head and wiped the sleep from her eyes. The stench hit her and it all came flooding back.

I am being held prisoner in a small hut, in a remote village in South Africa that is home to the most prolific AIDS death rate in the history of the world and is currently surrounded by a couple hundred thousand Africans who have made the pilgrimage to the village in the hope of receiving life-saving medication.

She shook her head. If she survived this mess, she had better get a book deal.

The stench crawled down Gina's throat as she squirmed to get the tube of menthol out of her front pocket. She pulled it out, put two large dabs under each nostril, then coated her chest. She took a deep breath. She could still taste the smell of the hut, but the menthol made breathing possible.

She peered around the small room. The men looked the same. Both in the exact same positions they'd been when the candle had fizzled. Their wounds were ghastly. Long, deep slashes of red. Bubbled up, green in some cases, purple in others. The men, if not dead already, and she was positive one of the men was in fact dead, would die from the infections within the week.

Gina moved her gaze to the tray at center. There was one bowl left on the tray. Gina stared at the two bowls next to her. She picked them up and silently crawled to the tray and set them down. Her eyes moved over the third bowl. It was empty. She looked at the man stretched out on his stomach. At one point, the man had gotten up, quickly eaten his food, then retired back to his cot.

The thought of the man moving around while Gina had slept sent shivers up her spine. What if he had touched her? What if she had awaken to the man on top of her?

Her stomach flipped just thinking about it.

She shook off the image and stood. The lighting was the best it'd been since she'd been thrown into the small prison and she started to look for weak spots in the thatching. Obviously, if light was getting in, then there were places where the thatching wasn't flush. And how strong could it be? There had to be a way out.

She began prying the thatching apart. But underneath the six inches of sticks, there was a thick layer of something else. Hardened mud or clay. Gina tried to punch through it several times. It didn't give. It might as well have been brick.

She moved to the entrance and stroked the large boulder filling the small entrance. The boulder was smooth. From the curvature of the three feet that she could see, she knew the boulder was enormous. Probably five or six feet in diameter. She put her hands against the warm rock, dug her feet into the dirt, and tried to move it. It didn't budge.

Gina let out a deep sigh.

She made her way to one of the cots and stared down at the wooded legs. They were stakes an inch thick. She rolled one of the cots on its side, careful not to make too much noise, and began prying one of the legs off. She wasn't sure if the guard would bring food again, so she turned the cot back over, and got it to balance on three legs.

She looked down at the wooden stake in her hands. Gina was quite certain she could do some damage with it. Maybe even knock the guard unconscious. But that was her backup plan.

She walked to the side of the hut. She looked over her shoulder at the entrance, making doubly sure the rock wasn't about to be moved, then thrust the stake into the side of the hut. There was a soft thud. Gina stopped. It had been a bit louder than she'd expected. She watched the entrance for a long minute, waiting for the rock to move.

It didn't.

She went to work. After ten minutes, tiny pieces of the clay-like material began to crumble off. After twenty minutes, a nickel sized piece chipped off and the sun shone through. Gina smiled. She covered the hole with the thatch. It disappeared. It would take her the better part of the afternoon, but she was certain she could make a big enough hole to crawl through. And the hole was on the back of the hut, so hopefully it would go unnoticed.

And then tonight, when the drums started back up, she would go.

She pulled back another section of thatching. Something caught her eye. It was black, about the size of a roll of nickels, with a flashing red light at the center. Gina plucked it from the thatching and surveyed it.

It was some sort of electronic device. But why here? And how?

The scraping of the rock filled the room.

Gina shoved the device back, then quickly began to move the thatching so it looked untouched. Gina stared at the entrance. The rock was only halfway moved. It was going much slower. Almost as if only one of the men were moving it. If it was only one of them, then she could smack him on the head and run. Or should she just wait for the night? Her heart was pounding. She thought about where the hut sat. If she hit the guy and ran, all she had to do was climb over the fence, then she could run up the hill and join the thousands camped out.

She made up her mind.

She darted near the entrance, gripped the stake in her right hand, and pressed her back against the wall. The rock moved out of the entrance.

Gina took a deep breath and raised the stake. The second the man popped his head in, she would bring the stake crashing down on the top of his head. Then she would duck out and not look back until she was at the Jeep.

A head poked in.

Gina started the stake down.

The man looked up. He brought up his hand and caught her arms as it was crashing down. He said, "Careful."

It was Timon.

Gina's breath caught.

"Let's get you out of here," he said.

He grabbed her hand, ducked out, and pulled her with him.

"Where are the guards?" she asked.

"I gave them twenty dollars to go away."

Gina shrugged.

"How did you find me?"

"You didn't come back. I think maybe they put you in prison."

Gina waited for him to expound on his detective ability, but he was done.

"Well, thanks," she muttered.

He smiled, then glancing at his shoulder, he said, "I should be thanking you."

They both clambered through the wide opening. The Africans camped fifty yards from the fence stared at them. Timon grabbed her hand and they slowly began their climb up the hill.

"Wait," she said, turning. "They have my backpack. And the phone. And the two boys?"

Timon shook his head.

Timon pulled the phone from his pocket and handed it to her. "How did you get it?"

"I gave them your clock," he said attempting to smile. "Sorry."

"What about the two boys?"

He shook his head. "They are not here." He explained how he had shown the pictures to many people in the village. The boys in the photo did not live there. Neither did the girl. The girl that Gina had brought back was different than the girl in the picture, though Timon could see how the deep dimples had fooled her.

ROAD TO PTUTSI
11:01 A.M.

THE SCENERY in South Africa was far different from both Kenya and Mozambique. Here there were rolling hills of green grass, lush forest, and open plains. The only wildlife we passed was a herd of buffalo. Twice we saw signs for diamond mines. When we were within fifty meters of the village, the pavement vanished and the bands of Africans began. Large groups of tattered, weak, and bone-thin individuals, walking alongside the road. It was bittersweet to watch them knowing they had hope in their hearts, that they would arrive at the village by day's end or the following day only to find the promised medical aid had not come. Or worse, that the village had been wiped off the face of the Earth completely. But these people would not die today. Maybe tomorrow. But not today.

Every so often we would pass another car, but for the most part, as we zoomed along at ninety kph. We were the only vehicle on the road.

"Turn here." Lacy pointed to a dirt road splitting the landscape of undulating green. "You need to stay on that road for the next twenty kilometers. It should take us directly to the village."

The badly maintained dirt road was the width of two cars. The clock on the dash, reading 11:15 a.m., bounced wildly up and down.

We had 45 minutes to traverse the 20 kilometers to the village, find some beacon, and destroy it. The fastest the bus could safely go on the bumbling road was about 30 kph, which would put us at the village at roughly 11:30.

That was cutting it close.

"Hold on," I shouted. "It's going to get bumpy."

I pushed the bus to 40, then 50. At 50 kph, it felt as though we were on some medieval rollercoaster.

"Slow down!" Lacy shouted. "There's a car coming."

Indeed there was. A quarter mile up the road, a Jeep was kicking up plumes of dirt. They were going as fast, if not even faster, than I was going. I pulled over onto what could be deemed the shoulder, where the dirt road met the beginnings of the thick pasture.

The Jeep was within a hundred yards when it began to slow, then stopped parallel with us. It took a moment for the wind to whisk away the dust, and then I was left staring down into the amber eyes of a windblown, yet remarkably attractive woman. There was an African man in the passenger seat whose face looked like a three-week-old pumpkin. In his lap, he was holding a little black girl.

The woman appeared on edge, like she hated to stop, but something had forced her foot to slam on the brakes. Maybe it was our white faces. Probably.

"Where are you guys going?" she yelled over the thrum of the two engines.

"The village up ahead."

"There's a barricade set up. They aren't letting anyone in. And for good reason. No help is coming."

"How do you know this?"

"I just do. I'd turn around and head back the way you came."

I saw her moving her hand around on the stick shift, she was ready to get moving herself. "We can't. If we don't make it into that village, I can promise you every last one of those people will be dead in half an hour."

"AIDS doesn't kill that fast," she scoffed.

"By a missile."

"What do you mean?"

My instincts told me this woman might have some insider knowledge of the village, which was why I was willing to waste another thirty seconds of precious time on her. Time I would have to make up by driving 100 kph. "Long story short, the promise of AIDS relief to the village was a ruse to get as many sick people together as possible so that they could be wiped out."

"Wiped out?"

"Genocide. The slate cleaned. A quarter of a million cases of AIDS simply wiped off the map."

"And who exactly would do such a thing?"

"I don't have time for details. A missile is going to hit the village in exactly thirty-seven minutes. And if we don't find some beacon or transponder thing that tells this missile where to go, then all those people are going to be vaporized."

She leaned her head out the door. "Did you say *beacon*?"

I nodded, then asked, "Who are you?"

"Gina Brady. I'm a doctor with the World Health Organization. I was sent to the village by some higher-ups in Washington."

"To find the three kids?" Lacy asked.

"How did you know that?"

I said, "We were on the ship."

"The cruise ship hijacked by pirates?"

"That's the one."

"Holy shit."

She jumped out of her Jeep and said some words to the African man. He nodded. She grabbed her backpack from the back of the Jeep, then ran around and jumped on the bus. She knelt down next to me and said, "I think I know where this beacon thing is."

I rammed the bus in to gear and eased back on the road.

Lacy spent the next five minutes detailing the hostage situation all the way down to the ship exploding.

Gina was leaning forward in the first row. I couldn't help but notice she had a nice profile. She said, "Fifty people died? That's horrible."

"That's nothing compared to what's going to happen in twenty-nine minutes. Now tell me why you think you know where this beacon is."

She described how she'd entered the village, found the small girl, then had the run-in with the guards, and had been locked in one of the huts. She'd seen a flashing red tube tucked into the side of the hut. She'd thought it weird at the time, like finding the fossil of a dinosaur with the imprint of a cell phone in its hand. The technology didn't fit the environment.

"That sounds like it might be it," I said.

Gina began rummaging around in her backpack, then she came out with a sleek phone. She dialed a number and pressed the phone to her ear. Whoever she was trying to call didn't answer. She left a message that the village of Ptutsi needed to be evacuated as quickly as possible.

I thought about telling her the evacuation of a quarter of a million people would take hours. We had minutes.

Rikki, who hadn't spoken much since the explosion, asked from the backseat, "Does that phone have internet capability?"

Gina looked at the phone, then Rikki, "I think so."

"Can I see it?"

Gina shrugged and handed over the phone.

I asked over my shoulder, "What are we going to do?"

Rikki smiled. "I'm going to get my father's money back."

I'd given Rikki the piece of paper Ganju had slipped me as well as the small electronic device. On the slip of paper were a web address, an account number, and two 20-digit passwords.

"Uh-oh."

I turned to Lacy, then gazed ahead. A half mile away was a massive roadblock: a quickly-assembled chain link fence that stretched across the road and well into the pastureland on both sides. There were two hummers parked on the road, making it impassable. Thirty armed soldiers were either standing near the fence, or sitting in the back of one of the hummers.

I told everybody to hold on.

When we were a long par three away from the hummers, I yanked the wheel to the right, sending the bus off the road and into the long grass. The small incline sent the bus airborne for a split second before it came crashing down. I could see the soldiers jumping from their Hummers, their weapons coming up as they did so.

"Get down," I yelled.

The bus closed in on the fence quickly. Fifty yards. Thirty. Ten. I braced myself for impact as the bus collided with the steel fence.

A crunching sound filled my ears, then I looked up. The bus was fit as a fiddle, save for the thirty feet of metal fencing it was dragging behind it. After a hundred yards, the bus broke free of the fence's clutches, leaving it behind for the scurrying soldiers.

The beginnings of the African camps were less than a hundred yards away and Lacy leaned over and repeatedly honked the horn. As we closed in on the thicket of black, the sick and weak slowly made their way out of the path of the large vehicle. As we moved through the masses of people, at right around four miles per hour, they stared. Some clapped. Surely, these people thought we were here to help them, the first of many buses that would soon arrive and whisk them away from the hand of death. We reached the top of a hill and I slowed. The village was at the bottom of a hill, surrounded by rolling green hills on all sides. And every inch, as far as the eye could see, looked to be covered in tiny black ants. I had never seen so many people. Probably a square mile of people stacked one on top of the other.

"Oh my God," exclaimed Lacy.

I pushed the bus over the hill's precipice. The Africans reluctantly moved out of the way. I looked at the dash. 11:38.

Slowly, methodically, we moved down the hill. I had long since put the bus in neutral and was simply easing up on the brake, which would send the bus rolling forward ten feet. The bus slid a couple times and several times I thought I had steamrolled a group of sick who were too weary to move, but each time the Africans were pulled from harm's way before the bus could crush them.

It took us seven minutes to move down the hill. We parked near the entrance to the village. I looked at the dash. 11:44.

Sixteen minutes.

"You guys stay here," I said. "Gina, you come with me."

Gina and I ran through the entrance. She said, "There are usually two guards at the entrance. They are probably looking for me right now."

I raised my eyebrows, but said nothing.

Gina yelled, "This way!"

I followed.

We ran for several hundred yards, passing hut after hut after hut. Some of the villagers stared as we ran. Others didn't even look up, two white people darting through their village evidently of little concern to them.

Gina approached a large hut. An enormous boulder was rolled in front of what looked to be an entrance. Gina said, "Help me move this."

It took the two of us nearly thirty seconds to roll the boulder from the entrance. She ducked into the hut and I followed. It was the size of an apartment living room. The air was warm and humid. There were three cots. Two of the beds were occupied by African men. One lay on his side. The other had his knees pulled to his chest. Both men had their eyes closed.

Gina said, "This is where they kept me prisoner."

"Quaint."

She went to the far edge of the hut and began clawing at the thick hatch that made up the side-wall. I guessed she stumbled on the beacon when she'd been testing to see how secure the walls were. I thumped my fist against the side. It hardly made a sound. The concoction of mud and thatch was roughly the same as brick. I mean it wouldn't take twenty years to break out like it took the guy in *Shawshank Redemption*, but it would be no simple task.

Gina said, "It's not here."

I joined her at the wall. I began peeling back layers of the thick hatch. I asked, "How big is it?"

"It looks like a roll of Lifesavers."

Right.

"Are you sure it was right here?"

"Of course I'm sure."

I wondered how many minutes had gone by since we'd left the bus. Three? Four? I guessed we had twelve minutes to find and destroy this thing.

We went over the wall a third time. Nothing.

"I swear it was here."

"Were these two other guys here when you were here?"

"Yeah."

I was thinking maybe one of these guys saw Gina messing with the beacon, and when she left, their curiosity got the better of them. I took a couple steps and surveyed the man on his side. He looked dead. I stared at his chest. It wasn't moving. He was dead.

I made my way toward the second man. His chest moved in and out, his hands were cradled together in front of his knees. I leaned down so I could get a closer look at his hands. A soft light was resonating through the gaps in his fingers. A soft red light.

"Found it."

"What are you waiting for?"

Good question. It wasn't that I didn't want to touch the seven-eighths dead African man with gangrenous sores all over his body, it's that I didn't even want to *think* about touching him. Gina pushed me to the side and grabbed the man's hands.

The man's eyes opened.

Gina screamed.

I screamed.

The man screamed.

The man rolled over on his side and I could see the beacon clutched in his right hand. Gina jumped on top of him and tried wrestling the beacon from his grip. It didn't work. The man continued to shriek. It sounded like a garbage disposal with a spoon in it.

"Pry his fingers off it," Gina yelled.

She had the guy in a bear hug and his left hand was dangling off the cot. I took a deep breath, darted in, and tried peeling back two of his fingers, which both snapped in half.

Gina screamed, "I didn't say *break* his fingers!"

Whoops.

The beacon fell to the ground and rolled under the cot. I ducked under the table and pulled it out.

Gina was staring at something wide-eyed.

It was a photograph.

I asked, "You okay?"

"Oh yeah," she stammered. She folded the photograph and shoved it in her pocket, then yelled, "LET'S GO!"

PTUTSI

11:50 A.M.

WHEN GINA and I were twenty yards from the bus, I screamed, "What time is it?"

Lacy, Rikki, Bheka, and J.J. were all standing just outside the bus. Rikki looked down at the phone and said, "11:50."

Gina and I joined them, sucking for breath.

"Was it where you thought it was?" asked Lacy, taking the flashing beacon from my hand and surveying it.

Gina and I looked at each other, and she said with a smirk, "More or less."

Lacy handed the beacon back to me, and I said, "All right, here goes nothing." I reached my hand up to smash it down on the metal bumper of the bus.

"STOP!" screamed Rikki.

I stopped. Everyone stared at her. "What?"

"You can't break it."

"Why?"

"If it's anything like a transponder on an airplane, then it will have a fail-safe built in. If you break that thing, the missile is still going to hit its last known coordinates."

Lacy chimed, "She's probably right."

I nodded. "How long do we have?"

"Nine minutes."

"All right." I looked up the hill where we'd come down. The path we'd taken was still open, as if the people were expecting more buses any second. I started up the bus steps. "I can get this thing a mile away in nine minutes.

"No!" Lacy yelled, grabbing my shoulder.

I shrugged her arm off and said, "Lace, it's our only shot."

Her eyes grew moist. "But what about you?"

I hadn't thought of this little nugget. "I'll be fine. I'll duck and cover."

She wrapped her arms around me and began weeping. "I love you."

"I love you, too."

I was probably down to eight minutes. But in eight minutes, I could get this thing over a mile away, then some. I threw Lacy off and climbed into the bus.

I placed the beacon in the cupholder and turned the ignition. I had this uncanny feeling the engine wouldn't turn over. But it did. The engine roared to life. Louder than I'd ever heard it. Too loud. Then it hit me. The noise wasn't coming from the bus. It was coming from above.

Through the windshield I saw the helicopter. On the side, it read, "SA NAVY."

I let out an exhale. Someone had listened.

The helicopter could get the beacon ten miles away in seven minutes. Take it and drop it in the middle of nowhere then zoom off.

Thank God.

The air whipped around us as the helicopter put down thirty feet to our left. For a moment, nothing happened. Then the door opened and I was left staring at a familiar face.

Shit.

I screamed, "Everyone in!"

The five of them jumped into the bus. I threw it into gear and slammed down the gas. The bus lurched forward.

Machine gunfire erupted from the helicopter, the bullets ripping into the bus, cutting through the engine. The bus stopped dead in her tracks. We'd gone eight feet.

"EVERYBODY OUT HERE!" yelled the Professor.

The six of us looked at one another in a daze. It was over. We were all going to die. I looked at the dash.

Seven minutes.

The six of us clambered down the bus steps and into the dirt.

"You again," I said.

The Professor was out of the helicopter and striding toward the smoking bus. He looked like shit. His face and arms were covered in bandages. He'd been burned in the explosion. Maybe he should have waited another minute before he'd blown the remote detonation switch.

"I told you about the village in confidence," he said. "And now you come and try to sabotage my perfect plan. Don't you see what you are doing? You are getting in the way of God's plan. God needs these people to die, so others can live."

"Save me the soapbox."

"The what?"

"You can rationalize this however the fuck you want. But it's murder. You are murdering these people."

I noticed a blur out of the corner of my ear. It was Bheka. He had darted toward the village. Maybe he wanted to be with his mother when the bomb came. The Professor watched him go. I could tell he'd thought about putting a couple bullets into the child's back, but it would have been a waste of energy. The child would be dead soon enough.

The Professor turned his attention back to me and said, "I will tell you what is murder. Having the means to help a country in dire need and not sending help. That is murder. Watching as millions upon millions of people die each year and doing nothing.

That is murder. No, this is the only way. Believe me. I have tried."
He waved his arms at the village and said, "In fifty years, long after
I'm gone, long after you're gone—which will be any minute now
—a new village will rise from the ashes of the old. A village that is
healthy and pure. A village where the word AIDS does not exist."

The Professor looked down at his watch and said, "Well, I'd say
this is cutting it a bit close." He started back toward the helicopter.
Over his shoulder he yelled, "Oh, and don't bother trying to break
the beacon, it won't do you any good!"

He climbed into the helicopter.

"You never knew my mother."

The Professor turned. "What gave it away?"

"She doesn't drink vodka," shouted Rikki. "And she wouldn't
have settled for a million dollars."

He nodded.

"So then Track was behind this whole thing?"

He smiled wide.

"What's he get out of this?" Rikki asked immune to the blow. I
guess she'd already known her father was behind the ransom.

"You'll have to ask him. However, you may never have the
chance."

"Well, seven hundred and fifty million of his dollars will die
with me."

"What do you mean?" the Professor's voice wavered.

She held up the phone and smiled. "You're not the only one
who banks in Monaco, you know."

"No. You couldn't." He grasped at his neck. He must have been
in such agony when Ganju had ripped it off that he hadn't
noticed.

Rikki held up the Random Generating Password capsule that
Ganju had ripped from the Professor's neck and said, "Looking
for this?"

He snarled.

I said, "Your friend Ganju was really good with numbers."

"Well, the money was just icing on the cake," he said, fighting back a grimace. "That you and everyone within a square mile will soon be compost is satisfaction in itself."

"But the money would have been nice."

He cut his eyes at me, then pulled the door closed. The helicopter's propeller started up, kicking up the village floor, then slowly began to rise off the ground.

I looked at Rikki and said, "Were you really able to transfer the money?"

She nodded.

But even with this small victory, we still had the problem of being blown to pieces in the coming minute.

The helicopter continued to rise. When it was twenty feet off the ground, it banked slightly. Then abruptly, it stopped. It banked once more and headed toward the bus. It stopped directly overhead, hovering. I stared upward. The door to the helicopter slid open. The Professor leaned out. He was holding something black in his hands. It weighed about fifty pounds. Bheka.

"I believe this belongs to you."

He released Bheka, and he fell into Gina's and my outstretched arms. The door to the chopper slid closed. The chopper banked to the left, quickly rose, and slowly disappeared from view.

I looked down at Bheka. I couldn't blame him. Trying to sneak onto the helicopter. I wished I'd thought to do the same. I rubbed his head and said, "Nice try."

He threw a shy smile.

"One minute," Rikki chimed, looking at the phone.

I let out a deep breath.

"Well, we might as well go ahead and break the thing," quipped Gina.

She was right. It couldn't hurt.

I jumped on the bus and checked the cupholder. It wasn't there. I sat on my haunches and peered into the sides of the seats where it could have fallen.

"Don't tell me you lost it," Lacy shouted, joining the search.

"It was in the cupholder," said J.J. "I saw it."

Gina and Rikki hopped aboard and began searching frantically for the beacon. I thought if we could just find it and shatter it, then maybe the bomb would misfire. That there would be some sort of complication. It had become our last hope. Our last gasp.

"It's 12:00."

I stopped my search and looked at Lacy. She was pointing at the clock on the bus's dash. She was right. And yes, the clock could have been off by a couple minutes like most clocks were, but this one was accurate. How did I know? Through the windshield a streaking plume of smoke was approaching from the horizon.

Lacy reached out her hand. I took it.

Lacy stared at me. Her beautiful blue eyes slowly leaked a single tear that ran down the side of her nose. I pulled her into my chest and closed my eyes.

The explosion was cataclysmic. A million times greater than the blast that had destroyed the *Afrikaans*.

But the explosion was not in the village. It was miles away, high up in the sky.

Lacy and I held each other and watched the orange mushroom cloud bellow high in the atmosphere. At the center of the mushroom, I was certain was a helicopter.

I looked at Bheka standing on the bottom step of the bus. His eyebrows were raised. He looked like he'd just been caught cheating on a test. I started laughing. Gina, Rikki, J.J., and Lacy still appeared to be putting the events together.

Lacy pointed to Bheka and said, "You? The beacon?"

Bheka smiled and said, "I thought he should have it back."

––––––––

Rikki smiled wide and gave me a big hug. That's when it clicked. I pushed her away.

She cut her eyes at me and said, "What?"

"The diamond in your tooth?" I said, holding onto her shoulders. "Where did you get it?"

"It came in the mail on my twenty-first birthday."

"Who do you think gave it to you?"

She paused a moment and then said, "Track probably."

"And what did we see two signs for when we were driving here?"

It took her a second, but she got there. "Diamond mines."

I raised my eyebrows. "You asked what your father would be getting out of it."

The air was sucked from her lungs. She still had the satellite phone and started flipping through it. She hit the screen several times and I knew she was searching, "Track Bowe and diamonds."

After several more seconds, she turned the phone to me and said, "Oh my God."

ELEVEN DAYS LATER

LONDON

4:40 P.M.

"ARE YOU READY FOR THIS?"

Rikki tilted her head to the side and gazed upward through the window of the cab. She appraised the skyscraper her father owned and said, "Yep."

After the explosion, the six of us had climbed the hill from the Zulu village, then hitched a ride in the back of a truck to the town of Ladysmith. There we hitched another ride, and by the time the sun was setting we'd found our way to King Edward VIII hospital in Durban. (Gina accompanied us as both Timon and the little girl from the village were being treated there.) When we arrived, Gilroy had just gotten out of surgery and was in critical condition. Susie and Frank had made the most of the hospital cafeteria and listened closely as Lacy, J.J., and I recounted the events at the village. We'd tried to get a hotel, but the media swell had made this utterly impossible, and we slept in hospital chairs. At noon the following day, Gilroy was upgraded to stable condition and we were able to visit him. Trinity hadn't left his side and was still wearing her bikini. Lots of happy doctors. Gilroy was groggy, but was still able to flip me off. What a guy.

Later that day, Susie and Frank said that they needed to get back to the States. There were tears (not from me), promises to stay in touch (from everyone), and threats made if Snuggies weren't waiting for us we got back home (from me). J.J. departed as well. His agent had him booked on all sorts of talk shows, and he needed to get back if he was going to cash in on the hostage "bonanza." There were tears (from him), promises to stay in touch (from him), and threats if we didn't stay in touch (from him). That same day, Bheka's mother showed up. She was a beautiful black woman, and I recalled seeing her about the ship. She didn't look the least bit sick and picked Bheka up in her arms and twirled him around when the two reunited. Gina took Llandee's information and promised to get her help with her disease as soon as she could. Lacy left as well. She could tell I was in detective mode, and she desperately missed her fiancée back in France. I would see her in three months at her wedding, but it didn't make the goodbye any easier (lots of tears from me).

This left Rikki, Gina, and myself.

We were finally able to get a room in a dumpy motel across the street, the owner of which—at the sight of Gina's wad of cash— kept our names off the books. The three of us spent the ensuing days searching the internet, making calls, and threatening careers. It took us a week to sort everything out and then another two days of planning.

Two hours earlier, we had landed at Heathrow airport.

Rikki took a deep breath and pulled the door open. Gina and I glanced at each other, then watched as Rikki made her way across the street and to the large turnstile entrance to the ninety-six-story Alidi building. I wished I could see the look on her father's face when he saw her. But she'd said she'd needed to do it alone. Fortunately, it would all be captured by the video camera hidden in her jacket and I, along with millions of others, would watch it soon enough.

I leaned forward and said to the black cab driver, "Let's go."

He eased into the downtown traffic and continued on. Gina's hand found mine.

Twenty minutes later, we reached an area known as the Albert Embankment, which stretched for a mile along the River Thames in Central London.

We stepped from the cab and looked at the building to our right that had been made so famous by James Bond. Known as the SIS Building or the British Secret Intelligence Building, it was best known as the MI6 Building.

I wonder if Q was in there somewhere.

We walked past the building and continued on for two blocks, then stopped in front of a three-story building with hundreds of small flags from different countries dangling from the roof parapet. The building was far larger than it had appeared online.

The IMO Building or International Maritime Organization Building, was home to an emergency two-day conference on the topic of maritime piracy, one elicited by the very attack I was part of eleven days earlier.

Gina and I crossed the street and sat on a bench near the river. Thirty-seven minutes later, thirty men and women—mostly men —exited the building.

Gina nodded at a man in a suit and said, "That's him." She pulled a walkie-talkie from her pocket and said, "White hair, blue suit, black briefcase, headed toward you right now...hold on...he's talking to two other guys...hang back...alright...go."

The cab we'd just exited a half-hour earlier pulled up to the curb just as our mark raised his hand in signal. A moment later, the cab pulled into traffic, then did a U-turn and stopped directly in front of us. Gina and I opened both back doors simultaneously and squeezed in around our mark.

"What? What the hell are you—" the man stammered.

"Shut up," I said.

He whipped his head from Gina, then back to me, then back to Gina. "Gina?"

"Roger," she said matter of fact. Then she punched him in the face, the sound of his nose breaking filling the small cab, and said, "That's for killing my father."

————

The moment Gina had seen the photo of herself flutter to the ground in the Zulu prison, she'd known. She hadn't been sent to save three kids. She'd been sent to die. She wasn't sure how the man in the prison had come to have her picture, whether he'd been the man who was supposed to do the job, or if he'd simply found the picture and clung to it, much as he'd clung to the beacon. But it didn't matter. Someone had her picture. Someone was supposed to kill her or make sure she was in that prison when the missile struck.

But who had supplied the picture? The photo was from the WHO website so theoretically anyone could have access to the photo. But how had it gotten to Ptutsi? And who had sent it?

She couldn't believe for an instant that Paul would send her to her death. Never. Which would only leave one man. His father. Roger Garret. But why would Garret, National Security Advisor to the President, a man that for many years Gina had thought of as a second father, a man that she'd always believed was destined to be her father-in-law, a man she knew loved her, want her dead?

She couldn't think of a single possible reason.

Back at the motel with Thomas and Rikki, she had racked her brain. The last time she'd seen Roger Garret had been at her father's funeral six years earlier. She'd remembered hugging Garret, wiping her tears away on his shoulder. She hadn't thought anything of it at the time, but looking back on it now, she'd remembered the way he'd said, "I'm sorry." The way he'd said it, eyes downcast, almost as if he were apologizing. Gina had always figured it had been some weird guy thing, like if he'd been in the car with him, or hadn't let him drink and drive, or if he'd only called him back maybe he might not have been on the road at that time, or some change of circumstances that would have altered the outcome. But could he have been simply apologizing because it had been his fault?

But it was the second thing that he said that tripped a wire in her brain. He had asked where her father's effects would be sent. Did she want him to store them for her? She'd been so distraught at the time, that she hadn't even answered.

At the motel, Gina had called her best friend who had been holding her father's belongings in her storage. Gina had forgotten about Garret's inquiry and the box had been sent to Bolivia, but it had been too painful for Gina to open, and she had sent the box back to the States. She had her best friend expedite the box to their motel in South Africa and it had come two days later. Gina had been going through the materials, tears dripping from her eyes as she looked at her father's many medals and decorations. Just some old papers, photos of her mother, and two worn copies of *To Kill a Mockingbird*, her father's favorite novel. One of the copies was a first edition. Gina pulled the book out and watched as three yellowed notebook pages fluttered out.

It was a letter.

It was from a missionary. His name was Doug Haniferr. The letter was written in a shaky hand. She doubted the man was still alive by the time the letter reached the States. In straightforward speak, the man detailed that he was doing missionary work in a remote village in South Africa called Ptutsi. The village was a hotbed for AIDS and nearly half the people in the village were infected. He'd been in the village for the past eighteen months trying to get some of the villagers to take Christ into their hearts before they perished. But now *he* was perishing. Although he had received all his immunizations, he had still contracted malaria. He knew without a doubt that he would be dead soon. This letter was a last-ditch effort to get some added medical aid to the people of the village. He knew that the U.S. could only allocate so much money to so many things, but he thought he had stumbled on an answer. While helping extend a mass grave, he had noticed a couple things in the soil. He'd been a geology major in college before going into the seminary. He'd done a rudimentary test, mixing one cup of soil with one quart of water, shaking, then allowing to settle. And as he'd suspected there had been a rainbow like oily film on the surface of the water.

Hydrocarbons.

———

"This whole thing was about oil," I said.

Blood gushed from Garret's nose, stemming over his hands, and I couldn't tell how he reacted to my statement.

After Rikki had shown me the Google results on the search for her father and diamonds, I had been certain that Track Bowe had been behind the takeover of the *Afrikaans*, the ransom of his daughter, and the attempt to flatten an entire village all in an effort to turn Ptutsi into a diamond mine. According to Google, Track owned two diamond mines in South Africa and he was in the process of hunting for a third site. I'd assumed he had somehow discovered that the land beneath the Zulu village of Ptutsi was brimming with the stones, but I'd been wrong. It was brimming with oil.

The first night at the hospital, I spent a good eight hours on Gina's satellite phone (luckily she had a bunch of spare batteries). I read everything I could find about the attack on the *Afrikaans*, the Professor (Baruti Quaroni), the Warlord (Keli "The Mosquito" Nkosi), and Track Bowe and his many operations, including his two diamond mines in South Africa. Other than Track owning the cruise line, I couldn't get the pieces to fall into place. Why ransom his daughter? Why pay one billion dollars? Plus, thinking back on what Quaroni had said to Rikki, it didn't seem credible. He'd told her that she'd have to ask her father what he was getting out of it.

But why wouldn't he just tell her. She was about to die. Quaroni didn't tell her because he didn't know? For all he knew, it could have been Track behind it; whoever was pulling all the strings was doing so anonymously.

So it was back to the drawing board. What was this really all about? And who was the one real person controlling everything.

It'd happened when I was visiting Gilroy. When he'd flipped me off I thought back to when he'd first flipped me off in the show lounge. When he'd said that everything always came down to oil, and how there was more oil in Africa than anywhere else in the world. They just hadn't found it yet.

So I started reading articles about oil and Africa, and Gilroy wasn't lying. They suspected there were enormous reserves hidden in the forgotten continent. There had even been four drilling ventures within fifty kilometers of Ptutsi. A number of different people felt there was a huge reserve in that general area, but it had yet to be tapped.

Two hours later, Gina had shown me the letter from the missionary.

"Are you guys fucking nuts?" Garret roared.

"I found the letter," Gina said. "From the missionary. I found it."

Garret's face fell. After three long breaths, he said, "He wasn't supposed to die."

"Oh what, he was just supposed to drive off a cliff and survive?"

"No, I mean, it shouldn't have come to that. He didn't need to die. All I wanted was the letter." From next to him I could see how long the words had been bottled up. They'd been fermenting for too long, and he actually breathed a loud sigh as they finally diffused into the atmosphere.

"What happened?"

I'd done enough interrogations to know when someone wanted to talk. Garret took a deep breath and said, "Seven years ago, a letter found its way to me. I'm not sure why I was the one to open it, but I was. How I wish I weren't. I take it you know the contents of the letter—a missionary who had a good suspicion there was a huge reserve of oil under the ground of an AIDS-stricken Zulu village. A missionary that was more than likely already dead."

"And suddenly you are the keeper of the Holy Grail," I said.

"Wrong, this made the Holy Grail look like a Styrofoam cup. Striking oil in South Africa, one of our biggest allies would not only mean trillions of dollars, it would mean an end to a war."

"A war? In South Africa?"

"No, the Middle East."

Gina and I gazed at each other. Neither of us had made the connection.

"We would no longer have to rely on them for oil," Garret said defiantly. "We could pull out all our troops, let them go back to blowing each other up. Do you really think we would be over there, still be over there, if it weren't for all that oil? If we found another oil resource, our troops would be out of there in six months. Guaranteed. This isn't about money. This is about National Security."

"Rationalize it any fucking way you want. You still tried to murder four hundred people on a cruise ship and nearly a quarter of million people in that village."

"Finish telling me about my father," interrupted Gina.

"Okay, so I'm the only one on the planet that knows about this oil reserve, or suspected oil reserve. But it makes sense because for the past ten years people have been drilling around this village looking for oil, everything points at oil, but no one thought that it might be directly under this village. So, I start thinking of ways to get this Zulu village moved. But because of all the apartheid shit, the South African government is strict, and not oil, not anything would get them to throw people off their sacred land, not to mention uproot a mass grave more than a half mile in radius. It would take an act of God to move those people."

"Or a huge fucking missile."

"Right," he said with a laugh, and I nearly broke his nose back into place.

"I started making some calls, a couple of friends of friends, and your father walked in. Heard me talking on the phone."

"Let me guess, you were gonna have some people just go in there and shoot them all."

"Indeed I was. And for quite cheap. But your father overheard me and when I looked for the letter the next day, it was gone. I begged your father to give it back. Told him that I wasn't going to do anything. I'd just been making some calls. But he didn't trust me. And after all we'd been through."

Gina stared at him.

"He was my best friend, Gina. Had been for nearly twenty years. I didn't want to kill him. But I needed that letter. And more importantly, I was sick of watching kids die in a land that we had no business even being in."

"Kill the few, save the many," I said.

"Exactly."

I punched him in the nose. It did not go into place. In fact, I think it was on his right cheek now. It took him a long minute to stem the bleeding.

"You were saying," I said.

He was having trouble talking, so I took over.

"So you kill her old man, he's gone, and you are sitting on this secret. You decide to take a different approach so you start researching this village and you stumbled on the name Baruti Quaroni. You know that he is an anti-apartheid activist, so I doubt you even mention moving his village, his hometown, elsewhere. He is living in exile and I don't know how you find him, but you do. You get word to him anonymously. You don't for one instant mention oil, instead you play the AIDS card. He has watched so many of his family members die from this disease, and from his past you aren't surprised when he thinks that your plan to kill a shitload of sick Africans is righteous. But how are you going to accomplish this? Death costs money. And killing a quarter of million people is no easy task. So, you come up with a plan. Ransom. As National Security Advisor I'm sure you tapped into a couple of favors to have some off-the-books work done for you. I'm not sure how you stumbled on Track Bowe. Maybe you were looking for a cruise ship and when you stumbled on the *Afrikaans*, you learned the principal owner was Track. Or maybe it was vice versa. Maybe you were looking at the richest men in the world and Track popped up, and from there you found the *Afrikaans*. Doesn't matter. It was perfect. A small luxury cruise liner. Small enough that it could be boarded by pirates, and in a safe enough body of water that piracy isn't too much of a threat. How Rikki comes into play, I don't have the wildest idea. You have access to basically any and all data-bases, and when you are doing research on Track, you discover he has an illegitimate daughter. You do your research on Rikki, entice her with an amazing African cruise via Facebook or whatever, and she bites. And when she books the cruise, you know that all the pieces are falling into place. How am I doing so far?"

He nodded. He was impressed. Who wouldn't be? I'm amazing.

"From here, you pretty much give Quaroni free reign. He brings in his own team, does things his way. All you care about is that he gets the money. You've probably already set up the purchase with the Russians for the Thermobaric Missile of increased whatthefuck and are just waiting for the go ahead. As for the bomb on the ship, I'm guessing that you used some back channels to get this or steal this, and before it made its way into the hands of Quaroni, I'm sure you had a remote detonation switch added that only you could control. Once the ship is taken over, it is pretty much out of your hands, and then all you have to do is play your part, trying to neutralize the threat, but not actually neutralizing it."

"Did Paul know?" asked Gina.

"No." You could see the pain on the man's face at the idea of his son knowing what he'd done.

Before we'd come, Gina had made me promise that none of this would ever get out. That Roger Garret would never be connected to the *Afrikaans* or her father's death. It was evident she cared deeply for Roger's son, even though he was married and had a family, but she wanted him to be happy. And knowing about his father would ruin him. It had taken me three days, but I had finally agreed to her terms.

"You texted him to call me," she said. "I don't know what you told this Quaroni, but you got him to add the rescue of three African children from the village to his demands. You didn't tell him why and he probably didn't care. You knew there was a chance that the letter from the missionary had been hidden amongst my father's effects. You probably searched for them, but you couldn't find them, and assumed they'd been sent to Bolivia. Which they had. But then I'd sent them back, and Vicky was keeping them in storage."

Garret looked up. I'm sure he'd checked countless places and had somehow neglected her best friend's storage.

"You wouldn't have known about it, the storage unit is under her stepbrother's name. So you had Paul ask me to go on this mission, a mission that I was never to come back from. You almost got your wish. I was attacked by a band of kids and nearly killed, then trapped it a Zulu prison with whoever you hired to kill me."

"Just a contact. Sent him your picture. Told him to go to the village. He was supposed to plant the beacon and to—"

"— kill me?"

Garret nodded.

"Well, he got there alright. But he did something to upset the villagers and they beat him to within an inch of his life. I'm sure he would have killed me if he'd had the strength."

"You saw him?"

"Yes, the guards put me in the village prison. He was there."

Roger nodded along.

"But it didn't matter that he didn't kill me because you knew that I would still be in the village when it was destroyed. You knew that I would stay there until I found the three kids. Three kids that didn't exist."

"You were always very persistent. I always admired that about you."

I quick flash of approval flickered over Gina's features, then vanished.

I took over again. "Everything goes according to plan, you get the money, wire the Russians, get the missile all set up. You made some calls, and you knew a team of SEALs were on their way to board the ship, and you probably knew within a ten-minute window of when they boarded the *Afrikaans*. And then in the single touch of a button, or a single phone call, you blew up the ship. You thought you were killing everyone, every hostage, every pirate, every SEAL. But to your dismay, you find out that almost all the passengers survived. But the passengers are the least of your worries."

I gave him a noogie. "At least you thought."

I continued. "I always thought it was odd that when we were taken aboard the South African Navy warship, no one would listen to our story. I'm guessing that you made some calls and you were the reason we were sequestered in that room on base. You didn't much care if our story came out, but just when. As long as the village was destroyed, then it wouldn't matter what we had to say. And we wouldn't be here right now."

I never would have been able to connect the dots from oil to the National Security Advisor if it hadn't been for Gina's letter.

And if we hadn't made it to the village, Gina would have been part of the mass cremation.

"But as you know, the village wasn't destroyed."

"Yes, how did that happen?"

There were only a handful of people that actually knew what happened in that village. And it would forever stay that way. Both the South African Navy and it seemed like the entire U.S. government had been trying to get in touch with us for the past two weeks. Lacy, Rikki, and I were the only passengers who hadn't been debriefed. I'm quite certain we would be presumed dead if not for the manifest on that warship. There were a couple close calls at the hospital and there were some news vans around our motel the first couple nights snooping around, but by the fourth day the story was old news and the U.S. was more concerned with the latest school shooting than something that happened a world away.

I recounted what happened, Garret even giving a snort of laughter when he learned his plan had been foiled by a seven-year-old.

"So what would you be doing right now if your plan had worked?" I asked.

He took a deep breath and said, "Well, I'd probably be at this anti-piracy conference all the same, but I'd also be silently making calls to prospective drillers. I had enough contacts and favors stored up in the South African government to ensure whichever driller I chose would be on that site. As for drillers, it would look too obvious if it was an American company, we already get a large portion of our oil from Canada, and the South Africans have a bad history with the English. Best case would be a Mexican company. In about six months, after the red tape was cleared, they'd start drilling, hit the jackpot. The South African government would get billions in royalties, and within a year, the U.S. wouldn't have to get a single barrel of oil from the Middle East. Without dependence on

Middle Eastern oil we would no longer need a presence or an influence in the Middle East, which if you ask any of these countries, is the biggest aggressor and liability toward U.S. National security."

"So you are saying that if all those people would have died, the United States would be safer?"

"Without a doubt."

"That's horseshit," I said. "That means that you value American life more than anybody else's."

"I do. That's what I am paid to do."

I couldn't argue with that. And I had about enough of this guy. I'd said my peace. I looked at Gina and said, "You about done here?"

She gazed at me. Then she reared back and punched him in the nose a third time. Then she opened the door. I opened mine.

"That's it?" he snorted. "That's it? You're just going to let me go."

I looked over the cab and Gina. "Your call," I said.

"Let him go," she said.

I closed my door. The cabbie took off with a backward wave. There was a small tattoo on the inside of his wrist. A saxophone.

———

Torrey Royal looked in the rearview mirror at the man in the backseat. His face was covered in blood. As was the cab. But Royal didn't care. He'd stolen the cab two days earlier, changed the plates, and in five minutes he would never see the cab again. "Are you okay?" he said over his shoulder.

Roger Garret nodded and said, "Just take me to my hotel."

After a couple miles, Garret said, "Are you sure this is the right way? I think it was back there."

"I'm sure."

He was just as sure as when he'd looked down at the bomb in the Computer Center and seen the pink bricks of LDX. The same pink bricks he and his fellow SEALs had recovered from the lab in North Korea six months earlier. It was then that he'd known that someone in the United States Government, someone *high* in the United States government, was conspiring with the pirates. Conspiring to kill a lot of people.

The only reason he was alive was because he'd been staring at the bomb when the numbers on the iPhone had disappeared and the phone had started beeping. Two seconds later, he was at the door leading to the outside deck, shouting into his headset, "Code Black." Save yourself.

He catapulted himself over the railing and dove fifty feet to the ocean. He hit the water and kicked, diving as deep as possible. And then it was as if a U-boat had dropped a concussion grenade five feet from him. His body was thrown violently, the wind knocked from his lungs as he was shot forward. The underwater explosion had ripped the radio from his ear, torn his dive knife from his thigh, and burst his left eardrum. When he finally surfaced, thirty seconds later, he knew all his brothers were dead.

He treaded water for twenty minutes and watched what was left of the ship burn, then sink to the bottom of the ocean. A South African Navy warship transferred all the passengers from the lifeboats, and Royal swam to the ship and snuck aboard. When they were a mile from shore, he jumped off the boat and swam.

Luckily he had his GTS—Gone to Shit—pouch, which had plenty of cash, a fake passport, and other necessities. He stole some clothes off a clothes-line, then walked seven miles to downtown Durban. The city was flooded with news media, but he was somehow able to get one of the last available hotel rooms. He was so emotionally drained from the mission, he slept for sixteen hours. When he awoke, his eardrum was on fire. He bought some clothes, then made a quick stop by the hospital. It was risky, because he would have to show his fake passport, but he had a second passport in his GTS that the U.S. Government was unaware of. Trent Montgomery was seen by a doctor, and given some ear drops, painkillers, and antibiotics.

Starving, Royal stopped by the hospital cafeteria. It was there that he overhead a small group talking. As he ate his sandwich and Sprite, he eavesdropped with his good ear. The group had all been passengers on the *Afrikaans*. And some of them had even been to the Zulu village.

Royal followed them back to a motel room across the street. The next day, he knocked on their door. He told them his side of the story. And they told him theirs.

"Now I know this isn't the way," Garret blurted.

"Shortcut," Royal said.

He took a right turn into a large park.

"What the hell?"

Royal ignored him.

Royal parked on the street and cut the ignition. He locked the doors. Garret said, "What the hell are you doing?"

Royal turned around.

He watched as recognition swept over the man's face.

Royal placed the tip of the silencer against the seat and pulled the trigger. Eight times. Once for each of his brothers. He tossed the gun in the backseat, opened the door, and walked back to the street.

THREE MONTHS LATER

VENICE
11:49 A.M.

LACY'S VOICE came through the door, "Is everything okay?"

I had been on the toilet for the last hour. And no, everything was *not* okay. "Just a little pre-game jitters." Combined with the 40 raw oysters I had eaten at the rehearsal dinner.

"You do know that I'm the one getting married, right?"

"Tell that to my colon."

She laughed. "Tip-off is in ten minutes."

"Okey-dokey."

Five minutes later, I stepped from the bathroom. Lacy was looking at herself in the mirror for the one thousandth time. She looked stunning. Her dress was custom-made by a French seamstress in trade for one of Lacy's most prized paintings. But Lacy got the better end of the deal, the dress would have cost somewhere in the low five figures and Lacy's paintings were lucky to go for the high fours. Anyhow, I didn't know the exact jargon, but the dress was strapless, had hundreds of little white beads, and Lacy looked beautiful in it.

She looked at me and said, "You ready for this?"

Was I ready to give away my baby sister, my best friend, so far the only love of my life, to another man? No, I was not. Hence the explosive diarrhea.

Lacy shook her head at me. "Don't."

"What?"

"Don't you dare start crying. If you start. I'm gonna start, and my makeup is going to run." She was already crying at this point. So was I.

She sniffed, walked toward me, and I put my hands on her shoulders. I had practiced the words I wanted to say for the last hour. While I was on the pot. I took a deep breath, wiped the tears off my cheeks and said, "Lace, I still remember the day you were born. I was eight. It was third quarter of my basketball game. Mom's water broke in the stands, dad runs onto the court, yanks me by the arm, and all three of us jump in the car. An hour later, you were born. You were just this tiny little thing. Ugly as hell."

She wiped her eyes and slapped me on the chest.

"For the last twenty-six years I watched as you went from my annoying baby sister, to a bumbling teenager, to a beautiful, funny, smart young woman. Mom and dad would have been proud."

Lacy pulled me to her and we held each other for a long minute. For the past ten years all we had was each other.

"I love you, bro."

"I love you, sis."

"Hey, can you guys wrap up the *Lifetime* movie bullshit? It's show time."

I turned. It was Frank.

I had remained close with the Campers over the past three months, visiting them twice in New Mexico, and them visiting me once in Seattle. And the three of us had gone on a two-week trip with Lacy and her fiancée Caleb to Italy. Anyhow, Frank was one of the ushers. Frank in a tuxedo was a sight. Like the penguin king.

I looked at Lacy and said, "You ready?"

She nodded and smiled. "Ready as I'll ever be."

Frank disappeared.

I slipped my arm through Lacy's, and the two of us walked out of the small room. The second usher was standing with his hand holding one of the double doors. It was J.J. Watkins. And yes, somehow, I had come to like the man. And I'd even found myself laughing at one of his jokes every so often. I'd say one out of every eight.

As Lacy and I neared, his jaw went slack. He gulped and said, "You look friggin' beautiful."

"Thanks. You look pretty friggin' handsome yourself."

J.J. blushed. Then he pulled the door open. The rustle of people getting to their feet filled the room.

Here we go.

The music started.

Dum, dum, de, dum.

Lacy and I started down the aisle. Lacy's and my friends were on the right side of the small cathedral. Strangely enough, the majority of the people who Lacy had invited were people we'd met aboard the *Afrikaans*. But, I suppose under the circumstances, it's only natural we'd made such close bonds with so many different individuals. Plus, they all had enough money to travel to France.

Dum, dum, de, dum.

Berta and Reen were in the back row. When they had returned to the States, they did what normal lesbian couples do: moved to San Francisco, got officially married, and adopted two Vietnamese children.

Dum, dum, de, dum.

We passed Walter and Marge Kohn. Three days earlier, I spent the day with my favorite three-quarters dead couple. In the span of twelve hours, Marge said the phrase "The French are idiots" 32 times. I know because I counted.

Dum, dum, de, dum.

A petite brown woman and a frail looking brown teenager with crutches were taking up the next row. Thapa's wife and son. On the slip of paper Thapa gave me there was information for a second bank account. His. I followed his instructions and the money was transferred into his wife's name. His son had already undergone two surgeries. Doctors were optimistic that after one final surgery his leg would be almost as good as new.

Next to them were another mother and son: Bheka and his mother. The two now lived in Cape Town where both Bheka and Llandee were going to school. Llandee's HIV had not yet progressed to AIDS, and doctors believed that with the right medications, she would live a long life. Bheka was tested. He did not have HIV.

Dum, dum, de, dum.

The next row was occupied by two of my favorite people: Trinity and Gilroy. I lobbied heavily against inviting the two, but it was Lacy's wedding, not mine. She and Trinity somehow became friends after the ordeal. Fucking Facebook. Anyhow, Gilroy had been somewhat tolerable the past couple days. I only thought about ripping his gold cane from his hand and shoving it up his ass twice. Maybe his near-death experience had softened his ego, it was hard to tell.

Dum, dum, de, dum.

Rikki was in the next row. Next to her, her father, Track Bowe, who just recently was named, "Philanthropist of the Year," by *People* magazine for his generous efforts to eradicate AIDS from rural South Africa. To date, he had donated three billion dollars and he promised another three billion over the course of the next year. He created the *Rikki Foundation,* which consisted of 3,000 private doctors who traveled around South Africa testing for HIV and distributing lifetime supplies of medication to rural villages.

The videotape Rikki had made of her meeting her father for the first time had gone viral on the internet with over 400 million hits on YouTube. The look on his face was priceless. Google it.

As for me and Rikki, we never did have the conversation, but we didn't need to. We both knew where we stood. And we would always have that one amazing night.

Dum, dum, de, dum.

There were three people in the final row. A beautiful black couple and a jaw-dropping brunette. Timon and his new wife. And Gina Brady. After hearing Gina's tales of Timon's heroics, Lacy insisted he and his wife attend her wedding. When they arrived four days earlier, Timon showed Lacy one of his clocks, and Lacy put him in touch with three stores in France that would love to sell his clocks exclusively. He'd already received advanced payment for two hundred.

As for Gina. She sort of, kind of, became my main squeeze.

Didn't see that one coming, did you?

She caught my eye as I moved past. I winked at her. She actually reminded me of Lacy. And yes, I was madly in love with her. But, I've said that before, so take that with a grain of salt. Maybe two grains. Hell, a whole shaker if you must.

Lacy and I reached the stage, and the music stopped. I looked at Caleb standing next to the altar. He looked like Keanu Reeves. But alive. My sister couldn't have found a better guy.

I took a deep breath, slipped my arm from Lacy, and watched as my little sister took two steps toward the altar and gazed lovingly into the man's eyes she wanted to spend the rest of her life with. I walked to my right, stood next to Gina, and slipped my hand into hers.

Lacy had spent the last couple months training Baxter to be the ring bearer. Everyone watched as Baxter walked down the aisle, a pink pillow tied to his head. He walked ten feet, fell on his face, and began to snore.

FREE BOOK

My #1 Bestselling 3:00 a.m. series was just optioned by Sony Pictures for TV development and it's about as fun a read as you will ever come across.

Get the first in the series free now!

>>>FREE BOOK

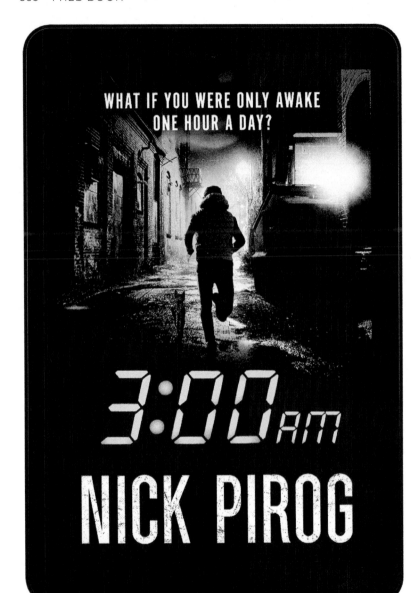

AUTHOR'S NOTE

I know there are millions of books out there, and I just want to thank you for choosing one of mine.

I hope you enjoyed *The Afrikaans* half as much as I enjoyed writing it. The idea first struck me in 2008 when I was searching the internet for stuff about pirates (Who doesn't love pirates?), and I read a story about a luxury cruise liner—the *Seabourn Spirit*—being attacked by Somali pirates. Then while deciding where I wanted my adventure to take place, I stumbled upon some AIDS demographics for South Africa. Devastating stuff. (As I write these words, South Africa carries the highest HIV prevalence in the world, with over 5.6 million people infected with the virus. In the KwaZulu-Natal providence, sixteen percent of the general population and over a third of the adult population has HIV.)

When the story began to take shape, and I started writing it, I kept forgetting where all the people on the cruise ship were. I printed out several sets of the *Seabourn Spirit* deck plan, which *The Afrikaans* is based on, then proceeded to account for every single person (passenger, crew, and pirate) for each important sequence.

Imagine a green dot for a passenger, blue dot for crew, black dot for pirate, red dot for Thomas, orange dot for Rikki, etc., etc. It was quite fun actually. I think the binder is in my parents' basement in Colorado. Knock on wood.

I took some creative liberties with diabetes, bombs, narcoleptic dogs, Zulus, diamonds, oil, and many other things.

I've attached a teaser for *Show Me (Thomas Prescott #4)*.

You can buy the rest of the series **directly** from me and download the books **directly** to your reader at www.nickpirogbookstore.com.

Use promo code GRAY10 at checkout to save 10% off your entire order.

For a 25% Off promo code, subscribe to my Mailing List at www.nickpirog.com.

Thanks for reading :)

God is love.

Nick

ABOUT THE AUTHOR

Nick Pirog is the bestselling author of the Thomas Prescott series, the 3:00 a.m. series, and *The Speed of Souls*. He lives in South Lake Tahoe with his two pups, Potter and Penny.

You can learn more about him at www.nickpirog.com.

ALSO BY NICK PIROG

The Henry Bins Series

3:00 a.m.

3:10 a.m.

3:21 a.m

3:34 a.m.

3:46 a.m.

The Thomas Prescott Series

Unforeseen

Gray Matter

The Afrikaans

Show Me

Jungle Up (April 2021)

Other Books

The Speed of Souls: A Novel for Dog Lovers

Arrival: The Maddy Young Diary

The Lassie Files: Four Ridiculously Silly Stories

Printed in Great Britain
by Amazon

33106669R00229